SOME OTHER TRAVELLER

LYN MCCONCHIE

Night to Dawn Magazine & Books LLC
P. O. Box 643
Abington, PA 19001

www.bloodredshadow.com

Copyright © 2022 by Lyn McConchie
Paperback ISBN: 978-1-937769-72-7
Ebook ISBN: 978-1-937769-73-4

Cover Artists: Abhijith Ar and Photowitch
Editor: Barbara Custer
Published in the United States of America

To Hugh and Maureen in Cornwall, to the real Cheryl, to Alpaca breeders everywhere, and to Tai who was my beloved half-Siamese cat.

The fire falls into coals and ash,

But if some other traveller came,

To stir the coals he yet might find,

Some flickering vestiges of flames

But looking at the flickering light,

That lives again as flames flare higher,

It could be asked by one who sees,

If this is the same – or another fire?"

CHAPTER ONE

Be prepared. ~Boy Scout motto

And if you aren't prepared, then move with caution. ~Donal McArn

I stopped at the fortified gate to Glen Mhairi, counting our people back home, and reflecting as they passed, that they looked like throwbacks to a clan's cattle-raiding past. Not that I looked much better. I was dirty and utterly weary. I had a graze on one cheek that still bled a little, and my husband, Donal, had bloodstains down the front of his jacket – although, happily, they weren't his blood. With us, we had a baby and three children in one lorry – rescued or kidnapped according to who defined their presence. We had a long line of utes and other vehicles with four trailers, all loaded with salvage, and some of our younger people had taken to wearing bandanas to keep their hair back – rather than cutting it – making them look like pirates. It was far from the civilization we'd had and far from the one I hoped would come back some day in the future, but we were doing our best, and you can't do better than that.

We were armed to the teeth. If this had been a year ago and I'd seen our group coming, I'd have vanished into the nearest cover and not come out for hours while phoning the police, ambulance service, and probably the army as well. But that was then, this was now, and I, along with Donal, was one of the war leaders of Glen Mhairi. I counted my people back and reflected on changing times and how people adapt or die when that happens. Since we had no intention of dying, we'd adapted, one of the few cohesive groups to have done so in our area – or so far as we knew.

The last of our warband passed me. Young Barry swung the heavy gates shut and rejoined his vehicle. I nodded to the gate guards as I followed my people home. Donal was waiting for me down the road and jumped into the Landcruiser.

"All right, dear heart?" I nodded. "No one injured, a total of twelve children added to the glens, more livestock, and some good salvage."

"Aye," he grinned, Donal's wide, infectious happy smile that I'd always loved. "Did you ever think you'd be doing this sort of thing at our age?"

I shook my head. No, I hadn't. My memory slid back to the start of it, and I shivered. So much death, so many unbelievable things. Desperate acts, difficult decisions. I was fit, healthy, and expected to live another twenty years or more in the quiet glen that was my home. Then the Laird had phoned, demanding we come to Edinburgh. Johnny didn't make unreasonable demands, and I'd heard the clear notes of grief and desperation in his voice, so we'd come running – and the world had never been – would never be – the same.

****

We were on the way to Edinburgh an hour after his call. It was a pleasant day, mild, windless, and I was with the man, my husband, to whom I'd been married for forty years and whom I'd loved all my life. I had no idea that this would be the last day on which things would be the same. But since I didn't know, I was listening to the car radio, a programme of old Scottish songs, and Donal and I were singing along to our favourites.

I'm Sheila McArn, and I've just turned seventy. Donal is six months older, and we'd been born in Glen Mhairi, owned by the Lairds of Glenrae. We'd gone to school together, got into mischief together, gone our own ways during our late teens and early twenties, come back together at twenty-five when we both worked for the army, and finally wed at thirty.

We'd never had children, and truth be told, I didn't mind. We were employed part-time, owned our own house in the glen, loved who we were and what we did, and most of our lives had been fairly smooth sailing. I had no idea that quiet morning how much would change in less than a week, and if you'd told me, I wouldn't have believed it. So we drove on singing, breaking off now and again to talk about small matters until the traffic became thicker. We went silent while Donal concentrated on his driving until late that afternoon when we pulled up outside the Kylen Research Institute, parked, and went inside to find the Laird of Glenrae.

Johnny McAlister is our age. He's been Laird since his father died when we were all about thirty. Johnny was an only child and inherited everything. That is, he was the only legitimate child; we'd always known his half-brother, Mac. Mac was the child of a local scandal; Johnny's parents had separated for a year - then got together again. Johnny's father had enriched that year by taking up with Silvie Tamman in the village, poacher's daughter, not above taking presents from men, and an all-around bad lot if you listened to gossip. Her elder brother was Jamie Tamman; something of a reprobate was Jamie the Younger – he'd taught us to poach - yet not a bad man and genuinely liked by many, including the four of us.

Then Johnny's parents got back together again, and next thing, the gossips *really* had something to talk about. His wife was having a baby, and so was Silvie Tamman, who didn't change her ways. She was as wild as ever, but she kept the baby despite everything. Both her father – also Jamie – and brother supported her in that, and Mac said she'd been a good mother to him. He went through school with the three of us, but Mac was a brain, and Johnny's father paid for him to get one degree, then another.

And in the end, we all wound up back where we came from, more or less, anyhow. Donal and I had my mother's old home at the back of the village, an ancient stone building to which we'd added rooms, and we had five acres around it. Mac had a small cottage he'd bought for himself. Johnny's home was only a few miles away from our glen – accessible over the hill by a walking track that made it just on a mile – and while Mac was only at his cottage a few weeks a year, although when he was there, we often got together. I broke the silence as we parked our Landcruiser.

"Why do you think Johnny wants us here?"

Donal thought. "Not sure, but it'll be something important."

Well, yes. I'd considered that myself. You don't phone people and ask them to drive most of the day – even on a main road that allows fast driving – to come and see you just to ask if you could borrow a cup of sugar. I said so, and Donal grinned.

"Aye, that'd be so. It'd have to be something major, but what it is, and why we're coming here, I've no more idea than you. I daresay we'll find out."

He led the way through the corridors of the old building and into the newer back portion, where Mac had his laboratory. There we found Johnny and Mac waiting. Johnny said nothing, just waved us to seats, and then to my surprise, went over and locked the door, pulled down the blind over the glass panel, and, hitching up his trouser leg, sat on a corner of the laboratory bench. He looked at us, and while I think I showed nothing, I stiffened. I've known Johnny all my life, and I know when he's serious – and this was as serious as I've ever seen him. The last time he'd been that serious was forty years ago when he told us that his parents had just been killed in a car accident in London and would we help him with the necessary ceremonies. (We had.)

"I want to ask a couple of questions first if that's okay." We both nodded. "Have you both been a bit sick lately?"

Donal glanced at me, I nodded, and he spoke for us both. "Yes, there have been sore throats going around the village. Half the place has had them."

Johnny looked at me; I work part-time as a nurse for the village, having trained in the army as a paramedic. "How did you treat them?"

"Allodaxin."

"Everyone with a sore throat?"

"Barring one or two, yes."

He exchanged looks with Mac, and Mac nodded. "Okay." Mac's grin was crooked. "There's the good news and the bad news."

"Tell us the bad news first," That was Donal; he always liked good news to end up with. Mac nodded slowly.

"The bad news is that most of the population is about to die," and before we could say anything, "The good news is that everyone who's had that sore throat and been treated with Allodaxin should survive it, initially anyhow."

I latched onto the last words. "Initially? What's going to kill them – us – afterwards?"

Johnny stirred. "Probably your fellow citizens."

We looked at them. Donal shrugged. "What do you know, what can you tell us, and when is this likely to begin?" That's my Donal. He doesn't sit around looking blank; he cuts to the core and goes on from there. Mac settled back and considered.

"All right, to cut a long story shorter. Something started in the Congo a year ago, some sort of viral mutation. Most of us carry Staphylococcus A. Now and again, it gives us a sore throat if we get run down or a stronger strain comes through. That's almost certainly what Mhairi Glen had, and with allodaxin being the new antibiotic and only out a year, that's what you used for it. Then the infection changed again, and now it's lethal. If you had both things, the earlier infection, and that was treated with allodaxin, you're immune according to how far in the past it happened."

"Parameters?" I demanded.

"If it happened within two to six weeks, you should be completely immune. About two to three or four months, you'll be sick, but you'll probably get over it if you can manage where you are." He gave me a sharp look when I would have said something. "Four to about six months, you may survive if you have devoted knowledgeable home nursing, over that, you'd need to go to Intensive Care in a hospital, and there isn't likely to be one of them around much longer. What that also comes down to is – if you have it and survive, you're immune thereafter."

I'd listened; he was saying that this would hit the entire population and that only those few who'd already had the mild version of the virus, and as well, only those that had then been treated with a specific medication would survive. Allodaxin was new; it was one of the antibiotics created to replace those older ones that were no longer effective. Many countries wouldn't have it yet, or couldn't have afforded it. And some of the more rural areas in the countries might not have received it for general use as yet.

I gazed at Mac. He'd been involved in some of the allodaxin tests, and as well, he had friends. I snapped out two words while even Donal looked at me in surprise. My voice was cold, hard, and demanded a truthful answer.

"Die off?"

Mac paused, and then I could hear the truth in his voice, along with the sorrow, the pain, and the quiet regret. They mirrored Johnny's voice when he'd asked us to make the long drive to the city – and it was that note that'd made us obey. "About eighty to ninety percent initially. After that, it may go up in some countries and places to as high as a hundred percent. In those that had the infection *and* allodaxin, about one or two percent will survive the virus and may survive what happens after that."

Johnny looked at us. "Sheila, I know you and Donal read post-apocalyptic books."

Donal and I nodded. I like them and have a shelf full, some dating back to the nineteen fifties, sixties, and seventies, like *Alas Babylon, Day of the Triffids, The Death of Grass,* and some that came later like *One Second After* and the *Home* series. Most recently added to our shelves had been several standalones: *Vestiges of Flames, Coals & Ash, Another Fire,* each set in a different country by an overseas author. They'd come out in the last seven years, and I'd bought all six. A chill washed through me. If what Mac said was true, this might not be the end of people, but it was the end of civilization as we knew it, and I did *not* feel fine.

Donal stood up slowly, balancing on the balls of his feet as if waiting for the attack. "When does this hit, and what do we do?"

"First effects will start showing in the UK in the next two to seven days. That's the hell of this variety; it's got a very long incubation period. But places like Mhairi Glen, well, some people may not be infected. Everyone who didn't have a sore throat, you take the swabs Mac will give you and infect them; that's the earlier type. Then the minute they show symptoms, you put them on the allodaxin. It won't save them all, but it should save most." He looked to see if I understood, and I nodded. "You take this," Johnny handed me a massive wad of cash and glared at me until I accepted it.

"On the way home, empty your bank accounts, then buy all the first aid supplies you can. Aspirin and stuff like that, band-aids, bandages, wound dressings, cough mixtures, and throat lozenges. Anything that treats minor wounds or sicknesses."

"What about more serious illness?"

Mac pointed, and I saw a stack of cartons on a trolley, half-hidden behind the inner-office door. "You'll take those when you go. It's everything I can get without questions being asked. And I can give you these." He handed over a bundle of written and signed prescriptions. "Stop at pharmacies all the way home and get them filled. They're written for you both, don't put in more than one list for each of you at any one place."

Johnny broke in. "And once the virus starts, wait a few days, then get vehicles and people who had the sickness, and go looking. Clear out pharmacies, shops, general stores, garages," his voice and face hardened. "Survive. If you have to shoot someone to do it, then shoot them. Once the sickness takes hold in the general population, there'll be no law, no doctors or nurses left, or not many. Some people will go crazy when they realize what's happening. You'll get looting, arson, rape, and anything else that happens where there's no law left."

Something occurred to me. "What about respirators?"

"Waste of time." Johnny's voice was sad. "There won't be many of them around anyhow. If you're thinking of the smell, dab perfume or *eau de cologne* under your nose, or tie a strip of material over your nose and dab it on that. This infection isn't airborne, and for any that are and may show up, I've included boxes of vaccination ampoules, needles, and the all-purpose saliva testers. However, it's likely that there won't be cholera, typhoid, or any of that sort of thing. The main danger isn't disease once you leave the glens; it's other people. Block off the glens, keep others out, if friends or relatives come, keep them away from the locals for a couple of weeks until anyone is either dead or known to be immunised. It's hard, but the alternative is worse."

Donal nodded once decisively. "Aye, we can do that. What about you two?"

Mac shrugged. "We have it. It'll go active in a couple of days, and we'll be dead a day or two after that. Johnny won't leave the city anyhow; Merryl's in the hospital." Johnny's wife was dying of cancer and had only days to go.

"The children?"

Johnny sighed. "Too late, Bel's been visiting friends in Australia. I phoned her, said to come home, but I couldn't get through to her until a couple of hours ago, and from what she said, the country's already starting to lose people. I doubt they'll make it home even if they're not infected; no transport. James and his wife and the kids are in the Caribbean on a cruise. I got through to them last night, but they'd just left port, they wouldn't be at the next stop until this evening, and the port there doesn't have an airport. They'll try, but the same applies, and I don't think..." his voice trailed off.

He took a long breath. "Donal, Shelia, you're my deputies. I'm placing my estate in your hands. You hold it in trust until someone you know to be of the blood comes to take it back. And be very sure they're genuine. Here." he handed us a document, two closely-written pages, signed by him at the bottom and with two witness signatures. I flicked a look over it and picked out several phrases that confirmed what he'd said.

"What about your house?"

"Take food, first aid supplies, guns and ammunition, any useful books from the library, then shut it up. Take the dogs and Tai, their food and gear. That's your choice; if you don't think you'll be able to care for them, give them a quick death." My gaze met his, and I nodded slowly.

"Now," Mac said. "Pack this lot and get out of the city."

Donal shook his head. "Not yet. We'll go and hire a trailer, a couple of tarps, and come back. Better no one gets any idea of what we have. Sheila, stay here, move the cartons down to the garage. I'll meet you there."

So that was what I did, Johnny and Mac with me. On the way, they quietly vanished into offices and laboratories and returned to add other items to the stack on the trolley until it was overloaded, then we had a second of those with an increasing pile on that.

"Take the trolleys," Mac said as we exited into the big underground garage. "You'll find them useful in your future." I noticed the way he said that, and a small involuntary shiver shook me as Mac handed me something else. A large bottle of tiny pills. "You know what these are. Don't tell anyone you have them, but you know what to do if you have to." Donal arrived before I could say anything. We loaded trolleys and contents, and Johnny went to his car.

"Take these." He handed over several items while Mac considered, went to his vehicle, and added other things. Johnny looked at me, and I saw tears in his eyes. "Sheila, Donal, you've been the best friends a man could have. My land is in your hands now, hold it in trust until the old blood returns, and if it never does, hold it forever and pass it down to those you trust."

Mac took us to one side while Johnny brought a few more items. "Listen, my cottage is yours." He chuckled, a genuinely amused sound, and I was taken aback. "No, I'm not crazy. But take the cottage; I'm giving it to both of you officially. There's a little cellar you may not have known about, a trapdoor in the corner of the mudroom under the shelving; that pivots to one side. Anything down there's yours too. Here." He pushed another document into my hand. "Title deeds. Signed and witnessed."

I'll not go into details after that. We hugged, spoke broken words of love and goodbye, until at last Donal broke away and thrust me into the front seat, took the wheel, and we left, both sides knowing we'd never see the other again.

We drove out of the city, waiting until we almost cleared it to make our first stop. We found a pharmacy in the outer suburbs, entered, handed over a prescription each, and while Donal waited for them, I went to the bank and withdrew everything from our accounts. I did more. Johnny would know Mac's account and PIN numbers, so there'd be money he could get, but I knew his. I'd banked for him the previous year when he was unwell, so I entered the bank and emptied his current account. I showed the manager the deed that gave me authority over the estate, and grudgingly he permitted it.

I left with the bag I had taken into the building, now stuffed with bricks of cash. Yes, I'd read end-of-civilization books, and I knew that when such a thing happened, it usually took time for people to realize that it was things that mattered; money had no value. But that could take days to weeks, and until the knowledge was general, shopkeepers would sell. The trailer Donal had rented was a large one, wide and with high sides. I could see he was still waiting for our prescriptions, so I went to our vehicle and made arrangements and a phone call to the glen. With that completed, I rejoined him. As I explained the arrangements I'd made while he was in the pharmacy, we collected the bottles and packets and drove to the next town.

Donal grinned. "What are you expecting?"

"Nothing, but just in case."

He pursed his lips. "Sense, yes. And let's stop at a gun shop. More ammunition might be useful." He went there when we stopped while I waited for the prescriptions to be filled. After that, we took a motel room for the night and were on our way again after a hearty breakfast. My phone rang as we drove, and I looked at it.

"Johnny," I informed Donal as I put it on speaker.

Johnny was laughing. "Smart lass, I looked at my bank account. You used the deed?"

"I did."

"I thought you might. If you hadn't, I was going to suggest it. What have you bought so far?" I gave details, and he approved. "Will you make it back by evening?"

I consulted Donal with a glance, and he shook his head. "We don't think so. It takes time to get prescriptions filled at each pharmacy, and we're buying other things as well."

"What about the glen?"

"I've told Janet to keep everyone at home. Said it was your orders, that there's trouble coming, and that if anyone leaves, they won't be let back in until Donal and I are home."

I could hear the smile in his voice as he answered that. "Janet, I see." He would too. Janet is the principal of our small school. She's a lady it doesn't pay to cross, and no one in Mhairi Glen would do so without an overwhelming reason. Not if they had the sense God gave a rabbit.

Mac came on and spoke briefly; more of a medical update. "Cases of the active virus are increasing in the city. By tonight hospitals will be full, and since many of the staff will be ill, there'll be too few to treat them. By tomorrow, people will panic as they see the numbers and can't get help. Johnny and I will go tonight to be with Merryl. I've medication we can take that will keep us comfortable until the end."

"And Merryl?"

"I'm taking something for her too."

I understood.

How long?"

"About the time I said. We'll talk to you regularly. We'd be pleased if you were back home by then." *So would I,* I thought. We chatted, needing the small personal connection until they rang off. I put the phone in its charger/holder and turned to Donal.

"We need to be back by tomorrow evening."

"Aye. We will be. How long would will people take money and fill prescriptions?"

"Maybe two weeks for cash, not so long for scripts, but we have options if we must."

He nodded, a pensive look on his face. "That's so, I don't like it, but when it comes down to survival, we'll do whatever we have to."

12

We were silent until we reached the next town where we bought more supplies, filled another four prescriptions – two pharmacies only a block from each other – and moved on. I was looking at the logistics of everything balanced against getting home without wasting more time than need be. Mac had given us a dozen prescriptions each. As we left the next pharmacy, I suggested we pause to rent another Landcruiser and trailer. Donal considered that.

"Aye, we'll stop at the last town before the turn-off, and I'll hire those and keep going. You get the people sorted with those swabs while some of the men empty the trailer, then explain to the responsible ones what's happening, and come find me after that. Have some of them bring vehicles too, utes, small trucks, trailers. Once we get a real stock of supplies in, we can hole up, so once we do go out, a lot of the dying is over and we'll be in less danger for a while."

I could see that. When people around them had died, for weeks or even a month or two, most survivors would be in shock or terrified they'd catch whatever was killing their neighbours. They'd stay wherever they were, and if we made sure to move around in a minimum of armed pairs, we should be able to manage safely, for a while anyhow.

We reached the larger town. Donal went to hire the car and came out with an even larger trailer and a Landcruiser like ours, only newer. We drove on, stopping to buy supplies and fill prescriptions until we reached our turnoff, then we parked, said goodbye, promised each other to be careful, and I drove to the village on our narrow, winding, gravel road while Donal disappeared along the main highway.

I watched him vanish and only hoped I'd see him again. Then I got back into my car. This was no time to be standing around. I had things to do, people to save, and … I came around the bend by the start of the village and found Janet arguing with two people.

CHAPTER TWO

When you engage in actual fighting, if victory is long in coming, then men's weapons will grow dull and their ardour damped. ~Sun Tzu, *The Art of War*

That really depends on why you're fighting and for what. If it's so everything you love survives, then mostly, it won't apply. ~Donal McArn

I recognised the minister and his wife. He was a saintly old man, she was a termagant, and I could see Janet was at the point where if the woman continued to shout, Janet might well do something regrettable. I drove up, stepped out of the car, fixed my gaze on her, and spoke slowly and clearly.

"Do you want to die?"

Mrs. Giles rounded on me. "Is that a threat?"

"No, it's a warning."

The minister intervened. "Can you explain?"

I did so in a few terse sentences, and he gaped. "Are you certain of what you say?" I nodded. He turned to his wife. "I think we should go home, my dear."

And to Janet's and my relief, his wife subsided. They started back to the manse, while I told Janet she should join me. We drove to the centre of the village where Janet got out of the car and rang the ancient bell there. People gathered, and I stepped up on the trailer linkage and spoke.

I was clear about what was happening and how bad it could get. I pointed out the dangers, reassured some, and to

15

several, I showed the deed Johnny had given me along with the letter Mac had written. There was a lot of talking, which died quickly when I added that I was looking for drivers who had vehicles that could carry supplies in bulk. Half a dozen stepped up. I handed over set amounts of money, a list each that Donal and I had made up, and gave them a town to visit. I queried each of them to be certain. Yes, all had had the sore throat that had been going around. When? Within the last few weeks. I let them go then with a warning.

"Your life is more important. If anyone starts asking too many questions, leave quietly. If you need an explanation for buying so much, look a bit embarrassed, say the wise woman in your village has said it'll be a tough winter, and your elders thought it would do no harm to buy extra." There was a concerted chuckle. "You can mutter you don't put much faith in her, but just in case…"

One of the men laughed. "I can do that. Are we to go alone?"

"Alone when buying, but two of you to each town watching out for each other. If anything goes wrong, we'll want to know who's in danger, what happened, and where we can find them. But remember what I say. Take no chances. We need you." I sent them on their way with my good-wishing nothing *would* go wrong riding their shoulders.

Janet had been waiting, and I looked at her. "Have you time to help me infect people?"

She grinned. "Sounds like a plan."

We played Typhoid Mary for three hours, and once done, she smiled cheerfully. "I've tea and scones. Come and talk to me."

I followed her to her cottage, sat, and allowed the stress to drain out of me. Then we ate, drank and talked. Janet nodded when I was done. "And Johnny's house, you should go now and get the animals. You don't know if his people are ill.

If they are, they may not have cared for the beasts. If they aren't, you should infect the people there too."

I rocketed to my feet. "Dear Heaven, I didn't think of that. Come with me?" She nodded, and, pausing only to tell someone where I'd be, Janet and I took my Landcruiser – now with the trailer unloaded – and we were gone, heading along the road which was three sides of a square that way, to the large old manor house and the spread of old and newer outbuildings that Johnny called home.

Johnny currently had two dogs, not the usual setters or spaniels, no. Cassie and Bruce were Dobermans, superbly trained, three years old, and, bless them, sensible dogs who knew me well. Their companion was Tai. His mother had been Siamese, but his father had, to Johnny's initial distress, been a Scottish wildcat. Tai had inherited hybrid vigour and was some twenty-five pounds of muscle, speed – and single-minded aggression when he felt it warranted. The dogs treated him as an equal, as well they might.

We pulled up by the front steps to find all three of them waiting. Janet stayed in the Landcruiser while I got out and the animals fell upon me. I made the required fuss of each before calling Janet and introducing them. Tai, once the amenities were completed, led the way into the house, complaining loudly. Janet glanced at me and spoke quietly.

"I know that sound. He's hungry. And if he is…"

Yes, if he was, it meant he hadn't been fed today, and that was a danger signal. Johnny's housekeeper lived-in, along with her husband, three cottages held the other staff, and I'd go there as soon as I'd checked the house. Once in the kitchen, we put down food, refilled the water bowls, and I considered those.

"They were dry."

"Yes. Upstairs?"

I nodded and led the way, down the back corridor and then up a flight of stairs to where the housekeeper had her rooms.

We found her there. She hadn't been dead more than a day, I thought, but she'd have been too ill to care for herself, let alone the animals, for perhaps a day before that.

"Help me." I wrapped the silent body in the fouled bedding. Tied it off, and with me at her head and Janet taking the feet, we carried her downstairs and to the back of the house.

"What will you do with her ... the ... this?"

I looked at her. "Over there. Johnny was planning to put in a row of saplings to shelter the new barn once it went up. The men dug a deep trench for them. We'll put her at one end of it and add the others as we find them." Janet glanced sharply at me. I saw her understand what I had not said, and she sighed.

"I see no one came to check on her or the beasts."

Wordlessly we went to the garage that held Johnny's cars, and there we found the husband, lying on an old couch by the vehicles. Mac had told Donal and me that it could hit hard and fast in some cases, and it had. The body was composed, as if he'd felt faint, laid down to see if he felt better shortly, and lapsed into unconsciousness too quickly to call for help. The couch had had a blanket over it, so we did the same as we'd done for his wife. After that, we went through the cottages, and when we were done, eleven bundles lay outside their homes.

Janet had picked up a phone from beside one of the girls. "She called for help."

"Any indication of it being answered?"

Janet held the phone up with the usual results. "No service. Landline in the house, but I suppose by then they were all too sick to make it there."

"Yes." I felt a wave of sorrow. "I'd say they were unlucky. It must have hit them all overnight at pretty much the same time."

"Johnny's still alive?"

"So far... oh, you wonder how come. Mac, I think he had something that could keep them going an extra day or two, but that's all. We'll get them into the trench; there should be a motorised trolley in the garage. That'll make it easier." It did. We spent another busy couple of hours – and went back to the main house where I phoned Mac.

"Is Johnny with you?"

"Yes. I'll put you on speaker."

"Johnny? It's Sheila. I have people out buying supplies. Donal is filling final prescriptions and getting more ammunition and medical supplies where he can. We're at your place. Dogs and Tai are fine. Otherwise, we're using the trench for the saplings." I heard the indrawn breath. "Aye, everyone. We're going to lock up everything now, but I thought of getting the barn moved to the village and put up there. We can use it as a warehouse if that's all right."

"Do it."

Mac spoke then. "Sheila. You may get friends and family coming to the glen and no place to house them. Once they're out of quarantine, you'll need something. Remember Comber beach. Apart from anything, you could make the manor a second glen with the track to connect them." I considered that; we'd planned a quarantine area, not because we needed one for actual quarantine, but because it could be helpful to keep some out of the village until we'd evaluated them.

"Johnny, do you mind?"

He chuckled. "Not in a position to mind, my dear."

"Are you…" I choked to a halt, words stuck in my throat, and his reply was gentle.

"Starting, yes. Phone us early tomorrow, may be the last time we can talk."

"Merryl?"

"I'll see to her," Mac said. "We'll go a lot better than others. You've infected what you can of the glen?"

"Yes. How long should I wait?"

"If they show symptoms by sometime tomorrow, put them straight onto allodaxin. But remember, they may have been latent; they'll die if they were. You could lose as many as half the glen depending on all the factors."

I cleared my throat. "I know. I'm hoping."

"Yes. If you ever get back to the city, you know where you'll find us. We'll be gathering supplies, then locking ourselves in and barricading the door and windows."

Johnny came back. "Take no chances, Sheila. We'd like to be buried in our own land, but only if it's safe. What you'd be getting if you come for us is shells, nothing more."

I spoke slowly and clearly; these could be the last words between us. "Johnny, Mac. I love you both. You've been my best friends all my life, Donal would say the same, and likely he will if we talk tomorrow. If we can, we *will* come for you. It may take years, but we'll come." The phone was laid down gently, the connection broken; I turned to Janet, my eyes filling with tears. She held me, and we wept together.

****

After that, we loaded the beasts, their food, bowls, blankets, and baskets, and I emptied the larders in the main house and cottages. There were bathroom cabinets, the gun cabinet, and ammunition chest, and I emptied them all. Janet drove us home, and Donal was back when I stopped outside our house, and he helped us unload the vehicle and trailer. The dogs and Tai knew him too and accepted being taken inside where he shut them, with food, water, and their baskets, in one of our spare rooms.

Janet left to go home, and Donal and I went into our lounge, and I slumped to the couch. "The television?" I queried.

"Aye, they're talking of nothing else. All the doomsayers are out, but I think even they don't yet realise how bad it'll be. The authorities may be hoping to keep it quiet. I got all the prescriptions filled, and I've marked pharmacies that may have supplies under lock and key. Looting's already started some places, and there didn't look to be many police about. I didn't run into trouble, but I heard you sent out three other pairs to buy supplies. Are they armed?'

"They are," I said grimly. "I told them if there were too many questions asked, to walk away. Not to start anything and try to avoid any trouble. They're moving singly in the shops, but they keep an eye on each other. If one gets into trouble, the other needs to be able to get back to us to say what and where."

Donal nodded approvingly. "I brought more ammunition, stopped off at the warehouse in Clerminster, and loaded up on tea, coffee, flour, powdered eggs, cocoa, hot chocolate, and all the salt, honey, and sugar I could get." He grinned. "One of the shops was having a sale on bread makers. It's quicker and easier than making it from scratch, so I bought them out. The owner was too pleased to ask what I was going to do with that many. Only question may be, where do we keep all the stuff?"

"The new barn Johnny was going to put up. It was delivered, and it's one of those that's prefab. It comes in sections, and there's everything needed, plus all the cement, sand, reinforcing rods, boxing, and so on for the foundations. They've delivered a couple of mixers on hire, and I don't think they'll be asking for them back." He raised his eyebrows, and I nodded. "Everyone at the manor."

"When did you talk to Johnny?"

"They're at the hospital. We talked three hours ago. They've started being sick too. Mac said to phone early tomorrow morning."

"He thinks…"

"Yes."

"Then we will. What about your patients?"

"We could lose up to half the glen. I won't know until they get better – or don't. But I infected everyone who came to me today; all those I know didn't have the original attack. Tomorrow, I'll start treating anyone showing symptoms. Then we wait."

"No, we don't. We'll be too busy. We sort out all the ones we know are immune and start them getting more supplies. We put a guard on the manor, and we put up gates on the Glen Mhairi end of the road and a guard there too." We sat up after that, eating a scratch dinner and talking about precautions we should take, things we should watch for, and how to fulfill Johnny's trust in us and his bequest. Donal spoke thoughtfully.

"We have one thing against us. Our ages. We expected to live another twenty or even twenty-five years, and we still could, *if* we don't have major accidents or get murdered. But it's unlikely we'll survive more than twenty-five years at the most, and we'll be losing effectiveness before that. We need to sort out deputies and decide who inherits after us if Johnny's family never returns."

"That's true. On the plus side, there are our professions and experiences."

He couldn't argue with that. He'd joined the army in his mid-twenties, he was an excellent shot, a reasonable gunsmith, a jackleg mechanic, and knew something about electrical wiring and plumbing – if neither work was too complicated. He might be seventy, but he was lean, fit, could walk many a younger man into the ground, and could be utterly ruthless when it came to those he loved.

I'd gone into the army, doing a specialised course where I'd been trained as a front-line paramedic. For those who complain the army they knew doesn't have paramedics, I would point out that I never said which army, or even that it was an official army. Donal was offered a very well-paid job, and I'd joined him.) I'd been in several hotspots under fire too. Apart from that, I'd grown up until I was eighteen on the estate where I'd used almost every calibre of gun. I'd gutted rabbits, plucked game birds, hand-milked goats and cows, and treated them for ailments. I could ride a horse, knew how to harness one, and I wasn't the sort that was left hysterical by mud, blood, or excrement. All of which attributes I thought we would need desperately in the times to come.

"When should we move the barn here?" I asked.

Donal shrugged. "Split our people. Dozen on the barn will do with Harry running things. I'll take another half dozen with me to go to the place that sells outbuildings. I think we need more than one barn. They have those compartmented ones. Flat pack system, get two, and they hook together side by side; you can run a line of them, many as you want. Johnny talked to me about them a while back."

"So, how many do you think we should get, and what do they cost?"

"Seven to ten thousand pounds each, that's with everything needed. Get five. Then there's the eco systems."

I looked up sharply. "We have those; we only put them in last year."

That is, Johnny had. Glen Mhairi was his land, so he'd paid and had his men install everything. We had wind generators, solar panels with batteries, petrol generators, and those were also linked into the national grid. Most of the time, that meant that we fed power back, and we paid nothing for our power, while Johnny got payment most months for power provided to the government. We'd upgraded all of the systems six months ago.

"And when did we upgrade things before that?"

"Oh, I see." It had been twelve years; the newest installations could last longer. But when they stopped working, we'd go on the spot from free power to nothing at all unless we chopped wood, and you couldn't run fridges on that.

"If we have a good supply of spares and more petrol generators too, along with petrol..." I nodded. "And other building supplies as well. We should alternate. Put up a line of barns, fill them, then put up more."

Something struck me; I beamed. "What did you just think of?" Donal knows me.

"The caves."

"They're over the hill."

"Not if we borrowed a council digger and a bulldozer. If we carved a path between Glen Mhairi and the cave glen, it'd give us more grazing land, another safe place, a ton of storage – the caves are dry – and the cliffs around that glen are even higher. It'd be harder for strangers to find or get into."

Donal considered carefully. "They're on a C-class Government heritage list."

"Because there was minor evidence that people lived there in the Middle Ages. Any artefacts that there were, Johnny's great-great-grandfather removed, and his father gave those to some official archaeological group in the nineties." I drew a breath and waited for Donal to see the result of that. I wasn't disappointed.

"And by now, there probably isn't any of the group alive – or there won't be in another few days – there'll be no government heritage section to stop us, and we need the storage, the grazing, and we have Johnny's document. Place will be safe too, it's blind at the far end, and a road from us to there will leave it that way." He summed up.

We sat there looking at each other before Donal moved. "Tomorrow. Now, numbers available. How many do we have in Glen Mhairi?"

"Total population is two hundred and thirty, ranging from Jenny Simmonds's new baby to the minister's mother who turned ninety-two last December." I pondered. "Tomorrow, we tell everyone to go with someone to the nearest banks. If we move quickly, they may still be able to get any money immediately available. You organise it, we phone Johnny and Mac before we start, then once we're back, you get the road between the glens started. I take people to gather more supplies while you get the barn up, and I'll bring back another set of those flatpack barns along with material for footings. Janet will want to keep the school going so that'll keep the children out of our hair half the time."

"High school?" I suddenly recalled.

Donal's gaze met mine. "You're *expecting* the school bus?"

No, I wasn't. "But what do we do if it *does* turn up?"

"We'll have guards at the gate. We say everyone is down with some sort of sickness, we're keeping the kids home for a few days, and no, they can't come in."

If the bus came, that would be good enough. And by the time the school heard what we'd said and truancy officers were informed, it was unlikely there'd be any left to investigate any-way. We moved on. Agreed we would alternate vital work so far as possible, set up the community hall as a hospital, if need be, and arm everyone who left the glen to do anything. We were late to bed, but I woke early, and Donal suggested we go over to the manor house. We ate a quick breakfast and walked, taking the shortcut and arriving there at 6:30 a.m. There I picked up the phone and listened.

"There's a dial tone." I pressed the numbers, there was a minute's pause, and a hoarse voice answered.

"John McAlister."

"Johnny, is Mac there?"

"Just. We've been hoping you'd phone early. It's good to hear you, Sheila. Is Donal there?" I indicated he was. "That's great. Tell me what you're doing, what you've decided, is anyone sick yet, and how are Cassie, Bruce, and Tai?"

We talked. Until I realised their breathing was harsher. I ended with assurances the beasts were well, that I was going back to check on people and give allodaxin to anyone showing symptoms, but after that, we were spreading out in smaller groups to bring back as many supplies as we could. Today and tomorrow should see supplies safely with us, and after that, we'd shut the gates and keep them shut a couple of weeks before venturing out again – cautiously and armed to the teeth.

Mac's voice was noticeably weaker. "That's sensible, but then you both are, thanks be. This is goodbye, old friends. We waited for you; now we know you'll survive. Johnny's just given Merryl something for the pain; she'll sleep soon. We haven't seen staff for the last twenty-four hours. I went looking, and they're gone." There was a pause then he spoke slowly. "I love you two, you never cared about my mother, and you never teased me about being smart. I'd rather go before you because it'd hurt too much to lose you first."

And a rasping voice chimed in. "Goes for me too. Sheila, Donal, remember us. Stay on the line a while if you can."

Mac spoke to him. "Johnny, brother, here. Drink this." I heard glasses clink together and then gulping sounds, and the glasses went down on a table. Mac spoke again. "Merryl's gone. Move the phone between us and turn up the volume."

Their breathing became louder as the volume rose, then breath by breath, it faded. I held the phone to my lips, speaking clearly. "We love you both. Go in peace."

And at the other end, the breathing stopped. There was a small gasp, an inhalation, a final gasp … and silence. I waited a minute, but at the end of the phone, nothing sounded, and slowly, gently, I replaced it. Then I fell into Donal's arms, my sobs racking body and heart. There'd been four of us; now there were two. Donal held me, and if he too wept, I didn't know. I knew he felt the same pain, however, and we sat grieving together until at last, he straightened, and I moved in his arms.

"I know, things to do." He nodded, and together we went out into the new day. Our best friends were gone, but the glen remained, and we had work to do in our friends' names.

CHAPTER THREE

Thou shalt not kill. ~The Bible

But if it comes down to your life or theirs, better it's theirs; after all, that quote applies to them too. ~Sheila McArn

That day would mark us, define some of what we were becoming. Donal had fought as a soldier, he'd killed and walked away, and I'd always wondered how he'd done it. I'd believed that if it happened to me, I'd fall apart. As an army paramedic, I'd seen people die in war situations, but I could stand aside. I hadn't been the killer, and then too, I was busy saving the lives I was tasked to protect. But that morning, I wasn't a paramedic. I was the leader of a small group, and they were mine. I stood sorting out who would go where and hoping nothing would go wrong.

"How many of you bank with…?" I gave names and had them separate. "Right." I pointed to the different groups in turn. "I'll drop you off in turn, you first, then your lot, then you. As you get your money, leave and wait outside for me. There may be less traffic today, so if you're all together, I can stop briefly, you pile into the vehicle, and I drive off again. With luck, I can get away with double-parking so long as we aren't stopping traffic."

I drove to the first bank, let out four people, and moved on, feeling grateful Johnny had had a people-mover in the manor-house garage. It took twelve and had been used to shift staff about for projects that would take a number of them working together.

It took little more than an hour before I pulled in to collect the final group again.

"Everyone got their money?"

There was a chorus of agreement. Some of them had been given the necessary numbers, cards, and PIN numbers and had collected on behalf of friends or family as well. It seemed the ATM had been sufficiently stocked with cash and had mindlessly accepted the information given. I mentioned that, and Jill, an older lady, spoke thoughtfully.

"The only person I could see in my bank was the manager. Today's the day they refill the ATM. I'd say it'd be a good idea for everyone that wants cash to get it today." *Before the money runs out,* was the unspoken addendum.

"Do you think the machine has been refilled?" I asked her, and she nodded. "One of the tellers talked to me about that ages ago. She said that security comes with the armoured truck to do it around three in the morning. Once when there was a delay, the manager put up a sign. There was no sign today."

It made sense, although of course, if half his staff were dead or dying, he could have been so distracted he'd forgotten, but as Donal said, "Cover your bets." I would. He was off with a small convoy of trucks and utes and a bunch of the men and older boys, picking up council machinery – they had a small depot out near us – buying the flatpack barns and supplies to erect those and buying reinforcing rods, cement, and so on. And before any of that, the men would also be visiting banks in a different town.

I collected all those I'd brought in and returned to the glen, gathered up another dozen, and went back to the banks. The second trip went perfectly as well, and as we'd started right after breakfast, I thought there was time for a third trip before I stopped for lunch. On the outer part of that, I passed several council machines being driven by people from our village heading back to the glen. I dropped off my passengers and noticed several lads hanging about on the pavement at the second bank. They might not have been obvious had there been more people, but there were few pedestrians, and all four of the boys had a furtive look that caught my attention.

I'd made arrangements in our Landcruiser during that first terrible journey home, and this morning I'd done so with the people-mover. Now, as I collected the final passengers, I ordered those who would normally have sat in the front seat with me to sit on the floor and that the windows and doors should be locked. Several of my passengers looked at me strangely, but they obeyed, and it proved a wise choice. We left town, and unconsciously I followed the road signs, slowing right down as we came to the last "*give way*" sign on the outskirts where it was flanked by a church and an orchard.

A motorbike pulled alongside our van, another pulled across behind us, and a rough voice shouted, "Stop right where you are, lady. Open the door or we start shooting."

I flicked a look around me. Their mistake, they hadn't boxed me on the other side or completely in front. I'd seen four lads, and each motorbike carried two, and if luck was on our side, that was all of them.

I yelled, "Everyone, hang on." Stamped on the accelerator, swung the van hard to the opposite side of the bike on our flank, and took off. One … two … three … four … five … and as they accelerated after me, I yelled again to hold on and stood on the brakes. One of the bike riders had fallen in behind us to follow, his engine screaming at full throttle, and when I braked unexpectedly, they hit the back of our people-mover like a ton of bricks – right into the heavy bull bar. By now, from the corner of my eye, I could see my passengers hanging on to anything that gave them stability. That was as well since I accelerated again, caught the bike still on my inside, and sent it spinning.

I called, "Everyone okay?"

Voices called back that they were, and I rocketed off down the road. Two bends further on, I spun the van to the side of the road and spoke in a hard voice I barely recognised as my own. "Get your heads down. *Stay* down until I say it's all right to sit up again." I stepped out of the van, hands full, and waited. Yes, I could hear a bike coming fast. One of them didn't learn from experience. No, two of them, one bike, two riders, it leaned around the corner. I recognised them and raised the shotgun, shot, racked the gun, and shot again.

There were two loud booms, screams from the van. The bike spun, smashed into the low stone wall – more screams – somersaulted over it and could be heard bouncing and crashing down the hillside. The riders were silent, something that could not be said for my passengers. I stood in the warm sun on a quiet road. Nothing moved, and after several minutes, I got back in the vehicle, locked the door, laid the gun on the seat, and drove towards home again. No one spoke until we arrived.

One by one, they got out, sliding nervous looks my way, and it was Claire who finally said something while the others hung within earshot to hear. "The police ... will you phone them or should one of us?"

I met her worried gaze. "If you think it'll do any good," I said quietly. "It's likely there's none left on duty, and all I did was see that four men who threatened us with guns weren't able to hurt anyone." I let her see me look sideways at Josie, eighteen, slight, lovely, and who'd taken out every penny of her savings – more than a thousand pounds. "That was what they were after, initially anyhow, the money they'd seen you get from the bank." I lowered my voice.

"And do you think she'd just have given it to them? They'd have hit her, one of you would have tried to protect her, they'd have lost it and started shooting, and once they'd shot someone, they'd think they might just as well hang for a sheep as a lamb. It'd have been a bloodbath, rape, shooting, people dead. And not them, it'd have been your friends. Did you want to see that?"

"No. No, I don't. It's just that…"

I took up her words. "It's just that you've never seen anything like that before. I have, in some foreign places where it was common, and remember this, Claire. It was common in those places because there was no law. Now that's us. When the virus started, I told everyone that most of the world would die, and here is part of the world. The police, the fire brigade, the ambulance, and medical staff won't be exempt. If we want to live, we have to defend ourselves and our friends and family. Those that aren't willing to defend will be killed by those that are willing to attack."

I turned away, picked up the shotgun, and walked to my house. Guns should be cleaned after use. I closed my door behind me, placed the gun on the table, dropped heavily into a chair, and started shaking. I'd known what to do, I'd just never done it before, and the reaction was setting in. After a while, I made myself a cup of tea, added a dollop of brandy, and relaxed a little while I cleaned and reloaded the shotgun. It had been strange, I thought. Once events had started, it had been as if everything had slowed down. I knew the phenomenon. In reality, things hadn't slowed down; my brain and reflexes had sped up. I'd been cold, calculating, seeing alternatives in fractions of a second. It had been invaluable, and I hoped that it'd continue for me if things went south again.

Donal didn't return for lunch. I'd thought he wouldn't, but by the time he returned for an early dinner, he'd heard all about it. He hugged me. "Good girl. We'll have something to eat. Then we'll go and check." I'd expected that. You clean up any mess you make.

"How is the gap between glens doing?" I asked

"Well. Another day, two at most, and it'll be through. I've got the line of storage barns going up down the end of our glen."

"And Johnny mentioned Comber Beach?"

"We'll go look at that soon. Now, let's eat, then go see about your bikers."

We ate dinner, very basic, and, pausing only to collect two of the men, we took the Landcruiser along the road to where damaged stonework indicated my confrontation. Donal moved soundlessly to the wall and stared over it. "Nothing." He stepped up on it, and with the added three feet of height, he looked down the slope and nodded. "They're still there. Let's go."

He took the lead, moving cautiously, I'd told him they had guns, and Donal doesn't take chances. We fanned out behind him, all of us armed, I glanced back every few paces, but nothing was moving on the road either. Donal reached the sprawled bodies, bent briefly, and straightened.

"Dead." He moved on to the motorbike and checked the saddlebags. "Well, well. Not innocent bystanders for certain." He held up a fist full of glittering jewellery. I joined him, and together we searched bike and bodies. Once we were done, the four of us looked down at the heap of plunder. There was cash, bank cards, watches, jewellery, their identification, and several passports. I stared at those.

"Passports?"

"They'd sell for good money on the black market," one of the men commented.

"*What* black market?" I demanded.

Donal grinned at me. "The black market that isn't there anymore, but their kind haven't yet realised it," he said. "We'll go and report this. I want to have a reason to see how the police are doing. First, though, we'll go and find the others you – met."

They too were still there, the bike's saddlebag had similar contents, and from their licence addresses, they all lived in the same place. A rundown boarding house, used mostly by the un-employed. The town's police station was empty. We walked through it, opening every door, and in their tiny medical room, we found a dead man wearing a sergeant's uniform. I checked and looked up.

"Dead around twenty hours, give or take a few."

"Likely when he died, any cops still here cleared out," Donal said slowly. "Let's take anything of use here, then go look at where that precious lot were living."

We removed a small stock of food and drink. Mostly bis-cuits, tea, coffee, and sugar. Added everything in the medical room to what we were taking and checked desks, finding a new laptop that wasn't password-protected, and some interesting per-sonal items, including a signed book by a writer I'd heard of. I took that. We left the weapons. As Donal said, there were more of those than we'd ever need, but ammunition was finite, and we took all of that along with anything from the evidence room we could use.

The sergeant had had a key ring on his belt that opened everything. It said something that anyone who'd outlived him had been too afraid – or perhaps too devastated by events – to take those. Outside in the police yard, we looked over the vehicles. There were motorbikes, cars, and two vans, all with radio receiv-ers/transmitters.

"They've got the main RT in the station," I said. "If we could dismount that and take it with us, we could take all these and stay in contact when groups go out."

We spent some time getting the radio station dismantled and placed in one of the vans. The larger of the two vans took all three motorbikes, and once we had both vans loaded, Donal looked at our companions.

"Take them home. Murray, you know how to set up that radio station, do it, and use the biggest back room in the community hall. Can one of you ride a motorbike?" Both nodded. "Okay, double up on one, and come back here, get the cars. Bring them all back, check that they're hooked into the radio frequencies. Shelia and I'll be heading for that boarding house to see what's there."

We left them and drove down backstreets, watching about us. The place was quiet, the occasional pedestrian scuttled around a corner, a dog or two rummaged in dustbins, and an old man went by blank-faced on a rusty pushbike. Occasionally, we saw movement in the windows of houses we passed. It was eerie. This was a time when most people were coming home from work or dashing out to buy the odd item before dinner at six, and there was no one. Five turnings later, we pulled up outside the boarding house, and Donal looked at me.

"Back me up. Stop when I say. Don't run forward, no matter what you see. I want a clear shot if I need it. Now, go."

I exited the Landcruiser in a smooth glide, went to cover behind the gatepost and rubbish bins, and watched Donal. He leapfrogged me, halting at the door which he tried slowly. There was an infinitesimal creak, and it opened. He nodded to me and I joined him, pausing while he slid inside into the brown-painted, cabbage-smelling corridor. He paused at the foot of the stairs, consulted the licenses he'd taken, and mouthed to me.

"First floor, rooms four and seven."

He took the stairs one at a time, pausing to settle his footing on the outer end of each and making no sound. We reached the first floor and looked at the doors down that corridor. I raised an eyebrow, and Donal paused to consider. If we started at the furthest door and there were people between us and the stairs, they could present a problem.

Donal made his decision, signalled me to flatten myself against the wall, and tried the furthest door. The handle turned freely, but a push against the door with increasing force showed it to be locked. He produced the keys taken and inserted one. The third key turned, and he opened the door an inch at a time while I moved to where I could see obliquely across the room. I caught his eye and shook my head, no person, no movement visible. He opened the door the final couple of feet, there was still no one within, and we entered, shutting and locking the door behind us.

It was what I would have expected. Unwashed clothes, dirty plates, and glasses, a bed that patently hadn't been made – or the bedding washed – for weeks. A window stuck shut with dirt and old paint and a smell compounded of all that plus urine, I thought. I donned gloves, riffled through the chest of drawers, finding the same items – cash, jewellery, and other things that might bring money or which could be helpful to us. I dropped them all into a bag, stuffed that into my largest pocket. We left the room silently, locked the door behind us, and moved to the next room for which we had a key. That, too, produced nothing unexpected and minor gleanings.

Before we left that, I moved close to Donal, and in a voice which would not have carried more than a couple of feet, I commented, "I haven't heard anyone moving in the building at all. Do you think they're dead or fled?"

He grinned down at me. "Combination, maybe. Or some of them could be out doing what that lot tried to do."

I thought it likely. There were several nursing homes for the elderly on the outskirts of town. If the police were no longer effective, it wouldn't take long for it to dawn on this type that they had easy pickings. We left the second room and silently advanced on the third door. That, too, opened with a key, but to our surprise, it was larger, cleaner, and there looked to be a built-in wardrobe. We searched to find that while there was more to take and what we found was of better quality, it was mostly the mixture as before – until something caught my attention.

"Donal?" I froze, listening; it came again, and I saw him register it. Not so much sound as a vibration. He laid a hand against the back wall of the wardrobe and waited. It came again, and this time, there *was* a faint sound, something so small I wasn't even sure I heard anything, and yet... Donal looked at me as I reacted.

"You heard something?" My hearing has always been good, better than most people, and he would trust that. I nodded, pointing to the wall, my voice a breath.

"In there, next room."

"Yes. We'll see, but very carefully." His breath tickled my ear. "It could be someone asleep there, and they may not react well to being woken up by people they don't know, who shouldn't have a key."

I grinned – an understatement that was. I followed him out, by now with bulging pockets and a bag, all containing a considerable amount of valuables. The jewellery wasn't that important right now – although it could be a medium of exchange later on – the money would be useful. The watches, most were the expensive type of windup which had become fashionable again this year. They were wristwatches mostly, but several were pendant type.

Donal eased the key into the lock, opened the door a fraction at a time, and we slipped in, shutting the door behind us. To my astonishment, the room was empty. The bedclothes were tossed back; the bed was a small double on legs. I ducked my head; nothing visible underneath. I drifted silently to the window and stared out to the street below; no one outside. I eased it up and looked down the side of the building. No other windows open. The boarding house could be empty, save for any dead.

Donal was checking containers, bedside cabinet, drawers, and a suitcase under the table hidden behind a tablecloth. Always check in places like that, you never know what may be sitting there, from a dog to a child – or a suitcase. He collected another stack of cash, and interestingly, a cloth bag of windup watches, pens, pencils, small hardcover notebooks, a seven-year calendar, a hand-engraver, one that was battery-powered, and a second bag that held plain gold jewellery, no gemstones, and all at least fourteen carets. Whichever of our attackers this had been, he had an eye for what might come in handy.

The faint sound came again. I grabbed Donal by the arm, and we stood motionless. I focussed; yes, it had come from *that* direction. I turned and realised I was facing the inbuilt wardrobe. I pointed. Donal moved towards the handle and depressed it silently. Then with a single heave, he flung the door open and waited poised for the attack while I aimed the pistol I'd taken from the dead boy, angling to keep Donal safe.

With the door open, the sound came again, clearer. A shifting. I moved to the side of the wall, flattened against it, reached out, and gently lifted away a crumpled blanket. Donal's eyes widened while I frankly gaped.

The girl looked up piteously. She was tied tightly. I could see how the cords cut in. Beside her, a younger boy lay, also tied, both comprehensively gagged, and the girl's face bruised. I would have jumped to help them, but Donal shook his head. He mouthed a word, and I subsided, watching while he went to the door, checked the corridor, and returned. Then, kneeling, he took hold of the girl's gag and lifted a finger, speaking quietly.

"Keep your voice down. When you can speak, tell us first, who you are, how you came here. At the least, we'll let you go, and we may help if you need it, but if you get us attacked, it may not go well for anyone. Now." He pulled the gag to one side, cut it, and lifted it away, dropping it on the floor. "All right, who are you both? Why are you here?"

I thought her to be about thirteen and the boy, kin from the resemblance, to be a year or two younger. She was too dry to speak. I fetched the bottle of water I'd seen, screwed the top off, and offered it to her. She drank eagerly and managed words.

"Thank you." She drank again. "My name's Kaylie, and this is my brother, Ricky."

She paused, and her eyes became unfocussed. I eyed her and spoke as casually as I could.

"Have you had a sore throat in the last few months?"

She looked blank. "No, why?" I saw Donal register that. Kaylie shivered. "Can you untie us, please? I want to go home. I want my mum."

I reached out and sawed through their bonds. "Lie still until you stop hurting," I said, and to Donal, "Check if anyone's around. If not, we'll take them home."

The boy looked up at me. "You really will?" I nodded. "I had that sore throat. Mum shut us out of their bedroom. I called, and she wouldn't answer. Kaylie said we should walk to town and ask someone to help. A man picked us up and brought us here. He made Kaylie cry. Then he tied us up, put that thing in my mouth, and locked us in here."

"Where was your dad?" I asked.

"Went out on the farm first thing. He never came back."

"Is it your farm?"

"No, sir, Mr. McMallan's. But we've been there long as I can remember."

It took time but gently rubbing welts left by the ropes helped, and in twenty minutes, they were on their feet. Rather, Ricky was, Kaylie was wobblier. In the end, Donal carried her to the Landcruiser, and with Ricky's directions, we found their farmhouse. I took the girl to her bedroom, laid her on the bed, found her fruit juice, helped her change her clothing, opened my mouth to comment on her bruises, and shut it again. With what I guessed, it made no difference, and she didn't have long. Donal came back in an hour.

"The mother?"

"Yes."

"Do you think their father…?"

"Yes." He glanced down at the girl. "Is she…?"

"Yes. I've given her painkillers. Heavy duty. She's asleep, and she won't wake up."

"The boy's fine. I told him to collect the eggs. He had a bad throat three weeks ago. His mother kept him away from this one, so she never caught it."

I sighed. "I see. We should take him with us in the morning."

Donal nodded slowly. "Aye. Seems like a good kid, says he turned twelve last week." He glanced down at Kaylie. "How long?"

"An hour or two. Once she's gone, I'll take him home, leave him with Janet, and come back with vehicles and drivers. We pack all of whatever's of use or value. The boy can tell us before we go where this McMallan lives. I'll let them know on the way."

"If they're in shape to hear."

I met his gaze. "If they aren't, I'll bring back extra people and vehicles. Once we get back from Comber Beach, we'll need more furnishings and bedding."

"True. I hear the lad now."

He was right. I took Ricky aside and spoke carefully. He watched me, listened, and I wondered if he understood a word. Then he spoke in a toneless voice, and I knew he had.

"Mum's dead, Dad's dead, an' Kaylie's dying. What happens to me?"

"You can come home with us. If you don't have anywhere else you'd rather go?"

His head drooped, and he thought, speaking slowly as he recalled. "Is no one. I mean, I think mum had family somewhere, but we never saw them. Dad said his mum died when he was at university, and his dad went sort of strange. He didn't ever visit us anyhow. Lives somewhere in Sussex, I think. Don't know the address." Even knowing it wouldn't be much help, I thought; the man was probably dead or dying.

Kaylie died an hour later. Ricky had all his things packed by then, Donal had dug a small grave, and we placed her in that, the teddy bear – a bright pink one that Ricky said she still loved – tucked in beside her. After that, he clung to my hand. The McMallans, when I drove there, were home all right. Dead, huddled together in their queen-sized bed. Mother, father, children, and one who may have been a grandfather stretched out in a recliner beside the bed. I told Ricky to pack all their food in the boxes I gave him, and while he did that, I checked for cash. There was a large amount in a drawer, and I heaved a sigh. Tomorrow we'd go buying, spend every penny on essentials before shopkeepers died or wouldn't accept money.

I drove home, and when I would have left the lad with Janet, he clung to me like a limpet, his eyes wide in fear of losing someone else. I put him to bed in the spare room, slept in the bed opposite, and took him with me the next morning. Janet took the accumulated cash, along with a list and several friends, utes, and her car with a trailer. We removed the Black and McMallan animals, several small portable sheds, and salvaged useful items from houses and outbuildings. During which time Ricky was never out of eyeshot, and when my hands weren't employed, he clung to one of them.

We drove home to eat dinner, I put him to bed, and when he asked, I answered, "Yes, this is your room now. You'll go to school here once it opens again. The place is called Glen Mhairi. It'll be your home." And then the tentative question that almost broke my heart. "Aye, you can call us Grandma and Grandpa if you want. We'd like that." He fell asleep still trustfully holding my hand, and as I looked at that peaceful face, I knew the truth.

After all those years and with never a child of our own, we finally had a grandson.

CHAPTER FOUR

"Don't let what you can't do stop you from doing what you can do."
~John Wooden

And don't make assumptions about not being able to do something.
~Donal McArn

The next day was even busier. It didn't help that over-night, seven people had died in Glen Mhairi, with nineteen very sick. The virus had finally caught up with our isolated village. Thankfully we had the space – our community hall and the med-ications – courtesy of Mac and our buying. People died, but we could keep them comfortable so that none died in pain. It was an awful week, one I'll never forget, but we came through it and lost fewer than I'd feared we would, thanks to Mac. I'd infected everyone I knew hadn't had that prior infection and who would accept the treatment. Then as soon as it showed, I'd given them the allodaxin, and it saved many.

Yes, a few families refused to take the chance; most died. For some, it had been too late; they too died. But of our original population – two hundred and thirty – in the end, we lost only forty-six, fewer than I'd expected. That is, that was the number lost to the virus. Of the families who'd refused the treatment, one of the women lived. She watched her entire family die because of her decision, and when the last passed away, she lay down with them and saw to it that she followed.

Two other people whose families had already been infected by the virus and died but who survived themselves did the same thing. It was a bitter time, and I was thankful we had the council machinery. Donal had foreseen what we'd need, and he'd had one of our people dig a long deep trench. As people died, we wrapped them in their bedding, placed them reverently in the trench, and covered them. And once those deaths attributable to the virus were over, we filled in the trench and held a service. Minister Giles spoke, and we wept. Then we turned back to living.

For the past two weeks, we had not set foot outside our glen. Presently, we ventured out again, mainly finding death and desolation. We had been incredibly fortunate, but now we needed to make plans and act for our safety. Donal called a meeting and spoke.

"We need to fortify the glen entrance."

Mrs. Giles spoke contemptuously. "There speaks the soldier. Everyone out there is dead, and he wants to start another war."

Donal looked at her. "Everyone is *not* dead," he said quietly. "The Laird's brother told us that eventually, the death rate could be as high as ninety-eight or even ninety-nine percent. And that is possible, but it's also possible that in this country, that may be lower. If that's so, we'll have a problem."

"Why?" another voice asked.

"Because civilization depends on numbers. Look at the glen here. Do we make our things any longer, or do we buy them? Can we make them? No, mostly we cannot. So what happens when the eco systems we have fail?"

"We have enough for years," was someone's comment.

"And what of our children? Will they have electricity, or will they have to go back to fires for cooking and heating, candles for light, and how will they make those anyway? Will they have to go back further, to getting up at first light and going to bed with sunset? It's not simple or easy; civilization gave us a lot, but it's taken away too."

"How?" That was the minister, and Donal eyed him gently.

"A village is no longer self-sufficient. It used to be that we had everything in one place. A blacksmith, maybe a tinsmith, a potter, a carpenter, we raised all our own food, many villages had only a bible, no other books, a midwife or a wise woman, but no doctor. If you were too injured, you died. If you were too sick, you died. A village was self-sufficient, and we may be moving back to that. Civilization requires numbers. But it also requires knowledge. And nowadays many people know only how to press a button, how to turn a lever. Then there are the cities."

"What about them?" Mrs. Giles again.

Donal looked directly at her. "They have people."

She snorted at this glimpse of the obvious.

"People," Donal continued patiently. "Who no longer have employment, money to buy food. And there's no food to be bought and no one to buy it from anyway."

She snorted again. "Nonsense. How did they manage before?"

Silly woman, I thought. I'd spent time in cities. Many city folks had only three or four days' worth of food in the house. At the least, they shopped each week, usually the day after payday. But what Mrs. Giles was overlooking was that food did not miraculously appear in city supermarkets. It was brought in from warehouses, depots, from the wharves, from many places which would no longer be sending it.

I could guess what would happen. People would live on what they had. Then they'd venture out in desperation. Those that waited too long would find shops looted and empty, the same for supermarkets. Fires would break out when looting became rife – looters always seem to set things on fire. But there were no longer brigades to deal with fires. Whole areas would burn, the inhabitants fleeing with what they could carry. Increasingly desperate, they would surge out looking for food, a way to survive. Initially, they might find what they needed on farms near cities. They could move into those where the owners had died. But they knew nothing about farming. Many would eat everything they found and move on. It would be like a plague of locusts spreading further and further.

Donal was explaining some of this. Other voices chimed in. One rose in quavering tones. Old Mrs. Giles, at ninety-two, she'd seen good times and bad, she'd been born two years after World War Two and knew from her family what times had been like then.

"The man is right. We need to take care of our own first. To make sure city folk can't come and take what we have, then leave us to starve. Or worst still, attack us for what we have, kill most of us, and leave a handful here with nothing."

I would have dismissed that as an exaggeration, but it was quite possible. If enough had had the initial infection in a city, been treated with allodaxin – and it was available first in cities – then there could be sufficient people surviving to overrun us. If they could find us, that was, and force the glen entrance, which we could make expensive for them.

I stood. "We have a choice. Do we go down into darkness, do we become the barbarians everyone once was, or do we retain what knowledge we can and slowly build back on that?" I let them see me searching every face for a response, as I added in a deliberately wicked tone. "You do realise that if we rebuild first, we can bring civilization to England, we can bring the benefits of our laws, our customs, our culture, we can have them singing our songs, the tartan worn everywhere?" Laughter began and rippled louder and louder through those present.

"Of course," I raised my voice. "We'd have to win against any invaders, but we've done *that* before." They cheered. "And we have more now. We have three glens to farm, to populate, as safe places from which we can grow. We'll take in the best that come needing a place; we'll take in children who have no one, we'll build a library and stock it with information along with books to read for pleasure. We fortify the glens and hold them against all others." More cheers. "We'll send out salvage parties and reclaim what we need not just to live but to build anew."

I raised my voice in a ringing cry. "We shall start our school again, we *are* civilization, and we *will* keep the lights on, we *will* live, grow, prevail, and in the end, all this land will be ours, and people will remember Glen Mhairi as the lamp upheld. In a thousand years, they will write books about us, trace their blood back to us with pride, they will make poems about us, sing songs, and our names shall live forever. *Glen Mhairi!*"

I was transported. I felt for the first time the power that comes when you speak the truth, say what people need to hear, and say it with a conviction that lifts them from their seats – and I did. They rose, chanting the glen's name over and over, tears on their faces. And amongst them, I saw the minister looking worried, his wife looking sour, and his mother waving her stick in the air and beaming. I let them rejoice in what they could do and be, then waved them to their seats.

"That's all well and good, but it's hard work," I said pragmatically, and a ripple of amusement came back. "It is. But the alternative is seeing our children, our grandchildren fall back further each generation. Right now, we have or can find the knowledge we'll need. We can take in others for genetic diversification, share the knowledge they'll bring, but from now on, we take in no one who hasn't been quarantined on the other side of our gatehouse to be certain they aren't bringing in sickness. There are others besides the virus. If anyone is a troublemaker, a predator, and continues that behaviour here, they'll be cast out. We can't afford them. We are a people. We stand for each other and against our enemies. *Glen Mhairi!*"

They cheered once more, shouting the name of our glen, until Donal dismissed them with a few well-chosen words, turning to me once we were home again, and Ricky was eagerly asking about the meeting.

"I had no idea you were an orator."

I laughed. "Cometh the hour, cometh the woman."

"The minister looked worried. And Mrs. Giles looked sour, I saw."

"Aye, we'll have trouble with them sooner or later, I'm thinking."

I nodded. "I know, now we need to get busy on some of what you said."

We had an enjoyable hour telling Ricky most of what had happened, and he groaned.

"School, when?"

"It'll start again next week. And it'll be bigger. All the children under sixteen will go to the school here."

Donal looked at me. "I saw you talking to Janet."

"Yes, she'll be principal, but we have Jill, who was a high school teacher before she retired. She'll come back. It'll be a scramble for the two of them, but there are people out there. To start with, we take in any family that has a useful profession, who's prepared to work hard and be a part of the glen. Orphan children we take in join a family, no house needed. New families, we have the older houses that were never moved, but we looked after, and there are houses left vacant by … by those who died. We fill the empty, unused houses first. And we go to Comber Beach. That'll give us a start on more housing."

His arm went around my shoulders. "We can do it."

"And we will." I hesitated, but Ricky had gone up to his room, and I met Donal's clear gaze. "However, we won't be around forever to keep the glen doing what's needful. We have to start passing on the torch *now.*"

"We will, we'll start at the school, with the kids who'll come after us, the older ones are living it, they'll remember and know what we lost. What we need to regain." I leaned into his solid strength and felt his calm reach out to me. We could do this, we would do this, and we would find those who believed.

"Donal, what about Comber Beach? If we begin there before we have the need, we can be ahead," *Best to be ahead where possible,* I thought.

He considered that. "Good thought, lass. Tomorrow, before school starts Monday, so we can use Jill and some older kids, Ricky could come?" I nodded, and it was agreed.

****

The wider road curved to Johnny's manor house from our glen, and all his glen around that was being well used. Johnny's estate had vegetable gardens, fruit and nut trees, an orangery attached to the old manor house, and an ancient walled garden he'd cleared and planted to berry bushes with netting from wall top to wall top to keep out the birds. By the house, there were outbuildings, many containing accumulated discards of generations – as did the manor house attics. Food was being harvested, and I had a team going through that accumulation, storing it properly, making notes of what we had, and repairing what could be mended and might be needed.

Tai, Johnny's cat, had settled happily with us, Ricky adored him, and the big cat indulged that since it included many cuddles, a comfortable bed and companion with whom to sleep, preferential treatment at dinnertime, and the right to come and go as he pleased. The dogs had somehow decided that they owned – or perhaps belonged – to the entire glen. They obeyed

Donal and me, but they roamed freely, greeting anyone who indicated a desire to be greeted, playing with the children. It seemed to me that they had reverted to the original system. We were all part of their pack, Donal and I the alpha pair, the rest on equal terms, with puppies to be indulged – and, as I came to see when I watched them one day, in effect walking the perimeter of the pack's territory.

Every day they went down the road to our guard-post, then over the two roads leading to their original home, and to the new glen opened up by the machinery, they sniffed the ground over the roads for a short distance, seemed to pause and listen, then relaxed, and it was watching their actions that something came to me. Johnny had bought them as well-trained guard dogs, but both were male – Cassie being short for Cassius. However, dogs' lives are a lot shorter than ours, they were only three, but that still gave us no more than ten or twelve years. If we wanted to keep the breed pure, we'd have to find a bitch or two. The ubiquitous Border collie we would find in many places. Dobermans were not so common, so I should keep an eye out; something else to add to a lengthening list

I spent the night sleeping very well. I will say this for the collapse of civilization, I went to bed so tired I rarely woke from the time I laid down until the sun shone in the window at first light. Unlike my earlier habits, when I woke once or twice and might read for an hour before sleeping again. Every cloud has a silver lining somewhere.

We ate early that morning, Ricky bouncing with excitement. He counted aloud as one by one the vehicles assembled. Once they were all there, our Landcruiser led off with Donal driving and me riding shotgun – literally. These days I was carrying two of them. Both cut down and the butts insulated to take up some of the kick. That way, they had more room to be swung into line, and I'd always been good with one. I started skeet shooting as a child on Johnny's father's back lawn, and of all of us, I was the fastest and most accurate. Now lives might depend on my skill, and while it wasn't obvious, I had other weapons. Apart from that, Cass and Bruce had come with us. I could put guards on the glen but not where we were going, or not as effective as the dogs would be.

It was a ninety-minute drive to Comber Beach, Ricky calling from the back seat as we passed places or animals that caught his attention. We took the journey at a steady thirty miles an hour. Hungry animals were beginning to break down fences on farms where the farmers were dead. Now and then, a crashed vehicle needed to be moved, and once, nearly to our destination, we met a barricade. I radioed back to the glen while we halted well short of it. If anything went wrong, they needed to know.

"Claire, Sheila here. We're ten miles short of Comber on the main road."

"Receiving, Sheila. Is there trouble?"

"Maybe. There's a barricade, not a natural one. We're about to check it."

"Claire, waiting to hear, Out." I turned. "Ricky, stay low. I'm trusting you to watch to either side. If you see anything unusual, any stranger moving, tell us." He beamed proudly at the trust and dropped down until only his eyes and the top of his head showed as he peered about eagerly.

Donal called instructions, and our people moved. Not army smart, but well enough. He moved with them, the dogs at his heels. A sweep of his hand, a quiet order, and they split, racing to either side and circled the barricade. Cass appeared on top of the blockade and barked. That was good enough. They were called back, Donal took his seat, and we rolled slowly forward. We spaced out. If any vehicle was attacked, the others had time to escape, but there was no need. We rolled ahead, and as we drove through the narrow gap, I saw that no one was there, and from the weeds starting to climb the bits of fence, old cars, worn tyres, and other junk, no one had moved anything there for weeks.

Donal slowed and glanced about. "Someone being paranoid right at the start of things. They expected ravening hordes and were making sure they could be kept out."

I imagined it. We'd had some idea of what was happening, here no one would have known. People had begun to die. Nothing that could be done for them stopped it. Maybe they'd guessed the outcome, but they had to do something. Maybe someone else liked SF, so this was what they'd done. Then they'd died, and their memorial was a futile barricade. I found tears in my eyes and blinked them back. I couldn't cry my way through another twenty years, not for all the sorrow, the death, and futility of a land scattered with bones. Donal reached for my hand, falling into the accent that was a joke between us.

"Dinna greet, lass, sun comes up in 't morning still, that's the main thing."

I had to laugh. "It does, although if we were all dead, it wouldn't mean much to us."

"Mean a lot to the creatures, lass, if humans were all dead, well, the virus isn't killing them, they'll go on, maybe become intelligent in the far future like that book of Andre Norton's. What was it?"

"*Breed to Come*. Intelligent cats, Tai would like that."

"Dogs wouldn't," was the wry response, and I laughed before radioing back to the glen that all was well

Ricky made the tiny sound that meant he wanted to ask something but didn't want to interrupt. I turned and nodded.

"I never heard of Andre Norton. Who's he?"

I smiled, remembering. A friend had introduced me to the author's books. She'd been older and had known both the books and the writer. "Andre Norton wrote science fiction and fantasy mainly. Her books are wonderful. I have almost all of them."

"I've never seen them?"

I laughed. "No, you wouldn't. They're in our bedroom."

Ricky eyed me suspiciously. "I've been in there."

"Yes, and you didn't see them because ours is a very old house." He looked at me, puzzled, and I elaborated. "You know it's a stone house?" He nodded. "Well, when Donal and I retired and came home, my mother had just died, and I inherited the house, and it has its secrets. One is a room off our bedroom. Maybe in older times, it was a strong room for valuables. Now we keep books there. The irreplaceable ones. My friend gave me copies of some of my favourite books. They'd been signed by their authors, and copies like that were valuable then. Not anymore, I guess, or not for money. But I value them, and they're safe where they are."

Ricky considered this. "Could I read them if I was careful?"

I looked stern. "You'd have to be really careful, not drop butter on them, or spill anything over them. If they're damaged, they can't ever be replaced." I set that thought aside for the moment. "Do you promise?"

"I promise."

"Then I'll show you the room when we're done with Comber Beach."

The road outside dipped down, and I looked ahead. We'd gathered every flatbed truck we could find, twelve of them. Half a dozen forklifts on one, and behind those another dozen of the more powerful vehicles equipped with towbars. Comber Beach was a small tourist hotspot; sites to park your caravan, with empty caravans and small chalets for rent. The chalets were mainly open plan and around thirty feet by twenty. Now, caravans could be towed home, and the best chalets lifted onto flatbed trucks. I wasn't sure how long we'd have petrol available, but while we had it, we needed to stockpile.

Books too, I thought. The damp of winter would ruin many, and books of the ordinary paperback kind were not made to survive for many generations anyhow. Our Landcruiser arrived at the start of town, and Donal slowed, watching keenly. I did too, and warned by our attention, the dogs peered out as well. A movement and Cass's head swung to follow. I patted him.

"Just a rabbit." And realised what that suggested. "Donal, if a rabbit's out and about in daylight, there's no people."

"Aye. Never was likely. They get tourists here from all over, other countries and all. They'd be carrying the virus. We lived longer because most of the glen had that minor virus to start, you got to our people quickly, and it would have taken longer because the glen's isolated, and we don't leave it that much so we were probably infected later."

"So there could be a few more places like us too," I noted. "Further north still, once we get the glens set up, we should think about an expedition."

Donal chuckled. "Aye, once we get the glens set up, and I'm thinking that'll be a lifetime's work in itself."

In which, he was quite right. Glen Mhairi was about two miles long and a mile wide. And could only be accessed in a vehicle by the single narrow strip of gravelled road leading off the main north/south road. Johnny's immediate land was also a glen although it was known as the Laird's estate, was twice the size with a decent road to it – and was thus more in danger of invasion – while the glen into which we'd driven a new road was a little smaller than ours, with the only vehicular access being through Glen Mhairi. But taken together, they made a fair bit of land.

In the old times, Glen Mhairi and Johnny's glen had housed five hundred people. We'd been down to less than three

hundred because of people getting work elsewhere, students going on to university, and some older folks entering a nursing
home rather than dying at home. Their houses had been left if
they could not be moved since they had little resale value, the
land belonging to the McAlisters. We'd kept the best houses in
good condition – while the ones that weren't in great shape to
begin with were quietly mined for wood until they vanished.
But we could see a population of several times that five hundred
if we found and chose new settlers judiciously. It wasn't quite a
civilization, but we could do a lot if we had those numbers.

We rolled slowly through Comber Beach, until at the far
end of the shops, we moved into first a small suburb, and beyond that, acres of bright chalets, caravans, and laid out sites for
those who arrived with their own quarters. We circled, slowed
to a stop in line, and Donal climbed out of our Landcruiser. The
dogs went with him, and he swept his right arm out.

"Cass, Bruce, people, seek."

The dogs took off, racing through the caravans and chalets. Now and again, they came into sight, running low, noses
working, and in silence. Looking in those moments at what
they were, dogs trained and bred as soldiers and warriors for
humankind, I determined we had to find more of them. We
would lose most separate breeds of dogs and cats, they would
combine, and the breed characteristics would go.

With cats, and in my opinion, that didn't matter. People
mostly loved cats for being cats. They were a comfort, a friend,
something to keep the dark away, and keep the vermin out of
food, so size, conformation, colour, or breed didn't matter. Just
an effective small killing machine for the vermin; and for humans, the love, the warmth, and the purr. But dogs were bred
to service. If we retained two breeds, it seemed to me that the
hard-working, intelligent Border collie would be the first and
the Doberman the second. Neither were huge dogs. They were

fast, smart, and instrumental in what was likely to become a new society.

Cass and Bruce returned, dropped to a sit at Donal's feet, and looked up. They were reporting no humans present, and Donal accepted the report. He nodded to me, and I spoke in a loud, clear voice.

"Each team choose a caravan or chalet. If you find bodies, you know what to do. Deep salvage where practical. Go." They went; me and Ricky with them.

CHAPTER FIVE

Common sense – isn't that common. ~Robert Heinlein

Smartest and most accurate thing the man ever said. ~Sheila McArn

It had been the height of the tourist season, but even so, many of the bright little chalets had no occupants. They had probably been in transition. One family had left, while another was due, but had fallen sick and not come. Sufficient empty chalets were found to take a load of twelve at once, and the flatbeds started on their homeward trip, which would be fast since the drivers would be dropping the chalets off on arrival and returning immediately. We had outriders ahead and behind the flatbeds for safety, with Jill in command of the initial convoy.

I'd let the glen know what we were doing and to have a team ready to remove the chalets. So far, it looked as if we could make at least two round trips in a day until we had everything useable. People could be housed in a caravan. If single or just a couple and planning to remain that way, a caravan might suit them permanently, or they could be moved to a house when one was available. For the chalets, Donal and I had plans.

About half a dozen caravans had no occupants. I'd had those taken in tow and sent off before the flatbeds, again with outriders. Janet back in the glen knew where they were to go. We'd discussed it earlier, and she'd made good suggestions.

"Split the caravans. A third to each glen. Stockpile most of the chalets by the school. You can use some as community buildings, and there is a good place. And some of the chalets you could drop off before the glen, say halfway down to us. You talked about quarantining new people. You'll need a place for that."

I hadn't thought beyond the idea, and that was a helpful suggestion. So the first lot of chalets would be dropped off there, and we would add water tanks and whatever else could be done to make temporary housing. There was a small flat area, about an acre on one side of the glen road, well sheltered by a long row of trees on the roadside. They would be put there, and the drivers and teams knew where and how to place them, spacing each chalet from its companions for health reasons. Once the virus was gone, we could reclaim the chalets if they weren't needed anymore.

"Sheila?"

I turned. "What is it?"

"Come and look at this?"

I followed Jimmie's call to a caravan. It was big, one of those self-contained, self-powered types, a late model in the Dutchmaster range. They had been downsized. The earlier models twenty years ago were so large; they'd been forbidden on roads in some countries. The new ones were narrower, lower, and lighter. However, they were still insulated, with a water tank, toilet and toilet tank, and large petrol tanks. They had a 3D 75-inch TV, surround sound, fridge-freezer, wardrobe, and two bedrooms, the master one en-suite. It had been parked in a half-circle hedge which was why we hadn't seen it before, and I paused to look at it in admiration before joining Jimmy on the steps.

"Fabulous."

"It is." I looked at him questioningly. "Aye, well, I thought you might want to go through it yourself. People that own this sort of outfit, you never know *what* they might have in here."

That was quite true. I sent him to look for other suitable caravans and opened the door. The most incredible stench wafted out, and I groaned. That might render the vehicle useless to us, which would be a pity. I entered cautiously. The bedroom doors were open, and I blinked. No bodies, then why...? A tiny movement caught my attention, and I focussed downwards, then spoke softly.

"It's all right, sweetheart. I won't hurt you. Come to me. Poor little fellow, did they leave you and not come back, and you've been alone all this time?"

Yes, that was a thought. It'd been over a month. How on earth had a puppy survived? On second thought, no, people who could afford a Dutchmaster would have a setup for their dog too. Water provided on demand from the tank, food delivered every x number of hours, probably dog biscuits. But that certainly explained the smell.

The puppy had wiggled his way tentatively to my feet and gazed up beseechingly. I scooped him up, laughed as a frantic tongue attacked me, and examined him gently. He was a boy, neutered, and probably vaccinated and micro-chipped. I'd have put him around six months old, and he was one of the designer breeds. Some time back, someone decided the collie type known as the Shetland Sheep Dog was a delightful but still too large breed. They crossed them with Pomeranians, stabilized the result, and Pomshees have been on the market for the past two years, guaranteed when bred within their breed to stay true to it. They were delightful creatures, beautiful, intelligent, a convenient size, and much sought-after.

The original breeder had had the right idea, however. He'd kept the numbers low, the prices very high. Culled for quality – in intelligence, size, and type – and sold only to handpicked owners who could afford the price. The puppy wore an expensive collar of gold plaques, etched with his name and the information that a reward would be offered for his return if he were lost. I sighed. There were people out there who'd see the collar, grab the pup, read the information, and hold him for ransom, whether or not he'd been lost initially. Dog people his owners may have been, but lacking in sense. Heinlein's quote came to mind.

I scoured the caravan, Laddie at my heels every step of the way. I found his food and water dispensers and thanked heaven for them. It would have been a brutal way for the puppy to die of thirst and alone, although it could have been from hunger. The toilet worked, and he'd have drunk from that. But sooner or later, food or water would have failed, and he'd have died. I wondered if he'd been their last thought as they died, wherever it had happened. Probably in hospital, people like that would have gone there at the first indication of sickness.

I looked down at Laddie and took a minute to mourn for beloved pets left to die and for owners who had no way of saving them. More so, I thought, for parents who had a still more bitter choice to make when knowing they were dying, of taking their children with them or leaving them to live on, in the hope they'd survive somehow. It had been Ricky's parents' choice – they'd just been lucky.

Laddie whimpered. I grinned at Bruce and Cass where they stood in the doorway. "Hi, boys, come to look at the puppy, gently now." I lowered Laddie to where they could sniff him, accept him as a new member of the pack, a puppy – no status, no threat – and then I placed him on the floor. He recoiled while he was checked over, his scent committed to memory, and I said his name to them. "This is Laddie." I got intelligent looks from amber eyes, and they moved on, but I knew they'd remember.

The Dutchmaster, I found, had been owned by a wealthy industrialist, even I'd heard the name. He was a philanthropist, a hard worker, an intelligent man who'd been happily married for almost fifty years to his childhood sweetheart, no children. He retired last year at seventy-five and announced they'd be taking a two-year vacation before deciding what to do with the rest of their lives. I sighed for them. Still, they'd had longer than I had so far. They'd probably died together; from what I'd seen, the virus hit harder and faster the older, younger, or weaker you were, and it was likely their only regrets would be years lost, their puppy's fate – and Laddie was fine; what had been lost was found.

But the caravan was a treasure trove. Everything of the best, the fridge-freezer would be useful, and the tool chest contained the highest quality tools. They had about fifty books, recent and all by fine writers. Their clothing was superb, the bedding and the furniture ditto, and there was a stack of small items which could be usefully shared over time. The wife had been into knitting and crocheting with wool and patterns, and while no stations were broadcasting, we could use the enormous television.

I suspected the husband had been taken ill first. She'd fled with him to a hospital or private clinic and left things undone. Why was that my conclusion? Because they weren't there, but everything had been left unlocked. I know men; they tend to be anal-retentive about locking up their prize possessions. A panicking woman with a beloved husband looking very ill would think it unimportant. You could always buy new things; you couldn't buy a life. So she'd helped him out to whatever vehicle had been used, and in her distress, she'd left the caravan unlocked, the inner doors and compartments all unlocked, and also, as I found in my prying, the safe remained open.

The safe contained jewellery, a magnificent knife, two handguns, vehicle registration, Laddie's pedigree, and other personal papers. There was a paper notebook with details of who to contact in case of emergency, and then there were the drugs. From the labels, they'd convinced their family doctor to part with these. However, I thought he may not have done that quite legally, since among others, he'd provided powerful painkillers not in general distribution. Well, they'd be helpful.

I shut up the caravan; it could temporarily be parked by our house. I'd clean it, salvage Laddie's food, sort out the contents, and I thought it could remain near us, to be used as temporary accommodation if we ever had visiting dignitaries of some sort. Ricky appeared as I exited the caravan, his eyes lighting up as he spotted the puppy, which promptly recognised another dog-lover when it saw one and strained towards the boy.

"Wow, he's great. Where did you find him?"

I gestured. "In there. He had food and water dispensers, so he survived, but he's been lonely, I'd say."

Ricky hesitated, then blurted, "Could I have him, please, I'll look after him, see to his food and water, and I'll train him."

"A dog is a responsibility," I told him carefully. I knew junior staff; they have enthusiasms and then drop them for something more interesting. However, I'd expected this the moment the puppy came to me. I knew Ricky wanted a dog, he'd been promised one for his twelfth birthday, but they'd been waiting until his father had time off to go and look at kennels. "You can't get tired of him and not bother, he wouldn't understand, and Grandpa and I don't have time to look after him. If you take him, you do the work. If you don't, I'd be sorry, but he'd have to go to someone else." It was harsh, yet I didn't think he would fail. He was an often silent child, intelligent, conscientious, a worker, and I thought nothing that loved him would ever turn to him in vain.

Ricky looked at me. "I swear, I'll look after him all his life, he'll be my dog, I'll love him and never forget he needs me."

No, I thought, *the way you needed your parents and lost them. Not their fault, but I think you're drawing a parallel.* I nodded. "He's yours then." I handed over the puppy and watched the wild enthusiasm as they ran in circles. Donal came up behind me and chuckled.

"A lad and his dog, not a much better sight in the world. Do I gather we have a new member of the family?"

"We do." I explained about the puppy, which led to a discussion on the caravan, a digression on the owners, and an agreement.

"Aye, I'll drive it back, and if the pup's been in it a month, it'll need fumigating. I can park it back side of the house where it'll be convenient for you. If anyone says anything, let them smell it, they'll soon enough shut up. Now, where are we on the next convoy?"

In the end, it took four days shuttling to and fro. Donal sat eating dinner that final evening looking satisfied. Ricky was exhausted, had eaten early, and gone to bed.

Fortunately, Tai had looked over the puppy on its arrival, noted that it respected him with every bone in its small body, and accepted it. He was used to dogs and had no problems with any that understood he stood first in any hierarchy. Laddie was delighted not to be alone any longer and was graciously permitted the freedom of the cat's home. Both now slept with Ricky, one to either side of the boy, and while Tai spent his usual time with Ricky, Laddie was Ricky's constant companion, loving and loved, and with brief periods of daily work, he was also turning into a well-trained little dog.

Donal looked up from his dinner now. "Got all the new vans and chalets sorted."

"How have you shared them?" I asked, knowing some but not all the final decisions.

"I can't believe how well we've done. We only took the portables in good shape and condition, but we've got almost fifty caravans, split among the glens; that's fifteen or sixteen each and thirty-one chalets here. Janet says that the school classroom was starting to be a bit crowded, but it's okay since we lost some pupils to the virus. But if we expand, it's useful to have classrooms right there waiting. And those chalets are a perfect size, they have a toilet, a kitchen alcove, and they can easily be insulated and have a rainwater tank added. We've set ten chalets aside for that, another two for staff rooms, four to amalgamate as a public library, and five more for whatever else we may need. The other ten goes five each to McAlister and Blind Glen." (We'd taken to calling the newly opened up glen by that name since it had no outlet save into Glen Mhairi.)

I felt a sense of deep satisfaction. There'd been the first twelve chalets in addition. They now formed a neat double line on the flat section off our gravel road. I'd put a team to making six into self-contained homes and the other half-dozen into three double homes for larger families.

"The road chalets, if we ever need to reclaim them, we can," I commented.

Donal's fork paused. "If they last, they're not under our eyes, we could get squatters, and you know what some of *those* are like."

I did, and I also knew some of them would have had the earlier minor infection. The question was, how many would also have been treated with allodaxin. I suspected that many wouldn't have. The minor infection died out if untreated for ten days or so, and many people had neither the money nor inclination to seek treatment if the problem went away within a reasonable time. I said so and Donal nodded.

"Verra likely. But there's others who had the money, could get the antibiotic, and would. Drug dealers, for one."

"With no more merchandise coming in, most customers dead, and how do they get paid now?"

Donal's face sobered. "They pay in service. Sex, killing whoever they're pointed at, manufacture from scratch or growing it, doing whatever's wanted or they're told."

"They'd stick to cities, surely?"

"Maybe."

I didn't like the thoughts I was having, not any of them. "But they won't live long."

"The original lot won't, but others will come along. Or a charismatic dealer who isn't a user may move into the Laird business. Take over an area and run it with serfs, soldiers, farmers, and all owning to him, grant rank for special abilities or events." He grinned at me. "You know enough of history. It's how many noble families started, or the equivalent of it. How do you think *our* glens are going to go?"

I stared. "Democracy."

"Modified, aye, that's likely with touches of the clan system. But in the end, when orders need to be given and obeyed quickly for survival, someone gives them. You may not have noticed yet, lass, but to date, that's been us. Janet, Claire, the minister, Jimmy, and a few others act as advisers, but we've made the major decisions, said what we're doing, and everyone's done it."

I thought back and had to agree. We had, and they had. Donal and I had come home with drugs that saved many people with early warning and solid information. We were used to taking command in dangerous situations. We'd told everyone what was happening, made some of the first necessary decisions allied to that - which had made sense to almost everyone, so they obeyed.

In the middle of the beginning, lawlessness, I shot the bikers. It was brutal, decisive, and I'd saved the lives of friends, who had told everyone in the glen about it. I'd been a reluctant heroine, and it had been noted again when we'd taken Ricky as our own. We'd brought back Johnny's animals, the dogs obeying only Donal and me. Then, too, there was the deed we showed them, naming us as Trustees of the McAlister estate forever - if no descendant of provably true blood ever showed up. In a way, we legally owned the three glens. For years, too, I'd acted as nurse-practitioner, medical technician, whatever you want to call it, to the glen, and Donal as Laird-accredited reeve – he'd taken the title since it was all private land and Johnny liked having a reeve. De facto, and without intention, we'd become the leaders.

I took in a long deep breath. "Truth to tell, love, I can't think of anyone better. Janet would be as good, but she would'na touch the job with a barge-pole. She loves her work at the school, and she's best there. Claire is a hard worker, but she's a natural second-in-command. She wouldn't be happy trying to run things."

Donal nodded. "She'd second-guess herself, hesitate when she should act." His face was quiet and solemn. "Part of it is, we may not be young, but that only gives us authority. I was in the army, and everyone knows I've fought and killed. This is a time when having a leader who can say that is reassuring. You, lass, you're a trained paramedic, you've stayed current, you've been under fire, you've had staff under your command, and everyone knows about the bikers." He chuckled. "I wasn't surprised when I heard, mind. But others were. Only Johnny, Mac, and I knew just how good you were with a shotgun. And you weren't a front-line paramedic without learning to act fast and what to do. You've never seen how it impressed some of our people."

I snorted. "I'd rather they were impressed by lives saved than taken, but what do you think of it all, Donal? What should we do about this?"

His gaze fixed mine steadily, and I knew what he would say before he spoke. "We take up the mantle, lass. We lead, hold what is ours, care for our people, hope for the years to do that, and we see that those that come after us are trained to do the same. And if we hold by it all, we can die knowing we did the best we could."

I sat silent a moment before I nodded, and so it was decided, on a fine evening in late summer, the world in ruins about us, that we would accept our people's unspoken demand, their expectation. We would lead them, and fates willing, we would do so wisely and well so long as we were able. We rose early the next day and went out to do our best.

CHAPTER SIX

Over the years apropos of various events, I've been told that the dice have no memory. ~Author unknown

That's where humans and dice differ, we expect patterns, and don't like not finding them. ~Donal McArn

After all the excitement at Comber Beach, I settled to make lists again. The first thing was to sort Mac's cottage. He'd given it to us when we'd said goodbye as we left his lab. Now I should see what that entailed. Then, too, there was the local poultry, and that would keep me busy. Until we started running missions up to a couple of hours driving time away, I'd had no idea how many people kept hens, and if I'd thought about it, I'd probably assumed that they were all in hen runs. They may have been initially kept that way, but I can only think that many people had been fond of their hens, and on realizing that they were dying, they'd freed their poultry and hoped for the best.

The average hen can flap a short distance up or along, but they don't fly well. Local foxes must be having a wonderful time, but considering how many hens we'd seen to and from Comber Beach, I thought the fox population was set for generations – and why should they have them all. Hens are a two-purpose species for humanity. They lay eggs, and they are edible. Only two glen families had hens. What we did have more of were geese. I'd seen in several places how useful they were – bigger eggs, more meat, *and* guard duty – and on coming back to live in the glen permanently, I'd gone out and purchased two ganders and seven geese.

They were Sebastopols, my New Zealand writer friend had them, and I'd long since known their uses. They couldn't fly, but they could certainly run, they were fairly aggressive, both sexes, and they tended to be surprisingly intelligent. They knew who belonged and who didn't, and they could make strangers or marauding animals very unwelcome. Our gaggle now numbered twenty-six, and I'd like to add more.

I'd also like to bring in more free-range hens, and I'd noted as we passed a side road on the way to Comber Beach that there'd been many hens pecking about in a field. I gathered several of the women, including Anna, whose family had hens, and in three cars, each towing a wide trailer covered with a tarpaulin, we set off on a poultry hunting expedition. We had three trailers because while I wasn't planning on bringing back hundreds of hens if we found them, we'd also look for feeders and other hen-type gear, as well as investigate the homes of deceased owners. "Time wisely used is rarely wasted," as my grandmother used to say.

Anna was with me and saw hens immediately; we turned into that road. "Stop here."

I signalled the stop and pulled the car up on the side of the road. Anne considered the hens and shook her head.

"Wrong breed. What we want is a breed that lays well but is also good eating."

"Such as?"

"Ideally? Orpingtons. Then there's Rhode Island Reds, Speckled Sussex, and Wyandottes. I'd go for any of those."

"And you'd know one when you see it? Or is that a silly question?"

"I'd know them, and I don't see any here. Let's go on, drive slowly so I can look over the paddocks."

I drove slowly. After a half-hour, I wondered if anyone in this area had ever had the breeds we wanted, but I said nothing. I learned in the army to trust an expert until they proved otherwise. Anna swung her small set of binoculars to look ahead as we rounded a bend and yelped.

"Pull in here."

I did so, and the other cars pulled up behind me.

"There," Anna was pointing. In the field, I saw hens, they didn't look wildly different to those we'd seen already, but Anna was smiling. She saw I didn't understand and explained quickly. "Look at that sign." I looked. It said that the Halcot Farm sold chickens, eggs, chicks, and equipment. It listed available breeds below, and I saw all four Anna had previously mentioned. Right, that was convenient.

I deferred to Anna, and she had us take the vehicles into the farm driveway. She marched up to the farmhouse door and knocked loudly. She waited and knocked again. The door remained shut, and I spoke quietly.

"They're in business. There are cars parked in the garage. If they aren't answering what could be customers, they're likely to be gone – one way or another but try again. I don't want to take property if they still need it." Anna nodded, knocked again, and called out.

"Mrs. Halcot, we'd like to buy some hens and equipment if you have it. Could you come to the door, please?" There was no response. She went to the back door, repeated her action and call, and again, nothing moved.

I flicked a glance over the house and noticed that a small window I took to be to the bathroom was slightly open. I walked over, placed my face to one side of the aperture, and breathed in. That told me everything I needed to know.

"I think you can stop trying." Anna joined me, sniffed, and met my look.

"Yes. Do we start with the house or the hens?"

"The house."

I took a tyre iron, wedged it into the window, and heaved once. It would have been a burglar's gift. The hinges gave way, and the window popped out, pivoting on the latch. Anna caught it, and I assessed the entrance. It was a small window, but I was lean. I accepted a lift and climbed through with a minimum of wriggling. I'd left the tyre iron with Anna, padding through the house listening for movement but hearing nothing. I opened the back door, and my team trooped in.

The power still worked when I used a switch, and in the better light, we could see this had once been a pleasant home, owned by people who looked after it. I assessed the contents and thought we'd deep salvage here. Many empty houses in the glen had no contents of any kind, and some of those we chose to welcome would come with nothing. Better to offer them a house fully stocked and this place would provide generously.

I found the owners in their bedroom as I'd both expected and feared. They were long since dead, and I saw that they had not been young, more of my age, and beside them lay a single sheet of paper on the woman's bedside cabinet. I picked it up, wondering what she'd found to say. It was succinct enough. Not a woman to taste words, she said what she needed to say, and that was it.

"We're dying. No one answers the emergency number. We let all the hens out. You can call them in with the wheat in the shed and clucking. If Maisie will come to you, please give her a home. She's a good mouser and a good mother. Take anything you want; we've no family but don't be vandals.

Mylie Halcot, wife to John Halcot."

I looked at the bodies on the bed and gave instructions. We wrapped them in the stained bedding, carried them outside, and buried them in a hole that may have been dug for waste. We tucked them in, covered them with earth, and I said a few words. These had been decent people who cared for their creatures; they deserved recognition.

"Sleep well. We'll give Maisie a home if she'll come to us. We'll take some of the hens and look after them so the lines you bred continue. We'll clear the house and use everything, and we aren't vandals. What you have will help to save others. Wherever you may have gone, know that and be pleased." Anna was crying quietly, as was Sue, her neighbour who'd come with us. Mary and Janis stood quietly accepting.

I turned on my heel and headed for the barn and henhouses. In the barn, I found Maisie. She was thin, around four, typically tabby, and nursing three kittens, still with their eyes shut. Far from fleeing, she came running and wailed urgently. Sue spun, trotted back to the house, and returned with a freshly opened tin of cat food. Maisie ate voraciously, and Sue stroked her.

"If no one minds, I'll take her." No one did. Maisie, the kittens, and all of the cat food were carried to Sue's car and ensconced in a curl of blanket on the back seat. Maisie settled without fuss and seemed almost happy. Sue certainly was.

"I haven't had a cat since old Timmy died. It'll be nice to have one again."

I hated to rain on her parade. "I don't know if Maisie will settle in a house. She seems to be a barn cat and may prefer to be."

"I know, there's a barn where she can live. I'll take one of her kittens for a house cat and find homes for the other two." I may add that she didn't have to look far. Mary and Janis had arranged to take a kitten each before we even made it back to the glen.

****

We investigated the barn where Maisie had been after that, along with a second and larger shed. There was hay, straw, bags and bags of various types of hen food, stacks of hen feeders, rolls of wire netting, hen water troughs which could be hooked up to a supply to stay filled, and an array of other items of the sort that accumulate in barns. There were two long henhouses. They were both set up but were empty.

Five brood coops did contain hens with young chicks. They had feeders and water troughs, both still full and working, but when I checked, I found a rather Heath-Robinson device that would have allowed the occupants their freedom once the food ran out – I thought the more of the Halcots when I found *that*. From their look, the gadgets were older than the virus, done perhaps because, as the lady said, they had no family, and if anything happened to the Halcots, the coops' inhabitants could have died unpleasantly.

I looked over what we had before we even began to hunt hens and decided to do something about it. "One of you, please go back home. Tell Donal we need help, we'll want to take everything here, and we don't have the capacity. Ask him to bring two flatbeds, three or four utes, and people to load them."

Anna stared. "We don't need the henhouses. We probably won't have feed after this lot. The hens will have to free-range in the day and be shut in at night."

"Exactly," I told her. "We take the henhouses for that. But we want all of the fodder, not for the hens. We need it for the animals we'll get sooner or later. Then there's the hen equipment, the coops, and the house contents. We won't fit all of *that* in three cars."

She looked around and nodded. "I suppose not."

Sue cleared her throat. "I'd like to get Maisie home with the kittens. How about I go?"

I agreed, and Sue drove off while the others turned to look at me. All right. "Let's see if we can get the hens in before everyone gets here and upsets them," I said in a tone nicely balanced between an order and a suggestion. Anna ran with that.

"I can do it." She opened the nearest big henhouse door wide, scattered wheat all over the floor from a bag she opened, went to the other henhouse, and did the same. "Stand well away. Don't move about, don't stare at them. Or better yet, go in the house and start there." I grinned, gathered my troops – all two of them – and obeyed as Sue began the imitation of a hen's clucking behind us.

We went through the house, and I concluded it could have been inherited. The house appeared to have been built before the First World War. The furniture matched. It was solid wood, made to be used for generations. I thought some were likely to be much older than the house since about a third of it wasn't nailed but pegged and beautifully cared for.

I ran my fingers over the surface of a dining table, touched the carving of the chairs, and decided none of this would go anywhere I didn't think it would be appreciated. Thanks to Donal's hard work already, we had a long line of barns set up near our home. He'd taken the sort made to be hooked up. You can – that is, before the virus, you could – go to a place that sold them and buy one. Then a year later, when you had the money, you could buy another which lacked that side and was, therefore, cheaper, and so on. Initially, while they were being sold and we had the money, we'd bought five.

Later, Donal had gone back, found the place deserted, and uplifted all of them there. We now had almost thirty, spacious, well-made, and about half with doors sufficient to admit a large lorry. And considering what we might be able to get, and what we would need in the generations to come, I must remember to suggest to Donal we found a lot more of that sort of barn and added lines of them to each glen – while we had petrol and vehicles to do so.

Anna came to find us. "The hens are all in. Poor things, they haven't had proper hen food for weeks, and they couldn't believe it was on the menu again. They fell over each other getting to it. I'd say all of them around are in their houses now. So do we catch and move them before our people arrive?"

I looked at my watch and calculated. It would take time for Donal to collect drivers and vehicles, then there was the trip back. No, better to get the hens now and send Anna back with them. I looked at her. "How long for them to finish what you gave them?"

"Half an hour at most."

"All right, we wait until they're done where they are, we scatter more food in the big trailer on my Landcruiser, back that right up to the henhouse door, and once we have all the hens we want aboard, you drive them back and wait until the first henhouse is in the glen. We'll load one of those first, you shift the hens into that, see they have water, and leave them. Is all that practical?"

"Yes."

So that was the way it was. We caught about twice the number of hens we wanted, letting some go again when Anna decreed they were too old, too scrawny, or the wrong type. In the end, we had sixty hens, a mixture of the Buff Orpington, Rhode Island Reds, Speckled Sussex, and Wyandottes we'd wanted. They wouldn't stay purebred for long, but they were all excellent layers and ideal for meat too, so it wouldn't matter. I smiled wryly. In a few human generations, we'd see a new breed, the Glen Mhairi hen. A thought hit me, and I glared at the hen-crowded trailer.

"Roosters, Anna?"

She laughed. "I wondered when that'd occur to you. I looked around. There's rooster houses down the back. They had food and water containers and another release gadget. I chose the best roosters and let the others go. I've got my pick of the ones I chose in carriers, and they can be loaded onto whatever ute we can fit them on."

****

Donal arrived with a positive convoy, and while it took the remainder of that day and most of the next, once we were done, we had chickens. They were free-range during the day, called in at night, and seemed to have already learned that a wise hen accepted safe shelter for the night. After that, we added another ten Sebastopol geese, found down the same road. Struck, quite a lot further away, a farm where the owners had been horse-drawn-vehicle enthusiasts. We gathered in the lot along with the harness and assorted extras and nine horses ranging from the cob type to half-bred Suffolk. Four mares and five geldings – while I added a stallion to my list of things required.

Ricky looked at the carts and wagons as they arrived while Laddie bounced around them. "Why did you get those? We've got cars an' the trucks and everything."

I noticed that several of the younger people were listening and explained. "We get petrol from overseas, when what's here, available, and not ruined by contamination, runs out, we won't be able to use the cars and trucks. We have a finite time in which to get ourselves on a basis to survive. If we waste time or don't collect now what we'll need later, we lose more and more of what we can have or be. Many things were made in big factories too far away for us to get there. We have those things if we can find them locally. If we can't, we'll never see or have or be able to use them again."

I saw that Ricky understood, although one of the Ross children looked baffled. "What about the government? Won't they fix things?"

I sighed. "Most of the government people are probably dead or trying to survive just as we are. We're on our own, we have each other, and that's it. We may find people who'll join us, but we don't know." I reflected that when birth control pills and maybe condoms ran out, our birth rate would probably rise abruptly. Note to self: *In ancient days, they used cleaned animal intestines as condoms.* And we needed recruits for the glens, or we'd start getting inbreeding. The Ross boy was still puzzled.

"What about the army? I seen them on TV, if things go wrong, they come an' help people. Yeah, an' I wanna watch *March to Glory.* When's the TV gonna be fixed?"

"Not in your lifetime," I said quietly, and when he gaped disbelieving at me, I added, "And there's no army, not anymore. It took a lot of people to run our civilization. Now that we don't have them, a lot of things we had we won't have anymore. People are dead, and things were often made overseas. No more big ships bringing them, no more big factories, no more food coming in out of season." *Heavens, yes, plant potatoes, lot and lots, put that on the list.* The boy gave me a sneer.

"Dunno why you're lying, but I guess you are. Can't be like you say, you'll see." He slouched away, and I went to find Janet.

I found her at the school, sorting out books. I spoke when she noticed I was in the doorway. "What can you tell me about the Ross family?"

"Trouble," she said tersely.

"Why, and who are they?"

"Kin to the Camerons. They came, uninvited, for the holidays. Myself, I think they come here for a few weeks because they'd stirred up some sort of trouble at home. They arrived, the virus started, and here they stayed. They came by bus," she said emphatically, and I understood. The bus service had been one of the first things lost.

"Do they come to school now it's started again?"

"No, and to be honest with you, Sheila, I wouldn't be keen to have them. They're lazy, dirty, and happily ignorant, as well as being troublemakers and bullies. I've heard the Camerons wish they could make them go, but they can't work out how to do it."

I went home to talk that over with Donal, and we came to the reluctant conclusion that for now, we'd let sleeping Rosses lie. That civilized attitude lasted a week. There were five Rosses, mother, father, two bigger boys, and a small girl around a year and a bit old who seemed to be named Weasel. I found her sitting naked in a puddle with a Doberman looking concerned beside her. She could have been a pretty child were she clean. She had blue eyes, and I thought her hair would have been white-blonde had it been washed any time in the past six months. She was crying, and I picked her up, carrying her back to the house. Here I handed her over to May Cameron, explaining how I'd found her.

She looked down at the child, and briefly, her pleasant face twisted into an unpleasant scowl. "Probably didn't get breakfast this morning. Ran out of disposable nappies and wouldn't take the cloth ones I got from the attic. I'm at my wits' end what to do, Sheila. They turned up out of the blue, dumped themselves on us just before you got back from Edinburgh, and with no buses anymore, they say they can't leave."

"How are they related to you?"

"They aren't really. My mother married again after my father died. Joe Ross was the son of mum's second husband. My stepdad was a decent man, but his first wife was a…" She hesitated. I took her pause for the word and nodded. She continued, her voice harsh. "So Joe's not related by blood, but according to him, he's family, and he's a right to expect us to take them in now."

"Are you supporting them?"

"Bedrooms, food, everything," May agreed.

I decided that it was time to be hardnosed. "Fine, tell them they work for what they get. The boys start school and behave, or I'll have the family removed."

The boys didn't arrive, and I had a word with May. "They said you can't make them."

I smiled. "Eat everything you have in the house and come to us for your meals once that's done." She did, and in a day, the Rosses were on my doorstep whining. Told that those who worked or went to school got fed. They held out for another week, stealing food, I suspected, but only until we had guards checking things. The father arrived on our doorstep one afternoon after the older boy beat up Ricky, saying – with many adjectives – that his grandparents were this and that, and his dad would get us. Ricky came home with a black eye. The older Ross boy went home with a bitten ankle. Laddie had been present and had resented the attack on his person.

I opened the door and faced Dougal Ross. "Good morning."

"Nae, it isn't, you..." I shut the door quietly. He hammered on it, and I opened the door again. "Mr. Ross, if you're rude, I shall ignore you. Tell me quietly and sensibly what the problem is or go away." He clenched a fist, and I moved with a speed he wasn't expecting. My sawn-off was pressed into his belly, not hard but in contact. He looked down and turned an odd shade of greenish-yellow.

"Whit are ye doing?"

"Mr. Ross, you feel free to behave like a freeloading lout because as you see it, there's no law. The problem with that is, when the official law is gone, people are free to make their laws. This is our glen, and while you are here, you live under our laws. If you don't approve of them, go home. Where is it that you live anyway?"

He named a town most of a day's drive away. No, he couldn't drive, wouldn't be any use getting him a car, and there weren't no busses no more. No, he'd go home if we took him and glad to get away from all of us self-righteous. I told him to go home, food would be brought for dinner tonight and breakfast. After that, he'd better be packed because he was going home, and that was that. We didn't need him any more than he wanted to be here, and he was about to be returned to sender.

Donal had been sitting quietly listening, and once the door was shut again, he chuckled richly. "Two birds with one stone time, maybe. I've wanted to go a bit further afield. You know there's a factory that refines all kinds of sugar down that way. It's off the beaten track, so the stock may still be there."

We sorted out the vehicles. All the flatbeds we had, the utes, and outriders in cars to lead or follow. The Rosses looked smug when they climbed into a car with Sam Cameron driving. From their smirks, they seemed to look on this as their due, a procession taking them home so they could show off to the neighbours. I wondered how long it would take to dawn on them that there was likely to be very few neighbours left, and it was probable any remaining wouldn't welcome the Rosses' return anyway.

The central part of our group quietly peeled off at the crossroads halfway. With Donal in charge, they'd see if the factory was unlooted and if so, they'd load every ounce of whatever they could find. I made another note, bees; they'd do well at the far end of Blind Glen where the cliffs rose high. The end was angled to the sun; also, that part of the glen was warm and in sunshine all day, with a strong heather growth.

The departed section of our people hadn't returned by the time we arrived in the Ross home area, indicating the factory had been intact. We wheeled into the town, passing looted shops, burned outbuildings, only the occasional scuttling animal to be seen before we stopped outside a house in which I'd have hesitated to kennel Laddie. Ricky, who'd come with me, stared.

"Is that where they live? It's awful."

The Rosses made a reply redundant when they scrambled out, marched down the path, and Mr. Ross unlocked the door. None of their surroundings seemed to have registered on them as yet, and I was just as happy. The family trooped inside while he turned and smirked at me, his eyes contemptuous. "Ye can **** off now, ye *****, we're hame, and we've nae need of ye." He slammed the door.

I smiled, signalled everyone to move out, wheeled the Landcruiser off down the main road, turned left at the cross-roads, and only halted when we came again to a small block of semi-looted shops on the town outskirts, in the middle of which was a large untouched library.

I pulled over, waved everyone down, and when they were listening. I pointed to the building. "Take any book you want. Don't make a mess." People descended like locusts on the five shops and library. Some found pickings in the shops, while Ricky came back with bagful after bagful of books, happy a Landcruiser has so much space. Once no one could cram another tin, packet, or book in – or find any more they wanted - we headed for home. Donal had sufficient people – and firepower – not to need us.

All in all, the last couple of weeks had been satisfactory. We were rid of the Rosses, we had hens, roosters, more geese, animal feed, all sorts of household items, including that beautiful furniture, and Donal should return with longed-for sweets. Which he did the day after, they'd managed to take everything edible in the factory. Although it had been a tight fit, we'd have enough now to provide the glens with some form of sweetener for years under a ration system or – until we could get hives up and running. Note to self, *find hives and apiarists*. Oh, and, as I discovered two days later, the Rosses had left their small daughter with May Cameron.

"Why?" I demanded.

"Didn't really want her; she was a nuisance and an expense. Welfare kept hassling them, they said, and I paid," was May's explanation. I left it at that, amused it hadn't occurred to the Rosses there was no longer Welfare *to* hassle them. But from what I'd seen, the child wasn't wanted, and she'd be a lot happier with the Camerons. They renamed her Ruth – and any time I saw her, she certainly appeared happier.

Later, I asked May *how* she'd paid and fell about laughing when I heard. On the Comber Beach expedition, Sam, May's husband, had found an unlooted back street jeweller's shop stocked with gold chains, rings, and bangles. He'd brought them home as he'd expressed it, "for you, love, for pretty." The Rosses, still not understanding events, had jumped at the chance to exchange an unwanted toddler for pounds weight of gold. Gold that could now be freely had in every house, town, or city across the land.

CHAPTER SEVEN

Don't count your chickens before they're hatched. ~old proverb

And don't count them after either. Time to count a chicken is when it's on the plate or laying, and even then, don't be too sure. ~Donal McArn

The hens settled in very happily. The geese considered them part of their territory, and the next fox that came looking for chicken dinner met an untimely end. Three ganders bailed him up, screaming an alarm. Donal came running and shot once. Exit fox. It may have gotten around since we didn't see other foxes in the glens for months.

After that, I had time to deal with Mac's cottage. That is, he had always called it a cottage. It had a sign on the gate saying it was, and he'd purchased it under that description. Initially, it had been a ground-floor, two-bedroom building. Mac had got in a local builder who raised the roof, adding a large room that covered two-thirds of the upstairs area and which was Mac's en suite bed-sitting room. Outside, one wall had been pulled out to make a much bigger lounge, a longer bathroom between the two bedrooms, a generous pantry, a larger kitchen, and a useful mudroom.

While the place might still be known as a cottage, it was twice the original size, and Mac had added quality furniture and other accessories. One of those had been a cellar with the access under a corner of the mudroom. I'd had no idea of the size or contents, so when Donal, Ricky, and I went over to unlock the cottage and inspect our inheritance, I was astounded when Donal opened the trapdoor and called us down.

Ricky and Laddie were there in seconds, and he yelped. "Gran Sheila, come on down, you have to see this."

I climbed down the steps, halted, and stared around. "Dear Heaven, what was he expecting? The apocalypse?"

Donal and I had been away when the cottage was brought in on an enormous flatbed. A master carpenter had built it for himself in 2019, bought as it stood, and Mac had begun the additions, so it was complete by the time we returned. We never knew that a cellar had been dug beforehand, roofed and shored up, and the house placed on top of it. The cellar was vast, shelved on three sides, and concrete-floored. There were not only electric lights, but candle lanterns hung from beams.

"Candle lanterns?" I said to Donal, and then suspiciously, "When was the last time Mac was here?"

"A couple of weeks before we went to Edinburgh," my husband responded.

"Did you see him then?"

"No, remember? We were away ourselves."

I did remember and bit back the desire to cry. We'd had army friends in the area, and because their time in the country was short, we'd gone to Glasgow to meet them there, spent a long weekend with them, had a marvellous time, and farewelled them off to Somerset before driving home. They had just retired, and the trip had been their retirement trip. I hoped that they'd survived the virus, that in the isolated rural area where they'd joined long-established family, they'd manage to survive, and I wished them well. Then I turned back to the cellar.

"So you think that's when he brought all this in? He couldn't have if the whole cellar's full. There's too much here; he has to have been collecting some of this long before. But Donal, that suggests either that he was, well, a secret survivalist of some sort and likely unbalanced, and I don't believe it, or he thought he knew something."

"Aye." We looked down the shelves of food, nothing in tins, all in heavy plastic sealed bags. Tea, coffee, flour, powdered eggs, sugar, salt, spices, and other herbs and condiments, and an entire airtight bin of candles. Not an ordinary bin either. It was around six feet to a side and would hold thousands of them. That was just one wall.

I turned the corner and gasped. "Donal?"

He was there in a stride and looked as surprised as I was, reverted to his childhood accents at that moment. "Och, I think he *must* have been expecting another war, lass, if not an apoca- lypse – or mebbe both."

The shelves were loaded with ammunition, again sealed and with silica gel packets inside to keep it dry over long periods. There were all the most common calibres, and down one shelf, there were handguns. Legally, no average citizen has a right to have fifty or so of them without special permits. With them were belts carrying holsters for the handguns and loops for ammuni- tion. It looked like a Wild West store. There were two shelves of knives and whetstones and an entire bin of … I looked, stared at Donal, dumfounded, and spoke. "Swords? Sword for the love of heaven, where'd he get *those*?"

Donal picked one up and examined it. "Army surplus. They're marked as from the old Indian Army, must have been in army storage somewhere for a century. What's next?"

We founded the corner. I was beyond being surprised by now and merely looked over racks of bolts and quarrels. I as- sumed they would go conveniently with the pistol crossbows, the full-sized ones, and ordinary long bows with their arrows, to- gether with equipment required to make new ammunition and keep the bows in shape and what looked like an entire bale of bowstrings. By now, stunned to silence, I walked deeper into the cellar and found something I'd been expecting after this. "Drugs."

Donal was beside me at once. "What sort?"

I pointed. "All sorts."

There were. I had not the faintest idea where Mac could have gotten some of them. These weren't the common medications any member of the public could buy. They were the sort of things for which you had to have prescriptions, and even then, there's a limit on what you'd be given. Along with them was a shelf of medical books covering whole aspects of disease, illness, injuries, and conditions from pregnancy to old age.

My brain kicked in. "Donal," I said slowly. "Did you ever hear odd talk about his mother's family?"

His gaze met mine in comprehension. "I did. They said his mum's great-grandmother was a McLeod, one of that line that had the sight. But..."

"I know, never mind whether it's sense or nonsense, but think about this, love. Mac may have heard rumours about the sickness quite a while before the general public heard anything. He said to us that it had a long latent period. What if," my eyes narrowed in thought. "What if there'd been an earlier outbreak that was kept quiet? What if those in charge assumed that was it – but Mac didn't? He could be a bit of a pessimist, and he used to say it's better to hope for the best but prepare for the worst. It wasn't as if he couldn't afford to do this. He made a substantial salary and spent damn-all of it."

"Aye, he knew there was McLeod blood in his line. He was proud of it," Donal said slowly. "With what he knew about the virus – if there had been an outbreak earlier – he may have believed that any dream was a prophesy. He'd not have said anything in case of being laughed at, but he could have done this, just in case."

"It's been sealed with those gel packs," I offered. "And the cellar's bone-dry. Kept like that, most of the stuff here could last for decades. Once the food started needing to go, if nothing had happened yet, he could just have donated it to a charity, got a receipt, and replaced it."

Donal looked at me and broke up. "Aye, and if this *hadn't* happened, if he'd died unexpectedly and we'd found all this, we'd have wondered about his sanity – but it's a windfall now. I wonder did Johnny know about this."

I shook my head. "I don't think so. I think he'd have told us."

Ricky came trotting towards us. "What's CID2097?"

I hadn't been an army paramedic without having the answer to that. "It's a very concentrated industrial disinfectant. Where is it, and how much is there?"

It turned out that there was a *lot*. It was conveniently in large airtight buckets that once emptied would be useful for many purposes, and there was enough of the CID to keep the place clean for a generation. The 2097 is *concentrated*. About one part of it to fifty parts water is a good solution for cleaning floors, walls, and bathroom fixtures. You can soak infected clothing in it – of course, too long or too often, and all you have is rags – but it prevented transmitted infections, and it had a pleasant lemon scent. We'd started using it a year before I retired from the army, and it'd been a real advance.

Ricky had vanished again, and Donal turned to me, his eyes serious. "I don't know if Mac dreamed, if he was paranoid, or if he knew something even Johnny didn't know." His voice was hushed. "But look at some of this lot, Sheila. Even with his connections, it's likely not to have come legally. Whatever reason he had, he believed that having it was essential, and he believed it enough to break the law."

I knew what he was saying. Mac had always been law-abiding – unlike the rest of his family. And I remembered that last conversation at the laboratories' garage. "He laughed when he said goodbye and told us if he didn't make it, the cottage was ours. He gave me the deed and said the cottage had a small cellar, said where we could find the trapdoor."

Donal nodded. "I found it strange how he seemed to find it funny."

I looked around the echoing space and grinned. "I see why now. If this is small, then the concert hall is a rabbit hutch."

Donal threw back his head and laughed. "Aye, and just as well neither are. What Mac's left us will save lives. He's thought ahead. Guns and ammunition won't last. We're fortunate in those that stayed in the glen. Most aren't so old, and we're healthy, from good stock. Between what we have here and what we can gather in, we have a foundation. If we build carefully on that, we cannot just survive but begin to reclaim what we had. We should encourage the older children to try the bows, make a competition of it with prizes every month."

"We'll have a head start with weapons, and I have it on my list to add more horses and horse-drawn items."

"More geese…"

"At least four more Dobermans…."

"Practical books, I want a library in each glen in case of fire…."

"More barns for storage," Donal added. "And people. We need recruits, people we can trust. We have to look for them actively, not just pick up the odd one now and again. If they don't shape up, well, we do as we did with the Rosses."

"The Rosses, I wonder how they're managing?"

"Well enough, probably. You saw their town, no one in sight, and most are dead there. They can scavenge all their lives and survive fine."

I considered that. "Horrible way to live."

My husband snorted. "You *saw* how they lived. They'd likely think it a step up."

I recollected the Ross house and agreed, changing the subject. "So what's next? Barns, people, or – I know, if we go to," I mentioned a seaside town known for its gardens. "We could get fruit and nut tree saplings, berry bushes for us and Blind Glen, vegetable seeds, fertilizer, gardening equipment, and look for people or connectable-barns there too."

And it was decided. Decided, too, was that we wouldn't waste time. We'd leave the morning after next, and on arrival, we'd find a list of businesses and begin there.

****

However, before that, we had arrivals that were rather more welcome. Claire's sister Anra had married James MacPherson. They lived in a rented cottage a hundred miles east of us with three small children. He worked as a clerk, and I knew Claire had worried over what might happen to them. I was, therefore, the more pleased to find they'd arrived while we were on the way back from the Rosses. Claire had seen the children were unwell and insisted the family stay in the quarantine chalets.

"It's not the virus, Sheila, but there are ten of them to spread whatever it is."

I blinked. "I thought your sister had only three…" I caught up with the most likely events and nodded. "Oh, I see. Orphans?"

"Yes. Three families were good friends of theirs, parents died, kids didn't," was her brief explanation. "They saw everyone was dying. Holed up for a few weeks." She grinned. "Then James stole a truck and trailer. Stuffed it with anything they thought would be useful. He stopped to check his parents; both dead. So they came here."

I looked over the eight children to find three had bad colds, so I kept them in the chalets a week. By then, we had a large old house chosen, garden sown, and trees pruned. They moved in, and so invisible were they that I often forgot they were even in the glen.

****

We set out two days later, almost at first light. It reminded me of the old song, "Convoy," on Cash McCall's *Black Bear Road* album that my grandfather had loved. It wasn't the dark of the moon *or* June, but we certainly had us a convoy. Over forty vehicles and everyone armed. We rolled, watching about us, and twice Donal sent vehicles to check something we might pick up on the way home again. At the moment, we had everyone living in our glen, but if we got more people, we'd diversify. That would make for more efficient use of vacant land and safer pasturing for the livestock and poultry – which needed human backup as predators began to thrive without human control.

At Thurston, I headed for the Information centre, levered the door open, and found helpful information. The power still worked in Glen Mhairi and Johnny's glen with our electrical eco systems. While we didn't have television programmes broadcast anymore, we could still watch movies and previous TV series in playable formats. Thurston had a shop that sold them. They had a pet shop I'd check out, three gardening centres, a library, petrol stations, three building-supply centres, and other outlets where we might find something useful, including more electrical eco-system supplies. I could see we'd be back and forth for a while.

Then, too, if there were people who might like Glen Mhairi and whom we might like… I collected Ricky and Laddie from the bookshop next door where they'd found some new volumes – now stacked in the Landcruiser – and we set out for a gardening centre. Donal left people and vehicles there loading everything functional; we moved on to the power place, left more there, while I took my Landcruiser and four other cars and went to look over the place that had the movies and TV series. The door was kicked in and the till emptied. The intruders had probably taken some items, but there were several thousand left, most of which we promptly loaded.

After that, I sent the people whose cars were full to head back to the glen to unload, and while I grabbed Claire and Sue as clerks, we sorted books from the library. We might be able to return for second helpings, but better we had ten thousand books with only one copy of each, than five thousand of two copies, at least to begin with. If we needed to, we could scan a book and print it out on a printer. Two loaded trucks later headed away, and I turned off to look at the pet shop.

That was interesting. The windows were boarded, the door was barricaded, and Laddie sniffed hard at that, whining softly. It wasn't an anxious sound, more, "I can scent humans, animals, and I'd like to meet them," comment, so I knocked.

"If there's anyone there, we're friendly. Our dog is friendly. Can we talk?"

A corner of material inside overlapping board gaps twitched. I grabbed Ricky, and he, in turn, scooped up Laddie while the puppy wriggled, beamed, and generally made it clear he wasn't abused in any way. An eye contemplated us, and we were apparently judged acceptable. The door creaked ajar, held there by a strong chain.

"Who are you, where are you from, how many of you are there … and is that a *Pomshee*?" A voice asked concisely, departing from that with the last surprising question.

Ricky giggled. "We found him shut in an empty caravan at Comber Beach. Gran Sheila thinks his family went to hospital, and…" he broke off, and I completed the sentence.

"They loved him; he had food and water containers. His name is Laddie; that was on his collar. We couldn't leave him."

The door was inching further open, and the voice was interested. "Yes, he looks like one of Gordon Jettan's lines. Do you know the pedigree?"

I did, it'd been in the safe, and I recited some of the names. The door opened further. "I know them. This would have been one of Sunshine's pups." I hadn't seen that name on the pedigree and said so. "No, that's her family name. She's Lady Penelope of High Noon Kennels. They called her Sunshine because she has one of the brightest gold coats you've ever seen." By now, she was coming into view around the edge of the door.

I held out a hand. "I'm Sheila McArn. This is my grandson, Ricky. You know Laddie."

She stooped and petted the puppy who was charmed to make her acquaintance and showed it vigorously while a smile lit her face. "Lovely boy, look, would you like to come in?" We would, we did, we shared a cup of tea, a packet of digestives, and we were shown around the big shop.

Miss Jane DeVenter was in her late forties – no exact age given. She'd lived here all her life, a maiden aunt with two sisters, a brother, and nine nephews and nieces; she'd inherited the shop from the employer for whom she'd worked since leaving school at sixteen until he died when she was thirty-seven.

"He had no family, you see. And – ah – he wasn't the marrying kind." I nodded my understanding. "But such a kind genteel man, and I thought the world of him. I've always loved animals, then all this happened. Someone tried to break in, so I got boards, and Bill helped me board up the windows, barricade the door, and add another chain to it."

"Is Bill still in town?"

"No. His family came from Edinburgh. He went back there in his little car to see if they were safe, and he's never come back. He wasn't feeling very well when he left, I said he should wait, but he said family was more important." I reflected that Bill and his little car were likely mouldering somewhere between Thurston and Edinburgh.

Jane DeVenter talked on, and I gathered her family, while none of them lived more than fifty miles away, were inaccessible because she couldn't drive. She'd hoped one of them would come to get her and didn't understand why they hadn't. I was afraid I could.

"I couldn't leave the animals, you see, but I've been so worried."

We considered the animals. She had eleven kittens, ten puppies – two of them to my unspoken joy, apparently Dobermans, the rest terrier types with a lone spaniel - six cages of finches and budgies, three cockatoos, nineteen rabbits and guinea pigs, and five aquariums complete with inhabitants, mostly cold-water goldfish and others of that sort with one containing a tortoise and another with three turtles.

Without making it obvious, I scanned the shelves. Many were empty, and I thought that her problems would multiply vastly in another week unless she had more supplies elsewhere. Her gaze met mine, and I saw she understood the realities of her situation, and she was terrified – both of what would happen to her charges and then to her if no one came and no one else would help.

I spoke, keeping my voice casual. "We live in three glens about an hour's drive from here. I suppose you could call us looters – although we prefer the term, salvage – we came to get supplies to store at home. Our glens are isolated, most of us had sore throats a while back, which made those that did and were treated with allodaxin immune to this virus. We're looking for people to join us, to work together and be safe."

I looked at her and let her see my understanding. "I'll help you restock here, but the truth is that you will run out of food for the animals soon, you can't let them starve, and if you let them go, their deaths may be even harder."

Her lips curved in a bitter smile. "I've seen foxes, rats, starving dogs. I know. I just couldn't bring myself to do it, not while I can feed them." She straightened in her chair. "What can you do? What would you be prepared to do?" I told her.

I collected all of our convoy, conducted them a group at a time through the shop, and asked if they would like a pet. It took some time since there were over fifty of us, with more arriving as drivers made it back after dropping off cargo at the glen. Donal and I took the two Doberman puppies. They were, Jane swore, purebred, but they'd come from family pets and were therefore unregistered, that was all. We believed her, and best of all, they were both females. Tai explained the hierarchy to them once we had them home, and they got it. The other puppies all found homes, as did the kittens. I'd expected that. The aquariums of fish, being cold-water species, were purchased by the school, as were the tortoise and turtles. That left the birds, rabbits, and guinea pigs.

I pointed out to people that rabbits and guinea pigs mostly ate grass that came free and kept segregated, they didn't breed. They were ideal pets, and children needed pets. They went, leaving the cages of finches and budgies. I explained to Jane that many years ago, I'd had a friend who lived in New Zealand. There they had bamboo thickets in a wet area at the back of a city called Auckland, where escaped budgies often ended up living free, nesting, raising young, and managing perfectly well despite hawks. Most of the finches, too, could live under similar conditions.

Miss Jane was worried. "But where?"

I smiled. "Donal and I inherited one of our three glens from a friend who died. Right at the end, there's a big shallow area that was swampy. Johnny had a bee in his bonnet and planted all the edge of it with bamboo. He thought it would drain the swamp."

"It didn't?"

"No. But there's about seven acres of bamboo ten or fifteen feet tall. Foxes can't climb it; hawks can't chase small birds into it. Little birds, however, nest in it safely, the way they did in Auckland. The bamboo's spreading, we have in mind to cut some of it now and again as building material for other things, but we don't want it gone. If we let, say, a single cage of the finches and a cage of budgies loose in that and see how they do, then if they're fine, we could let them all go. You may lose some here and there. But they'll be free, they won't starve, and you won't have to – do anything."

She sat silent a long time before nodding. So we packed everything from the store, took her and her creatures back to the glen, and while she stayed with us, we parcelled out her livestock, and I watched as she seemed to grow younger and happier with the burden lifted. Donal glared at me once we were in private.

"Puppies, kittens, budgies, *turtles*, for heaven's sake. What were you thinking?"

I gave him an evil smile. "Remember Colonel Martin. He always said a smart soldier has at least two agendas at any time?"

"Yes?" He abruptly developed a look of one on who light has dawned. "Another agenda, what is it?"

"You'll find out in a few weeks." After that, I shut up – for about three weeks.

CHAPTER EIGHT

Success is simple. Do what's right, the right way, at the right time.
~Arnold H. Glasow

Nice thought, but it's a council of perfection – and people aren't.
~Sheila McArn

It took three weeks for Miss Jane's creatures to be adopted, for her to be almost delirious with joy she wouldn't have to watch them die, or even more agonising, do it herself. We'd let a cage each of the budgies and finches out the morning after we'd all had a good night's sleep. We took Miss Jane to Johnny's glen, showed her the bamboo swamp, and she opened the cage doors.

It worked as I'd hoped; once a couple of them had been taken, they got the message and stayed in the bamboo any time a raptor overflew it. We released the remainder, and Miss Jane's face was a picture. She, too, was free. That was where the other agenda kicked in, and I casually raised the question of her missing family.

"You couldn't leave the animals before, but now that everything has homes, you could."

"I can't drive," her eyes implored me.

"Oh," I said judiciously. "But it wouldn't be safe for you to go alone anyhow. I've thought we should go that way soon and look around. We could take you."

It took little to persuade her. Her family lived along a motorway, both sisters and their families in the nearest town

95

eighteen miles away. Her parents were dead while her brother and his family lived in their old home, and his wife's parents lived where he worked, twenty-one miles past that. However, as we salvaged, we saw fewer people, but neither Donal nor I was happy about leaving the glens too defenceless.

In the end, because we wanted the opportunity of salvaging in new areas, we paused long enough to build gatehouses at the glen entrances before setting off with Miss Jane on another trip that would be further and take longer. Johnny had a gatehouse already, but we doubled the size, fireproofed it, and added a tower so inhabitants could fire downwards with better vision over the land. We built a tank stand with water tank, also shielded, and dug a cellar into which we stuffed sufficient supplies for a month. Let enemies get our people out of *that*! Mrs. Giles muttered for days about a waste of time and materials and encouraging people to look for trouble. I ignored her. Being ready if others cause trouble is *not* war-mongering, and we felt we could now leave in good conscience.

****

We hit the road, me driving the Landcruiser, with Miss Jane, Ricky, and Laddie as passengers and twenty vehicles behind us. We reached Thurston, turned off, and headed northeast. We'd decided it would work better if we went to the furthest point and returned, checking on Miss Jane's families on the way back. I knew where the last town was, and we passed through, halting on the far side of it after turning around. A small park was nearby, and I turned to the back seat.

"Ricky, Laddie's been in the car awhile. Take him for a quick run now." He looked at me, said nothing, opened the door, let Laddie out, followed him, and stood looking across the park while the puppy bounced joyously. Miss Jane turned and studied me. "You want to say something to me, and you don't want him to hear."

"Yes. His parents died of the virus, and his sister was dying when we found them. I've seen a lot of death since this started. I may be telling you something you already know, but I'd rather say it and be wrong than find you hadn't thought of it."

"That no one came to get me because they were all dead?" I nodded.

"Yes," she admitted. "I confess that at first, I didn't want to consider it. But after I was alone for weeks, I started thinking." Her voice was slow, and I could hear the pain. "I love my family and they love me. If everyone were well, someone would have come. I know. So maybe they're all dead, but I need to see, to be sure."

I kept my voice neutral. I didn't want to give too much hope. "Then again, the cell-phone towers aren't working. They couldn't call you, they'd have to drive to Thurston, and if they can't leave their family for some reason…?"

"I see, if some are sick, if there's trouble, if they can't afford to leave…"

"Yes. That," I said carefully. "Is why it pays to have a community. If things go pear-shaped (I used my New Zealand friend's term, and Miss Jane smiled), you have back-up."

I called Ricky. He and Laddie came back, climbed into the car, and I drove off with the convoy following. We'd go first to her brother-in-law's home. We stopped where Miss Jane signalled at the drive of a prosperous-looking house, well-maintained, although the lawn was starting to get away, and she looked at that before opening the door.

"He mows their lawn every Saturday, and he always has petrol in the shed."

I understood the subtext to that. The lawn hadn't been mowed for weeks by the look of it. She marched up the path and knocked briskly. There was no response, and she knocked again. I joined her and placed my face against the glass of a bow window. Dimly, through filmy curtains, I could see an empty room.

"Try the back door," I suggested, and we circled the house. My companion knocked again with no more response than previously and then stooped to pick up a rock, a quick twist of her fingers, and that opened to display a key. She opened the back door, and again we had no need to ask what lay within. She looked at me.

"Should we enter?"

I nodded. "Let's be sure. Did they have a pet?"

"No, they didn't like animals," she smiled briefly. "They didn't like me either – women should be married, not in business - and they didn't like it when I gave Benny, my brother, a puppy for the children, but you're right. We should be sure about them."

Her sister-in-law's parents were dead and had been for some time, in my opinion. At that point, something occurred to me. If they had been dead a while, it also looked as if their daughter hadn't come to check on them, or surely she'd have laid out the bodies, taken mementos, or done something that showed, not left the bodies sprawled across in the bed in a pitiful fashion that showed they had died hard. Miss Jane's look crossed mine, and I saw we were both having similar thoughts.

Quietly she walked to the chest of drawers, opened the bottom drawer, and pulled it right out. From behind that, she removed a zipped leather folder and a long narrow box made of rosewood. "Benny told me. I'll take these personal papers and their jewellery. If we don't come back, they won't be stolen, and if there's no one else, I'll keep them."

We locked the house again after I had walked through it. On the walk-through, I picked up a beautiful feather eiderdown, iridescent with embroidery, a magnificent naval sword with all its accoutrements, and a set of six expensive copper-bottomed saucepans. If we didn't return, it would be a shame to leave them behind. Miss Jane smiled.

"They liked the best of everything, and they had the money. We should come back and empty the house."

"What about the daughter?"

"Mara wouldn't mind, it will probably be her suggestion when we tell her, and if you don't want her grabbing those things back. I'd put them where they can't be seen."

"But you have no objection to me taking them?" I asked carefully.

"None at all," was the cheerful reply. I tucked my salvage into the Landcruiser with a sheet over them and re-entered the vehicle to drive on to our next destination.

I will not go into details of what we found there. Suffice it to say that the brother must have died last. He'd laid out his wife and children, left his sister a note – that seemed to be a human habit from the number of times I'd seen it now – and killed the dog. Then he'd lain down by his family and gone, if not in peace, then with resignation. Miss Jane wept while I hesitated, then closed my arms about her. After three or four minutes, she drew away, wiped her eyes, and sniffed inelegantly.

"He was a good brother, and I loved him." It wasn't a bad eulogy. "She looked around. "I'm the eldest. With my brother and all the family dead, I inherit." She lifted her head to meet my gaze. "It's quite a lot further to where my sister is. You liked Mara's parent's things, send some of your people back to…" Here, she managed a tiny smile. "To salvage whatever you can use. And the same here. I'd rather know someone else valued and used what they had than they were just rotting away."

We did that, but I deferred to her. I left the bed with its record of pain and fear, but other than that, we gutted the house. Miss Jane had been right. The furniture was solid wood, all excellent quality, the linen mostly was exactly that; *linen*, with an array of sheets, tablecloths, pillowcases, and napkins. The large side garage and backyard sheds were filled with tools, two electric bicycles, an electric car, and, to my surprise, several corded-up cedar chests of older items. They contained lamps, a silver samovar, five stunning fur coats of various sizes and styles, and several other items that looked to me as if they all dated to the late eighteen – or early nineteen hundreds.

Miss Jane looked at the chests. "Her great-grandfather served in the Indian Army. She had no use for the things, but she'd never have sold them. They were family heirlooms."

I nodded. "And now, in this day and time, they'll be useful again." A voice from behind told me that the house had been cleared. I indicated the garage and shed, and, leaving some of the vehicles to complete the clearance, I led the rest of the convoy back to brother Benny's home where, under his sister's guidance, we emptied that as well, all save the bedroom in which five people and a small dog lay still. I looked at Miss Jane.

"Do you want us to bury them or have you another idea?"

Some hours later, we drove away. The house had been on a corner site, the houses next to it were brick, and it had rained locally in the past forty-eight hours, and everything outside was soaked. We'd also investigated the adjacent homes, finding bodies but nobody living, and there too, we'd salvaged, lightly this time, taking only what was of real use. I glanced back as I drove away. The fire was starting to show at the windows, the structure was wooden, and it would burn well. Besides, everything flammable we hadn't taken was stacked around the bedroom.

A Viking funeral for a man his sister said had loved the stories of holm-ganging, going a-Viking, and had once told her he wished he could have lived then. It was the last tribute she could pay him. I suspected her sister-in-law would have been horrified, but my opinion was that fire cleanses, and the children might have enjoyed the drama. Anyhow, none of that mattered. It was her choice, and, as she'd said, she was the heir.

We stopped on the edge of the town when Ricky yelled and pointed. I signalled hastily, slammed on the brakes, swung into the roadside, and waved in the convoy. When we drove off again, we were richer by a shop's worth of electrical eco systems, nineteen household wind generators, and an enormous stack of the graphene solar panels with long-life batteries. I looked back as we moved off, and in the distance, I could see flames leaping up. It looked as if despite the wet more than Benny's house was on fire. If he'd really liked the idea of being a Viking, he was going out in style. I drove on to the next town, wondering what we would find there.

That was a pleasant surprise. Well, partly so anyway. The four children had survived. The parents – that was a different story. Amy, Miss Jane's sister, had been something of a hypochondriac. When the children had developed sore throats, she'd made sure that whatever it was, she didn't catch it – and she'd died of the later outbreak. Bevan, her brother-in-law, had been ill but survived. He and the children greeted their aunt as if she was an angel come to save them. They fell on her, hugged, kissed, told her in unison of all the events she'd missed, and demanded answers on everything she might know.

Somewhere in there, Bevan went to the window, saw the convoy, and his eyes widened. "Jane? Who are these people, what do they want? Are you with them?"

It took some explanation, and in the middle of that, I dropped a few hints. I saw at once that Bevan wasn't slow to understand. Live in the heart of a town he might, but, as I later found, he was of country stock. He knew – or guessed – some of what had happened, and he realised that it would be an extremely long time before people went to work in an office in a suit and tie again. He looked at me, his gaze straight and open.

"You have land, fortified, guarded, and safe. Would you consider new residents?"

I'd been summing them up as we talked. Bevan was in his early forties, lean, fit – probably played some sort of sports, I thought – his face was amiable and his eyes intelligent. The four children ranged from around nine to eighteen. Two girls, two boys, they seemed polite, sensible, and, like their father, pleasant-natured and intelligent. It looked as if agenda two was on the way to fulfilment.

I let them see me considering. "The glens can always use people who will work hard, who are honest, sensible, and understand they're part of a community," I said, a little pompously perhaps. "We can take everything here you want. I can offer you an empty house in the glen that's a bit larger than this one. It's on three acres and has two sheds, pens, and runs. It's sound, but the family that owned it were lazy. It hasn't had a proper scrubbing for quite a while. Would that suit you?" Their reply left no doubt that it would.

It took four days. By then, we had Bevan's family moved into the home left vacant by the deaths of one of the families that had refused inoculation on Donal's and my return from the city. At the final stop to check on Miss Jane's family, we found her sister and the child alive. The little girl had developed the bug and given it to her mother. They had been treated with allodaxin and survived. The experience, however, of her husband dying had paralysed her – the death dealt by the virus isn't pretty.

She'd been too afraid to leave the house apart from brief forays to the corner dairy, four buildings down from her. Other than that, she had blocked out everything, played with her daughter, made their meals, sung her to sleep, read to her, complained of the lack of anything to watch on television, and shut out the virus, the world, and everything in it. On our appearance, she reverted to a much younger sister relying on her older sister to take care of her, and Miss Jane stepped up nobly. We settled the two of them in a small cottage by the place Bevan had taken. I moved a caravan to sit by the cottage and explained quietly.

"I think she'll get over it in a few months, once she's had time in peace, taking Daisy to kindergarten and going herself to community events."

Miss Jane eyed me shrewdly. "And you think that once she does, she won't want me in the house anymore?" She nodded decisively. "You're right. Just now, she's using me as a sort of mother-surrogate. That'll pass."

"Yes," I agreed. "The caravan is a stopgap. Once she starts to regain independence, you can move into it. After that, you have a choice. Either you pick out another house, and that's yours, or you can have the caravan as home and move it elsewhere if you want when the time comes."

She took two days to decide on that, but she decided that she'd like a house. She chose a cottage on the boundary of Donal's and my land. It had belonged again to one of those older people that had taken the virus and died and still contained everything he'd left. Miss Jane cleaned all that out, sharing with those that liked the items, stored the rest in one of the storage barns, and filled the place with a judiciously chosen selection of things from her premises and from the in-laws' homes. Some she gave to her sister – whom, I noticed, from the slight sideways scowl, wasn't grateful either for her sister's care or the items.

I mentioned that. Miss Jane looked at me. "Jess has always been self-centred. It's all about her. She was the youngest and unexpected, my parents spoiled her, and her husband treated her like a flower. She had a char in every afternoon to do the hard work and a housekeeper in every morning. He was older, well-off, and he spent it on her. She behaves as if she was still in her teens. In her head, she knows things have changed, but in her heart, she still thinks everyone should look after her."

"Not here," I said firmly. "If she's like that, why did she have a child?"

"Her husband made it clear that it was the price she paid for having everything else," Jess's sister said dryly. "The housekeeper came in first thing, got the baby up, fed her, dressed her, washed her, and started breakfast. Kenneth went to work after that, while Jess got up when she felt like it. Housekeeper stayed until one. By then, she'd made lunch for them, cleaned up, and gone home. Charwoman came in around three. She did all the laundry, dusting, and cleaning. If Jess was fussy, she looked after her too, and she didn't leave until about half an hour before Kenneth was due home."

"Did Daisy ever go to kindergarten or something like that?"

"No. Kenneth didn't believe in them. He said they were just a way to slough responsibility for teaching a child how to behave."

I snorted. "From the sounds of it, she was being taught how to behave by a char and a housekeeper instead, unqualified personnel, when she might have been better off in a kindergarten learning to interact with other children."

Miss Jane's face broke into a smile. "We'd agree on that. And if I put it to her the right way, so will Jess." She must have done so as Daisy started kindergarten the next day, and was found to be good-tempered, sensible, and quite bright. Jess was delighted to find she had more time to herself, not nearly so pleased when she discovered she was expected to work for the glens.

"I'm a single mother, I have a child, don't I get some sort of allowance?"

I sat her down and explained some of the realities slowly and clearly, making sure she got the message that there was no longer any such thing as government assistance. If she wanted to eat, she worked.

"What about Daisy?" She looked sanctimonious. "You wouldn't let a baby starve."

I put a faint edge in my voice. "No, we wouldn't. If we found you could not feed her, we'd see to it she went to live with a family that could feed and care for her. Your choice would then be to work hard, show you meant to be a good citizen, and get her back – or not." I hardened my tone again, and she looked up. "There's also this. You were given a house. That's yours as part of the community, but if you decide at any time you don't want to be part of us, it's simple. You leave."

I saw two things then. One was that she might be self-centred, but that made her aware of realities if she had to be, and secondly, while she may have been spoiled, there was steel under the fluff. She stood up and nodded politely, her eyes hard with rage – and the acknowledgement times had changed, and she'd better change with them.

"Thank you. Don't worry about Daisy. She's a good baby."

There I was able to agree honestly, and I saw that she was pleased. She left and I looked after her, wondering what she'd do. What she did was adapt, to my mild surprise. In days she was working as a stores clerk, cataloguing items brought in, allocating them places in the barns, and keeping track of things as they were moved about. She proved to be good at that, and Miss Jane, smiled at Donal and me when told of it.

"Yes, she has the sort of mind that likes to see a place for everything and everything in its place. Now no one's doing that for her. I think she's quite enjoying doing it herself and being appreciated for it."

"Will you stay there a while?"

"Another week or two. After that, you can have the caravan back, and I'll move into my cottage. When are we doing another salvage run? I had a friend in Somerlee, I know all about the place from her, and it's off the main highway on one of those narrow roads. If anyone else is salvaging, they may not know of it, let alone bother to go there."

Somerlee, when I listened to what she could tell me and read what a couple of area guides said, turned out to be down the coast, almost a hundred miles from the glens and from the map and the gazettes, she was right. It had started as a fishing village, become gentrified in the 1980s, added some posh shops housing a few major names, and would be a wonderful place to salvage if all or most of its inhabitants were dead.

****

We gathered the salvages a month later. This would be an expedition in force. We'd use every flatbed, every ute, and all of the larger lorries. By now, we'd picked up extras in the first and third categories, we'd spent most of that month putting up more interlocking storage barns and stripping another block of country shops to add footwear, jeans, winter clothing, and extras like belts, socks, and underwear. I'd remembered hearing about a wool shop somewhere nearby, and we'd found that. I'd taken an entire lorry-load of wool, both genuine and acrylic, along with embroidery silks, cottons, sewing items like scissors and needles, material in bolts, nine spinning wheels, and four looms. If I'd found a partridge or a pear tree, I'd have taken those too. As it was, I found a pair of balloons in a back room, and added those. They'd be a pleasant addition to the next Valentine's Day.

We arrived in Somerlee mid-afternoon. Our convoy wound its way down the hill towards the sea, and I watched the streets below even as I minded my driving. Miss Jane beside me coughed gently.

"I see no one?" Nor did I. "Could we go to my friend's place. It's one of the first houses on the main road before the village. She kept goats. Nubians, nice animals."

That would be useful whether or not the lady had survived. "Tell me about her."

Her description was brief but informative. "Fifteen years older than me, never married either. Family well-to-do, bit snobbish. House is seventeen-sixty-four. Ten acres, all the goat shelters, and gear are new. Complete flock, pedigreed. Esme's a touch paranoid, retired to Somerlee because she thought it'd be safer. Oh, there," She pointed. "Her house is around the next bend, left side. You'll know it when you see it."

I saw the sign *Esme's Goats,* signalled, slowed, and one by one, the convoy pulled in along the road, the Landcruiser right by the entrance to the old house. A flock of goats looked curiously at us from a paddock. In the front of the house, a window slammed up. A voice shrieked something, and a gun went off like the trump of doom. A *bit* paranoid? And what did she have there, a small cannon? Miss Jane left the vehicle yelling back, the window slammed down again, and Esme Pemberlow appeared with what looked like an ancient elephant gun under one arm.

"Jane? Jane, is that you?"

After that, we were honoured guests.

CHAPTER NINE

"But before you all start leaving, I'll just find and load my gun. I've little experience at fighting, but I'm d****** if I will run." ~Esme Pemberlow's version of an old song

"However, with a gun that size, it'll do the job if you hit anything – and if you don't, it'll still scare them witless." ~Sheila McArn

Esme Pemberlow was a polite and pleasant hostess. I could see she regarded only Miss Jane as an equal; the rest of us were retainers, to be acknowledged kindly, then ignored unless she asked one of us for information her old friend could not supply.

I explained events as I knew them, and she regarded me steadily. "So most of the population will be dead, not just here but worldwide?" I nodded. She sighed quietly and looked at her friend. "I never really thought this would happen, but my father always said, 'Better to take precautions and look a fool, then not to take them and be one,' and I never liked the current government. When my great-aunt died and left me this place, I decided to move there. Once I moved in, I purchased the goats – an excellent dual-purpose breed – and this house has cellars."

I spoke quietly. "Which you filled, supposing they're dry."

"They are and I did. I'm an old woman. If I live for more than another ten years, it would be surprising. My heart is a little weak, and my doctor said I could go the way both my father and his did. Dead before they struck the ground. I have sufficient supplies to last me twice that time, and I intend to die here."

"What about your animals if you die?"

Her smile was sardonic. "You don't know goats. They stay in a field because they want to. But the moment they want to leave, they can and will do so. They will neither starve nor die trapped by a fence. Of the twenty-three I have, most are nannies drying off, with kids due shortly. I also have three billies, one older, one younger, and a yearling buck, none of which are related. The flock is not inbred, and even if they remain together without new blood for generations, they will not seriously become so. If I am unable to milk them, their offspring will do the job."

"Would you sell us any?"

Her refusal was composed. "However, I quite see that goats would be useful in your circumstances. There is – or perhaps that may prove to be 'was' – another breeder in Somerlee. Take the next right turn, about five miles across the uplands; you will find a farmhouse. They bred Nubians as well, not my quality but decent enough. They have all the necessary equipment for them, and..." she broke off and looked at her friend. "Your own animals, what of them?" Miss Jane provided a comprehensive description of her creatures' disposition, and Esme Pemberlow smiled on me. "That was most kind and thoughtful of you. If I can be of some assistance to you here, please tell me."

And so it was with her beside Miss Jane in the back seat, Ricky and Laddie now by me, that we descended the hill road into Somerlee. It was a bonanza, a cornucopia. The section of expensive shops held a largesse of items I'd never dreamed of owning. Donal looked at me when we got there, I looked at Donal, and we levered open a dozen doors and went slightly mad. Once half the vehicles were loaded, and mind you, we were taking only things we could genuinely use, we sent them on their way.

They'd unload and return first thing in the morning. Miss Pemberlow was amused.

"And there may be another place you will find useful." I looked at her. "There is what I might term a private orphanage school. They had over thirty pupils, teachers, a matron, and a principal, with several of the girls staying on to work with the younger children."

"Have you seen them since this started?" She shook her head.

"It was not until Jane told me how you have taken her and her family in and I understood you are building community numbers that I recalled them. Several wealthy people who wished to contribute to the welfare of children bought a property, retained staff, and set the place up as a trust. I say there are over thirty children there. It could be more - or fewer. There is one thing which may make you inclined to visit."

"What?"

"They were accepted if they fitted criteria. They had to be healthy, mentally stable, genetically clean, and of above-average intelligence."

I gaped at her. "How on *earth* did they get those conditions past a council? I can imagine the screams if some bleeding heart heard them."

"Quite so. But this was a private charity, and conditions were confidential. If a child was accepted, the board funded that child completely. They fed, clothed, and educated them, provided housing, leisure equipment, medical and dental care, and if they did well in their studies, they received scholarships to university. I was told that it paid dividends. Most children went on to become known and valuable adults in their fields."

Her smile was wry. "What council is going to turn that down or let the conditions become known if they can avoid it? I understand the board said if there were any trouble, they would close the school, hand the children back to the council, and cut off all charitable donations."

I winced. She was right. Apart from anything else, councillors are elected. Most of those in industry here would profit if the school bought locally everything they needed, or even almost everything. Cut off the flow, let everyone know the council had caused that, and watch if any of them could get elected to even collect the garbage ever again.

Miss Pemberlow saw that I knew reality when I heard it and nodded. "I've met them now and again; they came out once to see the goats. Nice children, not being spoiled or indulged, they have to work at their lessons. Nothing is given to them, and while they're comfortable, they're not living in luxury. You could do worse than to ask if any wish to join you. I'm sure you will know the points to make." Her eyes met mine.

So with her to point the way, we found the school. There were twenty-seven people alive there, and they were, as she'd said, intelligent, and they chose to come with us when I offered the option. We circled to the uplands on the way back and found the farmers there dead. We loaded all of their goats, all the goats' gear, a sampling of other useful items, then took Esme Pemberlow back to her home and her livestock, along with a load of supplies salvaged from other places. She climbed down from the Landcruiser and stood regarding her friend, me, Ricky, and Laddie.

"Thus has been a pleasant visit. It's been good to see you, Jane. It's unlikely I'll do so again, but please do call in to see me if you pass by. She moved closer to her friend and lowered her voice, unaware that I have excellent hearing. "Jane, if you do come back and I'm – no longer here to meet you. Take whatever you would like to remember me by. You are my friend, and I would rather you had everything than anyone else."

They held hands through the window, and I could hear the slight hoarseness in Miss Jane's voice. "Goodbye, Esme. I shall miss you."

"And I, you, my dear. But if forever, still forever, fare thee well." She looked at me. "Mrs. McArn, if it is possible, I would be happy to receive you again and your grandson and Laddie. Nice little dog," she added.

"Thank you," I acknowledged.

She stepped back and lifted her hand in a gracious wave. "Travel well, and may your journey end safely."

I moved off, and when I glanced back, she was gone. But I did intend to return. So far as we now knew, she was the last person alive in Somerlee, and we'd only salvaged half the shops. Meanwhile, once again, we would need more storage, and I had plans for the schoolchildren. Donal nailed me on that as soon as we were home.

"I get the impression that they want to stay together."

"I talked to Esme Pemberlow. She says the way it worked, they chose the girls at four, they were formally accepted into the school at five and stayed until they were eighteen. Those who liked small children often took a gap year before starting university and worked that year at the school, looking after the youngest classes as assistants. Some came back over the university break to do that as well, although they were paid. It was regarded as employment, and if they were studying in an allied field, they could get credit for it."

Donal pursed his lips. "So they think of themselves in a way as all family."

"I had an idea about that."

I took it to them, and it was well received. Once we were done, the children had a sort of manor house. It was four sides around a courtyard in which the smaller ones could be safely left to play. The front had common rooms: two lounges, a large dining room, a kitchen and pantry with banks of supply cupboards, and a laundry. There were four generous bathrooms, one at each corner, bedrooms along three sides – those on one side being en suite bed-sitting rooms for the teachers. Outside the block, they had hen runs, while inside, they were permitted three cats and a small dog. They were a family, happy, and it was amazing how soon it was felt they had always lived with us in the glens.

The Camerons came to me two days later. May, Sam, and their adopted daughter Ruth. May did the talking. "You remember the Rosses?" We all grinned wryly. They hadn't exactly been forgettable. "Well, we've been thinking. There's salvagers coming and going, but only once that way. Sam says a long time back, when he was driving for one of the big companies, he stopped over at a factory complex. It could still be there, might not be, but it'd be worth a look. And there was another place near it."

I heard the details. It'd be a major trip, but it could pay real dividends, as Sam said. However, just now, we were busy. We were developing Johnny's Glen. Much of the land had been planted in fruit trees, citrus trees, nut trees, and netted-in berry bushes, courtesy of a nursery twenty miles away. That was the advantage of those sorts of crops. They were labour-intensive, but they had long productive periods, and Johnny's Glen was ideal for them. The cliffs about it were higher, the bottomland there stayed snow-free and warmer, and the results would be a solid food and vitamin supplement for all three glens. We'd boarded up the old manor house. Somehow, it didn't feel right to move anyone in there, the land, the outbuildings. They were his gift to us, but somehow, we still saw the house as his home – and someone of the bloodline could still return. Note to self, make it to Edinburgh before too long.

We'd taken basic agricultural machinery and were planting potatoes as well. The Somerlee group had taken over the goats we brought back and produced milk, butter, and cheese plus eggs from the chickens we gave them. And I had my eye on some of the things that could be done in Blind Glen. Down at the end, there was a large deep hollow which filled with run-off all winter. Now that the glen opened into ours, I'd acquired a trenching machine, and with that, Jimmy patiently dug a trench into Glen

Mhairi, along one side of that, and out to our narrow road, which had deep culverts. The channel, once everything was done, would act as a spillway to prevent flooding.

Donal came in. "Trench is done, basic, but it'll carry overflow barring a real flood."

"Next stop, the lake again?"

"I'd say so. Sam can use a dozer; he says he'll start tomorrow."

It took weeks and considerable work, plus much of our remaining petrol. But once that was done, instead of the hollow, we had a fifteen-acre lake, depths ranging from three to over twenty feet, with the spillway to stop it flooding, after which it was time to use what Sam had told us. I'd looked up library materials, and so far as I could tell, the factories and depots he'd known about had still been in operation three or four years ago. However, I wasn't happy about how many able-bodied it would take from the glens. Donal went to the Somerlee group once a week and was training them in firearms and manoeuvres. The girls took to them like ducks to water which relieved some of my anxiety.

I counted numbers, made decisions, consulted, talked, asked questions, and it was just a year after the virus that our largest ever convoy started out. We had the flatbeds and fifteen utes but fewer outriders since every vehicle had a driver and at least one passenger. We were armed to the teeth, and I grinned as I counted our people past the Glen Mhairi gatehouse. Janet was manning that with a roster of older schoolchildren. It had become a fashion amongst our teenagers, too, to wear a scarf or bandanna about their forehead to hold back growing hair, and we looked like something out of bandit movies.

Mrs. Giles was near the road as we went, and I received her usual look, a compound of superiority and rancid dislike, which puzzled me. The truth was, we didn't know much about them. They'd arrived three years ago, old Mrs. Giles being the daughter of a man born here who'd owned a small house off to one side from most others. When he died, she'd inherited. The house stood empty until, out of the blue, the three arrived with personal possessions and settled in. All three were on some sort of pension, so I supposed a free house and three pensions gave them a moderately comfortable life. They'd had fruit trees there, and they'd put in a large vegetable garden on arrival.

Yet from what I'd seen of Mrs. Giles junior, it would never have been her choice. She was a city woman through and through. She didn't like pets, didn't like isolation, and – from what I'd seen – didn't like people either. I walk quietly; it comes naturally to me, and once, soon after they moved in, I overheard a comment from the old lady that made me wonder. She'd said to her son, the minister, that "…here is the best place until the fuss dies down."

He'd made a reply of which the only word I picked out was "scandal."

It had sounded too television series for words, and I'd pondered what it meant ever since. Frankly, I couldn't imagine any scandal that woman could generate. Now, as I drove, I remembered her hostile gaze, and I thought about it. The other odd thing was the son, Mr. Giles, was a minister. He seemed a kindly, decent, devout man, so was he involved in whatever had occurred? Sometime I should make enquiries.

I rolled down the highway, noticing the material was showing deterioration – cracks, some with grass coming up in those, washouts under the edges of roads, along with potholes that were becoming formidable in places. I wondered how long we would have roads. We had to have the glens self-sufficient, up and running, settled and ready, when the time came that we were truly isolated. That isolation could last a very long time – and when it ended, if it did, would it be because we'd thrived and spread out or because others took what we had?

I moved my concentration back to business. If or when that time came, I probably wouldn't be around to see it. Now was Donal's and my time, while we had health, strength, and people who followed us. I smiled to myself. Who would ever have thought two years ago that we'd have been where we were. Ricky, beside me in the front seat, noticed the smile.

"Grandma Sheila, what's funny?"

"Just thinking."

"About what?"

"That's it's odd. Here we are leading the glen on a raid, like the old clans."

Ricky shook his head. "*Not* like the old clans, Gran. They killed people and stole from them. We salvage. Like Miss Pemberlow, we didn't take her goats when she said no. Miss Jane came here because she wanted to, and we didn't take her pets, she was pleased to give them to the glen, and she set the birds free."

That she had. I smiled again, reminiscently. Amongst her other birds, she'd had three Sulphur-crested cockatoos. She'd let them go into the bamboo at the back of Johnny's Glen and what I hadn't known at the time was that they had been a male and two females. Possibly because they were the only ones of their kind, they'd amalgamated as a sort of trio. Both females had nested successfully and raised hatches. There were now eleven of them. They were effective too, beginning as a flock, to chase hawks away from the bamboo groves, so the smaller birds lived in peace.

Ricky was speaking. "If we find another Pomshee, can we take it?"

"That depends. Laddie's neutered so he can't breed more of him, and another one might already have an owner."

"I know, but if we find one that doesn't?"

"That's a provisional yes."

They're bright, sensible dogs, I wouldn't mind another, but they'd been a designer breed, and such breeds don't last. On the other hand, we had half a dozen terriers from Miss Jane's pet shop. I thought that the glens would probably end up with three types of dogs. A terrier-type, small, fast, suitable for vermin, a collie-type for herding and stock work, and the Dobermans, for guard and hunting. In the end, what they looked like would be less important than their efficiency. Laddie and any of his ilk that could breed would blend into one of those lines. The advantages of the dogs we had were that none were above moderate size, all were fast on their feet, learned quickly, and were intelligent, and none ate hugely or were lazy breeds. I intended to add as and where we found them to that base and on that basis.

We drove all day, nighted over in a small hotel whose sign we saw on the corner of a side road. Leaving Ricky to sort out rooms for everyone with Claire, I went wandering with Donal. He found the cellars and we descended. I stopped so abruptly at the foot of the steps as I held up a lantern that he almost fell over me.

"What...?"

"*Look!*"

"Good grief," Donal said mildly, surveying the cellar's inhabitants.

There were eight of them. All boys, none more than thirteen or so, clearly terrified, looking thin and dirty, and all clustered protectively around a cat. The cat looked smug. I spoke quietly, keeping my tone smooth and non-threatening.

"That's a lovely cat. What's its name?"

There was a pause then one of the smaller boys ventured a reply, "Fluffy."

That was true factually. I thought the animal to be at least half-Persian, or perhaps, since it didn't have the typical flat face, part Birman or longhair cat breed. The cat, having summed me up as another cat-loving sucker, rose, strolled to me, and made overtures. I scooped it up and confirmed its assumption, watching covertly as the boys relaxed.

"I apologise if we've taken over your home, we'll be on our way in the morning. But if this is your hotel, we should pay." I saw the oldest boy's look sharpen.

"How much?"

"Well, with money not being much good anymore, how about food?"

He bargained, face earnest, Donal stayed long enough to hear the terms, disappeared and returned with payment, and the boys fell on it. Donal then produced the piece de resistance, a bag of premium cat biscuits. I'd dropped one in the Landcruiser in case we ended up with a found cat. Well, in a way, we had. Ricky and Laddie had come back with him, and in between eating, the boys were talking. Laddie was a hit, particularly when they saw that he knew cats, liked and respected them, and Fluffy deigned to accept that.

"So this is your hotel?" Ricky was asking.

"Yeah, it was Dad's place. Me, an' Joe, an' Rod, an' Mick, we lived here. Others are our cousins. They lived down the road. Come here when..." he broke off, and no one spoke for a minute. "Fluff's the cat here, used to be her mum, now it's her."

I listened, learning how it had been. Two families, one with a smallholding, one owning the hotel. When needed, they would share work, and the smallholding would sell fresh food for hotel guests. A line prolific in boys, four in each family, tight, affectionate, and then the parents became ill one day. The children called for help, and no one came. They went looking and found either vacant homes or bodies. So they stayed where there was room for them all, and it became a base for them. They had each other and Fluffy. But time was running out. Every month, they had to go further afield to find resources. And after the second winter, many things were unusable.

Ricky was chatting about the glens, and I saw hunger light up the faces of those that could see what such a shelter could mean. "How'ja feel about cats?"

Ricky laughed. "You should see Tai. Gran Sheila says he's a Siamese Wildcat cross, he's huge, and even our Dobermans back off when he says. That's why Laddie's good with cats, Tai trained him." The boys laughed, and I saw what they should have been - instead of the dirty, half-starved waifs they were. I left Ricky and Laddie to it and went upstairs, where I found the parents' bedroom. I found papers that I read.

Joseph Matson senior, his sons Joe (junior), the oldest just past fourteen, Jack, the one who, at thirteen, did most of the talking, Rodney and Michael, their younger brothers. Joseph's wife had been Kirsty. I left the hotel and quietly walked to where I thought the other house would be, and it was. Papers there, too, were informative. Joseph Matson had been an elder brother. His younger brother – Jack – for Jackson, and after whom most likely Joseph had named his second son had lived here with his wife, Mary, and their sons: Will, Shane, George, and nine-year-old ... Coulthard? I wondered where that had come from and what they called the boy for short. Collie? I was to find that I was right; they *did* call him Collie. Later, I found he'd been named after his grandfather's favourite sportsman, a Formula One driver.

I looked over the farmhouse. The family hadn't been rich, but they'd kept it well. Some of the furniture was probably inherited. The parents' remains were still in their bedroom with old sacks heaped over them and an ancient voluminous fur coat atop that. I went to the children's rooms. They'd slept, two to a bedroom, and they looked to have been the usual boys, I could see nothing indicating trouble, and they read.

The house had stocked bookcases, one in each bedroom. In the parents' room, I found some of the classics and more recent works. In the boys' rooms, there were the sort of books readers of their age and sex would enjoy. I came away, and back at the hotel, I took down a large vacuum flask of hot chocolate, a tray of mugs, and shared it around the nine – Ricky having stayed talking. To say the drink was appreciated was a considerable understatement.

Jack drank his, and under the urging of seven pairs of eyes, spoke up. "Thanks, if you had a bit more of that, we wouldn't say no."

My reply was casual. "Of course. Ricky, can you ask Donal to refill this flask, please?" I handed it over, and leaving Laddie with us, he padded up the steps and returned in five minutes with more of the sweet, rich beverage.

The second lot of mugs were emptied, more slowly this time as they savoured it, and Jack nodded. "Good, that, where'd you get it?"

I explained the concept of salvage, storage, and the possibility of later production, all without giving anything away about the actual direction in which our glens lay.

"So you find it where you can and save it, but it's gonna run out sometime. What'll you do then?" I saw there was some self-interest in the question.

I sighed. "There are a number of things that are sweet. For a start, we have fruit trees and berries. You can dry some berries, powder them, and make a nice hot drink from that. Right now, we're watching for beehives, we already have a few in one of the glens, but we'd like more that gives us heather honey. Hot chocolate like this, cocoa and sugar, once that's gone, it's gone, but we can plant sugar beet – and perhaps sugar cane in lowland areas - for sugar too, so we can maybe make something one day that's like this, if not exactly. But with berries, honey and sugar beet, and maybe sugar cane, we'll always have something to sweeten our lives." Ricky laughed, and that set off the other boys.

Jack looked down, his first words a mumble. "'S been nice having you here. You could come by on the way back. Reckon Fluff'd like to see Laddie again, you wouldn't have to pay much like, and…" That trailed off to the mumble once more.

I was cheerful. "Of course, we'll stop in when we come back, and it'd be only right to pay." I left them to it and removed myself, nailing Ricky that evening before he and Laddie went to bed.

"What do you think of them?"

He eyed me seriously. "Second agenda, Gran?" I smiled. "Nice kids," was his verdict.

"They could come for a visit," I said in a completely neutral tone.

"They'd like that, I think, so long as Fluffy could come too."

"Would I expect them to leave her behind?" I was mock stern. "They could bring anything they liked. Stay a while, see what they thought. I won't mention it, but you could if you see them before we go … and we'll come back this way. Just don't give them directions. I'd rather no one knows where we live that doesn't have to know."

"You're not worried about *them*?" His look was incredulous.

"No," I said seriously. "But they could mention it to some-one else we *should* worry about." I saw him understanding that.

They lined up, all eight of them and the cat, to wave us off, and I thought I had the hook set solidly. So long as we survived to return, it was likely we'd have company on the way home. I suppressed a broad grin. They'd go well with some of the Som-erlee group. After all, we had to consider a new generation. I drove on down the main road until after another four hours, I could see Sam's car slow and signal. He'd been acting as forerun-ner since he knew where to find our destination.

We swung off at the crossroads, travelled another hour down that side road, and came to a massive complex of buildings that ran for almost a mile. Sam had said one of those was a depot for petrol tankers. They filled here and went all over. A second was, oddly enough, a fish farm, and a third was building supplies. Judging from what I could see, the number of businesses had grown since he was there, but I had no argument with that.

I pulled in behind Sam, cut the chains on the massive gates, and rolled into the huge turnaround in front of the first building. Donal joined us and considered the glass reception doors.

"Office, if we go there, it might save us time."

We walked over, found the revolving doors worked, and entered, cautiously, Donal moving to one side, gun ready. I tried the computers, nothing, not that I'd expected it. I foraged and found a side room filled with paper files that looked to have been printed out after the rolling outages of 2034, and although now seven years old, they gave a helpful overview. I scanned, talked to Donal and Sam, called in others, and we allocated areas. Petrol tankers were there, many of them already full, the new tankers with an inbuilt system that prevented water contamination.

The building supplies company had an entire fleet of lorries, fuelled, some loaded already, and the factory itself had been locked up securely. The fish farm had been an automated one. It was running down and almost out of supplies, but it still functioned, and there were lorries there that had the big fish transport tanks.

Donal grunted. "We could drop fish off in other places. There's that small lake over from the glens, just by McManus's place. Jackson's had a weir on their stream, and there's other spots where it'd make us a reservoir in case our lake dies."

I laughed. "What about real reservoirs? If we stock every decent-sized body of water in a fifty-mile radius of us, we could have fish for the foreseeable future, don't you think?" His slow grin was answer enough. Donal loves fish.

CHAPTER TEN

"Even when we were children, we learned not to go back by the way we had come." ~The Way That He Took, Rudyard Kipling

*Sometimes tiny things you don't consciously notice combine to give you a warning. It may be called a hunch, but it's reality-based. When that happens – listen. ~*Sheila McArn

It became both a working party and a glen party. Donal looked at maps, gave orders, and in bunches, lorries set out in different directions. Some to bodies of water elsewhere, some to our glens, and I watched as our survival possibilities improved. There'd been some accommodation here – perhaps for the depot's drivers, and we took that over.

Never less than six or seven vehicles left together. Each had a driver and a passenger riding shotgun – literally. By the time we were done, the glen had fourteen filled petrol tankers parked along one side. There was a double line of new storage sheds in Johnny's Glen, all stuffed with building supplies, while fish rioted happily in bodies of water in or near the glens. With most of what we'd salvaged staying in the glens, a smaller group was on the final return journey. However, when Donal gave the order to head home, nineteen vehicles fell into line with thirty-seven people in them.

I was driving, and Donal sat back comfortably beside me. "All right, lass. Let's go and collect those boys and whatever they want to bring."

I chuckled. "A certain cat for sure."

"Well enough. She's a nice beast, and they're good lads."

The countryside was quiet, the sun shone, and I drove without haste, our friends following. But something bothered me as we closed to within a few miles of the hotel. I couldn't have said what. Were I asked, just a prickling across my shoulder blades, a feeling that something had its attention on me. The further I got down the road towards the hotel, the more I felt it. I signalled and pulled into the roadside when we were three miles away. There I sat, trying to distinguish what was making me uneasy.

Donal closed a big hand gently on my wrist. "What bothers you, love?"

I shrugged. "Nothing I could tell you, I just have this feeling at the back of my neck. As if we shouldn't go this way."

"Have you seen something?"

"Nothing I know about. It's just something sitting there whispering in my ear."

Donal's gaze met mine, and there was an understanding in his "Ah," while at the same time, I realised what I'd said and identified its foundation. One of the things Donal and I have had in common most of our lives is a liking for the work of Rudyard Kipling. By the time we married, we each had a complete set of pretty much everything the author had written. And in this changed life, I was starting to think the man had been smarter than I'd realised. One of his stories talks about never using the same road to go back, and while I intended to pick up the Matson kids, there was a voice in the back of my head repeating the warning. I'm not one of these mystic Scots, but when that voice talks, I listen.

"Donal?"

"Mmmm?"

"You've got the maps. Is there a way we can detour around the Matson hotel and come up on it from a different direction?"

He looked at me. "Don't go back the way you came?" I nodded. "Aye." He spread out a map and traced roads. "That way," he said decisively. "We can park under the lee of the hill and not be easily seen. And you stay back. I'll take Jimmy and a couple of the others. We'll move in slow and easy, take a look before we call in anyone else."

I accepted that, and it was what we did – which turned out to be just as well – and I admit that after the events, I spent some of the following months thanking Kipling whenever I thought about it. I talked to Janet, and in the next few salvage forays, we spent time searching for the books and added them to our library until that, too, had a full set. Janet began making a habit of reading the stories to the children, which did mildly surprise me until she commented on it.

"Remember when they were written, Sheila. The times in which he lived and the ways of life were much closer to what ours are now than they were before the virus hit us. Now they have greater relevance again." I remembered the Matson hotel. She was right, and in the end, we had shelves of Kipling in various editions and combinations. I felt we owed him, and I pay my debts – not to mention that I love the tales.

****

But that day, all I had was the feeling and a husband who accepted that, a man who'd learned in the army that precautions taken were seldom wasted. He gathered up five men, all skilled stalkers, and they drifted into the fields, which were fast turning into an unkempt wilderness. He came softly back two hours later and slipped up to my window.

"You were right, and I think I know what alerted you as well." I waited to hear. "They're using little mirrors and Morse code. I think you caught a flash or two in the corner of an eye and knew it wasn't just a bit of glass in the sun."

"How many?"

"That's the trouble. Thirty we counted, and there could be a few more."

"*Thirty?* What are they?"

Donal laughed softly. "Believe it or not, I think they're football hooligans." I let out a startled giggle. "We split up and listened where we could. Talkative lot, fortunately. All young, none look to be more than the early twenties, no kids with them. Rough bunch. One of them is some sort of kin to the Matsons. He got out of Glasgow when the city fell to pieces, remembered the hotel, and came there along with friends, their girlfriends, and dogs."

"Fluffy won't like that," I said involuntarily.

"Likely not. They're bull terriers."

"Did they say anything about the boys?"

"Aye, and I don't like it." He frowned. "I didn't catch everything, but they've taken over the hotel, seem to be using the boys as servants, they brought a load of drink with them, and they're going through that like water. The ones I was listening to are planning to scout around the area. They want food, drink, women, and I have the impression they plan to set up as a sort of bandit clan, living off other people and taking whatever they want. They got here four days ago, and they know about us."

I jerked around to look at him. "*Do* they indeed. That isn't good."

"Nay, it isn't. And I'm worried about the lads. Sooner or later, one of them is going to push the line, and that lot of hooligans will come down hard. Could even be worse."

Abruptly I saw what he feared and shuddered. When there's no longer any law, the lawless take over, and while a group like this one might implode, in doing so, they could end up with people dead, with abused children, and half the immediate area in flames. Questions occurred from our army days, and I asked them.

126

"Can they move quietly? How well are they armed? Do they keep together, and how many dogs, are they trained or unruly pets?"

Donal nodded. "Good things to ask. I'll get some of the others in on this. But truth to tell, I want those lads out of there. Dogs are undisciplined and owners too."

We had a council of war that evening. First light saw another group of our vehicles taking to the road. Donal didn't want a fight, but he intended to be prepared if one came looking. We got the salvage our people would need away to the glens, and in return, we got back more fighters and a few things our football hooligans wouldn't expect. But I'd had an idea of my own. I waited until dusk and drifted silently across the fields under cover and towards the hotel. I'd judged the boys, from what I'd seen of them, to be on the lookout in case we came back without fanfare, and I was right. They were watching.

The hooligans were rioting. I could hear shouts, cheers, see the silhouettes of dancing figures, and a crash as if a bottle was flung. There was enough noise I could probably have arrived with a small brass band and not been noticed. I emerged under the line of hedge and looked up. A candle burned in a window where I thought the boys had their quarters, and I lifted my roughly-made catapult, tucked a tiny stone into it, and let fly. It was a little stone and twenty feet below and about twenty yards back, even I couldn't hear the tiny crack it made on arrival. The sound was more noticeable where it struck against the glass, and almost at once, I saw movement.

I let fly with a second tiny stone, and the candle was moved. I heard the faint squeak of a window being raised, and against the sky, I saw a figure descending the fire escape. It was who I'd expected it to be, and Jack Matson joined me, gasping a little from combined exertion and excitement.

I said the first thing that occurred to me. "Is Fluffy all right?"

He grinned. "She's fine, although she isn't happy, not with the place overrun by dogs."

"And uninvited guests?"

"Yeah." He paused, then talked, words falling over one another as he explained. "George is some sort of relation to mum. He came here sometimes with his parents before the sickness. When everyone started dying, he and his pals packed up, stole cars 'n stuff, and got out. He'd told them about here, they thought it'd be some posh place, and it isn't, so they're a bit fed up. But they've got plans. Trouble is before we knew them, Collie told about you, said you'd be stopping in to see us, an' said you had all sorts of things."

"Like hot chocolate."

"Yeah, so they figure they can ... that they could..." His voice faltered. "They say there's no laws, they can take whatever they want now, and no one can say nothing. One of them tried to get Collie into his room. George stopped that, but what if he isn't around next time or he doesn't want to cross his mates? We gotta get out, get away. We'd decided we want to go with you. But how, they aren't gonna let us just pick up our stuff an' leave? They like having us waiting on them, an' they want what you got."

"I see," I said. "So we do it in stages. Did Collie give them any idea when it was we'd be back?"

"Didn't know for sure, did we. They asked that an' I said it could be a month, didn't think it'd be more, but it could be that long."

He shivered suddenly. "It's real good you're back. I'm scared, an' I'm worried about Collie." I was too. Coulthard was nine, small for his age, with that angelic choirboy look that's a magnet to a certain sort of predator.

So we talked. Jack was thirteen – if my dates were right and I thought they were, his birthday had been ten days ago – and the last two years had taught him caution, to think things through before acting, and he had a ferocious protectiveness towards kin. His brother Joe was older, but Jack did the talking and most of the forward-thinking.

"How long is it safe for you to be gone?"

He sneered. "That lot? They wouldn't notice if I was gone all night. So long's they see me come morning, it's okay. They know none of us'll run cause of what they'd do to any as couldn't get away in time."

I led him back to Donal, and we sat up a while making plans, not the hard and fast kind, but contingencies. If that, then this, if this, then that. We watched, listened, and learned. There were, as Donal had thought, over thirty of them, including eleven women. I'd put the women's ages between sixteen and eighteen or late twenties trying to look eighteen. They'd looted a jewellery store somewhere. Most were bedecked in expensive necklaces, bangles, earrings, and they wore make-up, skin-tight clothing, and high heels, making them look incredibly silly in that country setting.

I was a little sad seeing their bright, chattering flock. I'd have liked to save them all, but we had to be realistic. They had no discipline, they'd never had to learn it, and they weren't interested. If we took them in, they'd be a focus for trouble, and once they got tired of being part of a community with the work and the cooperation that entailed, they'd run, and whoever they met after that would hear all about us, right down to exactly where we were. And we couldn't afford it.

The next night, Jack let down bags from the fire escape. They contained everything he, his brothers, and cousins couldn't bear to lose, with the final item a cage containing a muttering cat. Four of us made a quiet sweep of the hooligans' vehicles, and all was well. The cage came swinging down, Jack untied the rope, and brother Joe dropped down to join us. We started to where our vehicles waited, and the night came alive.

Lights, blasts from – quite incredibly – a horn and football rattles – and a shout. "You lot stay where you are, or we'll…" The

129

threat, expletive-decorated, was explicit. I ignored it, shoving the boys and the cage ahead of me.

"Get to the lorries. *Go!*" Fortunately, the older boys saw this was no time to be heroes and went. I was on their heels, and I knew that while we hadn't expected this, they wouldn't expect us either. The hooligans stopped shouting and using the rattles and started shooting. They meant what they'd said, and I thanked heavens that Donal meant what he said as well. He'd promised that we'd be guarded. I knew we were; I could hear the padding footsteps on either side of us.

But the steps behind were catching up, and I wasn't as young or as fast as I had been. Guns were firing all around. I could hear a shot now and then as it thudded into a tree or whined off into the distance. Then, from beside me, our people fired back. There was a scream from behind us, another, shouts of rage, the firing intensified, and – we broke out into the path to where the lorries were. The Landcruiser doors were open; I all but flung the brothers and Fluffy into the seats and dived into the front. In a couple of coordinated movements, I slammed the door shut, yelled for them to belt up, and took the vehicle away in a burst of speed.

Someone appeared in front of me, a dark figure rising, I hit it, and without thinking, I skewed the Landcruiser to one side and halted. Donal was there as I did so, a torch glowing in one hand. He knelt, the light lit up a twisted face, and a voice from the back seat said a name.

"George?"

The white face turned. "Jack?"

"Yeah. You okay?"

Donal's gaze met mine. No, George wasn't. I turned to the back seat. "Stay where you are. You can't help, and if you get out and we have to run, you could be left behind." I think Joe would still have got out, but Jack's hand went out and stopped him.

George was speaking between gasps. "I'm sorry... Shouldn't have ... taken your place, shouldn't ... have brought them here. Knew you ... were planning to leave ... didn't say nothing. One of the girls ... found out and come ... running in yelling.... My fault they were there. Didn't think, just had ... to get away, you don't know ... what it was like." His voice was getting quieter. "That's me, never think ahead ... Ma always said. Doesn't matter now. Better you're ... away from us. Sorry, sooooor..." Donal moved him carefully to one side of the track, straightened him, and stood looking down. He nodded.

"Aye, you were sorry, lad, you kept silent for them, and you've paid. Let that be counted for you." And to me. "Drive on now, love. Some of us will stop around and make sure they aren't on our tails."

I drove away, and from my seat, I could hear muffled sobbing. A fool George might have been, unthinking, casual, dangerous in what he'd done, but he'd kept silent when it counted, he'd been kin, and it was right they mourn him. When George jumped in front of us, I hadn't had time to do up my seatbelt, and I could feel a rising bump on one side of my face where I'd hit it against the steering wheel. I touched it with a finger. A little blood and a graze, not important. I could treat it when we stopped.

Behind me, I heard shots, and then a blast and another a minute or two later like the trump of doom. I smiled wryly. The building supplies depot had, in a large safe – with keys usefully found in the manager's office – a number of explosives. Donal wasn't likely to have been direct with those. It was more likely he'd waited until they came running after him and tossed something between them, enough to scare them all silly and into frozen immobility. Then he'd tossed a second one at the point where the foot-track broke into the road holding our vehicles. Between the double fright, the tangled destroyed vegetation and what our people had done to their cars, that would hold them while he and our people got clear.

It must have worked since there was no sight nor sound when we took a break an hour later. We'd turned down a side road Jack had suggested. "There's a village here, sort of. Not really, but there's farms and a few cottages and three shops."

I raised my eyebrows. "Salvage."

"Yeah."

"How'd you know the place?"

"Went to school with some of the kids."

And as I found, once we stopped, approached the shops, found no one there, and levered the doors open. Jack had done more than merely attend school with the owners' children. At some stage, they boasted of what their families had, of secrets and valuables, and exchanged information as children will. One shop was a small supermarket, the second was an agency with nothing of use to us. The third was a nursery with all sorts of saplings and seeds, and we gutted it and the supermarket. The buildings had upstairs living quarters and downstairs outbuildings, so Donal took the outbuildings and made an announcement immediately.

"Push bikes. Five, all sizes, and an adult's tricycle. And a couple of handcarts, home-made, pipe and bicycle wheels, those will be handy, let's get them loaded." I left him to it and retired to the upstairs of the first building with the four older boys.

There we salvaged. There were no bodies to be found. It had been where Jack's acquaintance had lived, and I thought it probable that the family had gone together to a hospital when they first fell ill. They'd never returned. Note to self: once we were done here, see if the boys knew where the nearest hospital, doctor's surgery, or any medical-type clinic was.

One thing I was taking wherever I found it was allodaxin. Mac had given me enough to dose everyone in the glens but to collect it when found cost nothing, and a good antibiotic treats other things such as infected wounds, some chronic conditions, and so on.

We found the boy's bedroom, and Jack looked wistfully at the array of computer gear. "Wish that worked still."

I pointed to a disk player, a game console, and other items. "They will, and so will the computers if you can get into them. It's just the internet that's down."

They stared. "You got *power* where you are?" Joe said eventually.

I grinned. "We do."

"Oh, *wow!*" They found bags, took the games, controllers, movies, and TV series, and emptied a bookcase. I left them to it and salvaged in the main bedroom, collecting a quilt, hand-made, a double one in autumnal shades of browns, orange, and gold, a charming set of green garnets in sterling silver, and in the wardrobe, boots. The lady must have liked them. They were flat – knee-high boots, one pair in black leather, a matching three-quarter-jacket, and ankle boots. All expensive and barely worn. I collected the lot.

The agency upstairs was a large room with nothing of value. We dumped our salvage in the Landcruiser, and I led the way to the plant nursery. Once there, I stopped and turned to the boys. "Let me go in first." They waited as I walked past the pried-open door and went upstairs, where I found what I'd expected. I tossed bedding over the remains, and in what must have been, by the size of the bodies, the children's room, I quietly picked up the now swathed bundles and moved them to be with the adults, shutting that door and leaving the others wide open. Then I called.

"Come on up. Only the rooms with open doors, anything you want, but not rubbish."

The pickings were good there. It must have been a thriving business because the children had owned some expensive things, most of which would be departing with us. Once the boys had all they wanted, I sent them to join Donal and returned to the parent's bedroom. I found a cache of sex toys in a bedside cabinet and

133

a shelf of pornographic books in the bookcase. She'd had some pretty exotic lingerie as well, and I smiled. I hoped they'd had a lot of fun and use out of everything before the virus hit.

Jack came in and touched my hand as he strolled past, books in one hand, looking for me to follow. I joined him and gave him a questioning glance.

His voice was low. "There's people in the far cottage. I went by, and I saw a girl. She looked right at me doing this." He mouthed words and did it again. I nodded.

"Have you ever seen her before?"

"No. Don't think so."

"Describe her."

"Red hair, about my age or a bit younger, I'd say, big bruise across one side of her face. She looked desperate."

It was the bruise and her age that decided me. I found Donal, explained what I'd been told, and he grinned. "Take them by surprise. That way, if we're lucky they won't fight, we can check the truth of it and do whatever needs to be done after that."

Donal wasn't in the army three decades for nothing. We hit that house like Atilla the Hun. In seconds, we were standing in the kitchen, a man cowering in one corner as he snarled at us, three children and a baby huddled on a couch. Donal had the man marched out while I sat down on a chair that I'd pulled close to the red-haired girl.

"We're here to help if we can and if that's what you want. What's the trouble?"

It came in a spurt of words. "Mum died with that virus thing. He used to work for her. When she died, he took over everything, us too. If you'll get us away, I'll work for you. Just take care of them." A jerk of her head indicated the children and baby with her.

I reached out and gently tilted her face to the light. It was a pretty face, except for a recent bruise. "Did you live here in this house?"

134

"No, farm a ways back. We ran out of drink, and he brought us here, said the shops'd have everything he wanted for a while. Once we'd had the best of it, we'd move on." Her eyes slid away. "He didn't like the baby crying. Said he'd dump her. I said if he did, I'd not be nice to him. So he let us keep her, but when she cries, he hits me."

I left her sitting and went out to Donal. It took only minutes to gather up whatever the children wanted to take. We looped past the farm, took the best of the animals that were there, and took from the house what was salvageable – not much, he'd left the doors and windows open. After that, we took the road back to the tiny village and passed the man where he sprawled on the doorstep a small hole showing in the centre of his forehead. The red-haired girl studied the body as we passed.

"Mum always said what goes around comes around. Guess it did."

****

I stopped at the fortified gate to Glen Mhairi, counting our people back home, and reflecting as they passed, that they looked like throwbacks to a clan's cattle-raiding past. Not that I looked much better. I was dirty, utterly weary, I had a graze on one cheek that still bled a little, and my husband, Donal, had bloodstains all down the front of his jacket – although, happily, they weren't his blood. With us, we had a baby and three children in one lorry, and eight boys with their large, fluffy cat.

We had a long line of utes and other vehicles with trailers all loaded with salvage, and some of our younger people wearing bandanas to keep their hair back, making them look like pirates out of our distant past. It was far from the civilization we'd had before the virus came and far from the one I hoped would come back someday in the future, but we were doing our best, and you can't do better than that.

We were armed to the teeth, and if this had been a year ago and I'd seen us coming, I'd have vanished into the nearest cover while phoning the police, ambulance service, and probably the army. But that was then, this was now, and I, along with Donal, was one of the war leaders of Glen Mhairi. I counted my people back and reflected on changing times and how people adapt or die when that happens. Since we had no intention of dying, we'd adapted, the only group to have done so locally – so far as we knew.

The last of our war band passed me, young Barry swung the heavy gates shut, rejoined his vehicle, and I nodded to the gate guards as I followed my people home. Donal was waiting for me down the road and jumped into the Landcruiser.

"All right, dear heart?"

I nodded. "No one hurt, twelve children, more livestock, and some excellent salvage."

"Aye," he grinned. "Did you ever think you'd be doing this sort of thing at our age?"

I shook my head. So much death, so many unbelievable things. Desperate acts, brutal decisions. However, someone once said that life was what happened while you were making other plans. It was true, but so far, we'd survived, making it a reasonable start.

CHAPTER ELEVEN

Warfare is based on deception. ~Sun Tsu

Aye, and it helps if the enemy can't find you, can't get at you if he does, and a strong defence costs less than a strong offence. ~Donal McArn

Winter arrived soon after that, and we hunkered down. It was then we found out, too, just how good Jamie Tamman was at poaching – not that it was poaching anymore. But he went out all hours and came back with rabbits, deer, fish, and birds, sharing them quietly about. I used to look at him, his flyaway white hair, his faded blue eyes, and the upright figure for all his age. Mac had loved his uncle, I knew, so I smiled, thanked him for what he did for the glens, and saw to it that now and again, a bottle of good whisky came his way from salvage.

Winter was a time to consolidate, and Donal had his list of things to be done or to be found. On it was a building programme in Johnny's Glen, and we got started on that shortly after we returned from the last salvage foray. We also strengthened the gate houses to the glens, building up complete walls across the roads with heavy gates. We'd started seeing people on the move. Not a lot, and not in large groups, but they were around, and Donal wanted it clear to any of them with an eye to what they could steal that we weren't good people to mess with.

Claire took in the red-headed girl and her three siblings. They settled with her, and Janet found me about a week later to report.

"That girl is bright. She's near fourteen, has ambitions, and survived trauma that could have broken many adults. She's ploughing through lessons; she soaks up information but not just as a parrot. She builds on it."

"What did you find out about her background?"

Janet accepted the offered mug of tea and settled back. "Her family were the Yarrows. Mother was a highland woman who went to England and worked there. Met a soldier boy, a lad from Sussex. Married him, and when her dad died, they came back to run the farm for the mother's mother. Grandmother died years back, and they inherited the farm, good parents from what the girl says. Sensible, practical, kind, and decent. Girl went to a school outside the area; father liked it better than the local one. She was hoping for a scholarship to one of the universities, and in my opinion, it wasn't unlikely."

"How old are the others?"

"Alex, our red-head, is thirteen plus. Next one down is Ann; she's eleven. The boy is Kin – short for Kinley – he's not quite nine, and the baby, unexpected tail-ender Alex says, is Iris. She was born three months before the virus hit, and she's probably the reason the children survived. She picked up a sore throat at the doctor's surgery and gave it to the others but not the parents. Father died first. He seems to have spotted what was happening and took the farm ute out, cleared their bank account, and spent every penny of it on supplies. Then they holed up. He died, the mother died, and that…" Her pause was eloquent. "That *man*, he'd been working for them a year, moved in and took over."

"How badly has it affected her, do you think?"

Janet thought. "Not as bad as it could have. She wanted to be a doctor. She understands the physical aspects, and I've been watching what she reads. She's been digging into some of the books, trying to understand how it affected her, I think."

I'd seen that sort of thing. It was a defence mechanism. If she understood it, then she could cope. "Then there's the sacrificial aspect," I said slowly. "She wasn't just abused. She consented to save her little sister. She was beaten – to save her little sister. And her brother and sister understand her choices likely saved them as well. It makes them look up to her rather than seeing her as a tart who traded her body for luxuries."

"Aye, whatever he gave her, she shared or gave to them entirely," Janet confirmed.

"So she wanted to be a doctor?"

"Aye," Janet smiled. "And she got a head start on that too. Girl at the school she attended, her father was the local GP. Alex spent as much time there as she could, talked to the father, listened to him tell stories of being a GP, he gave her a couple of books. She knew what she wanted, and she started right for it."

"How long ago?"

"Two years, maybe a bit more." Janet leaned forward. "You know, Sheila, you trained as a paramedic. There's ways you're better than a nurse. You learned some battlefield surgery, emergency medicine. That's the sort of thing to be passed on."

I'd been thinking about that myself. We had no other medical staff, not even a vet. If I died, all my knowledge was lost, not just my training, but the decades I'd worked, shortcuts and tricks I'd learned, substitutes for official treatments or medicines, ways of using what was available rather than expecting to have everything to hand. I made up my mind.

"You're right. Wait another month. If you still think the girl has too much potential to be wasted, if she still wants to be a doctor, bring her to me, and I'll start teaching her. Just a half-day a week to begin with, she can help me at the clinic I run Saturday mornings. If she is as good as you think, I'll increase time with her." And so it was decided.

Winter set in, and we were snug in the glens. Johnny always claimed one of the reasons his forefathers had taken this land was because his ancestor had come by one year when the winter was particularly bad. To his surprise, he'd found the glen to be snow-free, and beneath high cliffs, it was sheltered and even warm still. It was the old Laird's theory the land could have some source of warmth beneath it, something geothermal perhaps, but he was a man who didn't need explanations. It was sufficient for him that his land stayed unfrozen, and he did not need to know the mechanics.

I agreed that the geothermal idea was possible, and my belief was that the area of that extended further. Glen Mhairi also stayed snow-free, as did, we'd discovered once we made a road into it, Blind Glen. So before winter set in, I'd approached several of Ricky's friends, children of thirteen to fifteen, and offered them payment to explore the surrounding land about the three glens. With a bonus, if they found anything interesting, helpful, or important. Young Barry came to see me three weeks later, beaming with suppressed excitement.

"Mrs. McArn, I found something."

"Sit down." I offered hot chocolate. It had become something of a status symbol, and he accepted eagerly, not only for that, and drank the steaming drink with clear enjoyment. Once done, he put the mug to one side and brought out a rolled-up piece of paper.

"I made a map." He spread that out on the table and showed me something that for all I'd been born and brought up in the glen I hadn't known. "Found a cave." He described the location, and I saw why it was nothing I'd ever known.

"You think the cave is old, but it's been hidden? Interesting, I knew there were caves there in Blind Glen, but not this one," I commented.

"Yeah, not by accident neither. There was stone cut and fitted." Barry grinned

Well, well, well. And at the end of Blind Glen, while the others were down one side, I ordered the area in mind's eye. Yes, Blind Glen was ours, but before the virus, it was at the fringe of McManus land where it adjoined the McAlister estate. It had

140

been closed off, of no particular value. I was about to ask where the cave led, then let him tell it his way, his discovery after all.

He went back to explain some of it. "You know we had that week of rain?" I certainly did. If it hadn't been for Donal's trench, the far end of Glen Mhairi would have flooded feet deep. I nodded. "Looked to me as if water got under the edge of the wall's stones, washed earth away. They fell, and the cave was behind them. I saw the heap of stones and it sort of caught my eye. I went to look, and there was the cave. I went in a small way, didn't have a light, so I didn't go far, not that time."

"But you went back?" I encouraged.

"Got a torch from Ricky, said it was important, worth the batteries," Barry confirmed and looked at me anxiously. "Honest, I think it was." I indicated provisional acceptance, and he relaxed a little. "Cave's big, not much of an entrance, maybe three feet wide an' about five high, but it gets big once you're in. I reckon they put a wall up that covered the whole mouth and filled in earth behind that between the cliff and the wall."

Which was why, when that washed away, the wall may have destabilized and fallen. If the wall had been old enough, it could have been put up from cut stone, no mortar. Not that it mattered. What I wanted to know was what was interesting about the cave. I possessed myself in patience.

"I went in, and there's all sorts of stuff there, barrels, boxes too, odd-looking ones. Couple of lanterns, real old-looking. Didn't open anything," he flushed. "It's all corded up wi' huge old padlocks and chains. Barrel lids nailed down. So I kept going into the cave, tunnel beyond it, didn't go too far in case I came out on McManus land." Barry, too, was Glen born and raised. "You know that lot, so I came to tell you."

"McManus land?"

"Sort of. Tunnel stops, and there's another wall at that end. Couple of stones moved a bit, or maybe a corner cracked off, and I could see through the gap to their place."

"Did you see or hear anyone there?" He shook his head. I kept myself calm. "This tunnel, how long, how high, how wide? And the wall at the other end, if that was taken down, how big do you think the entrance would be?"

The figures caught my attention, and while I might be making assumptions, I thought them right. I smiled at Barry. "I want you to say nothing about this to anyone…."

"Told Ricky."

"I'll tell him not to say anything either. This is your discovery, but there could be danger. You said I knew 'that lot,' and I do. Before everyone starts running onto McManus land and we have trouble, I want to make a few quiet checks." I leaned forward. "Listen, Barry. This could be a significant discovery for the glens. You'll receive the acknowledgement for it, and I'll see you do well. But until we've checked, you need to keep silent about what you found, all right?"

His eyes were glittering with delight. He had an important secret. A war leader was asking him to do something for them. And it was him, quiet Barry, never-been-important-before-Barry, who was on stage. He nodded.

"I swear, Mrs. McArn. I won't let anyone know, won't say a word until you say I can, won't even hint, not to anyone."

I believed him. I farewelled him with sufficient ceremony, shaking his hand formally and holding the door for him that he flushed again with gratification, and I went in search of Ricky. He, too, I enjoined to silence on the matter.

"He really did find something important?"

"I think so. You haven't said anything to anyone?"

"No, Gran Sheila, it was Barry's secret anyway. Will he get a reward?"

"Something for sure. It depends on what it leads to and just how good things are. But it could be he'll do very well out of it."

Ricky beamed. "Good, some of them used to tease him because he's so quiet. I told them it wasn't right, wasn't the glens' way, and they stopped. That's why he came to me."

I went home thinking that several things in that discussion made for interesting items to ponder. I knew Barry was quiet, but there was nothing wrong with his brain. Then there was the assumption that anyone quiet must be stupid, and it was acceptable to tease him. I was pleased Ricky had stopped that and proud that he'd done what was right. There was another aspect of that. The other children had listened. Was that because he was Donal's and my adopted grandson, or was Ricky listened to as himself? Was he showing leadership qualities of his own? I left that to mull over when I wasn't busy – fat chance – and went to find Donal. There I explained Barry's discoveries, and once I was done, he took my hand.

"We'll go now."

"You think it's that important?"

"Aye, and so do you, we know what went on times gone by, that'll be what's in the cave, and it can wait. However, we know some of what's gone on since. Question is, and it's one we need answered, how much is still going on there and has anyone survived?"

"There's been no sight or sound of them."

"As the crow flies," Donal pointed out. "They're little distance. By road, it's a bit like Johnny's glen. We get to that on the glen track. It's a mile and twenty minutes afoot – thirty minutes by car, though. McManus land's the same now Blind Glen is open. Must be all of thirty miles there by road, from what young Barry says, it'll be far less via this tunnel. And if the estate there is occupied still, we're in danger the minute they find out there's a way into three rich glens."

I understood. Three glens, with resources, a population – the majority of them young - storage facilities, housing, livestock, and all of it ripe for exploitation by a superior force. We'd fight, but that was no guarantee we'd win. Best we found out what we might be up against before they found that they had something to fight for. We took the electric motorcycle Donal had salvaged from Thurston. It was fast, had excellent traction on rough land, could go a hundred miles before needing a charge, and if we added the small trailer, it would still do fifty miles if that wasn't overloaded.

We paused to eat a fast lunch, bread and goat cheese, a glass of milk, before we were gone, zooming quietly down Glen Mhairi, into Blind Glen, and to the end of that where we found the tumble of stones Barry had described to me. I was surprised he had found it at all. It was on the far side of the new lake, along a narrow strip of slightly raised shore that curved behind bushes and ended at the cave was screened by brush. When it rained, the water would come almost to the mouth of the cave, making it unlikely that anyone would bother. I said as much, and Donal snorted.

"Lads, there's nowhere they won't go if they think it a good idea. You offered a reward for interesting stuff, and Barry's a quiet lad but no fool. He'd think that the best place to go was where no one would think to, so he went there, and look what he found."

I'd wormed past the brush and *was* looking. The barrels I could identify. "Rum, brandy, whisky there…"

"Wine too," my husband agreed. "Maybe tea in the chests."

I laughed, keeping it down, laughter can carry, and the tunnel would amplify it. "Not that it'd be any good by now. It'd have to be two hundred years old."

"Depends on how it was packed," Donal said slowly. "The drink would be useable. Not important anyhow. We need to know about what's beyond. Let's go, love."

We walked with care. The tunnel footing had been smoothed off at some stage, but as Barry had told me, the height was about five feet, and it would be easy to knock your brains out if you got careless. We didn't, and we ended up where the boy had said, behind a beautifully built wall, where time had eroded a little gap we could look thorough. Donal put an eye to that, said nothing, and applied an ear.

"No one in sight, no sound of anyone. And I'll tell you something, love. There should be another way out of here into there. Why would you wall up a very useful tunnel with a load of contraband at the other end from you so you couldn't get to it?"

We went looking, breaking off now and again to listen for anything outside. No one turned up, but another way out did. It was Donal who found it, experience in special ops can be helpful, and this was something he'd seen before. There was a fold in the wall, which, when he investigated, turned out to be a door, disguised bolts held it shut on the inside, and – or so I presumed – there was something similar on the outside as well. We opened the door, slowly, carefully, until we could look through a six-inch gap. We stood there waiting for ten minutes by my watch. Nothing moved.

Donal stirred. "Watch the door, my darling, while the gentleman goes by." I grinned. He slipped out and vanished into the undergrowth. I had no real fear for him. He was armed. He was wearing body armour – one of the things we had salvaged from the first police station we found that had it. And he knows his business, does Donal. I watched, waited, and listened. There was nothing for an hour until I heard a faint rustle and he was back. He slipped past the door, pulled it almost shut again, and spoke softly.

"It's the back of the old McManus estate, all right. Greenhouses, and you can guess what they're growing, orchard too, the trees are quite new, full-grown but not much more, and there are bulls."

"Bulls?"

Donal grinned. "Defence in depth, lass. Police helicopter overhead sees little. Greenhouses are only about seven feet high.

Although they're a good fifty feet long, the orchard is planted in rows, and the greenhouses are between them. Once the trees get to a certain size, they cover the greenhouses, and those are done in green-tinted plastic panels that don't catch the light. I'd say they have the other end of this bit blocked off from the main estate. They've run bulls in to wander around this section, probably started as yearlings, now they're older and don't like intruders."

"Beef or dairy?" I queried.

"Mostly dairy, Jersey, a couple of Angus."

That would be handy, I thought, if no one was here to stop us salvaging, and we wouldn't have to round them up and go by road. "Police wouldn't easily find this section then, and if they did, they wouldn't just charge in, not with a bunch of bulls looking at them," I summed up. "What *is* in the greenhouses, just cannabis?"

"No, three are that; three are poppies."

"Do we both go and take a closer look?"

Donal hesitated, then nodded. We slipped by the door, pulled it to, and padded away into the brush. The bulls preferred the open grass areas, and so long as we didn't upset them, there was a fair chance we'd have no trouble. Donal led, I followed. Nor did either of us travel in straight lines. It took time, this inner glen was a mile long, but after an hour's cautious advance, we reached the end and could look into the central estate. We found a comfortable place to sit and watched for anything we could see. We both had army binoculars, the type that don't show lenses in sunlight. We scanned, listened, and nothing made itself apparent apart from animals. There were rabbits, careless, numerous, and fat. If they'd been shot at of late, none of them knew about it.

"The rabbits think it's a long time since people were here," I noted.

"Aye, I've been watching them."

"Not to say they're always right…."

"No, but when it's a beast's life, they tend to be wary," Donal agreed. "I know what's in your mind, lass. You'd like to go just a bit further and see what's what." How well my husband knows me. And he never minds indulging me either if it's not too dangerous – or expensive. He stood up silently, started for the wall at the end of the glen, and I moved to my position, following, wary as any rabbit, but far better armed and armoured.

The wall was about seven feet high, the gates were sheet steel, while the top of the wall was embedded glass, barbed wire, and angled lights to show it after dark. Serious business. But then, from what we'd heard, that was who and what they were.

The McManus estate had passed out of McManus's hands about fifteen years ago. The last of the direct line had died, and the heirs hadn't been interested in an isolated estate in the hills. They'd sold it as fast as they could and remained living in Glasgow. I wondered what had happened to them. Some obscure company had bought the estate. It had immediately posted the place, sacked all the local people, and hired men who scowled and said nothing but *yes, no,* or *go away.*

Rumour had it that the company was run by a Glasgow crime family. I'd vaguely recognised the name, but it was nothing to do with me, and so long as they didn't bother me, I saw no reason to bother them. Rumour had it, too, that the company specialised in moving illegal merchandise and luxury items that hadn't paid tax … at the thought, I smiled. Not much difference between the original owners and those barrels.

Donal was considering the wall. "We could climb it. Anyone waiting would see us first though. I wonder if it can be opened from this side?"

I'd already examined that possibility. "Not without special cutters. I've seen that sort of chain before. Ordinary cutters won't touch it. On the other hand..." I started walking along the wall line. "You know how it works, build a massive wall, build even more massive gates, fortify the wall, chain the gates – and ignore the ends of the wall."

We strolled the length of it – to our right, people go less often to their left, those on the other side would likely be that way – and found I'd guessed well. Where the wall met the cliff edge, it was crumbling. Out of sight, out of mind. We picked quietly at the wall; piece by piece came away. It looked to me as it had been built fifteen years ago and never maintained since. It took a while, but then we had a gap large enough to slide through. Donal went first.

The grass was hay-high. If anyone tossed a match down, there was going to be one heck of a fire. Donal signalled me to halt, and I did so, peering ahead to see movement. I inched forward. A step, another … *rabbits*! It didn't make us careless, but again it was an indication. The next movement was a pony. *A nice Arab and Welsh-mountain mix,* I thought. The wind was to us, so he didn't react. Beyond him, I saw others. And something came silently through the grass towards us. It arrived at my feet and wailed, a long tirade on the unreliability of people, a formal complaint of desertion, abandonment, and general ill-use – and what was *I* going to do about it?

Donal was grinning. "They know one when they see one."

I picked up the Siamese cat with ostentatious dignity. "Of course." The cat went into ecstasies. Finally, a human. Someone to feed him, love him, provide for him as he should be and… I ran through a mental list of cat-lovers in the Glens. Claire didn't have a cat, and the Yarrow children liked animals and were used to them. This fellow was neutered, probably vaccinated. I'd put him around four. I set him on his paws, and he paced after me as Donal led off again towards the house. Once he was sure which way we were going, the cat bounded ahead, and we lost sight of him.

"He looks well fed."

"Even crooks may love their animals. They may have had feeders. I tell you, love, I'm taking no bets, but I think the place could be empty." The path was going to creeping weeds. Donal halted us in sight of the house, and we stood waiting for any movement, any sign of occupation. There was none, and when he moved forward, I was at his heels.

CHAPTER TWELVE

Beware of people who dislike cats. ~Irish proverb

In fact, beware of anyone that doesn't like animals. It's often a warning that they may not like people much either – or be trustworthy. ~Donal McArn

The house was silent. The windows were closed, the door shut, and I leaped like a startled rabbit when the cat appeared on the doorstep and let go in our direction with what I can only call a commanding bellow. Donal touched my arm.

"Wait and see if that produces anyone." It didn't and the cat, indignant, issued another clarion call for service. I looked at Donal and started forward. If anyone were inside, they'd have to have been deaf from birth not to have heard that. Besides, now that we were closer, I could see leaves banked up against the door. We advanced on the door, and I tried it.

"Locked. What about the back?"

We circled the house. The back door was ajar, blocked that way by a large stone on either side of it. The cat passed us and began issuing orders again. It felt a bit like *lese majesty*, but I joined him, found a can opener, cat food stacked in a cupboard, and fed the cat. He ate tidily, paws tucked in, purring bliss. Things were back to normal when humans came when called and fed you.

I looked about and found what we'd expected, a feeder and water system. The feeder was empty, but while that might be so, I suspected it hadn't been so for long; the cat showed no signs of actual starvation, although with the number of rabbits around... Donal went to the foot of the stairs and listened, more silence, and step by step, he moved upwards, making no sound. I waited below, my gun out, covering his climb. He reached the next floor, moved to guard in turn, and signalled my ascent. We advanced along that floor the same way, one up in turn, the other watchful. There was no movement, but partway I smelled a familiar scent.

I joined Donal in a doorway and pointed. "Something dead down that way."

"Aye," he said heavily. And we went to see.

It was a variation of the usual scene. I walked in to find a male sitting in a large chair. If he had sight still, he would have been looking directly at me as I entered. Laid out on the bed were bodies: an older woman, a younger one, two children, and a baby. I wanted to see what the rest of the building held before making any decisions. Donal lingered, and when I turned to see why, he was bending over the man on the chair. He nodded and went to the bed, considering those on that before turning to me.

"Most of these were shot."

"Shot?" I came back and looked down. He was right. "Do you think they were some of this crime family?" Donal was bending over the baby. Now he peeled its shawl aside and pointed. I stared. "The *baby* was shot. What kind of person shoots a *baby?*"

My husband took my arm, leading me out of the room, and, once we were peering into other rooms, he spoke sadly. "Who'd shoot a baby? Maybe a man who knew that the whole world was dying, that if the baby lived, it would only die later. It couldn't survive on its own, and who was likely to find it? Then too, a man who'd lived his sort of life, maybe he didn't want someone else raising his child. One of them can't have been all bad, though."

I looked at him, and he pointed down towards the back door. I blanked for a moment before understanding. "The cat."

151

"Aye, someone made sure it had food and water, some- one at the least blocked the door open, so once the food and wa- ter ran out, it could go out and hunt."

I remembered the signs I'd seen and smiled wryly. "Not sure they knew about cats. He didn't hunt for a fair while, not with a secondary food supply right here."

Two of the bodies had shown signs of predation, but then many cat-owners didn't understand the feline mindset. Alive, you were their beloved human; the moment you died, you were food. Cats are what they call "opportunistic feeders." I'd always known that, and I was a realist. Rather than have a cat I loved starve, I'd have happily given permission – not that any cat would ask.

Donal halted at a shut door towards the end of the corri- dor. He tried it. "Locked. Now, why?" He produced the short tyre-lever from where he carried it hooked over his trousers' waistband and applied it to the door jamb. I moved quickly to one side before he could wave me to. Donal grinned. "Smart girl." He levered again. The door came open with a crack, and there was a bellow as a full charge of shot slammed into the opposite wall.

I took in a deep breath. "Nasty."

"Yes, stay back in case he's a belt and braces type." He moved to where he could see around the edge of the door and then sidled cautiously into the room. I received the *all clear* and joined him, then stared. Donal was carefully opening drawers, feeling under the edges of those, and looking into the build-in wardrobe. He emitted a satisfied sound from the back of his throat and came out of the wardrobe holding a single key.

"There'll be a safe somewhere."

I contemplated that and snorted. "And it probably holds his money and her jewellery. What use is that to any of *us*?"

"None if that's all, but there could be papers, other things, we won't know until we find it. Better not to miss anything use- ful."

To abbreviate a long story, we found the safe downstairs, and Donal opened it with care again. Just as well; that, too, was booby-trapped. It contained, as I'd expected, several bricks of cash, a stack of jewellery cases, three handguns, and the cat's pedigree papers. He was Champion Apollo of Helios, neutered, vaccinated, micro-chipped, and his fourth birthday had been the previous month. I took the papers, not that they had any relevance these days, but if he went to Claire and the Yarrow children, they might like to have them. Donal rifled through other papers and looked up with a set in his left hand.

"Take a look here, love."

I deciphered what I was seeing. "Some sort of bunker?" Mutely he handed me another set, a list this time, and I scanned it. "Phew," I said quietly. "What was he *planning*?"

The list included sheet steel, sheets of material commonly called glasscrete, and weapons enough to outfit a small army. It struck me then. "Donal? Do you think maybe someone hinted at him? Mac knew – and look at the delivery date here." I pointed. "That's only three days before it started." Donal pointed in turn to the bunker plans. "I know they're much older, but what if he'd wanted that all along as a place to hide drugs or other stuff the police could come looking for? Then, just before everything fell over, he heard what was coming. He had the bunker, so he got in other things to help them survive – but they had the virus, and they all died."

"If we find the bunker, it could be useful, never mind what he knew or didn't," Donal commented. "He's got food on this list too. Bulk stuff, long-life supplies that'd last a decade or more if he has them properly stored."

"Do we look for that now?"

"It'll keep. Let's see what else is around."

What was around was a massive garage. That contained two three-ton lorries, a Landcruiser with armoured glass windows, four e-motorbikes, and three fancy cars, the sort used for showing people how rich you are. At the back was an elaborate workshop, and behind that, a door. I exited and found I was loomed over by petrol tanks.

"Donal?"

He looked up at those from behind me. "Wonder how full they are?"

I shrugged. "Either they are or they aren't, but I'd make a small bet they're full. He had all those vehicles. It's cheaper to buy in bulk."

We checked, and he had enough petrol there to keep all the vehicles that used it running for a year. I started for the front of the property. I wanted to know how secure it was and just what else might be here we could use. Donal moved out ahead of me, silent and deadly, although, as we found, there was no need. There was no one alive, the entrance to the estate was secure, and it was ours now. We could access it through the cave, there was a gatehouse here, and it had been heavily fortified too. The land belonging to the place was a goodly amount, and we had added to our domain by one glen and everything within it. I collected Apollo, and we went home.

The cat settled down with Claire and the Yarrow children. He liked Alex best, and she adored him; I think he helped take her mind off some of what had happened. We returned in a week with assistance, took the bodies out and buried them, not in McManus Glen but on the uplands above it. We gave them no headstone, no markers, just a deep grave where they could lie together forever. Janet asked me afterwards why I'd bothered.

"You could have dumped the bodies somewhere. He was a criminal."

"Who left us food, petrol, weapons, and a fourth glen," I said slowly – we'd found the bunker. "It felt right, we took what he left, and we gave him and his kin a decent burial."

"He gave us land, aye, I suppose that's fair." She grinned. "Land for land."

So now we had Glen McManus together with everything it held, and that was a lot. Janet raised another question as we scoured the place for hidden items.

"What about settling the other glens? Right now, everyone's in Glen Mhairi."

That was true, and it was something Donal and I had discussed. At the moment, we felt we had insufficient numbers to divide them. I said so, and Janet inclined her head.

"True enough. So what we need now is more people, ones we can trust, maybe a profession or two. We haven't needed a dentist yet, but we will, and you need to start teaching your skills to Alex or someone."

Both comments were right. It was just that I needed time and didn't have it to spare.

****

I had managed to start one thing of late, however. Archery contests. The Matson boys had taken it up with enthusiasm, and several children around their age had followed suit. To my carefully suppressed delight – at least in public – Ricky was a natural. One of the things I'd seen to it that we collected were sweets. Humans crave sweetness, and winning a single bar of chocolate wasn't just a token of ability. It was something to share with your best friends. I noted with interest that when Ricky won, he shared with Barry, Jack Matson, and Alex.

In the old days, a leader was open-handed with his followers, his ability to do that showed he was an effective – and perhaps a lucky – leader. As time passed, we seemed to be falling into some of those original patterns where they felt right. Well and good, if they worked, we'd be none the worse for them.

The Giles were around, the minister going about the sort of business a minister has, and so long as he wasn't preaching fire and brimstone and terrifying people, I had no objection to it. His wife rarely did anything that I saw, but his mother, old Mrs. Giles, was often found reading to the smaller children. She had

155

a lovely voice. Soft, expressive, and she could catch a listener up in the story she told. Their house had a large vegetable garden, several fruit trees, and Mrs. Giles, the younger, worked there most of the time. It did strike me as unusual after a while that she joined in nothing, spoke no more than a phrase or a word or two, and kept to herself with an almost hostile fervour.

I learned the reason for that one day. The trees in Glen McManus had fruited, and I'd declared them open to all. Half Gen Mhairi had gone, including, to my mild surprise, the minister and his wife. I'd stayed, and so I was home when old Mrs. Giles came calling.

"May I speak with you, dear?"

I ushered her in, made tea, and we settled in the kitchen. She drank composedly before saying something that riveted me.

"I've not got much longer."

My gaze at her sharpened. I was used to people telling me as soon as they felt unwell, but she'd never done so. I'd noticed signs that she had health problems, but as she never complained, I'd done nothing. I had more than enough to do without looking for work.

"Your heart?"

She nodded. "Yes, now and then, I have a giddy spell. I have tablets for it, and I'd just filled a prescription before everything happened. It was for three months officially, but usually, it lasts a year or so since I take them only when I need to. And when you did one of your early runs to Thurston, my son saw some in a pharmacy; he should maybe not have done so, but he took them for me."

I saw the faint blue tinge around her mouth. "And now they aren't working so well, you increased the dose, but you still have the turns." She inclined her head. "I may have something that will help."

"That would be good, thank you. However, you can't make old bones young again. I'm ninety-three, my dear, and no one lives forever. I'm content, I've had a good and long life, I had a fine man, and I have a good son."

I spoke without thinking. "No grandchildren, though?"

She remained composed. "No, and just as well."

I showed no sign, but abruptly I understood. This was why she'd made sure her son and daughter-in-law were away. She wanted to tell me something. I stood up, refilled the teacups, sat again, and showed her that I was listening. She took a sip of the tea and nodded approval. "I do like a good cup of tea. Now, my dear. I know you've wondered about us. The truth is that my daughter-in-law can be a problem. She dislikes children, and we came here because there was legal trouble where we were." She took a breath. "My son didn't know any of this when they married, and afterwards, he would never consider a divorce. But he came to see that should she have a child, it would be – unsafe."

"Legal trouble," I said as encouragement.

"He persuaded her to teach Sunday school where we were. One of the children there – a Letty Simon – was difficult; disruptive, rude, and unpleasant, and after a few weeks, Hazel refused to have her in the class. Her parents were furious, but even my son couldn't change her mind, so the girl didn't attend anymore. She resented it and often hid as Hazel passed, throwing stones in her direction to make her jump, and she told stories in which Hazel featured in unpleasant ways. Hazel heard them, and she came home and told my son and me. She made threats against the girl and was quite frightening in her fury."

"And then?"

"And then Letty made a mistake. Now and again, after church, Hazel would go to the small stream behind the church to pick watercress to bring home for Sunday afternoon tea sandwiches. The stream was on common land, you understand. On this occasion, Letty followed her. Hazel was picking the watercress when she saw Letty spying, and from the fragments Hazel let fall to me later, I think Hazel flew into one of her rages and so scared the child that she picked up several stones and flung them. One quite large stone hit Hazel in the temple and cut her badly. Hazel attacked the child, flung her into the stream, and I cannot be sure, but I believe she held her down so she drowned."

I kept myself composed. To show anything would derail the narrative, and apart from wanting to know what had happened, it could be vital that I heard the story.

Old Mrs. Giles faltered. "Hazel returned home with a gash on her forehead that was bleeding profusely. She appeared dazed, staggered inside, and collapsed. One of Letty's friends had seen some of what occurred, although not the final actions. The police came, and Hazel testified that she had been at the stream, that Letty had attacked her, that she had been so stunned from the blow to her head she had known little but that she must get home. She suggested the girl had probably run after her, tripped, fallen in, struck her head, and drowned. There was little proof, either way. Letty's friend admitted Letty had thrown stones and made threats and that she had then run home and seen nothing more."

"So the police laid no charges?"

"They told my son that there was insufficient proof. They were not prepared to lay charges based on what they had. They knew Hazel would be acquitted if it came to trial. We moved away and had begun to rebuild my son's ministry when we found that Letty's parents were bringing a civil suit. It failed, but such was the gossip – and we had threats made against us as well – that I said we should go where no one knew us, where we could live quietly for some years and then set up my son's ministry again."

She looked across the table. "Hazel was furious. I insisted, and she lost her temper and said many things that confirmed my belief of what she had done. She agreed, however, when I put my foot down with my son's agreement, and we came here."

I summed it up. "You believe that in her rage at being hurt, she attacked Letty, killed her, and successfully hid that fact from the authorities." I made a small leap. "You have watched her carefully, kept her away from all children and most people here. You are afraid that she may harm someone else when you are gone or endanger us in some way. Your son cannot control her, and if she is sufficiently angered, she could even turn on him. What do you want me to do?"

"Watch her." She went to speak, faltered, and I could see her govern herself to say more. "Hazel is, I am convinced, not always in her right mind. Having a temper is not an indication that one is – that, but in her case, I think it is so. Hazel works hard; she is faithful, honest as to valuables. She is a devoted gardener, as am I; she has always been polite to me. I think she genuinely loves my son, but in the wrong circumstances, I think she could be a danger to all about her. Because of her temper, if she thinks of someone as an enemy, she may go to extreme lengths against them."

Old Mrs. Giles looked at me imploringly. "You had to know. Life now is so uncertain, so dangerous. You don't need trouble from someone you don't expect to act badly." She stood up. "I leave it to you, my dear. Do whatever you must, whatever you think is necessary." She smiled then. "And I'd like to be buried outside the glens, up on the small hill on the other side of the road. I don't need a headstone or a coffin. My son knows what I want. And thank you for listening."

She opened the door, and I saw her small erect figure walk away in the direction of her home. I never saw her alive again. Nor did it surprise me. I've seen people who knew their time was upon them and waited only to pass on something important. Her son and his wife came home laden with fruit from Glen McManus and found his mother already in bed saying that she was a little tired. They woke in the morning, brought her breakfast in bed as a treat, and found that she had passed into that eternal silence during the night. Her son, at least, mourned her deeply and sincerely.

We buried her where she had wished, on the small hill that could be seen from the Glen Mhairi gatehouse. Her son led the service, and she lay, wrapped in what he told us had been her grandmother's wedding present, a rabbit-skin bedspread, and dressed in a simple green velvet gown given her by her husband when they were young. Under one hand, she had a book; under the other, a framed photo of her late husband. Why, I wondered? So she could recognise him? So he could find her? Or as proof she'd been married? And the book? Did she plan to re-read it where she went?

Once the grave was filled in, we sang. The strains rang out across the land before we walked back to the vehicles waiting. One of the people of our glen was gone, and I had a trust, a danger to watch for in her place. I told Donal everything, and he sighed.

"You think she knew the woman did kill the girl?"

"Yes. I think she didn't want her son vilified as the husband of a murderess and a madwoman, but she knew all right. We could toss them out, and I will if she makes real trouble. Otherwise, I'll watch her."

And I did, as winter passed, spring came, and we decided to make a second – and possibly final visit – to Miss Pemberlow and complete our salvage of Somerlee.

CHAPTER THIRTEEN

Is faodaidh sinn èirigh gu bhith nar Rìoghachd a-rìs

But we can still rise now, and be the nation again ~from the song, *Flower of Scotland*

Aye, and it is to that end we work, that from the ashes of the world, we shall be Scotland and the Scottish people again. ~Donal McArn

The road was in even worse shape than it had been before we battened down the hatches for the cold weather. Winter had been no worse than usual, but without the council road-menders, without drivers reporting damage or potholes that had appeared overnight, nothing was done. I could see that in a generation, even the main road could become impassable to ordinary small cars – fortunate it was that we didn't use them.

I steered the Landcruiser down the long hill to Somerlee, pulled into the roadside by the large, ancient house, and noted that the nearby fields had Nubian goats grazing. Miss Jane, who'd been in the back seat, was out in seconds calling her friend's name in a loud, clear voice. There was no reply. I exited my seat, grabbed Miss Jane as she would have headed for the gate, and brought her to a halt.

"No, just in case someone came and took over the place, I go first."

"No," Donal said from behind me. "*We* go first, one up at a time." He advanced, and I moved well to one side and backed his move. We moved silently from room to room until we came

161

to what, from its placement, was the main bedroom. The door was ajar, and Donal eased it open a fraction. I touched his arm, put my face to his ear, and spoke quietly.

"Someone is there. I can hear them breathing. Hoarse, not well?"

He shifted us against the wall and reached out, the door in response to a gentle thrust opened further, and a weak voice spoke. "If you come in, I shall shoot you dead."

"Does that apply to Jane if she comes in?" I asked, and there was a choking sound.

"Jane? Jane, is that you?"

"No, Miss Pemberlow, it's Jane's friends, Sheila and Donal McArn. Jane is waiting by the gate. We didn't want to take chances if someone had come here and taken over." That, I thought, was a nicer way of putting it than that we were afraid she'd been murdered and was quietly decomposing somewhere about the house.

"I'm a little unwell, Mrs. McArn, but you are welcome. Please make yourself a cup of tea, and if you would ask Jane to come and see me, we could have a pleasant visit."

I went out to collect Miss Jane and halted by the front door. "I think your friend is ill, and if she's really unwell, she may not be able to manage any longer on her own. Let me say this clearly: if that's so, and you can persuade her to come back with you, I'm for it. We can collect everything, the livestock, their equipment, her personal things, everything in her bedroom, whatever she wants, and take it back. She could stay with you."

Jane DeVenter studied me and smiled. "You mean that, don't you? Esme treated you politely last time, but I could see you recognised her attitude. She comes from a very old family. To her, you are – not servants – but perhaps like farmers who lease a farm from her family's estate. There is a certain lower level where you belong."

I laughed. "I know. It doesn't bother me. She sees me, shall we say, as a free person, but of lesser rank, it's all right, Jane.

162

If you'd like to have her stay with you, we'll see to it. Ask her first if there's anything that needs doing immediately. Once we do that, we'll go on to clear the shops of whatever's worth taking. Judging by last time, it could see us coming and going for days. If you'd like to stay with her while we do all that, I could leave Ricky with you to run any errands."

"If Ricky wouldn't mind, I think both of us would be pleased."

Ricky didn't mind. I left him, Laddie, and Miss Jane, and we went on to Somerlee. No one seemed to have been there since we'd called last. The shops were shut up. There was no movement apart from birds, a rat once, and leaves shifting in the gutters. We salvaged. I left our people clearing two shops – one of fabrics, the other a small up-market version of a chain store – and with Barry, Jack, and Alex at my heels, I went from home to home, investigating bookcases and other interesting items.

Now and again, one of the three came back to me waving a treasure. Barry found a large book: complete with diagrams, sketches, and photographs, on raising chickens, Alex took one on crochet and knitting patterns, and Jack found an entire set of space adventure books by an author I'd met once at a convention in Bangor in Wales. I said so, and all three regarded me in awe. I knew a real author. Actually, I knew several; a friend in Maryland was one, my New Zealand friend another, and I met a mystery writer in Somerton. We collected the items, including another load of books from a hobbyist who seemed to have accumulated "how-to" books for years, although I doubted he'd done more than collect the books. There was no indication of actual activities.

And now and again, I added an item I fancied. Salvage. The owners were all dead. It made no sense to waste what we could use, and having useful, attractive items meant I could give them out to make a point when I needed to. Every time I filled a box or case, I sent one of the children to stack it in the trailer. Untouched cans, bottles, packets, or bags of food went into one of the lorries. While we were here, I wasn't leaving that for the tins to rust away or the vermin or insects to get into packages. I found expensive horse gear and added that as well, everything from bridles to covers – along with a box full of cans of leather cream for cleaning saddles and other horse items.

The first lot of salvage went off toward the glens. They'd store it in empty barns, stay the night, and return the next day. I went further afield. In a paddock, I found an emaciated Jersey cow I thought to be around six, complete with a new calf at foot and a yearling heifer. She'd broken through one fence and had just managed to keep herself and her offspring alive. We could put them in a two-horse trailer one of the utes was towing. Donal brought it and looked from me to the cow.

"Soft-hearted."

"Maybe, but she's a good cow, and brave, didn't sit in her paddock and watch her calves die. She broke the fence, so there was feed for them."

Donal frowned. "So she was hungry. She just did what any brute beast would do."

I took his arm, walked to the end of the shed we stood behind, and pointed. Donal studied the pathetic corpses of seven cattle that had eaten out everything, then died of starvation behind fences barely as strong, and he pursed his lips, saying no more. The cow and her offspring went back to the glen with the next convoy that day, and I claimed her as my own. Bess was a good cow all her life, and her daughters after her.

We kept checking. Vehicles came and went, and on a side road, we found a depot that held over a hundred packs of barn sections that could be added in a line. I had them taken home and ordered some of our people to begin putting them up in all four glens. A second depot held stacks of graphene solar panels and household wind generators. They went as well until finally, we had everything of use to us. I made sure a final selection of vehicles returned, and without being noticeable, I walked back to the Pemberlow house and made myself a cup of tea in the kitchen. Miss Jane found me there.

"She won't go. I think she has pneumonia, but I can't budge her. She's going to die if we leave her, and I can't make her listen." Her small pointed face was set in sorrow, and her eyes showed the pain she felt. I indicated the teapot.

"The kettle's close to boiling. When it's ready, make the tea, find something to eat, and bring it up. Don't hurry. Tap on the door when you come up, and then wait, don't come in until I call you."

"What are you going to do?"

"First, I'm going to deal with the pneumonia – if it is – and then I'm going to talk sense to your friend," I said grimly. "By the way, rub hard at your eyes. And deny everything."

Miss Jane showed a glimmer of amusement. "If anyone can talk Esme around, it's you. I'll wait until you're done."

I went to the Landcruiser, collected my medical bag, and stalked upstairs with it. Esme Pemberlow did have pneumonia. I treated that, assured her she'd feel a lot better in a couple of days, and when she thanked me, I sat in the chair by her bed – uninvited, to her apparent surprise – and eyed her sternly.

"I thought better of you as Miss Jane's friend."

She drew herself up in the bed. "What do you mean?"

"She has missed you ever since we were here last. You are her oldest friend and the only person left to her from her younger days. Yes, she has family, yes, she loves them, and they love her, but she lives alone. They've never had a lot in common. She's lonely for someone of her own, for a friend. And all winter, she worried about you. She was so happy to be coming back to Somerlee to see you again. Then, to arrive and find you unable even to get out of bed…"

"I could. I was…"

I overrode her. "Oh, yes, you could get to the bathroom. You couldn't get downstairs to the kitchen. You'd have died here, and no quick heart attack either. Even if it had been a heart attack, I can tell you from experience that it isn't always quick, family history or not. Miss Jane knew it too, and she was heartbroken. Right now, she's making you a pot of tea, finding something you may like to eat, and while she does it, she's crying her heart out for fear of losing her oldest friend. It's selfish to make her go back without you, and what if something happens and we can't return? She'll wonder every day if you're alive and if not, how you died and whatever the truth is, her imaginings will be far worse."

"I couldn't … you can't bring…"

"We can't bring everything? Nonsense. We have the vehicles and the people. We can bring the goats and all they have. If I put my people to it, we could strip this place to the foundations in forty-eight hours." I allowed my tone to soften. "I know it's hard to leave home, to choose to walk away knowing you'll never see it again, but better that than dying alone, a martyr to an old building, and being a bad friend."

Esme Pemberlow looked at me, and I saw she knew what I was doing. Yet, it gave her an acceptable excuse for changing her mind. I thought that while she lay here, knowing she was going to die – alone, slowly, and even for a strong-minded woman, the idea would have been terrifying. What if some predator found its way into the house, and she was eaten before she had time to die, unable to defend herself – she had prayed for a saviour. It had come in an unlikely guise, but she was going to accept salvation.

I heard a faint sound, a tap, and went at once to the door. "Oh good, tea."

Miss Jane entered, silver tea-tray in hand, and laid it on the bedside table. "I brought biscuits as well and a cup of hot chicken soup. There's nothing quite like it if you're feeling a little under the weather, Esme dear." I noticed that her eye-rims showed pink. She's rubbed them as I'd demanded. I saw the sick woman's gaze resting on those reddened eyes and drawing the conclusion I'd wanted.

Esme Pemberlow cleared her throat. "Thank you, Jane. And I have been considering. I've no wish to be a nuisance. As a Sussex friend used to say, after three days, fish and guests start to smell. But if something could be arranged so I must leave nothing behind, and I will be in circumstances where I will not infringe upon your privacy nor become a burden, I confess it would be pleasant to spend time with you again."

Miss Jane looked at me. "I would be happy if that could be arranged."

"It can and will be," I promised. And to her friend." Eat your soup while I give a few orders." I left them to soup and reminiscences while I found Donal.

He grinned. "You persuaded the old biddy?"

"I did. We'll leave moving her until last. But the chalet set-up will work. You know what to do. Goats go first, take their shelters and everything in the big shed. Settle them in that field at the back of Miss Jane's place, and set up their shelters and the shed there."

"And the house?"

"Goats, empty the cellars, then start on the house, Oh, and set up a trio of barns by Miss Jane's place for storage for the house stuff. I'll see you this evening."

"I wouldn't bet on it, love. I remember what's in this place from when we checked it last time." With that comment, he left to begin the list of what was needed, and I returned to the kitchen. There I cooked. Ricky, who had gone with Laddie to see the goats on my return to the house, came back and sniffed.

"Smells good. What are we having?"

"Baked potatoes, peas, a canned ham, gravy, and if you get me them from the garden, fresh butter beans. Dessert will be a pavlova." I knew all about those from my New Zealand friend, I'd always loved them, and Miss Pemberlow's hens were laying. "And I'll open a tin of peaches to go with it. How does that sound?"

Ricky made a blissful face. "Great. Are we eating with Miss Pemberlow?"

"We are. And listen carefully." I explained some of what I'd arranged, mentioned that I didn't want the lady to change her mind, I'd murder anyone that caused her doing so, don't speak until spoken to and then engage gears before opening mouth, and…

"I *get* it."

I thought that he did. He is a singularly sensible boy, and in the just under two years now since we made him our grandson, he's shown courage, common sense, and considerable musical talent – which we were not expecting. However, we'd found once he'd settled in that while he had no musical instruments of his own, he'd been taught to play the smallpipes at school. Once we were where we could find such things – just a month ago now – we'd raided a shop and brought back half the portable contents. Guitars, harmonicas, flutes, recorders and other woodwind instruments, four trumpets, a bugle, and three saxophones. However, there'd been no bagpipes.

Ricky had stood there as we emptied the shop with an ear-to-ear grin you couldn't have widened without moving his ears back. "Bags I first pick."

"Yes."

He'd spoken, I think, without really expecting anything and was surprised. "You mean it, Gran Sheila?"

"I do. Neither Donal nor I can play anything, and, sadly, we haven't any musical talent. However, we value anyone that has, and maybe we'll find someone who can play and teach. It was all the sadder when I saw him droop a little and found that he'd hoped for bagpipes somewhere amid the instruments. It was on those his heart was set. He'd been taught the bagpipe by a teacher of whom he spoke highly.

To date, none of those we'd taken in could play anything well. Joe, the oldest Matson boy, could manage simple chords on a guitar; Janet played the piano well enough for the schoolchildren to sing along. Some of the Somerlee girls and young women could sing well and played recorders, but I mourned the loss of bagpipe music. It was to me the very essence of my country.

I was thus completely stunned to find, while we ate dinner and Miss Jane and her friend chatted, that Esme Pemberlow could not only play the bagpipes but that in the past, she had taught them to select pupils. I must have looked so flabbergasted that a wintery smile lit her face. "Is it that you cannot associate me with the instrument or because you are surprised that I'm musical?"

"I'd have thought you more likely to be a pianist," I answered without thinking.

The smile defrosted. "No, my dear father wished me to be, and I have some competence, but the bagpipes were always my great love. I play both the smallpipes and the great pipes. I also have considerable sheet music for both, plus cleaning kits, replacement items, and music disks."

Ricky forgot he was supposed to stay quiet and burst out, "Miss Pemberlow, I was learning the smallpipes at school, and I want to play the great pipes as well. If you come with us, would you teach me? Please, please?" He paused, then offered inducements. "I'll shut Laddie away if he howls, and I'll work for you. Anything you want me to do?"

It would overstate it to say that her face lit up. But I could see she was delighted to have a possible pupil, and they plunged into a discussion of what he'd learned, who his teacher had been, and veered into technical comments that completely lost me. I listened and rejoiced in the possibility that in time the glens could have their own pipe band, that the true music of the land would live again and not be lost as I'd feared.

Dinner over and the hostess looking as if she desired nothing so much as a long sleep, I left Miss Jane to settle her friend comfortably, swept Ricky and Laddie out, along with the tray of dishes, and headed for the kitchen, Ricky and dog at my heels.

Once there, he eyed me. "I'm sorry I butted in, but isn't it great? She can play and she'll teach me, and I *missed* not playing."

"How long were you learning them?"

"Three years. Kaylie could play too. Dad's father was a piper, and he..." He fell silent.

I kept my face blank and my voice a little absent-minded. "Yes, we really must find somewhere that has pipes still. Miss Pemberlow can teach using hers, but if she has more than you as pupils, we'd need more bagpipes. You said you learned them at your school. I wonder if they're still there?"

That led to a discussion on where the school was, how the instruments were kept, what their quality was, and if they might have been appropriately stored so that they would be worth retrieving. Miss Pemberlow, consulted the next morning, was doubtful.

"I know the sort of instruments schools buy. They tend to be of mediocre quality and are not always well treated. However, there's a place where we *can* find several fine instruments. It is, or that may be, was a private conservatory on an estate. A hobby of the wealthy owner, although from what I know, hobby is an understatement. He took in those who wished to play, gave them free board and lodging for periods ranging from a weekend to several weeks, and while many had their own pipes, he also had sufficient to cover any who did not."

I brought out the map, found where the place was – not far from her home but off the beaten track – and resolved to go there right now. Miss Pemberlow was explaining the owner still. "An American of Scottish ancestry. He returned to look over the place from which his ancestors had come, fell in love with it, and purchased a small estate. He may even have survived this catastrophe."

And if he had, he could be of use, I mused, if he was interested. I tuned out the conversation, making plans until we'd finished breakfast, after which I left in search of my Landcruiser, some support in case of trouble, and in an hour, I was on the way to Craydon estate. Ricky and Laddie with me, and six other vehicles following, passengers and drivers all well armed, as was I.

It was as well the road had been described to me. It ended in a winding lane, which, as we found partway, was blocked by fallen trees. It took an hour to clear those, and we were on our way again to find the main gates locked, chained, and barricaded. *Drat!*

I turned to Ricky. "I want you to circle the place. I don't want to smash in the gates or even cut the chains if it can be avoided. Don't enter the estate, circle outside it, see if you can observe or hear anyone. Find any other entrances and check if they're barricaded too. You're our scout, and *be careful*. I've gotten used to having you around."

He grinned at that and slipped away while I held an upset dog. Donal had taught many of those interested the army ways of scouting, not that some had needed to learn, those that stalked deer were already experts, but making a game of it based on army tactics had left a number of the older children able to slip through the landscape unseen in an way that was near uncanny. Ricky was one of them since he'd had more time with his Grandpa Donal, and right now, a child was less threatening should he be seen, and also with the boy's expertise, less likely to *be* seen anyhow.

Ricky was back in an hour and a half. "Back way in has locked gates, no barricade. No signs of anyone or anything left against the door. Animals loose."

We went by the back way. Sam Cameron – who had a misspent youth in the city before he wed and came back to the glen –

picked the gate lock, and we drove up the curving drive and parked in the centre of the main turnaround. There was no sound. I stepped out and called. And again. No one replied, and I approached the front door to find that too locked. Sam opened it, and I walked into a hall, brave in banners, a tapestry, a display of swords on the wall, and a massive coat of arms done in iron and enamel.

Ricky was halfway up the stairs, and I called him to a stop. "We don't know what or who may be up there."

I joined him, and we advanced cautiously – to find no one. I found the owner's papers and reading a filed letter copy, I saw why. He'd gone back to America weeks before the virus. Whether he'd died or still lived, I had no idea. In any case, he wouldn't be back, so we salvaged. We found musical instruments and collected the lot. I added food from the kitchen, alcohol, some excellent bedding, and other valuable items.

Ricky dived into the man's wardrobe and backed out with a magnificent Scottish outfit, it had everything from sporran to dirk, and I promptly claimed it.

"Any more like that?"

He vanished and emerged with two more, each slightly different but equally well-made and striking appearance. I dived in and took casual country clothes, sheepskin coats, tweeds, even a tweed cape. The drawers yielded expensive gloves, scarves, socks, packets of unopened underwear, shirts, and a top drawer containing tobacco, pipes, cigar holders, and several antique lighters, along with an even older flint and steel set. I left the tobacco, pipes, and holders, but took the rest. We trooped back to the Landcruiser, disposed of our salvage, and left with our gleanings. The others had raided the barns and out-buildings and found items they, too, deemed useful.

Back in Glen Mhairi, Miss Pemberlow was settled in. The bagpipes we had found were pronounced to be of fine quality. Ricky had his first lesson; five other children, including Will

Matson and Alex Yarrow, wanted to learn, to the teacher's gratification. She was almost well again; she would begin actual classes, she said, on Monday. Donal and I were preparing for a mission that would see us achieve something we'd had our hearts set upon since the dying began. The army says, "never leave a man behind," and it was time we found our own and brought them back.

CHAPTER FOURTEEN

Nine hundred and ninety-nine can't bide the shame or mocking or laughter, but the thousandth man will stand by your side, to the gallows-foot – and after! ~Kipling

And there were two of them for me and Donal. Half-brothers to each other, and heart-brothers to us. Even with his wife dying, even already infected as they were, Johnny and Mac thought of us and the glens, and we lived because they stood by us to their deaths – and beyond. ~Sheila McArn

It was the largest convoy we had ever led. We were going for two reasons, one being to see what had become of the city and salvage if we could, but we'd have gone for the other reason alone. In the great hospital, in a private room in the cancer ward lay those we would bring home. We boomed down the road, a hundred and fifty people of the glens – once again the Clan was riding – as we passed villages, towns, and came at last into the outskirts of the place where Johnny and Mac, and Johnny's wife, Meryl, might be found.

Donal marked the map and glanced at those around us. "We go in groups. Drive along parallel roads, keep a watch in case there's trouble. If there is, you know the drill. Start nothing. If someone else does, finish it without holding back."

I was driving our Landcruiser while Donal had the one he'd rented – and never returned since there was no one to return it to. They had extra armour, and we drove, Donal first, then me. Ricky had come, but I wouldn't have him in a place of greatest danger. We wound through the streets, groups moved up, fell back, shifted into different roads, and rejoined. If there was anyone here, if they were enemies, they weren't going to trap us together.

We did see people, all of whom took one look and disappeared into or between buildings. We made first for the Kylen Research Institute where Mac had worked.

The convoy halted in a line that circled the block while Donal and I went inside. We'd visited a score of times while Mac was there, and we knew the place. We went to his laboratory, and I opened the door. Donal looked at me, and I found I was crying. It was all Mac, the smell, the memories, the arrangement of beakers and Bunsen burners. There was a gap on the bench where his computer usually rested, and his lab coat was gone.

I walked to the desk and opened that, pulled out each drawer in turn while I sifted the contents. I took pens, pencils, a whole bag of small items that he'd touched, used, and that was Mac, right down to a large box in the lab corner containing the hardcover notebooks he preferred to use for working out problems. There were fifty, unused, left behind – what use would he have had for them by then – but I'd use them. When I was done, Donal shut the door and placed everything chosen on a trolley.

The other laboratories contained items we could use, and we took those. They went into a lorry, the things from Mac's lab came with me, and our vehicles moved on. Again, we saw deserted streets, the occasional person diving for cover, a dog trotting along an alleyway, and over and over, shops that had been looted, windows smashed, some blocks burned out. We drove up Little France Crescent at last and halted in the empty car lot. It's an enormous place, but we knew where we were going.

We'd have gone alone, but Janet spoke sternly. "There could be people in there and we'd rather not lose you. Ten of us will come too, and we'll bring stretchers and body bags. I'll have some of our people look for the morgue than find us."

Janet was practical, and I accepted what she said. So we were twelve strong as we negotiated the corridors, where Donal saw a sign and turned down that passage to the ward we knew. There, at the end of the corridor, we found a private room block-aded. The big window was covered, the door wouldn't open, and when I poked under it, I found something was there to prevent my explorations.

Janet was watching. "This one?"

"I think so. None of the others are blocked like this. It has to be."

It was. We broke down the door. Our people stood back, and Donal and I went in together. In our passing through the hos-pital, we'd found masks and something to put on them, so the stench wasn't as foul as it could have been, although it was bad enough. There were three bodies, a woman on the bed and two men lying in long chairs beside her. I knew who they were. We wrapped them gently in bedding brought from Johnny's home and slid those into body bags, placed the bags on stretchers, and slowly, solemnly, we claimed our people back by Clan and glen right.

It was dark, and we had no wish to navigate the city at night, so we found a spacious hotel and camped there. We had candles and lanterns with us, along with a portable generator. We set up comfortably, took over the largest bar, broke out food – there being none in the hotel – and I chose to sit behind most of the group, nearest the door to the street. Donal joined me. Ricky brought out the smallpipes and began to play "Johnny's Gone for a Soldier." I felt tears coming. Or I did until I felt Donal stiffen.

His voice was a breath. "Outside by the front door."

I turned my head slowly, and only as far as I needed. Now I could see a small dark figure. It moved forward cautiously, and

I knew it was a child. I reached out, took a handful of biscuits, placed slices of cheese on them, and spoke softly while holding them out.

"Are you hungry?"

The child was there in a jump, snatching the food and cramming it into its mouth. Mute, I reached for more, signalled everyone to do and say nothing, and proffered the second helping. I couldn't see our guest well, but s/he looked to be around seven or eight. Eventually, they ran out of stomach space and stood there looking at me as if they were grateful but no longer remembered what to say.

"My name is Sheila," I offered.

"'Mick."

"Pleased to meet you, Mick. Do you have friends or family who'd like some food?"

"You gimme some?"

"Of course." I filled a cloth bag, handed it over, and saw the shadow fade into the street. Beside me, Donal nodded.

"I wonder how many of them there are."

We slept peacefully that night and were just talking over how we would proceed home when I saw a movement. Someone dodged around a building, almost slithered along the front of that, and I saw they were not alone.

"Donal?"

"I see them. Child from last night, I'd think, and someone desperate who thinks we may not be so bad if we feed children."

We didn't leave that morning. The "someone desperate" was Susan Dunlop, the child was her youngest brother Michael, and they were two of an extended family. We made an offer, being careful to explain what would be required of them, and it was not so much accepted as seized on so that when we did move on, it was with fourteen more people for the glens. City folk who'd been too afraid to leave the city, at least they had some food here they could find, but that was running out, and they were all but starving.

That gave me an idea, and as we left, we detoured through suburbs, driving not much above a brisk walk and pausing now and again to look around. I made sure Ricky and Laddie were front and centre, along with Mick and Susan. That was enough to bring out others who saw the writing on the wall but were afraid to leave a familiar environment. Children and a dog were, it appeared, something of a guarantee of our benevolence. By the time we cleared the city, we added thirty-nine people. And I was beaming.

****

The journey home was both sad and joyous. Those we had lost were coming home, we had new people for the glens, and yet I remembered Johnny and Mac as we had last seen them, as we had last spoken to them. I missed them with all my heart and I mourned.

Donal broke the silence partway since we were together for the return trip. "I would wish we knew what happened to the family."

I did too. James and Isobel had been Johnny's children, both married and overseas when the virus struck. "He talked to them."

"Aye, I remember he said Isobel and her husband were in Australia. He couldn't reach her until things were so bad he couldn't believe they'd make it home."

"Do you think they could have survived there?"

Donal scowled. "I don't know, but I'd think not. The people they were visiting have no children, and their place is isolated, so where would they catch the initial infection? They didn't have it so far as I know before they went."

That was true. James, Isobel, and their families stayed with Johnny and Meryl since they'd been gone for some months. "What about James?"

"He and his wife and the children could have lived," Donal said thoughtfully. "Initially, that is. They have two children, and the cruise was one for families with children. Get several hundred children together, and it's not unlikely one of them would have had a sore throat and passed it around, and that's a major line. They'd have their medical staff on all the cruise ships, and almost certainly, they'd have had allodaxin available."

"So they could have survived?"

"It's likely, but look at it this way, lass. After that, what?"

I thought about it. Johnny had told us that he'd got through to James, but when they'd just left port, they wouldn't be at the next stop until the following evening, and the port they'd arrive at didn't have any airport. They could hire a car and drive, then take a ferry and reach a major airport, but by then, planes would be long since grounded, even if there were pilots left alive to fly them, and even if there were still air traffic controllers to help them land. Apart from that, there was the sheer distance. We'd become so used to crossing a world in a day. We forgot how far it really was.

"No," I said, a small pang of grief striking me for James and his family, who, even if they lived, were never likely to see their home again.

"That's why Johnny left the glens in our charge," Donal told me quietly. "A thoughtful man, Johnny. He knew the chance of any of them making it home, and he prepared for it. Remember too what he said on that?"

I did. I remembered every word. He'd said, "Hold it in trust until someone you know comes to take it back. And be very sure they're genuine." I repeated that aloud to Donal. "Be very sure they're genuine." And then it hit me. I knew Johnny. "You think he believed some of them could survive, but if it took a generation to make it home, he didn't want them taking over unless we thought it right?"

Donal nodded. "James was a good man. He'd have done his best for the estate and the people. But his kids were already spoiled stupid. That wife of his, rich socialite, never spent a minute in the glens she didn't have to. Last time I saw the boy, Jonathon, he spoke to me as if I were his servant. Johnny jumped all over him, and the kid apologised, but I could see he didn't mean a word, and he was furious."

"If they make it back, he could have improved, learned to be sensible. He'd hardly have been spoiled if they do survive?"

Donal glanced at me. "I've seen that kind before. He'll blame everyone for the deprivations he suffered. He'll feel entitled to get it all back as soon as he's home. He won't learn, love; he'll be more arrogant, not less."

"And the girl, Meria?"

"Young Jonathon was thirteen, and Meria was ten. I'd say his character's set. She might improve. They could be badly damaged by trauma…"

I'd seen enough of that as an army paramedic to know how right he was. "So if James gets back, you think we could just hand back everything safely to him. But not to his wife at all or the children if it's been too long?"

"Rule of thumb, yes. Take a long hard look at them before we agree."

I frowned. "But if they are Johnny's family, how can we not agree?"

Donal smiled. "And who's to say they *are* his family? They aren't likely to still have their papers. If it's been years, they'll have changed. If they return and we say no, our people will back us. Let things lie, time enough to make decisions if any of them return, depending on which of them do and how they are."

I said no more, we were passing through a small town, and I signalled a halt abruptly. I'd seen shops down a side road that looked undamaged. Salvage was always on my mind.

Everything we stored was another chance at life. There were so many things we wouldn't be able to buy again in my lifetime, some we might be able to make, grow, or build in time, other items we might never see again. I had a list of things I hoped we could produce, but many required a population to implement. Note to self, take a group around every town or village and try to find suitable people who'd join us.

The shops I'd seen were a typical grouping. A small supermarket, wholly emptied. A pharmacy – the shop emptied too – but a large hidden back room that was fully shelved hadn't been touched; possibly it hadn't been found. We stripped that, finding a lot of prescription medications that delighted my paramedic soul, heart medication, pills for gout, preventing kidney stones, and treating arthritis. I beamed as we loaded everything into one of the lorries.

Donal came to find me, his face too creased in a wide grin. "Shoe shop, everything from boots to kids' slippers. And a butcher's shop, no meat of course, but there's a lot of equipment. Choppers, knives, hooks to hang meat, I've had everything loaded." He grinned again. "Other two, well, I've called Miss Jane for one. The other was a bike shop."

"Bikes, push or motor?"

"Both. And a mix in that." I looked a question with raised eyebrows. "They seemed to have kept to bikes, but they're mostly e-bikes, lower cubic centimetre e-motorbikes, several e-tricycles for adults. They're the type that comes equipped with overhead adjustable solar panels, so on a fine day, you can ride from sunup to sundown, and as I said, a large amount of equipment to repair, add to, and upgrade them. I've had it all loaded."

I didn't want to ask, but I did. "And Miss Jane and Esme have gone to the other shop. I presume it was a pet shop?"

"Yes."

I didn't want to, but I went to where they'd be and entered. Once in, I heaved a long silent sigh of relief. All the cages were empty, the aquariums silent, their usual bubbling stilled. Thank heaven for that. The owner must have seen what was coming and acted before they became too ill.

Miss Jane turned to glance at me as I came in the door. "Owner cleared the place of livestock. We can take cages, though, pet gear, and there's other supplies, cat and dog biscuits, cuttle-fish, a *lot* of bird seed, and the back room has shelves of worm and flea treatments, vitamin supplements. You don't have any problem with us taking it all?"

It was politeness, and I shook my head as expected. "Take everything you think will be of any use. You know what you're doing, get people to help if you need to, say that it's my order. I'm just happy to see there's – there was – nothing else left here." They understood what I meant, and Esme Pemberton nodded.

"As were we. Clearly, the owner was a genuine pet-lover. Either he let everything go, or he euthanized them elsewhere and probably buried or burned the bodies." She, too, sighed quietly. "I don't wish to think of all the other places where that didn't hap-pen. Although one thought did occur to me."

"What?"

Her smile was surprisingly mischievous. "I wonder how many who worked in zoos or wildlife parks may have released their charges rather than kill them."

I gulped as that sank in. "Lions, tigers, leopards, *wolves*," I said hollowly. "Oh, good grief, do you think it's likely?"

Esme Pemberlow glanced at her friend, and in turn, they looked at me. "Yes," they chorused – and grinned cheerfully.

Miss Jane chuckled. "Scotland *did* have wolves. If we have them again, I daresay we'll cope – and with all the wandering farm animals, it isn't as if they'll have to turn to eating us any time soon."

"We didn't have lions, tigers, and leopards, though," I pointed out. "And they're more likely to attack people. What else could they have released?" It hadn't been a question, not really, but they answered.

"Monkeys, lizards, snakes, bears perhaps, and *elephants*..." Miss Jane offered, the list taken up by Esme.

"Rhinos, vultures, cheetahs, wildebeest, zebras..."

"If that lot starts heading north, we'll have to deal with whatever arrives," I informed them. "Sufficient to the day is the evil thereof, and thanks be we can close off the glens for anything large."

Esme Pemberlow's lips twitched. "Birds fly. We could see the vultures and a whole lot of other non-native avian species."

I produced a nasty look. "Well, many of them may be edible. It could add a nice variety to our diets."

Both women gave me outraged looks and turned to stacking sacks of animal biscuits and bird seed while I left them to it. I'd mention this conversation to Donal. It wasn't urgent yet, but we might have to think about it in time. I most emphatically did *not* like the idea of coming face to face with a wandering tiger or a pride of lions.

We cleared the shops, and the convoy moved on, to halt again for something to eat and a break from driving. Donal glanced at me once we were done. "This was one of the towns where we had Mac's prescriptions filled. I remember where too," he waved a hand. "It was that way. Shall we?"

Now that he'd mentioned it, I recalled the place where I'd gone. They'd been only two blocks apart. I took his arm, and we strolled down the street, enjoying the sunshine, a few minutes alone, and mourning looted and/or burned-out shops and businesses. On a corner, I stopped in mid-stride, and Donal looked where I was looking.

"That'd be useful." It was an equestrian shop.

"Yes, motor vehicles won't last forever, and we have no saddlers."

What we did have were barns filled with weaponry and horse equipment, however, and we'd have more of them. Most of the children were already good shots with a bow from our regular competitions, and most could ride. We had stored horse-drawn wagons, pony carts, and ancient but working horse-drawn farm machinery too. When the time came, we had that as a start, and in a few more years, we would start using it in a paddock here and there for hay or oats so that when the last petrol or diesel-powered machinery failed, we would already know what we were doing. I'd made a beginning by picking up horses too, ranging from Welsh cobs on up, mares plus a couple of medium-sized stallions, and pasturing them in the rear portion of Glen McManus.

We called our people, left them to clear the saddlers, and wandered on. One of the pharmacies was burned out, and from the looks of it, looted beforehand. The other had been looted, but we did find some valuable items when we trawled through the mess. We turned onto a parallel street and found a shop down an alleyway that hadn't been touched. It looked like it catered to smallholders and contained everything from chick incubators to farm clothing. We took the lot.

Donal suggested we move on after that, and I took the wheel. We rolled past small towns and villages and halted once more an hour from home when a woman appeared waving at us. She was a farmer's wife. Everyone she knew had died, so she'd come into town where there was at least food to be had. In the past two years since, she'd found five people: a man with a small daughter, a brother and sister in their teens, and an older woman. They asked questions, we answered, and while the elderly lady was doubtful, in the end, they agreed. We'd return for them in a week, and they'd be ready.

Our home was in sight. I knew every inch of the lands we passed. Another bend, the old farmhouse that was falling– the man that had owned it died, and there had been a long-running row over the will – the stone wall here, a hedge there, and then turning in to the Glen Mhairi road. The gatehouse, with two of the Matson cousins waving us through, and we were wheeling the Landcruiser to a halt by our house. Vehicle after vehicle fell into a long curving line behind us as engines switched off. Home.

CHAPTER FIFTEEN

Neighbour: one whom we are commanded to love as ourselves, and who does all he can to make us disobedient. Ambrose Bierce. *The Devil's Dictionary*

And one of ours fitted that to a T. ~Donal McArn

Donal caught me as I was making dinner. "The funeral. When?"

"Three days' time," I told him. "It'll take that long to finalise everything. The bodies are safe enough in the sealed body bags. They're laid out in Johnny's main room, and there's relays of our people sitting with them. Esme will play the great pipes, Ricky the smallpipes, and we'll lay them in the earth as they are." We'd discussed this before we set off for Edinburgh; nothing had changed.

"And we bury them on his land," Donal confirmed.

I dished up the food, called, and Ricky came running, Laddie at his heels. Knowing my husband, he'd guessed why it would be three days to the funeral. That would be the anniversary of two years since we'd received the phone call and driven to the city, two years since we'd known what was to come, and two years since we'd last seen those beloved faces.

And in three days, we marched, bearing three body bags on biers, all of Clan McAlister walking from Glen Mhairi to Johnny's Glen to honour those we'd lost. Ricky led us, playing

186

the smallpipes, the tunes echoing from the hills and through the glen – *Heilan Laddie, The Rose of Kelvingrove, 79th Farewell To Gibraltar, Going Home, Farewell to Lismore, Bonnie Mary of Argyle*, and *Ae Fond Kiss*. I walked with tears in my eyes, knowing those who had known Mac and Johnny would be walking likewise.

And at the grave dug deep along the side of the great house of Glenrae, we halted. Esme Pemberton stepped forward and played then. The trio of songs that are forever ours, *Flowers of the Forest, Scotland the Brave*, and *The Laird of Glenrae Comes Home*. The last written by a Laird minstrel half a thousand years gone and always played at the Laird's funeral – luckily, we'd had the music. The last note sounded, and there was silence. I looked about me and saw old Jamie standing, tears running down his face, a great claymore sheathed down his back. He'd loved Mac and Mac had loved him, and maybe it hadn't been only for our lifelong friendship that Mac had saved us. His mother and father were long gone, but his uncle Jamie lived, and Mac often visited the glen.

Donal walked forward and turned to face us. "Johnny McAlister and Mac Tamman are gone. Yet we shall remember and honour their names so long as the glens live. When the world was dying, they gave us warning, a way to save many of our people, and even as they lay dying, they thought of us. Into mine and my wife's hands, they laid the glens, biding us care for them, biding us live and see that the blood of the people endures. That is our trust, and so it shall be. Let them lie in peace in the land that was theirs, let them be told each year of how it has been for us, and let them welcome each of us when our times come. And when that is so, be proud to tell them that we yet endure."

I joined him. "We are Clan McAlister in Johnny's name. All of us, those born here, those that join us, these take up the name. We are the Glens and the Clan of McAlister, and here we stand, here we live, and here we die when our time comes. Let enemies beware. We are the Clan, and the flag of McAlister goes before us. Clan McAlister and the glens, the people and the clan, we live, and we ride. *Clan McAlister!*"

Esme Pemberton came in again with the *March of the McAlisters,* the great pipes ringing out, and we sang. We were the clan; what we had, we would hold. *Fiat!*

****

I admit it was something of an emotional letdown the day after. I had to oversee the disposition of some of our latest salvage. Donal had disappeared somewhere, and Tai had slaughtered a rat and hauled it into the kitchen, expecting praise and petting. I provided them, removed the rat, and sorted the question of salvage. I wanted peace after it and slipped away to where the cave at the end of Blind Glen led into the McManus estate. There I walked the land, looking over my notebook, and considering what we should do next. And there, Donal found me.

"What's to do, lass?"

"Just a bit of a letdown after yesterday."

"Can't live on excitement forever. There's a time to slow down and think."

"I know, and I have."

"What about?"

"Population. We've as many by now as we ever had, but we need more. I don't want to take chances, though."

"Aye, leave it be a year, let the ones we gained settle in, and us get used to them. Then we'll go looking. I've a mind to go north sometime. There were glens up there with the same problems as we had."

I knew what he meant. It had been the age-old problem between isolated rural areas and cities. The children grew up and couldn't find employment, so they moved to the cities and stayed. Their children grew up in cities and no longer understood farming or delighted in the peace of a glen. The first generation would come home often, the second now and again, but the third turned their back on the land and saw no reason to return.

It was to them a boring place of mud, cold winds, manual work, and they wanted none of it. Now, however, there were no bright warm offices, well-paid jobs, easy meals from takeaways in the teeming cities' fast becoming rat-infested ruins. They had a choice. Die or come home if there was yet a home – and any kin – to come home to.

Donal was nodding. "And for many, most in their glen may have died. They've been gone a generation or more, don't know the land, how to work it, how to survive if they go back to it, and those who could have taught them are dead. Then, too, in some of the glens, there will be survivors, but they'll be the older folk and may need being looked after themselves – if they've survived until now."

"Who will know if they have managed to stay alive?" I speculated. "Where their children and grandchildren lived. If the adults haven't come back, it may be because only the younger children survived and we can offer to get them."

"Aye. Something to think about while we settle our incomers."

We went home and did so with those we'd rescued. Janet, Miss Jane, and Esme Pemberlow were towers of strength in that. It took time. Many had been city folk all their lives and didn't even know how to feed chicks. Still, they learned, none being foolish enough not to understand survival now meant learning new ways, and truth is, that privation does wonders for making folk settle when they get safety and food again.

And all of the next half-year, Donal was working quietly on his project. I knew something of it but minded my own business. He'd driven to Thurston, found the place where they had blank gravestones, and selected one. He'd brought it home – using a forklift since the stone he'd picked was huge - and now he carved letters into the black granite. Once he was done, he painted white then gold into the letters, and with that complete, he hoisted it onto the back of a lorry and took it without fanfare to the grave by Johnny's house. We'd made the grave in a small bay in the hillside. Out of the way of foot or any other traffic, but slightly elevated so anyone passing could see it.

"Want to come with me, love?" I did.

I found some of the other glens folk there, Janet McIntosh, May and Sam Cameron, Anna, Sue, Mary, Janis, and others, all of whom were Glen Mhairi born and who'd known and loved Johnny and Mac. We watched as Donal sing the hoist, lowered the stone onto the graves, leaning solidly against three shallow triangular blocks of matching stone. There was nothing fancy about the words. They listed the names, dates of birth, death dates – and then there were two lines below that. They said:

"Their land, their people, nor shall we whom they loved and saved forget them."

We sang *Amazing Grace* and went home quietly. A day after, the minister's wife confronted me with a grievance.

"You had a funeral service and didn't ask my husband to officiate."

"It wasn't a funeral service. We placed a memorial stone, and it was for us who knew them well to see that done."

"You should still have asked him. I think it was very rude. He's your minister and…"

I was tired. Watching the stone put in place had stirred up all my sorrow at the loss of two of my oldest and best friends and, while it takes a lot to anger me, the woman's stupidity managed it for once. It added to my annoyance that I'd never liked her, deeply distrusted her, and now she was pushing into something private. I opened my mouth just as Donal came around the house corner to stop as I spoke in a tone he rarely heard.

"Mrs. Giles, your husband is not *our* minister. He lives in Glen Mhairi and nothing more. Placing the memorial stone on Johnny and Mac's grave was a private ceremony for his friends. We did not require you there or for him to officiate. Good day to you."

She stared at me, astounded, I think, that I would gainsay her. "How dare you, we're part of this community. We should have been asked to attend." And with a sneer. "I suppose that guttersnipe you took in was there?"

With the attack on Ricky, I said the unforgivable. "Why should he not have been, woman? There's no nearby stream for him to drown in."'

Her face went white, and the skin tightened on it like a skull as she caught the reference to her legal problems before she came here. Her voice was bitter with a savage undertone. "I see my mother-in-law couldn't keep her mouth shut. Don't worry, I wouldn't touch the brat with gloves. You never know where he's been."

At that point, the look on my face must have become so lethal that Donal brushed past her, took a grip on my shoulder, and spoke in a quiet, deadly tone. "I bid you good day, Mrs. Giles." He hauled me inside, shut the door, leaned against it, and surveyed me. "What did she say to make you so mad, lass? It's been a long, long time since I've seen you like that." I told him and he scowled forbiddingly. "Not a pleasant woman."

"No." I sat down suddenly, feeling the rage drain away, taking my strength with it. "She's trouble, that's what old Mrs. Giles said. She told me everything to warn me."

"Well, we're warned. Now, what's for dinner, and should I make it while you put your feet up a while?"

I did, he did, and Ricky came in with Laddie just as the meal was ready. We ate with talk of small events, and I was myself again by the time we went to bed. But over winter, I remembered the minister's wife's words, and I talked to several trustworthy friends. She'd not do anything unnoticed now. Spring came, then summer, the world was warm again, and we planned a trip north to see if we could find those that might like to join us – along with more salvage, of course. The more we had, the better cushion against the time when we'd have to make it ourselves

– what we could – and our work would be less with machinery, and more and more the harder work of our hands.

In autumn, we'd moved some of those that came earlier, so now they lived in Blind Glen. Barry's family had taken over a smallholding in Johnny's Glen; that was given for his brilliant discovery of the tunnel to McManus Glen. Before everything there went back to ruin, I wanted to find more people to use the land.

So a month into the following summer, we set out at the head of a long train, a hundred of the Clan McAlister, with thirty vehicles, armed and ready for anything. *That* was as well. We pulled into a small town and were met with a hail of gunfire. For a moment, I felt myself in some western. Donal, however, had planned for such things, and it took little time before we prevailed. I'll not describe events; they were brutal. We lost one of our people – Jimmy McFarlane – with four wounded. We killed more, aye, and the wounded Donal had us kill too, saying that where their injuries would see them die slowly, it was merciful, and where they might have survived, it was safer, quoting one of our superiors from the old days. "A dead enemy lays no second ambush, nor comes hunting you."

I might have felt bad about it had it not been that we combed the town and found where they'd holed up. There we found a locked room with five women, all brutalised – and a dozen children – many the same. I offered them refuge, and they couldn't agree fast enough. I decided not to subject them to the longer journeying, and sent them back with half a dozen vehicles, none without a woman in it, so they would be comfortable. Janet would see to them when they arrived. We already had lists of available homes, and they'd been stocked with food and other things in anticipation. They could make their choices as to how they combined.

We moved on, and in a village, we found a school and an overburdened young teacher. She came out waving frantically at the sound of engines. She bolted up to our Landcruiser as soon as we stopped, and I powered down the window.

"Oh, thank you, thank you for stopping. We need help. I don't know what happened, but everyone was sick. Most of them died, and all that was left were the children, and I couldn't leave them." She clung to the window, her words tripping over each other as she tried to explain everything in a breath. "Please, we're running out of food, and there are dogs. One bit Andy, and Shona isn't well. I don't know what to do about her."

I swung the door open, she fell back, staring at me imploringly, and I gathered her into my arms. She burst into a storm of tears, and a red-headed boy of eleven or twelve came out of the woodwork looking belligerent. "Don't you hurt my teacher."

I smiled at him, seeing the dirty bandage on his left hand. "I won't, Andy, don't worry. We're here to help you all." Although, perhaps I should have used other words because he too joined his teacher in tears.

Once we'd resolved that situation, we followed them to the school and schoolhouse, where I completely understood why "teacher" was so overworked and overwhelmed. She'd been in her second year of teaching when the virus came, having obtained her teaching certificate via a partial scholarship which came on the condition she spent five years teaching in the country. She'd been sent to a small school. There had been only the headmaster – and his wife who did clerical work – besides her. Most of her pupils had come from the village and a few from a nearby estate.

She sat forlornly in a chair and explained. "The headmaster and his wife died. Then the children started coming back to tell me their parents, their older brothers, and sisters were dead. I went to see, and it was true. Not everyone, but almost and three of them were sick." Her eyes filled with grief. "They died after a while. I don't know why. I did my best." I made soothing noises, and she went on. "We had ten pupils, all of them were all right, four of the older children were fine too, and Mrs. Symond's baby. Well, she was a toddler, really, and now she's four. I was thinking of starting her at the school."

I patted her arm, and she grabbed my hand. "I did my best, I swear, but it's been so awful, and I want to go home. But I couldn't take them all, and it could be worse anywhere else, so I stayed here because there was food and I looked after them. I don't know what happened at home, and I've worried so about them. Please, if there some way I could go *home* now?"

Home, it turned out, was about forty miles more or less north, the way we planned to go. Her family lived on a small-holding off the main road near a crossroads that provided all they needed within walking distance – a village shop, a church, a community hall, and bus depot, one building on each cross-roads' corner. I counted children. Fifteen, eight girls and seven boys, including Andy. They ranged from the Symonds' four-year-old to the class that would have gone to the larger school via a daily bus the year following if the virus hadn't intervened, and who, three years later, were now around thirteen. Andy, younger or not, seemed to be their leader, and from what their teacher – Miss Jenny Hannach – told us, he was a boy of inde-pendent spirit, protective, clever, and sensible – most of the time anyhow.

"He likes dogs, says his dad promised him one for his birthday, so since his family died and couldn't buy him one, he tried to steal a puppy."

Donal smiled. "And the mother resented it."

"Yes," Jenny Hannach said simply, and both Donal and I laughed.

I stood up. "I'd better have a look at Andy's hand." And when the teacher looked as if she might protest that, I added, "I'm a trained paramedic. When all this started, Donal and I had retired from the army, but since then, it's been back on duty." I left Donal explaining some of what we knew and searched for Andy.

I found him alone, standing, looking over towards farm-land. Upon reaching him, I spoke gently. "Is your home over there?"

"They died." His voice was hard, and I might have been fooled, but for his eyes glinting with tears he refused to let fall.

"I'm very sorry. I lost my two best friends. They died making sure I'd have a chance to live, and I think about them every day."

"You do?"

"I do. I grew up with them. I knew them all my life, and I miss them. They were wonderful men, and as long as I live, I'll never forget them." I spoke with heartfelt honesty, remembering Johnny and Mac, and found tears in my eyes. Andy looked up and saw them, and as if my own emotion gave him permission. His face screwed up, and he cried again, great shuddering gulps as he wept for those he'd lost. My arms closed around him until he cried himself to silence and stepped back.

His voice was gruff. "Thanks."

I nodded. "That's what friends are for."

"It's been awful, teacher's good, but she doesn't know what to do a lot of the time and nor do we. I came away from home, I couldn't bear to be there anymore, not with mum and Dad, and Jessie and..." I nodded, understanding. "I let every-thing go. Dad would have been mad at me, but I couldn't stay and look after the animals..."

"You did the right thing," I said.

"I never went back after I came here. Could we, I mean, would you...?"

I had no trouble with that. "Yes, I could and would. Let me call a couple of friends, and we'll go now if you like?" He liked.

His family's smallholding had been only a few miles away, and I went in first. The bodies, now mostly bones, lay on the parents' bed. The older sister had, as had many, gone to die with them while she had just enough strength to walk the few yards required. I found her bedroom, took bedding, wrapped what was left of the bodies, then I called in the four who'd accompanied us. Miss Jane's brother-in-law Bevan carried the bodies outside one by one. I'd scanned the property on arrival, but now I consulted Andy by walking to where I thought we could bury his family and looking at him. He nodded mutely. Once the grave was ready, we laid the three inside it gently, picked flowers from the straggling flower beds, and I signalled everyone to gather around.

I tossed my flowers down one by one as I talked, not knowing if the people we buried were religious, or if so, of what denomination, so I spoke simply. And once that was done, and everyone had added their flowers, I sang. My voice does well enough, and although I can't play any instrument, I can carry a tune, and *Abide with Me* is always suitable. Then I spoke again, looking down at the blanket of flowers.

"The Scotland you knew is changed. Yet the people live, and while we live, Scotland lives. Your son shall join us if he wills it, and from his blood, a new Scotland shall be. He will remember you and tell stories about you that you are not forgotten. Sleep well, knowing that your blood and Scotland live yet." I sang *Scotland the Brave*, and they joined in, Andy singing with a clear soprano that was pleasant to the ear.

We finished, stood in brief silence, then Andy looked at me. "You mean it? I can come back with you? What's it like?"

I told him briefly about the glens, and he nodded. "Makes sense. The more people, the more you can do stuff." Then, shyly. "You got dogs? I don't suppose I could have one?"

I beamed at him. "We do have dogs, and it's glen policy that anyone that wants a pet has one, so long as they look after it properly. A dog has to be trained, fed, and exercised, and if you have a cat..."

"It has to be trained, fed, and exercised?" A cheeky grin showed.

I laughed. "You don't know cats."

"Yeah, I do."

"Right, then if you have a cat, it has to be fed. It'll exercise itself, and it'll train *you*."

In return, I got a shout of laughter and I grinned back companionably. I glanced about us. "You have a choice. Do you think you'll want to go home with us?" He nodded. "Very well. How did you get to the village when you needed to?"

"Bike. It's there."

"Then we'll take you back now. We'll be leaving tomorrow, taking your teacher to see about her family, but we should be coming back in five or six days. If you decide to come with us, come here on your bike. Pack everything you want to take, mark it if it's too heavy for you to move, and we'll collect you in the village again. If we need to come back here for whatever you can't move, we will. Understand?"

"Yes."

We explained that later to Jenny Hannach, and she protested. "I can't leave them alone. They need an adult."

"Some of our people volunteered to stay until we return. We'll be going on past your home as well. So the same as I told Andy applies. If there's nothing there for you anymore – I carefully refrained from saying no *one*, then you pack, and we'll collect you as we come by again. That's if you want to come back, either here or with us. I can tell you Andy's made up his mind. He wants to join us."

She said nothing, and I kept my mouth shut.

We moved off late morning, the children waving us and their teacher goodbye. We drove steadily alongside roads that were in increasingly poor condition, but by afternoon we arrived where Jenny indicated we should turn off. Her home was two miles further, and almost before we had halted, she was out of the Landcruiser, shouting names. She tore open the door, vanished inside, and standing by the vehicle, I waited. It took only three or four minutes before her shouts died and a similar time before she came staggering out of the door, helplessly retching.

I knew from her attitude during the trip that she'd managed to convince herself her family lived, that they'd not answered phones or come to find her for some reason that meant they were still well. As Donal says, there are times when a silly belief is functional. Hers had allowed her to do what was needed for the children, in the expectation that someone would come, relieve her of her post, and she could go home, where everyone would be waiting to greet her. In the face of decomposed bodies, you can't cling to a fantasy of joyous reunion any longer.

Donal went over and stood by her, patting her shoulder gently. "We'll bury them on their land. They'd like it that way, no doubt?" She nodded and retched again.

He went into the sprawling house, and I followed. There had been, so far as I could tell, nine occupants, all long dead. We covered the remains, took them outside, and buried them with a short service while Jenny alternately cried and retched. Once that was over, we were briefly occupied. I thought she was with Donal, he thought she was with me, and it took a little time before we realised that she was with none of us.

"Jenny's gone," I said when I found him and saw him alone.

"*Magairlean!*" said my husband, who rarely swears.

We found her in the hay barn. She'd slashed her wrists quite competently on a scythe, and she was dead. Beside her lay a sheet of paper. The message left to us was only a few words that covered anything we needed to know.

"Put me with my family. Take anything you want for the kids."

Donal snarled. "I've a good mind not to."

I looked down at the girl who'd taken an easy way out. "Put her with them, love. What use would she have been to us if she wanted to die? At least she stayed with the children until we came. She'd known her people were dead; she just shut her eyes until she could get back home. Then all she wanted was to be with them. Let her be."

We buried her with her family, I said *The Lord's Prayer* and asked that wherever she was now, whoever she was with, they understand her decision and accept it. We sang *Flowers of the Forest*, emptied the house and outbuildings of everything useful, spent the night camped outside, and drove on in the early morning.

****

We circled a dozen small towns, two occupied glens, and several estates. We added livestock, horse-drawn items, came upon three enormous empty, fuelled lorries behind a garage, filled those, and added them to the convoy, along with five large trailers. We also filled those with salvage and a petrol tanker, also full when we checked. There were people too. In ones, twos, and small groups, we accepted them, where they agreed once they'd heard of the glens and where after some evaluation we thought they'd do well with us – and us with them. Several had pets which came too — our agreement to that tipping the balance on more than one occasion.

Andy was watching as we came over the brow of the hill and into his village. His eyes searched our vehicle and slowly blanked. "She didn't come back. Did she?"

"No," was all I said, and he asked no more. We gathered up everyone, all the children having decided they'd come with us. Not a coerced decision, yet what other choice did they have? But they chose, they came, and we turned for home taking different roads. We stopped often at villages and towns, adding another person or two here and there, along with dogs, cats,

goldfish, birds, and – to my amused surprise – five alpacas, together with the lady that had bred them for years.

"I know where there's more," she said, and before I could
object, she added, "They're dual-purpose, wool and meat, and they
come, or I don't." So we included Cheryl and her five alpacas. We
went on to the other place of which she knew and found another
dozen, which plodded calmly onto a large trailer under her urging. As we continued, now with seventeen strange beasts, I wondered what the glens would look like in a hundred years with
that lot wandering about - not that they weren't attractive, but
they were hardly the essence of Scotland.

We reached home. It took three days to unload everything,
settle people into homes, tell the children that no, they were going to school again and woe betide anyone that played truant
and introduce our new settlers around. Mrs. Giles sneered privately, or so I heard. She thought we'd chosen poorly and that
most we'd taken in were ill-educated yokels. I clamped my
mouth shut and said nothing. She wouldn't have been happy
whoever or whatever they'd been. The fact was that the woman
complained for love of complaining. Short of gluing her lips
shut, we had to live with it.

Our fourth winter came. Andy had gone to live with Bevan
while Miss Jane and Esme Pemberton taught him to sing and
play the smallpipes. Slowly the cold weather passed into spring,
and I went out one day on a solar tricycle. I ran it up and down
the main road a few miles each way and concluded that the
streets would be impassable in another few years. We had to salvage for items and people before that happened. This summer
and autumn, we should be out hunting the whole time. I went
back to tell Donal and found he agreed and had a mind to seek
in some of the larger cities. This would be our search year, and I
hoped the salvage would be good.

CHAPTER SIXTEEN

Every citizen should be a soldier. This was the case with the Greeks and Romans, and must be that of every free state. ~Thomas Jefferson

Laws and justice should apply to all, man, woman, child, or creature. That shall be how our glens live. No one is outside the law or beyond it. ~Donal McArn

Ricky was sixteen that year, and we had a birthday party. Two of them really, one with just his close friends – eleven of them – at our home on the evening of his birthday. The other was one to which all the children came and took place at the community hall by the school. It was fun, silly games, small gifts to every child, and we even had homemade jelly and ice cream. I thought that we might not have those forever, so while we did, we should enjoy them. Donal shook his head at that.

"Ice cream's likely to last our lifetimes, love. We've solar panels and wind generators on every building. We'll lose the ability to generate electricity sometime, that's true, but not yet and maybe not for generations. And if we gain sufficient population, we can hope for someone who's a born engineer to repair such things and maybe recreate them. That will be the real race, learning to make things before the old machinery dies."

I glanced at the new refrigerator and chest freezer we'd brought back from an un-looted shop. "I know. The truth is, I think we'll lose some things for good. The time comes when you can't fix them anymore, and you can't make them either."

201

Donal shrugged. "When the last fridge dies, we'll go back to ice boxes or putting some foods in the stream. Times will pass, someone will be born that can read the books, learn from them how to make something, and that'll be up and running again. Can't keep the human race down, love, the trick is to keep the glens all reading so when the time comes, they'll have the books that'll tell them how."

"I know." I collected books wherever we went, Miss Jane, Esme, Janet, Claire, whoever was with us when we salvaged knew to seek out books, and we'd had to expand the libraries. We took fiction and the heavy-duty scientific tomes that we found in odd places. For that, too, I joined with Donal in saying we'd go to some of the major towns or smaller cities. They were where you found books by the hundreds – or by the thousands – and I had computerised lists of what books we already owned.

We waited until the spring had stopped being quite so windy and wet, set up rosters for guard duty, made lists of things we *really* wanted, sorted out who wanted to go and who'd go if asked but would rather not, and set out one bright morning with a convoy that would have startled Cash McCall. I said that, and Donal began singing the song. I was doing the CB talking – "Ah, breaker one-nine, this here's the Rubber Duck." and we joined in the choruses. "Come on and join our convoy. Ain't nothing gonna get in our way…" Many vehicles had a radio, and we all tuned in at the same frequency, so the chorus came to and from us, carried on the air and RT.

I laughed as we finished and went on to another song. When we'd started going out, I'd often sung that song and early decided that the last line of the chorus was wrong for us. So now we sang instead that "we were going to roll the convoy across the far Strathspey." Other popular songs had been slightly adjusted in the same way, and it amused me again that, in a hundred years, those who sang them wouldn't know any better.

We came to the chosen city late that afternoon, found a hotel that hadn't burned, and parked. Cassie and Bruce came with us. We'd leave them in the Landcruiser, and if anyone came sneaking around, we'd hear about it. Cheryl was with us, having a breed book that listed every registered alpaca breeder in Scotland and pointing out to us that, "Their wool's better than sheep. It's lighter, warmer, and stronger, and where they come from, they're Highland animals." So at some stage, we'd probably make a detour. Cheryl was driving a vehicle that would allow her to take as many as twenty of the animals, and I thought that would probably do.

And for those that wonder, alpaca fleece had turned out to be all she claimed. The other advantages were that she could shear them in a pinch and that her own were Suris, and that's what she continued to choose, taking no over-pale animals as she pointed out to me when I asked about that. "You have all the white sheep wool you need. And white dirties easily. My alpaca are black or shades of brown. They're excellent at blending into the landscape, and they don't show the dirt." I agreed and decided the lady could use help if I came across someone that liked alpacas, whom she also liked.

We had Esme Pemberlow and Miss Jane with us as well. They had Nubian goats in mind, and what with one thing and another, I thought it'd be an exciting trip. I can record that it started as more panic-stricken once we hit the city, spent the night, and moved deeper into what had once been crowded streets the next day. I turned down the main road, a woman shot out of a side street screaming like a banshee and leaped for the top of one of the vehicles that had climbable sides. She ended up on top still screaming. The driver braked hard in fright, she fell partway down the back, and something hurled itself at the vehicle, hit the windscreen – the screams, almost impossibly, became louder – and I finally registered the pursuer.

"Is that a *tiger*?"

"Damn right," Donal assured me, stepping out of the Landcruiser, gun in hand. He sighted, shot once, and the tiger went down. He fired again; it spread out on the road, became a late tiger, and I found I'd been holding my breath. The woman dropped down from her perch and looked at it as if waiting to see a reanimation.

I approached, remembering some of what I'd once discussed. "Are there many of those around here, miss, ms..?"

"Jackie, and there's a few more lions, though."

Miss Jane, who'd arrived in time to hear that, nodded. "I expected it. Even zoo keepers get fond of their animals. I'm surprised there aren't kangaroos and zebras."

"There are," Jackie informed her dryly. "The ones the lions and tigers haven't eaten. There were koalas, to begin with, too, but the leopards got them, and the kangaroos are vanishing. I think they don't like the climate."

Esme came up and looked at her. "How are you finding the climate yourself?"

"A bit hot for my liking. I just haven't been able to decide where would be better."

"Any more people around that you could recommend as decent, sensible, hard-working, and who might like to live in the country?" I broke in.

Jackie faced us and nodded. "I would. If you have a community that could use me, if you have laws about abuse and enforce them and if no one demands I marry and produce children, whether I liked the man, whether I wanted to or not," she said flatly.

I absorbed that. "You mean someone else expected that from you?"

"Yes, a rather nasty bunch came through last year. Two friends went with them. One made it back in bad shape six months later. She lived long enough to tell me about it."

By now, half our people had come to see what the hold-up was and was listening. I made up my mind. "We'll night here. Jackie, do you know a hotel we can use?"

"Down that way." Donal went to see and reported back that she was right. We moved there, dinner was started, and Jackie gave us an overview of her story while she ate.

"University qualification, parents overseas when this started, and I never heard from them again. City girl, done some work in the country, came back to my boss here. Rented a place from an old lady, a garage made into an apartment. She died. I stayed, couldn't think where else to go. Raided local shops, hauled back everything to my place—emergency rules. Things started going bad last year. Rats, tigers, lions, dog packs – feral people too. I'd have liked to get out; I couldn't decide where."

"How many others are in the same boat?"

Her grin was a wry expression that was more a grimace. "A few. I'd recommend maybe twenty and be sure they're okay. Another dozen could be. After that, I wouldn't make promises. We run across each other, lending a hand now and again. Talk a bit. Tell you, too, one pretty good way to know if they're okay is if they have pets. Do you?"

I beamed. "We most certainly do." I raised my voice in a call. "Ricky, here!"

He came running from where he'd been talking to the Camerons. Laddie was with him as usual, and Jackie stared.

"A Pomshee? You've got a Pomshee?" Laddie barked, and she laughed. "Sorry, fella, not insulting you. You're only about the third I've ever seen, and it's incredible you've survived this long."

Ricky promptly sat and started telling her how we'd found Laddie, segued into some of his history, talked about the glens, and got back to Laddie. "You've seen others, where, could they be around still? I'd love another one?"

Jackie's face clouded over. "Sorry, no." And Ricky knew not to ask anything more. When someone looked like that, you didn't ask questions.

Jackie stayed the day with us and excused herself when it was dusk. "Must go, things to do, places to go. But if you're around, I'll see you again."

I hoped so, but for a week, there was no sight of her. However, we did get people. They came wandering in, not mentioning her name but suggesting we'd been vouched for. We made offers to the twenty she'd listed to me, and about half of the dozen she hadn't been sure of. I wasn't sure of half of them, so we dined them but made no advances.

One man made his own. He came walking in, nodded to us, and asked: "Who's the leader here?"

Donal turned from where he stood, talking to several of us, looked the visitor up and down, and stated quietly, "I am and my wife."

Ignoring me, the man nodded. "Okay. My name's Russ. I was in the army. Reckon you could use me." That last was a flat statement.

Donal moved, turning to me slightly, his sign I should take over. "I don't know. What were you in the army? We don't need cooks. Have you any actual fighting experience, and what about your discharge, honourable?"

I got a look that should have dropped me in a small heap of ashes. "What? She does your talking for you?"

Donal looked at him. "Nay, I can talk well enough."

"Then what do you say?"

"We dinna need you. I'll have no man with us who doesn't know how to take orders. You've just shown you can't. Sheila asked if you'd been honourably discharged. I'd say not. Good day to you now."

This time the look was turned on him. "You're making a big mistake."

"Mine to make," Donal said laconically.

Russ gave us a comprehensive scan. "Yeah, while you've got friends at your back."

Donal laughed. We both knew that taunt. The idiot was expecting my husband to come over all macho and want to fight to prove he could. Soldiers learn early that attitude is a waste of everyone's time – and sergeants don't like it. Donal half-turned his shoulder and continued the original discussion, making it clear he wasn't silly enough to get caught. Russ waited a moment, then stamped away.

I spoke softly. "Not army, or not for long, they'd have taught him better."

Charlie, one of the people sent by Jackie, nodded, also keeping his voice down. "Nasty piece of work that one. Funny thing is, he's new around here. Never saw him before last year. No one knows him. Now and then, he seems to disappear, be gone a month or two, then he's back again."

Something in me sharpened. "What else happens around the times he disappears? People go missing, shops cleaned out, anything you've noticed?"

"Both those and petrol tankers vanish too."

Donal looked at me, and I looked back. Neither of us spoke, but I thought we both had the same idea in mind. The glens were a long day's run from this place, but we'd keep a watch. We went back to talking logistics, supplies, possible recruits, and animal control. Of which we did a bit of that over the next two days. Locals showed us where lions infested one of the biggest parks. We gathered up a dozen good shots, moved in slowly, surrounding them, and shot every lion we saw. I felt a pang at shooting cubs, but they'd grow up to be killers, and by now, we'd heard some of the stories.

Locals also knew where tigers laired and where we could find leopards. We saw to them as well when we had time and ended up with a stack of skins. Ricky claimed a lovely one from what had been a dark leopard and was working on it every night. We left it mostly to locals to claim which of the skins or other bits they wanted. We were doing a public service. Something that, it was brought to my attention, was appreciated. I shrugged at that.

"We're happy to help. We get to know people, people get to know us, and you have fewer predators to worry about."

Besides, I hadn't liked the story I'd heard about a small child taken by a pride, where he'd been used, from the sound of it, as a training exercise to teach the pride's cubs how to kill. Her mother, a disabled husband, and two children joined us the minute she heard we were accepting people. The tale of how she'd had to watch her small son die, knowing she was unable to do anything but die herself and leave her children without her if she intervened, had been heart-wrenching. Yes, I knew it was natural behaviour by the pride. That didn't mean I liked it.

We moved on after ten days, almost thirty people up in numbers, and with about half the vehicles loaded with judiciously chosen supplies. We circled to the east, entered another large town, and had similar results, including information about a man. I found that caught my attention since hearing about another of Russ's sort wasn't usual. He didn't appear – and we found that a point of interest as well since we were present for just over a week – but we heard about him.

One of those that approached us, and under apparently casual questioning about whom else was around, mentioned the man. "Aye, not a nice one, doesn't socialise, won't have your back, and…" Dan scowled. "I can't speak against him. I don't know. I do know since he turned up here, we've lost people. Shops some of us were using for supplies suddenly show up empty, and I know a petrol tanker depot where there were half a dozen there, and they vanished overnight. Comes and goes too; he does. Never know when he'll be around. Makes me wonder about him, what he does, who he is, where he does go."

"Come to any conclusions?" Donal asked.

Our informant grinned. "Maybe he's got a holiday place somewhere. Maybe he's stocking it up for a time when you can't live here. I dunno. And I'm sure as hell not asking *him*." We exchanged glances and said nothing. Donal changed the subject, and in response, we were offered a few names of those who might be interested in joining us.

"You could talk to Marise. She and Bel are sisters, husbands were down in London when it happened; never came back. Sisters moved in with their mum, big old house out on the edge of town. Took in another sister and her family, and three, four friends. Reckon there's a dozen or more of them. They manage, but the last time I saw Bel, she said they were worried about the future." He made a face. "Hell, who isn't? Don't matter so much to me. I've got no one, I can use a gun, I get by, but those with families, I guess they've a right to think about what's to come for their kids."

Donal leaned forward, and their gazes met. "We have no problem taking singles. All we ask is if that one is of decent character. We don't like rapists, child abusers, thieves, or those that are completely selfish."

He flushed. "Hell, man, I'm none of those. There's people that could speak for me."

"Then consider joining us," I said flatly.

There was a pause, then he spoke shyly, a little embarrassed. "What about a cat?"

I made it clear I was impressed and pleased. "I have two dogs and a cat named Tai. We *like* people who have pets. It shows stability. What's your cat's name?"

Dan told us all about Miss Toughy. It seemed that she was the feistiest, the smartest, the most affectionate of cats. He had a huge store of cat food. "Worried I'd run out, so I got half a dozen of them cat feeders too. She knows how to work one. Give her tinned cat food when I'm there, but she can work the feeder if I'm out."

I cut the paean short and offered terms and conditions. When we left the town, we had Dan, Miss Toughy, and everyone from "the big old house on the edge of town," whose numbers incidentally had been higher than Dan knew, to our benefit.

****

By the time we made it home again, we'd been gone a month. We acquired fifty-three new people for the glens, many of whom had pets, and we'd gathered major salvage on the way, including livestock – nineteen alpacas and two small flocks of a type of sheep that had been taking over many small-holdings. The Easycare breed was one I knew of but had never met before. I heard more about them from the owners who wouldn't come without them and were ecstatic that, on the contrary, we'd be more than willing to accept sheep and shepherds.

The literature that family had on their beloved flock said, "The breed requires minimal shepherding and veterinary care, sheds its fleece in the summer, does not need shearing, and yet offers excellent meat yields and lambing ratios. The ewes seldom require assistance at lambing. They have strong maternal instincts and will rear their lambs without human intervention." So far as I was concerned, they'd be an ideal primary sheep breed for the glens.

"The fleece, when shed, goes back to the soil quickly," the book continued, but we could send some of the children to gather it, and if mixed with shorn fleeces, should be fine for spinning, weaving, or felting.

I liked both the families and the sheep. We'd stayed long enough to gather up everything they owned, and on arrival, to allocate them a substantial piece of McManus Glen, along with a large barn, a smaller outbuilding, plus two houses that had belonged to staff and which were well appointed. The McKays and the Campbells settled in, started their children going to school, and submerged seamlessly into glen life. Mrs. Giles considered the sheep and made several comments about them, of which the least was that they were "unnatural."

That came to my ears in due course, and I advised both families to ignore the woman. "How can your sheep be unnatural? Doesn't the information say they were bred up from ordinary sheep? Where's the unnaturalness in that? The woman's a trouble-maker and a fool, don't listen, and she'll shut up after a while."

If she didn't, at least I heard no more about unnatural sheep. However, I heard about something else when Bevan came to me quietly with a sighting that disturbed both of us.

"You know I didn't go on the last trip?" I nodded. "We're doing well, but we were short of meat, so I took a .22 out rabbit hunting most days while it was fine. Not in the glens, down to the main road and far side of that. And it was there I saw Mrs. Giles."

"How far from the glens?"

"A fair way. The side road's five miles, and I was a couple of miles beyond that," Bevan said thoughtfully. "Wouldn't have thought the old lady could have walked so far." He realised what he'd said, and I listened while he tied his tongue in a knot trying to explain he'd only meant *that* old lady, and not another old lady and…

"Yes, but Mrs. Giles *does* walk," I said to cut short the embarrassment. "She's fit, and for all she looks to be older, she's only in her early sixties. Where was she when you saw her, how long were you watching, and did you ever see her that way again?"

Bevan could be concise when not embarrassed. "When I first saw her, she was over by the ruined house. I watched her for ten minutes or so, but she wasn't doing anything much. It was just odd to see her there. I saw her over that way again five days later."

"Describe what you saw."

211

He did so, and I let him leave after that while I sat thinking. Once I'd thought, I went in search of Donal and talked. He agreed, and we mentioned casually to several people that we would be going to one of the nearby towns in the morning, no, just us, and maybe Miss Jane, Esme Pemberlow, Janet, the Camerons, and a couple of others. A salvaging trip for animal food, nothing major – in which we lied but feared it necessary.

CHAPTER SEVENTEEN

If it were done when 'tis done, then 'twere well, it were done quickly: if the assassination could trammel up the consequence and catch, with his surcease success. ~*Macbeth* by Shakespeare

I've always thought that decisions should be made after consultation; it's well to act quickly but take the time to think beforehand. ~Sheila McArn

Those who went with us knew something of why, but they wouldn't talk. We left them salvaging and drove down the road to where Mrs. Giles had been seen. We both knew about the old house there. It had been abandoned years ago when the owner died. He'd been living in utter squalor. There was no electricity, and he cooked on an open fire. He'd had dogs and ferrets, and they'd done what they needed where they liked. The council had an order on him, but he'd died before it could be enforced. The authorities had removed the animals but couldn't rehome any since everyone knew they'd been hungry and … well, you'll guess. So the house remained, falling more each year but not quite gone yet.

We circled and came at it from the far side away from the glens, and there I looked at what we found and then at Donal. "Someone's been here."

"Regularly, by the firewood and those ashes."

There was a large stack of cut wood in the kitchen, and ashes lay thick on the grate. Not a single night's worth, and why bother to cut so much wood and leave it if you didn't intend to come back? I walked to the next room. Nothing but a bed in

213

pieces … hold on. I went back to the kitchen and found the piece of furniture there.

"This matches the bed. Why move it to the kitchen?" I was opening the drawers. Donal moved to join me and took each drawer from my hands, turning it over and placing it on the floor. We found nothing until he stooped, turned the chest of drawers on its head, and peered to the inside back.

"Something here, love."

I slid my arm in and reached, bringing out an envelope. It was sealed, and I glanced up. "Put that old pot on the fire with some water. It may better no one knows we found this." The envelope was old, the glue weak, and we had it steamed open undamaged soon after. I laid out the sheets of paper, and we read them. Donal sighed.

"Here's trouble unlooked for."

I agreed. "Douse the fire, seal the envelope, put it back where we found it, and let's get out before we're seen."

We talked over our findings two nights and did not decide until Cheryl and the alpacas roared back into the picture. She came tapping quietly on the door at dusk that evening and looking as if she'd seen a ghost. I let her in. She collapsed, shivering onto a chair, and took a breath, let it out, and made a five-word statement that startled us.

"I've just shot a man."

"Who?" Donal recovered first.

"I don't know. I've never seen him before. He was in Johnny's Glen with a dog, big vicious-looking brute."

Donal handed her a cup of hot chocolate. "Drink that, then tell us from the beginning."

It was easy enough to picture. The alpacas had recently been moved to graze near the gates to that glen. There was a considerable gap in lawns. As a result of the configuration and the wind blowing towards her, no one in the houses beyond that could hear a shot, not even two from a sawn-off. So she'd felt free to come to us with no witnesses and hope for no trouble to go with that.

"This man had one of them, my Chiquita. That dog – filthy brute – it'd already killed her baby, and he had Chickie. He was going to cut her throat. I asked him what the hell he thought he was doing, that was my alpaca. He had a handgun on a belt. He grabbed for that, sort of snarling at me, so I shot him. The damn dog started for me, so I shot that too." She was breathing hard, her face twisted in distress.

I patted her arm approvingly. "You did quite right."

She heaved a huge sigh. "I didn't think. I just did it. They're both dead, so I came to tell you. Oh, and I checked his pockets. He had a driving licence." She dug it out of her jeans and handed that to me. I opened it, looked, and while Cheryl may not have noticed, Donal did. I gave it mutely to him and saw him register the same thing.

He stood up. "You were patrolling Johnny's Glen just before coming back to make dinner for yourself," he said, emphasising the words in a way that told her this was to be her official story to everyone else. "You found a stray dog had got in somehow and killed Chiquita's cria. You shot the dog. The dog was alone. You saw no one and nothing else with it. You are to be commended for your prompt actions."

Cheryl went away comforted, and I started putting what was to have been dinner in a few minutes into the warming drawer. With that done, we took torches, straddled two of the very useful solar tricycles – one of their uses, in this case, being that they were silent and moving at a comfortable speed – and headed for the further glen. There the situation was as reported. The dog had been some sort of mastiff, I thought, and the man was Russ. I'd taken one look at his driving licence and knew him immediately.

Donal glanced at me, and I nodded back. Two minds, a single thought. "Liaison for a group where he was, picking out the best people, places that still have something worth taking…" Donal said.

"And," I added heavily. "Maybe I can guess what group. Remember Jackie's friend?"

"Aye, her friend said they'd gone north."

"Building a fiefdom, where women are property, breed the next generation whether they like it or not." I continued, remembering Jackie's pain and anger at what had happened to her mate.

"So," I knew the decision before he spoke it. "We'll clear up this mess; leave the dog where it lies. We'll drop in on the Camerons on the way home, tell them about it, and ask that they bury it in the morning. As for this piece of *caoch*, we'll haul him outside our glen. Who's on gate duty?" I gave names. "Can you distract them?" I grinned. "Okay, love, silly question."

And that was the programme. We hauled Russ's body onto Donal's tricycle. We took it close enough to the gate for me to dismount and go in, where I chatted to the lads, said we planned an evening's hunting – sighing quietly for my uneaten dinner. Before I operated the gate, Donal went through silently while I focussed their attention on me, and once he was clear, I got my tricycle and followed him as the gate closed again behind me.

About a mile on and up a hillside, there was a hole where a badger or a fox had dug a den. We rechecked Russ since I doubted Cheryl had done it thoroughly and found a pouch of gold coins attached to his belt, a box of ammunition – very useful, it fitted the revolver he'd had and which we'd collected with him – and a wicked little knife tucked into one sock in a thin leather sheath. The leather belt he wore seemed very thick, and with my help, Donal had that off and was checking it. In small slits on the inside, it contained a razor blade, a couple of Krugerrands, and five tiny pills.

I eased them out. "Look at *these*."

Donal did, using one of the torches and rolling the pills over in his palm. "Same as Mac gave you?" Despite what Mac had said, I'd told Donal.

"I'd say so. What I'd like to know is where this one got them?"

"Could be he had them officially some way?"

I hunched a shoulder. "We'll never know. He can't tell us, and who cares. He struck me as *leam-leat* the minute I saw him anyhow."

"Aye, and me, lass. Two-faced as ever was. Well, he'll double-cross no one else if that was his trade. Get him into the hole and leave me be a minute." We heaved, pushed, and wedged until all but the upturned face was gone from view. I walked away to the tricycles and heard the sound of dull sodden blows behind me. If the man was to be found, they'd not identify him by his face, and the stink of blood would bring the local vermin running. With luck, he'd be gone in a few days, and I was glad of it.

We went home in silence two hours later. We knew where to find rabbits once the moonlight was up, we had silenced .22s, and we came back past the gatehouse with a dozen, sharing a couple with the boys. There was little gossip after that about the dog attack on Cheryl's alpacas. Everybody felt she'd done a good job, and few people even talked much about it, except those in Johnny's Glen. I took a quiet tour a week later, and we'd been right. There was nothing left of the dog's master. However, what we'd found in the old house had been an alert, and we stayed wary, with a dozen of the best hunters watching down the road from the south and reporting regularly.

Then, late one afternoon, Dan arrived on an e-bike, his face showing that he bore news. "Some group's coming in this direction. They've stopped fifteen miles back."

"Description?"

"About two dozen vehicles, around seventy people. Can't be sure of that."

"Why not?"

"One of the vehicles is a bus, doors shut. I could see faces, looked to be women."

"How many?"

He considered. "I never saw more than five or six at a time, but I wasn't close enough to be certain it was the same ones. That's why I say I'm not sure of their numbers."

"Did they look to be planning to stay the night there?"

"Nope, they'll all around another vehicle. I'd say it's a breakdown. They could move on if they get it fixed or swap over whatever's in it. I left Jackie watching them with Joe Matson. Jackie'll let you know if they move on or stop anywhere around here."

"All right, go and get your dinner."

Once he'd gone, I turned to Donal. "Jackie may recognise them if it's who we think it could be."

"Aye," was all he said. I grinned. My husband can say a lot in a word or a look. And we had our fears and suspicions verified at first light. Jackie came in, muttering about the chill and wrapping her arms around herself.

"It's them," she stated, a savage look in her eyes. "The bunch that talked my mates into going off. What's more, Marni's still with them. I saw her. Saw one of them hit her too." She frowned. "They parked over by that old building that's falling. One went in the minute they stopped. Came running out waving sommat. Joe's still watching."

Donal and I waited until she had gone, and Donal nodded. "They'll be the ones then. So we know, and they don't know we know. Useful that."

I heartily agreed. There's nothing as useful as an ignorant enemy.

****

218

Jackie would have approached her friend, but we forbade it. If there was the slightest suspicion, it could get her friend beaten, tortured for information, or just executed. Jackie accepted the order, but she spent most of her time watching the camp with an extra pair of good binoculars. What we'd anticipated on that came three days later when she stormed into our house and slammed a hand on the table.

"I'm going to ..."

Donal took her by the arms and bent one of his best *I know what I'm doing, now shut up and listen* looks on her. "We know everything you're telling us. We've long since made plans to deal with it, and yes, you'll be part of that."

He sat her down, and we talked – late into the night while she switched from looking mad enough to bite and began to look anticipatory with a side order of evil.

"When?"

"Their decision. Defence is safer and more effective most of the time than offence. We'll do both; you can be part of the offence. Suit?"

"*Yes!*"

We sat back, hoarding our time and strength and making flexible plans. In a sly way, it amused me. They assumed we knew nothing, would be caught with our pants down, and they had only to march in, guns waving. Their intelligence was flawed. They didn't know that on the last two runs, we'd bought back people. They didn't know of the cache of items we'd found in Glen McManus either. They believed they were dealing with a bunch of mostly women, children, and older people who couldn't fight or wouldn't be effective if they did. I chuckled softly. They were in for a surprise, and I was looking forward to providing it.

They came slinking towards the glens three mornings later. Their boss man knew one or two things. Somewhere he'd heard that the hour before first light is the best time. It's when people sleep the deepest, and he'd assumed we wouldn't have sentries. We had them, and they had Night Vision Goggles. Army gear had been one of Donal's priorities, and he knew places to find it. The goggles lit up our enemies nicely, and we let them get past the gatehouse. They didn't even ask why the gates were open.

There were around fifty of them, and it was a killing ground. Once they were all past the gates, Dan pressed the lever; the gates swung silently behind them and locked, while ahead of them Alex, who could imitate the sound perfectly – or perhaps that should be purrfectly – produced the squall of a startled, angry cat. It covered the lock's click, and they were all looking for the cat, so they saw and heard nothing. They came on, a flamboyantly-dressed, armed but casual mob that halted when they came around the bend and sighted houses, school, library, and grazing cows, all silhouetted against the sunrise.

The leader held up a hand. "Hold up," he snickered, his voice low but carrying to us. "Looks like they're still asleep. Let's keep the noise down 'til we're inside. After that, it won't matter. Now, watch it. I'll kill any man that makes a row before we need."

Remaining in that tight group, they advanced. Donal let them get another ten paces on, by which time they were all bunched in the open, the sky was lightening further, and we were in position. He whistled, the long carrying call of a local bird that we knew to be the signal. Not that we needed it. I had one of the items we'd taken from the McManus cache, Donal had another, and Sam Cameron a third. At the whistle, I aimed and let go. A grenade dropped neatly into the mob's centre, a second grenade took out some of those behind where mine had landed, and Sam took a grip of the spade lugs and let drive with the ancient machine gun on its folding tripod.

Half of them were down, from somewhere behind us, the great pipes were howling bloody murder, and near me, old Jamie Tamman rose screaming, stark mad with the skirl of the pipes and outrage at the invasion of his glen. I grabbed for him and missed, and he was gone, over eighty, and armed with the claymore he'd had from his great-great-great-great grandfather, a weapon supposedly wielded by an even earlier ancestor at Culloden. It might be ancient, but it had an edge like a razor, and the weight and balance of one is a killing machine in the hands of a man who knows how to wield it. Jamie knew that wielding very well.

He had an honour guard for his going. One of them shot him dead, but when we had time to look, we found his body lying over three men, two dead and one dying – and all of them slain by that ancient weapon of the clans that he'd carried. He had a satisfied look on his face did old Jamie, and we buried him as he'd have wished, on the rise overlooking his home, claymore in hand, the largest bottle of whisky to be found, by his side, and him swathed in good tartan, lying straight in his grave with them curled naked and dead at his feet as dogs lie.

The battle was a pure slaughter. He was the only one of us that died, although we'd injured to be aided afterwards, some badly hurt, yet they all lived, and the enemy died, which was the way we'd wanted it. Nice for once to have what you want. And then too, while we killed, Jackie and Dan had been with others of us at the bus that held the group's women. They'd strolled up, hailed the guards politely, said they lived down the road and had just come back from shooting deer. Would they care for some venison?

They would, and while they were distracted, our people pounced. Jackie's friend exploded out of the bus, yelling her name, the other women behind her, and their guard lying dead in his blood on the floor. Our people might have taken prisoners. The friend was in no mind for that, and nor were her companions. It was a bloody melee, but at the end of it, while three of the women had wounds, all their captors were dead, and Jackie and her friend – Marni Gilson – were hugging as if to drive their bones through each other. Aye, it was a famous victory; or so we saw it anyway.

We celebrated all that day and half the night, between bouts of my having to care for the injured, arbitrate claims, and praise those that had done incredibly well. Minister Giles appeared, gentle and shy, wanting to bless the dead and asking that they be decently buried. Donal agreed, saying privately,

"If it were up to me, I'd burn the bastards and piss on the ashes, but we aren't savages, and it's a bad precedent to set. But they'll not lie in glens' earth."

Nor did they. After the celebrations, we quietly searched the bodies, laid them out on one of the flatbeds, then took them to a deep gully. There, before the minister arrived – having told him an hour later for the time – we tossed them in, bulldozed soil over the bodies, and dumped in stones together with lumps of old concrete to cover the raw earth. We ran the dozer over the mound to flatten it, and once he arrived – Mrs. Giles with him wearing her usual sour face – we stood patiently while he recited verses, prayers, and hoped God would take them to himself in forgiveness. For myself, I doubted it. The Devil was more likely to claim them, but Minister Giles was a good man, and I wouldn't offend him by saying anything of the sort.

He and his lady left for home, being given a lift by one of those in a car, while Donal and I walked home talking.

"What do we do now?" he asked.

I looked him in the eye." We canna let it go, love. There could be a next time."

"Aye, but what's to do?"

"That's for me, love, leave it to me."

"Sure?"

"I am."

Time passed after that. It had been getting close to our fifth winter, and before I did anything else, we had to be sure the glens were snug.

Marni and Jackie came to see us about then. "Marni would like to move in with me, but we could use a bit more room. Can you do anything?"

I could, we still had some of the Comber Beach chalets tucked away, and I had one hauled over to Jackie's small cottage and positioned against their second door, that connection made snug by Mick Francis, our carpenter. It would add a good-sized bed-sitting room, en suite too, for Marni, which should do fine. I was right about that, and they settled in happily.

Dan accepted a cottage in McManus Glen and proved to be a helpful handyman. He could fix almost anything, knew something of electronics, and using whatever was lying around could slap together most of whatever was asked for. I noticed him at Jackie and Marni's door now and again and said nothing. Not my business.

What *was* my business was the question Donal had posed, and I'd promised to sort. I had to do something about that, and it took time to consider my options. It couldn't become known. It would do the glens no good at all for whatever I did to become talked about. Nor would it be wise for any steps taken to be admitted or guessed at. Nothing was likely to happen before summer, so I let be and did other work, although I believed none of those might be quite so important for the glens in the longer run.

****

Midwinter came, and we celebrated. I counted people, and my heart rejoiced. We'd been less than two hundred once the virus had done its worst to the glens, and now we'd more than tripled that. We had pregnant women, and by my count, the next baby born would bring us to precisely six hundred. For the past two or three years, we hadn't only gone looking, a steady trickle of our folk had come back to us, remembering in death and danger, fear and hunger, the peace and the safety of the glen. They'd returned, in singles, pairs, and families, in a wide assortment of vehicles and with some curious items from which they'd refused to be parted even if the way was long and the road bumpy.

They'd come, the Camerons, the McDonalds, Iresons, MacFiernans, and others. And where we knew them for good people, they'd been welcomed, given homes, work, and settled in. Now and again, we'd found ourselves mistaken, and then we'd do what we must, and they'd been blindfolded and set down seventy or eighty miles away, usually in someplace that was unlooted yet, with large comfortable houses, and told not to come back. So far, none had. Either they'd felt themselves better off, been overtaken by others more ruthless, or remembered what we'd said and reconsidered any return.

Midwinter passed, and there was a minor epidemic of colds despite our glens being warmer than many other places, even warmer than we were before climate change began to raise temperatures. The cold virus is always with us, and I was not surprised when Mrs. Giles sent a message complaining that she was unwell. I called to find that while she complained, her husband was the worse off. I left remedies and planned to call again.

That second visit, I looked him over and took her aside.

"He's ill…"

"I don't need you to tell me that," was the reply before I could finish.

"Then maybe you'll listen when I tell you that he needs nursing, not just checking on before you go to bed and when you get up. He needs an eye on him all night and medicine at two-hourly intervals."

"I can't do that. You can't expect me to."

I remained patient. "I don't."

"Then what are you suggesting?"

"I'm suggesting that he comes into the hospital. Someone will see to him there, you'll be able to get a good night's sleep, and it'll be better. Don't think I don't see his coughing has been keeping you awake too. You look tired out."

There was a glimmer of satisfaction at this acknowledgement of her service. "Yes, well, it's my duty. You are right, though. You're the nurse."

I bit back a correction on that.

"If you think it right, then take him. I can manage."

I had Minister Giles collected with his belongings, and he was tucked into a hospital bed. Alex had become my paramedic apprentice, and she liked him, he liked her, and she nursed him well. It took more than two weeks before he was well again, and there was a setback when someone reported Mrs. Giles hadn't been somewhere she was expected, and on investigation, was found to have died in her sleep. He was well enough by then to conduct her service, and when he went home, I had a roster of neighbours who would bring food or ask him to dinner.

And once the service was over, once the attendees – I won't say mourners – had departed, Donal and I went for a stroll. He cleared his throat.

"Those pills of Macs?"

"Yes."

"How?"

"I put them in her medicine. I took her a single dose over that evening. I said it was so she'd get a good night's sleep because we'd be bringing her husband home the next day. I wasn't going to do that, he wasn't quite well enough, but she didn't know. I said she should take the medicine then, and she did."

"And?"

"I waited, she said she felt exhausted, and I told her to go and lie down. I opened and shut the door so she'd believe me gone. I heard her in the bedroom, and when she went quiet, I checked. She was on the way out by then. I went back and waited in the kitchen. If anyone came asking, I'd have said she suddenly seemed very tired, and she'd gone to bed. I'd been tidying the place for her so she wouldn't wake up to a mess."

"And you being a paramedic, they believed you when you said it was a heart attack."

"As they'd have believed me when I said how tired she'd been – if anyone had come calling, seen me there and asked," I agreed quietly. "No one did, no one knows I was there that evening, and we're rid of a traitor who schemed to betray the glens to that bunch that had Marni and the other women."

Donal's voice was sad. "Aye, so her man would be the official minister, and we'd do as she told us. I wonder how she met them in the first place."

"She used to go walking." I laughed harshly. "The thing is, I'd take a large bet if they *had* taken the glens, he'd have killed her and the minister. That sort wouldn't want a man preaching at them. They liked what they were, they enjoyed what they did, and they wouldn't change for him telling them not to, and they get sick of it in no time at all."

"True, lass. I'm sorry you had it to do, but as someone once said, there's times the good of the many outweighs the good of the few – or the one, in this case." His grin was a little sad. "Or as my old Sergeant used to say, 'it's a dirty job, but someone has to do it,' and it was one for a leader to do." His eyes on me were warm, and I smiled back with all our long trust and affection in that exchange.

Which was how we left it. Should I have regretted what I did, felt bad that I'd used my medical skills to kill, that I was a murderer? Not to my mind. Better one treacherous woman died than four glens. Better her peaceful death than the kind of deaths Alex Yarrow and her siblings, the Camerons, the Matsons, Miss Jane and her friend, all those that I knew, who were good, honest, decent, and hardworking people, would have died if those men had taken the glens. If her evil was done willingly – and it was – then she could be counted as a willing sacrifice, and with that, I had no trouble nor ever would.

CHAPTER EIGHTEEN

Security against defeat implies defensive tactics, ability to defeat the enemy means taking the offensive. ~Sun Tsu, *The Art of War*

Combine that, let your enemy come to you on your ground, and remember something. Even if you win and live, you need more than survival to make a life. ~Donal McArn

The MacFiernans came to me that month with a request. They'd been kin through great-grandmothers to Jamie Tamman, and they wanted his house.

"We liked the old fool," Rob MacFiernan told me frankly. "A wicked old man but none so bad and by his *fearchas*, he died a hero. Since we made it back, we've been in two chalets, but there's nine of us and it's not enough room. If we added them to his place, we could have the land, animals and start an orchard and a real vegetable garden." He ducked his head, glancing at me. "We could look after his grave too. We'd like that."

I granted what they asked, and they did everything they promised. I was invited to visit once they settled in, the orchard planted, and the garden dug. I found the house changed. It was neat – old Jamie had kept it clean enough in his time – but now it was orderly besides. There was a claymore and two crossed skean dhu, the small knife traditionally worn with the kilt, over the mantelpiece – anyone could take weapons from stored salvage, and I noted that these had been sharpened until they were as good as the weapon Jamie had carried. Below them, I saw a parchment. I angled to that and read it while the lady of the house made tea.

It was handwritten in black ink, the capitals picked out in red and gold, with the flag of Scotland in two corners and the thistle in the other two; those were painted in softly glowing hues. And the parchment read:

"In memory of James (old Jamie) Tamman, who five years after the virus stood with the people of the glens (Mhairi Gen, Blind Glen, Johnny's Glen, and McManus Glen) the Clan McAlister, against invaders. Eighty and armed with the claymore his ancestor bore at Culloden, he slew three enemies, dying himself at their hands. Let all of this house cherish his grave. Let none of this house do less if the need comes again. Let none of this house forget Jamie Tamman and let them do him honour so long as his blood and his memory lives."

Grace MacFiernan bustled in, saw me reading the parchment, and blushed. "I would not have you think us overproud..." she began and felt silent as I turned and she saw the tears in my eyes.

"Overproud?" I repeated softly. "No, I was there that day. I saw him fight, Grace. I have never been so proud of any of our people as I was that day. And we need heroes. We need those that children can hear about. When he asked for this house, your man said that Jamie was a wicked old man, but your family liked him. That's true, but when the winter was hard, his poaching often helped a family. He was never cruel to the beasts he took; he killed them cleanly. And, at the last, he died as a man should, with his face to the enemy, his blade bloody and his foes dying at his feet. You do very well to honour him."

I turned the subject a little. "Who did the parchment? It's beautifully written, and the painting is lovely."

"My daughter, Joss, we were talking of old Jamie one night. She's an imaginative child, wanted to be an artist." Grace MacFiernan sighed. "Her father described what he'd heard of Jamie's fight. Said he was buried up on the hill back of the house

228

like a chief, and that it was a pity few would remember him in twenty years. Next thing we knew, she'd gone to barns, come back with the sword and daggers, and got hold of that piece of parchment stuff and paints and ink. She did all that."

"How old is she?" I thought from what she said, Joss would be maybe thirteen or so and was interested to hear that she was in her twenties.

"Aye, she wanted to be an artist, and she would have been. Had a scholarship to the Glasgow School of Art. Would have gone but for the virus putting an end to everything."

"So she was about eighteen then?" Grace nodded. I thought furiously. The girl had to be good if the GSA would have taken her, and she was right. We needed to remember. We needed a record of the times as they changed. "Ask her if she will come to see me. I may have work that would suit her."

I shared tea and scones, listened to several minor problems, and suggested a solution to one. "Here's a salvage ticket. Get paint, boards, nails, and screws, and fix that wall, no charge, but once you have a good harvest in something, bring a tenth of it to share with those that may be in need."

She beamed. "I've no trouble doing that. It's only right, aye, and I'll see Joss comes to you this evening if that's suitable?" I indicated that it was. "She's over at McManus today, helping there. She'll be home by five, and she'll come by then."

We parted with mutual esteem, and I went home, had a word with Donal, who thought it a fine idea, and waited until there was a tap at the door that evening. Joss MacFiernan turned out to be a small slim girl who looked nowhere near twenty-three. Her black hair was in an almost waist-length plait, her skin was clear, and she moved like a cat, all balance. She was no great beauty, but I thought her intelligent, honest, and sensible, that'd do me any day – and she'd be a fine-looking old woman, she had the bones for it. I gestured to the kitchen table and the nearest chair.

229

"Come in, sit down and be welcome, Joss MacFiernan. I have a few questions to ask, and if you're happy to answer, you may be happier yet with what I may offer." I wasn't making any offers yet, I wanted to hear what she had to say, and I was pleased to see she asked no questions but sat composedly and waited.

"Your mother says you were for the Glasgow School of Art before things went bad."

"I was. I won a scholarship."

"You would have made art your profession?"

"I would. Dad said it would be a hard life, and I said life was as hard as you made it. I could have got work doing advertising or book illustrations and lived on that while I painted. When I made a name at that, I could let the other work go."

"And if you never could make a living selling your painting freelance?"

"I'd still have the other, better doing art of some sort than not. I'm no snob. It's what you make of it, and I've seen some fine work in those areas. I'd have painted as a hobby and maybe made a little on the side."

I thought that was both smart and sensible. A lot of artists cut off their nose to spite their face by refusing to compromise. "Were you well taught?"

She considered that carefully. "I believe so." I noticed she did not point out that she'd hardly been offered the scholarship had she not been well taught *and* showed further potential for improvement.

"Do you know if anyone here in the glens could continue to teach you or paints or draws?"

Joss shook her head slowly. "I know of no one." A quick urchin grin flashed out at me. "They do say artists are impractical; possibly few survived."

I smiled back companionably. "On the contrary, being impractical means you don't deal with a sore throat until it gets

230

so bad you need allodaxin. More artists may have survived – initially anyhow than you'd expect. So, I have a proposal. I want you to come with any group that goes out. Your specific job is to hunt for materials, canvases, paints, pencils, charcoal, art paper, anything of that sort. And when time allows, you sketch. If, on your return, you have the materials and feel the sketch is worth it, you do a painting from it in whatever medium suits you and the work or subject. You can sell paintings if others commission you for them."

Joss looked as if I'd just given her the keys to the kingdom. "You want me to find art supplies and paint, you mean as a job?"

"Yes."

"*Why?*"

"Because I am determined the glens will have a future," I said passionately. "There's a saying, those that don't remember the past are damned to repeat it. I want pictures. I want our descendants to *see* the ruined buildings, the bodies, us bringing salvage home because we could die without it. I want sketches showing Jamie's battle, the graves, *bairns* playing with a puppy, old folks with a cat, farmer milking a goat, a cow, Cheryl's alpacas, fruit being picked. I want scenes of glen life, and I want people to remember a thousand years from now, what we were, what we did, how we survived, and how we paid with lives, blood, sweat, and horror. And I want those then to know, so it never happens again."

Joss bowed her head, then straightened, and her eyes were fiercely proud. "If you'll trust me, I'll do it. There may be others better than me, but my great-grandmother was of this blood, and I'll not let it down. I'll waste nothing, give you nothing but my best, and honour Jamie's memory."

I took her hand. "I believe that. Now go home, we go out in the morning, Be here ready at ten. Bring bags to carry supplies you find and a handgun in case. Old clothes, you can get grubby foraging, and lunch in case you don't want to leave where you are."

She drained the last of her tea, ate the final scone in two bites, and took her farewell. I watched her across the glen and went inside, shutting the kitchen door while Donal, who was in the lounge, looked up at me. "I heard all that. You think she'll do?"

"Yes, but it put me in mind of something we'd discussed before the invaders came."

"I wondered, she put me in mind of that myself. You're thinking of Glasgow?"

I met his look. "I know it's far, but if we don't make the longer trips soon, the roads will have reached the point where we can't. So long as we can travel, we should. "

Donal inclined his head. "As you say, love. There'll be a plan or two that'll need to be made, but come early summer, we should go."

I hummed softly, his words reminded me of the song, and Donal began singing, not the old song as it was, but the song that it had come to be here...

> *I will go, I will go*
> *when the fighting is over*
> *to the land of the glens*
> *that I left to be a soldier*
> *I will go, I will go.*
>
> *When the virus came we*
> *were called all together*
> *those that led us saying,*
> *Brave lads and lasses*
> *Will you fight for our heather?*
> *I will go, I will go.*
>
> *Yes, we lived and we saved,*

Those we loved, all together,
Our glens have survived,
To grow purple yet in heather,
And we a people are,
Facing life together,
I will go, I will go
And returning stay forever
Bide with kin and friends
That I left to be a soldier…

We finished the song smiling at each other, sat up over dinner and then a wee dram, discussing what we should do come warmer weather, and went to bed where we did a little rejoicing in the truth of the song – and other things – before we slept.

****

The convoy went out the next day, Joss MacFiernan in the back seat of the Landcruiser with Ricky and Laddie beside me. Donal for once had stayed behind; there were things needed doing in Glen McManus, and he was directing what was in effect a working-bee dealing with half a dozen items that should be done *now*. Joss had taken my advice, I saw. Her clothing was whole but worn. She had on flat boots, a capacious shoulder bag, and her face was alit with excitement. I saw Ricky look her over as she came to the vehicle and something in that appraisal abruptly reminded me that he wasn't the twelve-year-old we'd taken in five years gone. I hid a smile.

"Joss, I've a mind to assign you an assistant. I want your mind on what you're to do, and you can't concentrate if you have to watch your back as well. Ricky, would you mind going with her and being her guard, you and Laddie?"

I received in return a thoughtful look from the boy. "I don't mind Gran Sheila, not if Joss is all right with me and Laddie tagging along?"

Joss laughed. "I like dogs, and a guard is a useful thing. Besides, I can maybe use a helping hand if heavy lifting needs doing."

Ricky grinned, flexed a bicep, and nodded. "Always happy to help a lady."

We parked up in the small town where we hadn't been before, and I scanned it. It had burned in one section. I saw blackened bones in the ruins, but much of it was unharmed save by the past five years' weather, and from where I sat, I could see at least one un-looted shop. I gave the signal, and our people exited the vehicles and scattered out in pairs or larger groups to salvage whatever could be found that would be of use to us.

I wasn't as casual as I'd appeared to be in choosing this town. It was a bus depot for several surrounding towns and had had schools – always a happy hunting ground for art supplies if not the expensive kind. But as well, it had had an art supplies shop. I parked only a block away and pointed Ricky in that direction. From where I now stood, watching our people diving in and out of shops and public buildings, I could see Ricky and Joss suddenly stop. He unhooked a short ram from over his shoulder, swung it at a door, and they vanished into the shop now open to them.

They were back in a few minutes—Ricky in the lead. "Gran Sheila, can you bring the Landcruiser? It'd be quicker. We found an art shop. It hasn't been touched, it's loaded with stuff, and Joss wants it all. Oh, and do you know where the schools were here? Joss thinks if we got whatever art stuff they had, we could start art classes at the glens."

"All that sounds good to me," I endorsed. "Hop in, and I'll drive down there." I parked outside the shop, left them to their salvaging – Laddie to his pursuit of several rats – and walked back and along to see what else we'd found.

Dan caught up with me. "Come and have a look at this. Not sure there's anything we can use, but I'm certain there's stuff there."

He'd found a pharmacy on the edge of the burned zone. The shop had burned, all down one wall and the front. Looters had emptied it, either before or after I couldn't tell, but at the back of the shop, there'd been a locked room. The door was solid, the lock was heavy-duty, and debris had fallen across it, so if the looting had been after the fire, it was probable no one had known the door was there.

I examined the lock. "You won't get that open in a hurry."

Dan laughed. "I wouldn't bother." He produced a small hacksaw. "The best method is not to attack the strongest point, but the weakest." He set his blade to the hinges, and in less than thirty minutes, the door could be lifted away, pivoting on the lock. I considered the room's contents and developed a wide smirk.

"Oh yes, I think we can use this." It was riches. Three walls' shelving held common remedies, elastic bandages of varying lengths and widths. Wound dressings, sticking plaster both in rolls and in packs. Pairs of steel scissors of assorted sizes, five commercial bottles of standard painkillers, packs of throat lozenges, an assortment of bottles of hand sanitizer, an entire bin of unwrapped soaps. I estimated there could be five hundred in that – and then my gaze reached the furthest wall.

"Allodaxin," I breathed. "The massive advantage of the new antibiotic was that it wasn't just better than anything before it. It was that even the first version had a shelf-life of twenty years. The second version, usable for thirty-plus years, had appeared only six weeks before the virus. Yes, we had some of the early one left, but I wanted all I could get, and this was the second version. Once it was gone, we'd have to go back to herbs and people dying of a cut that became infected.

I reached for the bag Dan offered and scooped all the packs into that. "We want everything, but I'll take this lot and lock it in the Landcruiser." Dan cleared his throat.

"You might want to keep looking?"

I saw where his gaze rested and agreed. Along with the antibiotic were heart and anti-stroke medication, the costly – and very effective types – preventatives against gout, kidney stones, diabetes - with a range of vaccines last. They, too, had an excellent shelf-life and would be useable for a decade or more.

I kept my voice calm with an effort. "Yes, pack everything on that wall first. It's to go in the Landcruiser trailer. Then pack up all the rest. That can go anywhere it'll fit, and someone has room, but remind them if anything happens to any of it, I won't be pleased." I left Dan and two of his friends who found us to complete the job and went searching again to see what had been uncovered. The trail led me to the schools. They, as was not uncommon, had been built on the town's outskirts. I found Miss Jane and Esme there, and they greeted me with enthusiasm.

"Look what we found."

It seemed that the principal had hobbies, or perhaps they had thought that the children should since there was a bookcase filled with "how-to" books, pottery, science projects, build your own telescope, and a line of other similar subjects, many of which I was sure no one knew about in our glens.

"Take them."

"We planned on it," Esme stated in a tone of *teach your grandmother*.

"Sorry."

"That isn't it, though." They marched me to a laboratory, opened the door, and displayed the contents. Chemicals. Fifty-litre glass containers of them, all marked both with their chemical symbols and common names.

I read my way down the line and nodded, keeping my face bland. "That is a valuable find. I'll leave it to you to pack and transport them. I authorize you to ask anyone to help, and have them take anything else at the schools you think we need or can use. In that order."

I walked back to the Landcruiser, thinking. I'm no scientist and never was, but I know a few things. One of them is how to make explosives. And apart from all the other uses for what Miss Jane and Esme had found, there was that in particular. Explosives deteriorate. Many army bases may have disposed of their stocks when they realised what was happening to the world. But chemicals would last longer in those glass carboys. We had only to make up a batch when required – and the ingredients that would make explosives were predominant in this room – probably why they were kept aside.

And I had a secret no one knew. Decades ago, when Donal had broken his leg in a silly stunt, I'd been at a loose end. Johnny was away with his parents – I can't recall now where – while Mac was studying and not interested. So I took my lunch, and one morning I went exploring. I climbed the hills into Blind Glen, went on over the hills behind that, and found another place there. A long valley that widened then narrowed again, and at the far end, it turned sharply, and through what was almost a hole in the wall, it let out on a tiny steep beach down to the sea. I came home with a secret and kept it, for what reason I couldn't tell you, save that it pleased me to know something the boys didn't.

One day I looked up the estate map in the McAlister home and found my valley. It was marked as "not worth cultivation," from the notes that went with it. I saw that it was fertile enough, but there was no suggestion whoever wrote them had known there was an opening at the far end, and it was stated because of the inaccessibility, it wasn't worth using as yet. I wondered if the entrance to the beach had come later than the notes, but I never asked. I grew older, spent time overseas in New Zealand, in Canada, and then in Somerset, and joined the army after that, working with Donal and our history went on together. And all of that time, the sea valley had lain in the back of my mind.

I remembered it as I'd seen it last, the steep climb from Blind Glen to there, and what use we could make of another sheltered glen that would be neither easily found nor attacked, one moreover with an outlet to the sea. The small gap in the cliff that led to the tiny beach was high above the waves, I thought it unlikely anything short of a truly massive storm would reach that far – and the entrance could be fortified.

And now, as the sight of those carboys had struck me, now between what we had in storage and what my friends had found at the school, I could be in a position to offer the glens something we hadn't had. A road by which we could travel that in the years to come would not disintegrate. A way to land unexpectedly, a way of voyaging, trading, exploring, and, I grinned at the thought, to go a-viking if we were so inclined, a way to strike against any that had shown themselves to be enemies. That would be if, or when, we found someone that knew what he was doing in that department. Yes, once our salvaging was done, I would finally talk to Donal about my secret.

CHAPTER NINETEEN

History – an account, mostly false, of events, mostly unimportant, brought about by rulers, mostly knaves, and by soldiers, mostly fools. ~Ambrose Bierce, *The Devil's Dictionary*

Aye, that's what the man said, and if Donal and I have anything to do with it, that's not what the history we'll leave the glens will be. It'll be truth, important to our people, with no rulers, just a couple of ordinary people, and as for soldiers, just now we're all those with few fools about of any profession – they don't survive that well. ~Sheila McArn

Joss painted once we were back. She painted the town where we'd been, showing the burned shops, our vehicles, and the whole buildings with our people in the foreground as we went from place to place. She titled it *Salvaging Life,* a clever pun. Once it was completed and fixative applied, it hung in the community hall, and I think everyone in the glens went to look at it. After that, she sketched anything that stayed still long enough, and if it didn't, she followed.

"People should have something. A time will come when there's nothing that'll work, just a sketch to remember someone. They should know what family looked like."

I agreed – yes, we still had digital cameras with working computers, but if the power failed, you'd lose everything – so she sketched. Walking around the glens, pencil or charcoal stick flying, now and again adding highlights in coloured pencils or chalks. The next painting was of a farm we visited. Cheryl had it on her list of Alpaca breeders, and we went that way because there was also a good-sized town towards the coast. We salvaged the town first, finding, to my delight, an entire untouched shoe shop that had been left locked up with a solid steel grid across the door and front window. It had shoes for all ages and both sexes, and we took every last item, including the steel grid, the mirrors, footstools, padded seats, and a huge sheepskin mat.

Then we went to the alpaca farm. I went into the house, breathed in, and nodded. "They'll be all dead. Go and look at the alpacas. Take whichever you want but nothing too old, poor quality, or neutered. We want productive animals." I got a look for that, but Cheryl bustled off in the direction of the occupied fields while I went inside, not noticing Joss on my heels. I'd been right about the dead. By now, I'd had more experience than I wanted, and I knew too where farmhouse bedrooms usually were and went directly there.

Behind me, Joss made a slight sound, a sort of sorrowing mixed with disgust, and I turned. "Yes, the dead stink. The doors and windows were all shut so no animals got to them. If they had, the place would smell sweeter. They're dead, but you're alive, which would you rather?"

She looked at me, saw it was a genuine question, and answered it. "Alive."

"Then remember it, mourn for those who died, then move on. Live, share, pass on what you are, what you know, and if possible, and it's your wish, your good genes, and your talents, and know the other half of that is what you see here." I grinned and quoted something I'd heard from my New Zealand friend, an old joke she'd told me. "The only thing we know for sure about life is that we don't get out of it alive."

Joss choked and started laughing. "I'll remember that. What do we do about – them?"

I sobered. "I have a policy. If we salvage what they had, we give them a decent burial."

Cheryl returned just then to report that there were seven suitable alpacas. I said, "Tell Dan and get them loaded. Is there anything else worth having in the outbuildings?"

"Usual gear, a real stack of bags of feed too, all okay, they were in a loft, and the stairs pull down, so nothing got to them, heavy plastic sacks, so the rats seem to have left them alone as well." She turned to go. "Oh, how about timber?"

"Good stuff?"

"Boarding, studding, looks fine…"

"I'll come and see." I did, and that was how we added a flatbed's worth of building timber, roofing iron, nails, roofing screws, tools, paint, and other items, all from an enormous barn where it had been sitting under cover. The owners may have intended to build something. Whatever they'd planned wasn't going to be small either, and it was all excellent salvage. I went back through the house. We were here now, and it would be foolish to ignore anything. Joss was behind me every step of the way, and I didn't mind. I wanted honest depictions of how we lived for those who'd come after.

I toured the house, adding good bedding from the linen cupboard. Unopened food from the kitchen – cans and packages have dates, and many things like flour, salt, and sugar last a long time past those anyway. Older tea, coffee, or hot chocolate can lose a little flavour, but it's still safe to drink. I sent Joss to look over two unoccupied bedrooms while I checked the one that was – well, occupied still in a way. The usual thing. Two older people, one younger, a woman from the clothing remnants, probably their unmarried daughter, or if married, her own family were already dead, and she'd come home to die with her kin.

I quietly opened drawers and cupboards. A full-length fur coat, two jackets, a man's knee-length leather coat of fine quality in the wardrobe. I stacked those ready to go. There were five longer dresses, velvet, silk velvet, and plain silk. Designer brands, worn only once or twice from its looks, and I added them to the pile. I gleaned from practise, overlooking nothing, and was done before Joss was finished. By the time she came back, I had what I had chosen in large suitcases in the hallway and looked over her selection.

"Nothing but bedding and pillows?"

She winced. "It feels like robbing the dead."

"No," I said gently. "It's not, Joss. Do you think these were good people?"

"Cheryl said their animals had been really well looked after. I guess they were,"

"If you were dead, but someone could ask you, if they said, may I take what you'll never need again, to help me and my kin and my children stay alive, would you say no?" Joss shook her head mutely. "Then you aren't robbing the dead, are you?"

She shook her head again and, without being asked, went back to the rooms and began bringing out the better furniture, items from their wardrobes. I moved my own selection to the deck outside to be collected and went back to the bedroom. There I shut the door behind me and bundled the bodies, talking to them softly.

"Thank you for all we are taking. We'll care for the alpacas that come with us. Their bloodlines will live on. We'll take the fur coats and jackets apart and remake them for winter. Ours aren't so bad now, but some people feel the cold. Your bedding and pillows will see to it good people sleep warm and comfortably. I've taken some of your jewellery, one set I'll wear and remember you." It was a lovely set of amethysts in sterling silver. I've always had a partiality for them as well as green garnets and opals. "The rest of it goes as tokens to our people who do something well. I don't know what form of religion you followed, but you'll be buried on your land, and we'll sing you to rest."

I'd just found the box containing important papers most kept somewhere, and I smiled as I read one. That we could indeed do for them; they'd have the very funeral they wanted. I finished bundling the bodies securely and went out to make arrangements – for those who had been proud Scottish Nationalists and members of the clan McLeod.

We buried them deep, and with them, I buried their papers in another box I found in one of the sheds. I thought it possible that the contents might survive a very long time with the small box inside the larger airtight one. If anyone from the future found the grave, they'd know who lay there.

And once we were done, we gathered there, laid flowers, and sang the songs of Scotland, concluding with the original version of *I Will Go*. I spoke a few words, as did some of our people, several of who recited Burn's poems, and we ended with *Scotland the Brave* that was not so much sung, as hurled in the face of the fates that had given us what had been wanted, a free Scotland, but at the expense of millions of lives, a price none of us would have found acceptable had we been asked. We drove away, Joss content with the myriad of sketches she'd done, Ricky pleased with his guardianship, and Laddie simply happy to be with his humans.

Joss's painting showed all the starkness of that bedroom. It was dark, little clear detail, although you could make out the bed and the pitiful bodies, but behind it was a great window. Through that, you saw our people, Cheryl leading a mother alpaca with her cria, Ricky, with Laddie bouncing and barking, as the boy carried paint cans to a waiting flatbed, and behind them others, all busy, some laughing. You could see they were exchanging jokes and making light work out of hard. She titled the painting *Death – and Life*. I hung it in the medical centre, and again everyone came to see it.

She did another painting on that one's heels, asking me beforehand of the subject's character. I had shown her a photograph, taken when Donal and I had returned permanently to the glen. It was of the four of us in our sixties, with Jamie Tamman – eleven years older than our quartet – and had been taken by Janet.

"Why did he really attack the invaders, do you think?"

I did my best to explain, and she listened, her eyes on my face as I talked, recalling Jamie in that instant when he rose to fight and die – like a wolf, his teeth in the foes' throat. I did *not* tell her something only Jamie Tamman and I had known. That his heart had begun to fail, and Jamie could never have endured lying in bed. It was a professional secret, and while I knew it had had its place in his decision, it had not been everything. If it were to be known, people would make assumptions, and I would not have them think the less of his pride and courage. Nor had I retained my medical notes.

That was the painting Joss called *Scotland the Brave*. It showed a kilted Jamie Tamman, claymore raised as he charged, his mouth open in a shout of defiance, white hair blowing wildly. The enemies he faced were men in modern clothing, stained and ragged, their faces twisted in savage sneers, guns in their hands as they advanced. Above them, the skies were grey clouds, but the sky was blue above Jamie, and he was lit with faint sunshine. The grass under his flying feet showed a brighter green, the sheen on his blade a brighter grey. The picture was painted on a slant, so you saw both sides, and someone behind him held up the Scottish Flag so that it blew in the wind.

Joss kept that one, and I was happy she should. It glorified a bloody sorrowful mess, and I thought that war should never be counted as something wonderful – although the truth is too, that I shall never forget Jamie and his shout of "*Ith mo chac ye blaigeard!*" (Which I shall not translate for any that do not have the tongue.) His death had been so very Jamie, and while I mourned his passing. It would become a legend, that I knew. I sighed. I know what war is, and still ... that charge was something I could never forget.

****

And a week after we returned, I spoke to Donal, asking him to rise early next morning and come with me for the day, asking no questions. My husband chuckled and agreed. So it was that we left Gen Mhairi on the tricycles at first light the next day, took them the length of our glen, down Blind Glen to where the hills reared behind and left them there, to climb obliquely along the faint thread of track I thought to be made by deer. And when we stood at the far side looking down to the sea glen, Donal whistled softly.

"Another glen here; I'd never known that. How did you find it, lass?" I told the story and he laughed. "All this time, you've kept silent. Ah, but I can see why, a good secret is a warmth to the soul. How we opened up Blind Glen was in your mind?" I nodded. "Aye, it'd be a major job, but I think it's possible. It'd add to our lands, and as you say, the place is almost unfindable and difficult to access even was it known. The work is the only drawback. Everything else I see is an advantage. Let's be away, and tomorrow we can talk to some of those that have done such work."

That we did, and in a discussion a week later, it was decided that we would break down the section of hills between Glen Mhairi and Sea Glen. Jack Wistal was the voice for that. He'd been from a family with not much money, so he'd spent his days on a road gang and his night studying to be a civil engineer. He'd completed about three-quarters of the degree when the world fell apart, and now he was of invaluable use to the glens. He'd lived in Thurston, having been known by Miss Jane, who'd told us where to find him and what to offer. Now Jack was our Public Works Manager, proud of his title and what he was accomplishing. He had a Shetland Sheep Dog named Bonny, who went everywhere with him, which was how he'd known Miss Jane.

"I looked at the old map you told us of, and look here," he traced his finger down a sketch Joss had made of that for him. "If you walk over the hill, you go best there from the end of Blind Glen, but a ravine runs back from Sea Glen and into the hill at the end of Mhairi. It runs deep, and if we break through there, it's half the work. It should be done now, while we have the machines, the fuel, and the explosives."

Dan winced. "I'm for that. I'm no ancient Egyptian to be building pyramids with a pick and shovel. Although in this case, it's reverse and we're tearing down, still, running a bulldozer is easier either way."

We agreed, grinning at that. Jack laid out plans, marked the place we'd begin, and as the autumn was mild and winter looked likely to be the same, we started then and there. We ran out of the explosives found in Glen McManus when we were two-thirds of the way, and it was there the glass carboys of chemicals came into their own. We blew even larger holes in that hill until we broke into the Sea Glen ravine. Our people came running when word spread and marvelled at the glen unknown before now. With machines, we cleared the way, making it wide enough for a lorry, but at the intersection between the glens, we began a gatehouse and a massive wall. If invaders ever came, we would not make it easy for them to reach one glen from another – and Glen Mhairi was our heart.

Donal oversaw that with our Public Works Manager and made certain. "I want slots deep into the cliff at each end of the wall. The wall goes right into the cliff then, together with its concrete reinforcement, and leaves no weakness." I knew he was remembering how we had broken into Glen McManus and agreed.

246

So it was done, and then we trenched in the flatter areas at the glen sides. In spring, we would plant fruit and nut trees, and in a section of the ravine which could be closed off, we would plant berry bushes where livestock could not damage the growth. A bay into the cliff in that section was five acres, and I planned to cultivate that with potatoes in spring. The winter was mild as hoped, and we had the work done before the real cold came. We settled in then, proud of what we'd accomplished and knowing that there was room for expansion at need.

Donal sat back one evening and spoke to me of that. "It's why we should go to Glasgow. We need people, and we need enough interested that we can pick and choose. We've five glens since we opened Sea Glen, and a properly worked self-sufficient glen can support from two to nine hundred depending on the glen's size and fertility."

"I know," I said thoughtfully. "Our glens' land is fertile, particularly Mhairi, Blind Glen, and Johnny's. None are small, and with climate change, the winters are warmer and things grow that would never have done so three or four generations back and this far north. How many people do you think the five glens would support all year round?"

"Two and a half thousand," Donal stated after a pause. "A run of good years, and we'd be all right with more. That's with the lands we have, but not all years will be good."

"And we're just over twelve hundred," I said ruefully. "Yes, we need Glasgow – we should go back to Edinburgh too. Drive it as a triangle."

"It's what you said a year or so back. While we have the roads, while we have the fuel, we need to salvage for supplies, livestock, and people, and we *canna* sit back and rest until we ha' what's needed."

Donal earnest tends to be Donal going braid Scots, and I smiled affectionately at him. Tai, who had joined us and was on my lap, brought up a paw and patted my hand. I hugged him gently, and he purred. That reminded me. "Something else, there's Ricky."

"What about the lad?"

"Two things, one is that he's eighteen soon. That's an important age. We should have a good party for him."

"What's the other thing?"

I hid a grin. Donal wasn't going to like that one. "He's started seeing Alex."

My husband sat up. "Wee Alex Yarrow, the redhead?"

"Aye, and if I'm not mistaken, it's serious. So you'll have to have the *talk* with him."

Donal groaned. "No, no, anything but the *talk*."

"'Fraid so, he was barely twelve when he came to us, and he needs to hear things in plain language. Claire took in the Yarrow children, so I'll talk to her in the morning. We've supplies for that sort of thing for a generation, but after that, any *talks* may have to be stern. Alex is only a few weeks younger than Ricky, and if they get careless…"

Donal gave me a pawky grin. "If they get careless, we could be adding to that needed population sooner than you approve." I nodded. "Aye, I'll talk to Ricky; you see Alex."

I called on Claire the next day, and she was reassuring. "I saw it start, but you remember the trouble Alex had with that man who worked for the family." I remembered. "It's left her gun-shy. As soon as I saw which way the wind blew, I spoke to her. She said she liked Ricky, but … I told her 'but' has a habit under pressure of turning into 'maybe,' then 'yes' when she's more feeling than thinking. We talked that over, and she's on the pill in case. She says she won't, and I believe she won't – not for a while yet. But you know girls."

"I was one once," I said dryly.

"So was I," Claire said, still more dryly. "That's why she's on the pill now."

248

I turned the conversation to Ricky's birthday and the expedition to Glasgow. Claire was happy to help with one and didn't want to join the other.

The party was a huge success, Laddie was sick from all the titbits, and Ricky was gratified to find we now treated him as an adult and brought him in on policy discussions. With spring, we planted in Sea Glen – including those five acres of potatoes – and with early summer, plans were made and actions put in train for the expedition.

CHAPTER TWENTY

If you are careful of your men and camp on hard ground, the army will be free of disease of every kind, and this will spell victory. ~Sun Tsu, The Art of War

In which he was right, we went further. All our people were vaccinated against everything we thought likely – if we had the vaccine – and I'd found an untouched pharmacy that had just begun a special sale on multivitamins. I started everyone going to Glasgow on those a week beforehand, and they stayed on them until we returned. ~Sheila McArn

The drive was slow and tedious. We stopped in towns that showed any hint of life and looked for people there. We found some, many desperate and willing to listen. To those we thought would fit into glen life, we suggested they pack. We'd return and ask if they were of the same minds still, and if so, they could join us.

By now, in the sixth year after the virus, survivors tended to have split into three main types. There were the families, by blood or necessity, which trusted each other, had each other's backs, and could mostly, I thought, be trusted to have ours in the glens if or when, they joined us. There were loners. Mostly men but a few women, who could manage on their own, didn't much like people, and had settled in a place they could fortify, stocked that, and enjoyed the solitude, the lack of nine to five, and the adrenalin rush of life as it now was. Then there was the third group. Predators, ranging from thick as porridge to lethal because some didn't care if it were you or them that died.

We reached Glasgow two days after starting and found it dead. Almost the entire city had burned. We stood on an eminence that overlooked most of it and stared, Donal and I, hard-eyed in disbelief.

"What in *taigh na galla happened* here?" Donal asked as he stared at the devastation.

I eyed him. "They had a fire," I offered ironically.

Donal was serious. "They had more than one." He pointed. "Look here. There's green stuff starting to grow again. But look over there; that was recent." He registered what he'd said and spun on a heel, calling orders. "Everyone out of sight. Get those engines running and follow me." He was into the Landcruiser, I dived into the passenger seat, and we were backing off the rise, down the street to turn and away, angling across the fringe of the city and toward a road that was wide, but not the main one.

Belatedly. I realised what I should have seen. That if the city was being burned section by section, that *could* just be by intent. And if someone was organised enough to be doing it and thought they had a reason, we might also be a target. Donal drove, keeping to a speed that would give us time to brake, accelerate, or dodge down a side street. We'd come via Lenoxtown, through Bishopbriggs, and now we were entering the heart of the city, we could see it too was burned.

We circled, finding every place we looked was empty or destroyed – or both in some places where there'd been sufficient left for us to see that was so. It wasn't until we were near the Botanical Gardens that I saw someone, then a second person. I nudged Donal.

"Slow down and pull over. There's people. I think if we don't scare them off, we could learn something." One advantage of being older, people are less likely to be frightened of you, and once out in the street, I whistled Laddie. He came bouncing happily as always, and from the shrubbery, I heard a giggle. I glanced in that direction and laughed. "I know, he'd got more energy than three cats," Another giggle, and a woman's amused voice.

"He'd not have to have much to beat that."

"True," I agreed. "I'm Sheila, the dog is Laddie, my grandson's dog, and this great lump here is my husband, Donal. We came down to see how much of the city is left and if there's anyone that'd like a safer place where no one starves."

A scrawny woman moved half a step from cover. "You army?"

"Not any longer, but I was a paramedic with them for thirty years."

"You know medical stuff?"

"I do. Are any of you sick?" I found I'd asked a silly question. Rona, the skinny lady, was sick, her daughter was too, and so was a steady trickle of people who came as word got around. I treated for rat bites, infected flea bites, malnutrition, heart trouble, bones broken and never properly set, and a multitude of human problems, some of which boiled down to "everyone around me died, and I'm having trouble coping."

Once the sick parade was over, it was almost evening, and Rona, who'd been sitting on a low wall watching events, stood up. "I know a place if you want. Used to be a good hotel, it's empty now, but it hasn't burned down."

We went there and she was right. It had been a good hotel once, and while, by empty, she'd meant that there wasn't a drop of alcohol in the place, that didn't matter to us. Rona, her daughter, Annie, and three others stayed. We invited them to dinner, and there was no doubt about their enthusiasm for a well-cooked meal, which included meat, a dessert, and tea, coffee, or hot chocolate to go with those. They ate politely but with a speed that suggested food shortage, and I asked about that once they'd slowed down.

Rona laughed harshly. "Druggies. There was a proper epidemic of sore throats month before the dying. So a lot had it and survived. They started looting hospitals soon as the law was gone, and when some of them were high, they set fires. Once they ran out of hospitals, they started on doctor's surgeries, dentists, vets, and with some of the stuff they found, it killed them, other stuff sent them crazy, and there were more fires."

Annie nodded. "They'd end up burning down whole blocks, didn't care if there were supermarkets, they went too. Once they got as far as surgeries, well, some of those were in doctor's houses, so they killed them if they couldn't say where there were more drugs. Course most are gone now, druggies, I mean, but there's still some, you watch for them, kill you soon as look at you." That had all come out with little pause between sentences. Now she reached for the cup of hot chocolate I'd refilled.

Her mother nodded when I raised my eyebrows at her. "'S true. Wish it wasn't, but who's left, we're starting to get desperate. They burned down so much an' it's still going on. If we find food, we take it home as much as we can before anyone sees. If it's more than any few of us can manage, we send the word out and everyone comes. We put it in places that won't burn, but often that's 'cause they're damp and the food goes rotten. Now and again, we can't find anything for two, three days."

I didn't need an expansion on that. If there was no food to be found, they went without. That explained almost everyone I'd seen being so thin, and it explained most of the sickness I'd seen; that and the "druggies" burning down what was probably most of the pharmacies as well once they'd had everything *they* regarded as usable out of them.

Rona had been darting quick looks at us since she and Annie sat down. "Don't look like there's a food shortage where you come from?"

"No," Donal said. "We've land, we raise crops, we've livestock, and we hunt, so there's meat aplenty eggs and milk too.

253

We have barns for storage and them full of clothing, footwear, medical supplies, and weapons. We're forted up where we are. Last lot that came to take what we had, we were generous. They each got a bit of land."

There was silence while that sank in, and Rona started laughing. It was genuine laughter, all of them laughing then until tears ran down their faces. One of them, a man in his early thirties, I thought, with a scar almost bisecting his face, nodded to Donal.

"That's the way to deal with that sort." His voice went wistful. "Don't suppose you'd have room for a mostly-trained vet?"

"We would," I told him. "Name. qualifications, circumstances?" I barked the queries, and to my approval, he gave answers, not questioning I was female nor that I had the right to ask. A sensible man, seeing that antagonising possible saviours was *not* the way to go.

"Dave McPherson, cousin to Annie here, Rona's my aunty. My dad was a vet. Druggies came a few weeks after things went bad. I was in training, year to go, but I'd been in and out of Dad's surgery all my life. I was away scavenging when they came. Like Annie said, they took anything the vets had, then killed them if they couldn't show where there was more. Dad died quickly."

He looked sick. "I got back and found him and mum. She'd been … they'd … she died just after I got there, but she managed to tell me, describe them. I found them later. Killed every last one. Then I went looking for aunty and found her and Annie. They lost most of their family too, so we teamed up. I've been saying we should get out of here."

Another man sitting quietly beside them agreed. "So I've said, but people who live in a city their whole life, they're feared to go into the country."

I smiled at him. "That's right enough. They don't think they'll manage. But if they had a house, land, and people to show them what to do, to help them with food to start, they'd manage fine, others have."

The five visitors exchanged glances, and Rona spoke for them. "If you'd be interested in taking us, we'd be interested to go. Oh, and these two are brothers, friends of Davie's."

After that, it was long discussions. Rona knew a lot of those in the area. They came in and talked to us. I treated them where I could and where what they had was treatable. I asked for nothing, but now and again, one would offer payment anything from information up to a kitten. I accepted mostly – the kitten going to Alex's sister Ann, who didn't have a cat and wanted one.

Dave came running into the hotel the day after that. Donal and I had just crossed the lobby and were almost at the door when he rocketed in. "Druggies, they're coming."

Donal caught his shoulder. "Numbers, direction, weapons, do they know about us?"

Dave took in a quick deep breath. "Couple of dozen, from that way," He pointed. Weapons, mostly guns, don't know if they know about you or not, and they'll be here in maybe ten minutes unless something else attracts them away."

I began to smile. "Donal, you do what you do best. I'll decoy them away a while."

I dived for our room, snatched up items, and was back outside in seconds. I had the Landcruiser keys, and I was into the seat and gone while I heard Donal's shout. He wasn't addressing me, so I kept going.

I met the druggies, they met me, and I spun the vehicle in a U-turn, then, using all my skill, I allowed it to give the impression my turn had done something to the engine. It coughed, spluttered, and with them emitting screams of excitement, I stayed barely ahead, veering in a half-circle. I skidded, and allowed the door to fly open and bottles of pills to bounce out; then I slammed the door shut and took off. I looked in the rear mirror at the end of the street, and if anyone had seen it, they'd have thought my grin evil.

I had a good reason for that. I turned a corner, circled back to the hotel, and rejoined our people, who were lined up ready. Donal surveyed me. "Everything fine?"

"Very."

"How long?"

"Half an hour. Then about a day, more time depending."

Donal gave orders. Two of our people peeled off to keep an eye on the enemy, while Dave eyed me with fascination.

"You did something?"

"I did." I agreed uninformatively.

"Um, is it a secret?"

I lost it and shrieked with laughter. "I gave them pills."

He, his cousin, aunty, and several others present looked bewildered. "Um," Dave explained to me as if I was a little thick. "That's what they want, pills. It'll just make them keener on finding you and getting more."

Donal chuckled deeply. "You forget my Sheila's a paramedic. What did you give them, love?"

My grin widened. "Purgatives."

Dave stared then whooped. "That's what you were talking about. Half an hour and about a day. Half an hour for the pills to hit them, and a day to get over what happens, more depending on health and how many pills." He sobered. "They'll know you did that on purpose, and once they're back on their feet, they'll come gunning for you."

His aunty stepped in and explained. "Yeah, and by then, we'll either be gone or something will be done about them." And to Donal and me. "Which is it?"

I looked at my husband, he looked back, and we both understood our preference. There were some good people here still. Donal nodded. "If they come looking for us after that, we'll take it amiss," he said quietly. "Dave, you said there were around two dozen?"

"That's how many I saw."

I spoke quietly. "They've amalgamated then because, by the time they were fighting over the pills, I saw closer to forty."

"They're like rats," Annie said in disgust. "See one, and there's always more. Would there have been enough pills for all of them?"

"I took five bottles full. Each had fifty pills," I informed her. "I unscrewed the lids, so they'd come off as they rolled out of the Landcruiser. The pills spread all down the road."

"So everyone should get one or two," Dave mused. "What if someone got a lot?"

I answered clinically. "They're heavy-duty. One pill, and it'll take twenty-thirty minutes to work. One pill and the patient will vomit moderately, sufficient to clear anything eaten in the past three or four hours. Two pills, and they vomit comprehensively as well as getting diarrhoea. If they take a large amount, anything over three or four, it could be an unfavourable outcome if they have weak hearts, are prone to a stroke, or are medically unfit in some other way."

Dave gaped, then flung back his head and howled. "A day, medically unfit? They won't come looking for anyone for a month."

Donal eyed him. "Druggies, lad. I wouldn't take any bets on it."

In which he was entirely right. It took them longer, but it took us longer than we'd hoped as well. Rona came back the next day with news that a group living on the west side of the gardens was interested. I'd have suggested we come back another year but for their professions. They were what remained of eight families who had been related or close friends and included a junior English teacher, two nurses, a dental hygienist, a master carpenter, and to my suppressed amusement, a sewage inspector. I wasn't sure what we'd do with that last, but I could find immediate employment for the other five. The rest, who were – so Rona swore – all good people, would be useful too.

I drove over with her, talked to them, and agreed. They had pets, and I had to relieve their anxiety over whether those would be welcome too, and once they heard their cats and dogs could come, along with two canaries, a budgie, a tortoise, and three white mice, they started packing. We could go to them, but they wouldn't be ready to leave until the next day – and upped time taken by talking a third group they'd met a time or two.

"Deaf," one of this bunch informed me. "She had some disease as a kid. Went deaf, but she talks okay, and she lipreads as well as knowing sign language. Her sis is fine. They've got five kids between them. She used to look after the lot while her sis and the husbands worked. Women and kids got that sore throat you were asking about. Husbands died. The sister goes out scavenging, and four of the kids are old enough to go with her. Deaf one stays home with the rest of their kids. I ran into the sister the other day, told her what Rona told me. She said she'd like to come if you're okay with the sister."

I'd been evaluating as she talked. The sister had likely had measles. Heaven alone knew how; everyone'd been vaccinated for a decade. The main thing was that her deafness wasn't hereditary. It would do no harm to look at them, two women, seven children, and they'd survived six years, so they were competent. But it was another holdup, and by the time we'd added them, if we did, any druggies who had survived my donation to their cause would be starting to look for us with unpleasantness in mind.

****

I found the deaf woman and her kin to be all a glen could wish for. Apart from anything else, all of them knew sign language, something useful in both stalking wild game and when trouble came. Right now, we might have radio transmitters in the vehicles, plus handheld radios, but they wouldn't last forever. A way of talking silently – if many learned it – would last. I left them packing and went back to Donal, who was listening to one of the handhelds with a bland expression on his face. I know that look.

"They're coming?"

"Aye. Dan thinks a number died, but they've found others. It looks as if we've drawn every druggie in the city. From some of what he's heard, they aren't counting the deaths as down to us, but from the potency of what you lost from the car."

I said something regrettable. "In other words, they think we have more and want it."

"That'd be it."

"So we fight?"

"Aye," Donal said placidly. "Not that it'll be so much of a fight."

In that I had to agree. In some of his original army missions Donal faced odds of ten to one. On this expedition we'd brought just on a hundred and fifty of our people. At most we faced odds of two to one in our favour. Our people were well-armed and knew how to use what they had. The past six years we'd welded a core of them into a genuine fighting force and, usefully, many of those who'd been children six years ago had now grown up with bows. All types. Crossbows, pistol crossbows, long bows, and the shorter re-curve bow of the rider. *And* they could use them.

"Bow ambush to start?" I queried. Donal nodded. "Then guns," I concluded, "You plan to wipe them out, all of them."

"It's reasonable, and any folk still here will have a better chance. We can't fix everything, love, but where I can do something that costs us little, I think it right to act."

I wasn't arguing. In the past six years, I'd done some of that myself. Come to think of it, any of the dead druggies were down to me, I'd used medical knowledge to kill them, and I admit to no sorrow in the doing of it. "When?" I glanced around.

"Five minutes, no less and not much more."

The handheld cleared its throat, murmured a number, and announced it would now go silent. I moved into cover, looking where Donal was watching and seeing a movement at the end of the road. I unsnapped my holster, took out the gun I carried and waited.

They came then, not in silence, not stealthily, not in any way as I'd expected without considering what we faced. Instead, they came down the street, in a loose pack, some running faster, some half-staggering, and as they ran, they screamed threats, insults, demands for what we had, and some just howled like dogs. They were armed – if you could call it that – with weapons. Knives, iron or steel bars, guns of all descriptions, and one, to my amusement, with a scythe. A miracle if he hurt anyone with that but himself. One at the rear fell. Then another and another, and I saw the beauty of Donal's plan. He had them in a crossfire, killing those at the back as they ran on oblivious, making so much noise they could hear no cries from those who fell.

It worked. By the time the attackers reached where we waited, half of them lay in a line down the street, most unmoving, one or two twitching still – which usually attracted a second arrow in it was more than minor. The leader, a man who would have been massive, had he not been wasted almost to bones, halted when Donal stepped out. His arms were crossed, and I knew he had a gun held along one arm. I'd seen him do that before in other times and places where his ability to shoot would be underestimated.

The big leader stared. "Come oot yer hole tae gi' us what we want, hae ye?" The accent rendered his words almost unintelligible even to me. They were slurred, a parody of the Scottish tongue, possibly because he had no teeth as I now saw. I moved slightly, and he saw me. "Yer th' one as has it. *Gi' it tae us, ye piseag*, else…" He explained what he'd do to me, lingering on the details. Without speaking, Donal shot him dead.

His followers stared blankly before a small man behind screamed and charged. I shot him, Donal and I stepped back behind an entrance column, and our people opened up. It was a slaughter. We were under cover, and we knew what we were doing. They were fighting mad, so drugged they felt neither pain nor fear, and they kept coming. All they wanted was our drugs in their hands, their teeth in our throats. I shot the last of them as he reached for me and only realised as he fell he'd have been no older than Ricky.

I'd put two bullets into him, and he wasn't quite dead. I bent over him cautiously, and his eyes opened to look up. "Kill me!" His voice was a quiet demand, and I could see that balanced between the shock and pain and the drugs he'd taken, he was momentarily lucid. "Kill me!" He ordered again, and I felt a huge rush of pity. His voice was that of an ordinary lad, even an educated one.

"Why?" Was I asking why he wanted to die or how he'd come to this? I didn't know, but he answered the latter and within that lay the other answer too.

"They all died. Everyone. I asked people for help, and they ignored me. I was starving, so I stole food. Killer found me, took me in, gave me drugs so I didn't feel so bad, didn't miss my family." His gaze shifted to the big man, and an eerie half-smile came and went.

"He was the only one who helped. He told me he was a bad man, but he wasn't into kids. Wouldn't let anyone else hurt me. But with hospitals, he could take anything he wanted, and he wanted it all. Then there was less to find. We got word there were new people with the stuff. Killer said we'd have it off you. Guess he was wrong. Is he dead?"

"Yes," I told him. "One shot. He wouldn't have felt it."

"Good. He was decent to me. Kill me, missus, there's no more drugs, my family an' Killer are gone. Let me go with them." His voice was down to a whisper as he bled out. There would be no need for anything further. I took his hand and held it, he smiled at me, and in that final expression, I saw everything he'd been once – before the virus came. And as he died, I wept for a civilization lost, for the dead, the abandoned, those we would never find or aid, and behind me, Donal laid a hand on my shoulder.

"We'll bury them together, lass. As the boy said, his friend was nae so bad."

We tossed all the bodies but two into a collapsed cellar and caved in the ruins over them. Killer and the boy we took to an overgrown park and buried them there, deep, with broken concrete piled above them, and Ricky playing a lament on his smallpipes. It may have seemed odd or foolish to some that we should treat well the bodies of two druggies who'd come to rob and murder us, but we did so, and I was not the only one who'd heard what the boy had said or the only one that cried for innocence lost.

I'd had no name for the boy, and I doubted his friend had been christened "Killer." But Ricky, who could be kind and sensitive, found a tin of black paint and a plank. Alex found a brush, and they carefully lettered a line I knew they'd seen in a churchyard where some lay who'd been unidentifiable bodies washed up by the sea. *"Known only to God,"* it said, and Donal laid a length of flowering branches beneath the words.

We returned to our convoy, collected those we'd offered a home, and drove out of the ruined city. I looked at it in the rearview mirror, not knowing if we'd ever return. We'd had the best of it, killed the worst of it, let the city die in peace. It'd be a tale, then forgotten, until a people rose again to go out in search of new places. Maybe then they'd find the ruins and marvel at what their ancestors had done.

In Edinburgh, where Donal had decided we should also go since we'd come so far, we found those who remembered some of the people who'd joined us and were now willing to follow suit. One of them directed us to what had been an alpaca farm, and we saved all of those we could, all in shades of brown. We added, too, a girl who came to see us and who'd lived nearby, the only one of her family, good with animals and needing a home. Cheryl added *her* to the flock too and drove off, looking just a trifle smug.

We salvaged even as we interviewed and talked to people, listening to what they knew and adding more of the things we would be long in making ourselves. One of the couples took us aside and talked to us alone.

"We both worked in a laboratory. We can take you there if you want. When this started, the boss said he'd heard it could be very bad, so he sent us home, paid an advance, said we should get it in cash, should get food, first aid stuff, and a gun and ammo."

"Did you?" I asked.

"He was a smart man, he had friends, and he knew people, we believed him. That's what got us through. But the thing is, Tommy may still be there, in the labs."

We went there, and he was. It took persuasion, but on the outskirts of Thurston, there'd been a private laboratory where advanced studies were done. He knew of it, and we were able to tell him that the small complex had survived. Our people packed everything he wanted – with him watching every move and screaming to be careful. We added more recruits, stuffed every vehicle with salvage, and lined up.

Donal stood up on the Landcruiser door edge where he could be seen and waved in a circular motion that ended up pointing forward. I giggled. Too many westerns. I touched the accelerator. We moved forward, Donal dropped into his seat beside me, and Ricky and Alex in the back seat with Laddie between them cheered. We were going home.

CHAPTER TWENTY-ONE

East, west, home's best. ~Old saying

And none the worse or less truthful for the banality of it. ~Donal
McArn

Once home, it was busy all the way. It took summer and
autumn to sort out homes, school, and work for those we'd taken
in, and there were many. Cheryl brought the girl she'd taken under her wing to our house and introduced her as Meli, short for
what I had no idea and didn't ask, but it was clear they worked
well together. Apart from that, we'd stopped twice on the return
journey to collect people who'd let us know they would like to
join the glens, and we'd brought back over two hundred folks.
Not all fitted in. We took those that didn't to Thurston, where
Tommy Branson – no relation to another man of that surname –
had taken over the laboratory there. It came with a large house,
and we fitted that out with his possessions and more acquired
from properties nearby.

He took on staff, and they settled to working out ways to
retain or regain some of the amenities of civilization. We had a
rotating team that salvaged and brought them all they needed so
that if they had no money, they still lived warm, dry, and well-
fed. An investment in the future, Donal called it, and I was in
agreement. The winter was harder than the one before. Still,
we'd prepared, and we thrived. Donal and I talked during that
quiet time and made a decision. Then we called in Ricky.

He came looking worried. "You both all right?"

"Yes," I told him. "It's just time to discuss a few things." He looked relieved and sat watching us while I began.

"I don't know if you were ever told how old Donal and I am?" He shook his head slowly, and I nodded. "We were both seventy when you came to us. Donal's half a year the older, and now he's just turned seventy-seven, and I will shortly. Life makes no allowances for people, Ricky. We were old when the virus came. Yes, we're fit still, and we come of long-lived kin, but we won't last forever, and there's no way of knowing when, how, or if it'll be slow or fast that we die."

Donal took over. "If we have time, as we hope, we want to spend some of that seeing you become the Clan McAlister leader when we're gone."

I smiled at the reaction. First, a tinge of surprise, then a movement of his shoulders, as if he settled for a load he knew he could carry. "You lead naturally. Those around your age already look to you. Those younger look up to you. We think you'll do fine," Donal assured him.

"You guessed some of this," I commented. "We could live another fifteen or twenty years, but if not, we want you known and accepted as our heir. Read this." I handed him the deed to Glen Mhairi and Johnny's Glens, and once he'd read that, I met his gaze.

"You've heard about Mac and Johnny. Johnny McAlister was Laird of Glenrae, that's the real name of his glen, but we use his forename for it now. He and Mac and Donal and I were children together, we loved and trusted one another, and when he knew he and Mac had the virus, that his two children and their families were overseas and would likely never make it home, he gave us that. We'd sworn to keep the glens safe until one of the old blood returns. If they never do, we're sworn to the glens, to lead, to care for them, to protect them, and to uphold their laws."

"And if I become the leader, I should do the same," Ricky said. "I can do that."

"And have whoever becomes the leader, in turn, swear also," Donal said quietly. "It's a sacred trust, an oath before the graves of the men that gave the glens a chance to survive. Without them, many more of us would have died, they sent us home with the knowledge, the drugs, the information we needed to make it through, and we have. We owe a great debt that must be repaid by each leader, in turn, taking the oath – and keeping it. It's not only words. It's something they must know bone-deep. Protect the glens and the people and keep the law. Keep it for themselves as well as asking that of the people."

Ricky nodded deeply, almost a bow. "I'll do it. When do we tell – them?"

"At the spring telling."

And so we did. We went, as had become the custom since we brought Johnny and Mac home to where they lay, and in spring, the day after the first flowers showed on the cherry trees in Johnny's Glen. At his and Mac's grave, Donal spoke. He told of the events since the previous spring, of new people, the development of Sea Glen, our trip to the cities, and the smaller events here, of crops, and livestock and new babies. It was in some sense the sort of report a man might make to his landlord. Donal spoke as if to a cherished friend, and it was the more touching for it.

He finished, and I stepped forward a pace and addressed those I remembered, old and dear friends, who I missed and would miss all my days. "Before you died, you gave us a deed and a *geas*. That we should hold the glens." I read the deed slowly, and those that had not heard it before listened with interest.

"Until the old blood comes again if that shall ever be," I added softly. "We know that unlikely now, and we to whom you gave this are no longer young." I wasn't naming myself or Donal as *old*, not for anyone. "We think it wise that we should choose an heir to carry the *geas*, to hold the deed and the word, and the glens and their people, and so we have chosen Ricky Black, who

266

has chosen to be, from this day on, to be known as Ricky Black McArn, as our heir and inheritor. Let you look on him, and if anyone knows a reason he should not lead after us, say so now."

There was a vast deep silence that seemed to echo, broken by Janet. "Aye, a good choice. I'll follow the lad when his time comes." Others called their agreement which swelled into a roaring acclamation, and I saw hints of red on Ricky's cheekbones, and under the noise, I bade him to remember this minute when the people's whining and demands fretted him past sanity. He grinned.

So we came back with an heir established and were promptly deluged with all the minor problems that five glens, Thurston town, and the surrounding countryside, could produce. That began with an announcement from May Cameron as she arrived on my doorstep and gasped the information while I was still in my dressing gown.

"The Rosses are back. They want Ruth. They want to stay, they've others with them."

I groaned. "Tell me everything new you know about any of them."

It wasn't a lot. I already knew about the Rosses. They were related to the Camerons via marriage, but not by blood. They had two boys – whom, now I thought about it – must be in their twenties. They'd had a girl-child, a toddler, whom they'd called Weasel, and whom they'd traded to the Camerons for gold jewellery – by then worthless, which shows the type. May and Sam had renamed her Ruth, and she was now eight, a sensible happy child who was best friends with Jane DeVenter's niece Daisy. I scrabbled in my mind; yes, the Ross boys were Colin and George, known as Geordie.

"Who came with the Rosses, and what do they have?" I demanded.

"Three families. Janet said there's fourteen of them." If the fourteen were suitable, we could use them, but from what I recalled of the Rosses, we wouldn't be taking *them* in.

"Where are they?"

May laughed. "Parked on the roadside of the gatehouse. Janet wouldn't let anyone in until you came to talk to them. She said it was for the Leaders to say and not for her. She shut the gates, said they'd have to wait until you got there, and that was that."

Our gazes met, and we both started to laugh. I recovered first and considered. "Did you see the people with the Rosses? What was *your* evaluation of them?"

May pondered that. "They have five vehicles. All covered utes with trailers, all loaded to the top. I saw two dogs, but they may have other animals. It's possible they're an extended family since there's an old lady who seems to give everyone orders and they obey them. She's the one I saw, and if they're all like her, I'd think them suitable. She's neat and clean, decent clothing. I saw three of those with her, and they're the same."

I'd started walking towards the gatehouse, and May looked at me. "Meg Ross says since they're here now, she'll have her daughter back."

"What did you say?"

"Nothing."

"Tell me, May, which of them sold Ruth to you? What did they say about that?"

"You know some of it. Joe said she was a nuisance, brought the Welfare down on them, said he'd swap her if I had anything valuable."

"What did Meg say?"

May's face screwed up as she tried to remember. "You know, she kept quiet. I thought she'd speak once, but Joe sort of turned on her, and she didn't say anything."

I remembered things. The dark hair and eyes of the rest of Ruth's family, and that Ruth was very fair and eight to ten years younger than the boys. I chose my words carefully. "May, would you find it possible Ruth could be Meg's daughter *only*?"

May Cameron stared, then her expression went thoughtful. We had walked a hundred yards or more and were almost at the gatehouse when she spoke again. "I wouldn't say it's *impossible*. I've little to base that on, you ken? But she looks nothing like Joe or the lads, and her character's nothing like."

"No," I agreed. Ruth was intelligent, sensible, a hard worker, a kind child, and an animal-lover.

"You think…"

"I remember wondering about possibilities when they were here before," I said thoughtfully. "Remember when I brought her to you that time. It wasn't so noticeable then; she was dirty and her hair unwashed. But once they'd left and you had her a while, I noticed how fair she was and remembered the others the last time I'd seen them.

"Meg was never that fair," May said slowly. "She has middling brown hair with hazel eyes, and her skin's sallow."

"Yes," was all I said as we entered the gatehouse, Janet, having seen us coming, opened the door. I nodded as I passed, and she spoke very quietly.

"No trouble, and apart from the Rosses, I don't think the others plan on any. I have people standing by, and if anyone starts anything, he'll be dead before he takes aim."

I grinned. "I've no doubt. Stand ready." I opened the small window and spoke through the bars. "Who speaks for you, someone who isn't a Ross?"

I saw at once that May was right. The old lady in the lead vehicle stepped out and walked to the window. She met my gaze calmly. "I'm Joanna McHain. Those with me are kin. We were told you have a safe place and may take in those that are honest, hard-working, and have trades; the more so if we do not come empty-handed."

That sounded promising. "Would it please you to come in and talk about that with me?" She inclined her head. "Then you and two others, one male, one female."

She turned, said two names, and they joined us. Janet had a kettle on the hob, and once we'd all sat down, we poured tea, shared a plate of biscuits, and Joanna McHain began.

"We lived in the village of …. here." She named a place that was around sixteen miles from where we had returned the Rosses. I knew the area. It was picturesque, with many there making a living from various crafts. I indicated I knew it, and she continued. "My man and I owned a mixed farm. He died ten years gone, and I came to live with my son, who was a builder and a good one. My daughter had a few acres and took our beasts. Her man worked with my son, which was how my daughter met him. With us, we've my son-in-law's sister and her second cousin. The sister is a potter, and the second cousin makes herbal medicines and cosmetics." That, I reflected, could be useful indeed, and apart from the cousin, we could use builders and a potter too.

"Six adults, including you?"

"Five. My son's wife left him and is somewhere in France. She left his children with him while she was gone, so he has them safely." Her look was a combination of rage and amusement as the snarl before that turned into a smug look of satisfaction. "Took him for every penny, did Gillian, and laughed that she'd spend it on a fancy holiday while he stayed home to look after his children and make more money for her next holiday. I doubt we'll be seeing her again."

"So do I," I agreed. "And your son-in-law's sister and her second cousin, they have no man with them?"

Joanna McHain hesitated. "Ah, well, they'd no wish for any, do you see. They had friends who could help with the other, so they've children and no need for anybody asking questions since they earned a decent living. Sue's pottery's been in exhibitions, and Verna, she did a degree in what she does, and she had a website." Her tone was respectful. "Made good money, and the older two kids were helping with orders. They were paid," she added hastily.

I'd realised by then what she was saying about Sue and Verna and nodded. "Your son and son-in-law, what sort of building did they do?"

She explained that and more besides while I listened. Joanna said that the combined families had moved some of their people into the nearer town to continue foraging there, while Joanna, the younger children, and Sue and Verna had stayed in the village. Finally, the son – Lachlan – had met the Rosses and heard their grievance. The father, Joe, had explained how we'd taken his daughter, tossed the rest of the family out, and how he planned to return and demand his rights.

Joanna's gaze met mine in a direct stare. "I'll tell you now; I didn't believe it. I'd met him by then, and he's a waste of space. His wife's a slattern, and the boys are bullies. However, he said he knew the way here, but unless we took his family, he'd not tell us. It was a gamble, but there's fourteen of us, so I thought if they were planning to take us by surprise and have all we own, they'd be in the *caoch* and sinking fast."

"So you owe them nothing?"

She frowned. "Joe said if we took his family, they'll point out another portion of the way each morning. We did and they did. One of the trailers has everything they wanted to bring. What's your thinking?"

"That he made the bargain, and you kept it," I said slowly. "There's some things too he may not have made plain to you. He wasn't tossed out; he was told to leave because he would not send his sons to school, and he was unwilling to do any work for the food they ate. The relation-by-marriage who took them in,

271

unwillingly, I may say, finding them dirty, lazy thieves *bought* the girl he calls his daughter, and he was delighted to sell her."

Joanna McHain showed herself no fool. "Delighted? What did she offer? And you say that he 'calls' her his daughter. Is she not?"

"He took gold for her, and the child is white-blonde, blue-eyed, and with a fair complexion. You've seen the Rosses."

"They've dark hair. Most have brown eyes and sallow skin. The woman's bastard?"

"That's what was in my mind. He'd go along with it since if he didn't, she'd only have to leave, and he'd have to work. The welfare would make him pay maintenance."

"But with what happened, he could afford to sell the child," she chortled. "He had it half-right. No welfare after him any longer, and his woman couldn't walk out, gold though, no value, no one would trade, and I wonder what he *did* do with it?"

"You never saw any gold?"

"No. Maybe he found someone else who didn't know it's pretty much worthless. Anyway, you say we owe him nothing?"

"I say he bargained to ride with you to our gates and for you to carry here such of their possessions as they wished to take, that in exchange he said he would show you the way, and that both sides of the bargain are fulfilled," I stated precisely. "You did not bargain to get him past our gates, to fight us, to persuade us, or to speak for them?"

"We did not."

"Then I declare your bargain complete. And I have a suggestion."

Joanna McHain heard, smiled appreciatively, and agreed. That night while the Rosses slept heavily, we allowed the McHains and their kin to pass. Their vehicles – in neutral – were being pushed by our strongest people. Outside we left the trailer and the tattered tent in which the Rosses slept, together with whatever they had in it. It was a pity they didn't like dogs. It would have been much harder to get by them if they'd had a dog or two. As it was, they woke long after daybreak to find themselves hungry, alone, and with nothing more than what they themselves owned, and to say they were furious is an understatement.

They moaned, complained, threatened, and after two days, they realised I was obdurate. They could sit on our doorstep until they died for all I cared, and no, I would not feed them or provide alcohol. They could squat in our quarantine chalets, but if they did any damage, they'd be out. Nor would we return Ruth. We'd discussed that, and since too many of us recalled the conditions in which they'd kept the child, and May repeated how she'd bought her, it was our Glens' united decision that she remain with the Camerons, and on being asked, that was Ruth's wish as well.

We drove them home, their trailer attached to the Landcruiser, the Rosses making threats under their breath – at roughly a threat every twenty miles. Donal recalled the way, and we halted outside the place they called home. He unhitched the trailer, left it in the gutter, and stood facing them.

"Listen carefully. I shall say this only once." I developed a broad grin at that point. "If you come back on your own, the gates will not be opened. If you come back with others, if we find them acceptable, we may allow *them* in. If we don't, neither you nor they will enter. If you bring an army, we'll fight, and we have what we need to win. If they fail, they'll likely kill you for it, and if they retreat and leave you behind – we'll kill you. Believe this, or learn it the hard way."

He turned on his heel and swung back into the Landcruiser seat. Out of sight of the Rosses, I clapped softly. "As good as a speech by the French resistance any day. Can we go now?" He nodded. I pressed a foot down, and we moved off, our people driving after us. Behind me, the figure of Joe Ross, standing rigid with rage at his door, grew smaller and smaller until I took the corner, and he was gone. Forever if we were lucky.

****

A month later, I found that we weren't done with the wretched man, although not in the manner he'd hoped, I believe. Dan came trotting up to the house and hailed me.

"Problem, Dan?"

"New settlers applying."

"Any good?"

"I'd say they're likely ones."

I came to the gatehouse, allowed two in, and heard the story. They'd been farmers on the main road well to the southeast who'd developed bandit trouble. Everything they had was stolen, eaten, and finally, their house burned down when the latest bunch found there was nothing to steal that the marauders thought worth taking.

"There's three of us families, missus. Been neighbours all our lives. Got so bad we couldn't live there anymore. We went to the town further south to look for food and met a man scavenging. He said he knew about a place, said we should sneak into it, take what we wanted and get out, that there were places where we could settle and no bandits. Said not to let you know we were around because you murdered people."

I studied him. "Why did you come to us then?"

"Got a telescope, went up the hills, and watched. You got a school, a library, a clinic even. Saw the kids running about with dogs and people laughing. Didn't look like murderers, we reckoned. We decided we'd rather take a chance."

In which they made a good choice, since we gave them the requested chance in McManus Glen, and they did well – as had Joanna McHain and her people. Scott Bradley came to me once they'd had their land for six weeks and thanked us with tears in his eyes.

"Dunno who that guy is to you, but he's an idiot. You've been as good as kin. If I ever see him again, I'll tell him a thing or two." I could see he was bursting with curiosity, so I told him a little, and he was aghast. "The father sold his kid? What sort of man does that? I'd have starved before one of mine went anywhere else."

I smiled. "You don't have to, not now. By the way, we'll be taking a run back to Edinburgh in a year or two. Know anyone there?"

"Used to, not sure if they're still alive, but I can go and tell you where they were."

I thanked him for saying his name would go on the list I was compiling and watched him head homewards. If that was the best Joe Ross could do against us, I hoped he'd continue. I said as much to Donal, and he scowled.

"I had scouts out, and they missed them. Could have been dangerous if there'd been more and they weren't Scott's type. Next time they may be, I'll up the level."

He did, starting with another dozen scouts, all on e-bikes – which are silent, don't require feeding, and don't leave hoofmarks or other evidence of passing through – and which, in this case, spread out both ways up and down the main roads. I've often thought that Donal has a nose for trouble, and when he acts quickly, it can be a pointer to that. For my part, just in case, I reinforced the gatehouses, added still more weapons and ammunition, and talked to Janet, who suggested walkie-talkies.

"They have them."

"One pair per gatehouse. Get more, and spread the glen sets to different people, not just to your place." Come to think of it, that was sense, and like Donal, I acted immediately. It was just as well. We got a call three nights later from Jackie, who'd gone out with Dan.

"Group is coming your way. All male so far as we can tell, about fifty of them, heavily armed, they're in buses that look to

275

be steel-plated, and they've front and rear outriders. Dan says to tell you that the way they move, he thinks some could have been army." I did *not* like the sound of that – and nor did Donal when I told him.

"Hell! Okay, say we fort up and fight them off, then they sit around and pick us off any time we go out."

I smiled slowly. "I wonder if Joe Ross told them anything about Thurston?"

Donal's smile matched. "I don't think so. He wasn't here long enough to overhear anyone talking about Tommy Branson, and he wouldn't know about him from when he was here because Tommy's lot hadn't arrived then." We called a conference.

Once most people had blown off steam saying what they'd like to do to Joe Ross, Janet stood up. "It's simple. Look at the choices. We hole up; we lose no one, but we can't go out again without someone probably being kidnapped, raped, or killed. So we'd still lose people, just more slowly. They don't sound like the sort that'll talk peace, and it makes us look weak if we try. Or we ambush them once they relax. If we wait, we can see what they intend, what they plan, so we know we aren't killing innocent people."

Donal had primed her, of course, but she said nothing she didn't believe, and that came across to our people – who, after discussion, agreed. Messengers went out, Tommy Branson came to see us, and we added to our scouts. We code-named the group "road riders," and Donal commented that whatever they were, they weren't professional soldiers – although he thought their leader could have done something in that line.

"What sort of something?" Ricky was interested.

"Territorial in another country perhaps. If he was stranded here from overseas, he could feel it's better to make some sort of safe place before he settles down."

"Scouts say he's a bad 'un, Grandpa Donal. They took out a family the other day, and…" his voice faded away, and I winced.

"I know, I heard," I informed him.

I *had* heard, and I'd had a report on the state of the bodies once the road riders moved on. It was gruesome, and I made sure that the report was known, the more so because two of those that had died were children, and a description of how they'd died would make sure no one with half a brain would take the chance of getting anywhere near the road riders from now on. They didn't. A number of them came to us instead. I assayed them, and about two-thirds of them I let in. The other third I had taken well away from the road riders' line of advance, along with everything they valued that could be moved.

The glens settled to wait, while, unknown to the road riders, our scouts circled them, watched everything they did, and reported back. Donal was our great advantage there, he'd done decades in special ops, was an expert in guerrilla fighting, and he'd taught our people for years, particularly those that had been around ten to fourteen when the virus hit, it had been half fun for them, but they'd learned well, and now they were old enough and sensible enough to be precisely the scouts we needed.

The road riders started scouting us, and Donal was sure when they would attack since they'd brought in extra supplies and weapons. They came at first light two mornings later, and we were waiting. Ricky charged through the gates, his vehicle a light civilian-type jeep, but unobtrusively armoured, and beside him, Alex, armed with a crossbow. Being the fast and excellent shot she was, she sent bolt after bolt into the road riders while Ricky skidded the vehicle back through the gates as they slammed behind him. With four of the enemy dead and two badly wounded, that concentrated their attention on us nicely.

An hour later, they were fully embroiled. Donal looked at them and abruptly chuckled. "Now I know one of the things he was. Look at that. He's a siege in mind." I looked and understood what he meant.

"He could still have been some sort of soldier somewhere?"

"He could. It may be that one fostered the other."

"Dungeons and Dragons," I had a fit of the giggles and couldn't stop for minutes. "What else will he try, I wonder?"

"Probably a trebuchet." And when, two hours later, they wheeled one out, we almost collapsed. They knew the principles of the thing – vaguely – but they got too close and lobbed the missiles far over us. Then when they backed off, the rope they were using snapped and dropped a missile on one of the men, who went hopping about, holding his foot, screaming, and took a swing at one of those operating the trebuchet.

A walkie-talkie crackled softly. Donal spoke to it, opened the door, and waved his arms. Once there'd been time for everyone to look his way, he began to signal, while I reflected how convenient it had been that a whole family who knew sign had joined us. They were scattered around where they could see Donal through binoculars and pass his commands into the places where radios didn't carry.

We held, waiting … waiting … waiting, until high in a tree where Ann Yarrow perched, I saw her moving her hands and read the message. Tommy Branson and his people were ready. That message flashed via a small mirror to her from behind the road riders. Donal signalled us to stand by, flicked the signal to Ricky and Esme Pemberlow, then as the road riders attacked again, there was the hollow booming echo of the single great drum we'd salvaged from a museum. The pipes screamed, and from behind the road riders, Tommy's people attacked, movement hidden by the pipes and drum. The road riders spun once they realised they were attacked from behind, and with their backs to us again, Ricky and Alex took to the gatehouse tower and shot again and again while men died.

I think Joe had never told them how many of us there were. But in that year, almost nine years after the virus, we had fourteen hundred people of the glens, and Tommy had another hundred plus in Thurston. They'd brought fifty against us, less well-armed, less trained, and with less to gain. We were fighting for our lives and homes; they come seeking plunder – and found death instead, just as the last invaders had. We reaped them like corn, and when the last dozen made a stand, we met them with swords and guns. They fell, and there were no more, while at our backs the drum roared, the great pipes screamed triumph, and our people, mad with blood and death, danced.

That was the *Road Rider Battle*, since when Joss painted it as a mural on a library wall, with a smaller painting hung in Johnny's home, she named it so. We buried the men who'd come to kill, salvaged what they'd brought us, and we went back to our work, Tommy to his laboratory, and in the spring, we told Johnny and Mac, so they knew they had saved no mean folk. The old blood of the clans lived on, and we fought and danced to the great drum and the pipes, and let all beware who came against Clan McAlister.

CHAPTER TWENTY-TWO

Mine: belonging to me if I can hold or seize it. ~Ambrose Bierce,
The Devil's Dictionary

*Unfortunately, too many people follow this as their definition. Then
again, as Sheila pointed out when I said so, what we call salvage may
be called something else by others.* ~Donal McArn

Time passed quietly in the glens. The twelfth year after
the virus, Donal and I talked with those who had become a council and advisers.

"People have come in, but we could do with more yet,"
Janet was saying.

I nodded. "Donal and I think another expedition to Edinburgh should be done."

"What about the roads?" That was Cheryl.

"There's several roads go there. If one's blocked too badly
to pass, we try another. We have the maps," I responded.

Donal looked around the big old table. "You all know the
roads are failing," he said quietly. "From Thurston to the glens
is fine because we keep it that way, but we can't do that for the
whole country, not even for anything outside our area. And once
the main roads go, that's it. We'll be confined to the coast."

I gave thanks to whatever there was that had given us Sea
Glen. The husband and wife – Jay and Teresa – of a group from
the last trip to Edinburgh had been from a sailing family. He and
his had settled in Sea Glen, and once they were snug, they asked
for a run to the coast, to a marina the couple knew about. We'd

gone in a smaller group, and he'd picked out several sailing yachts. Different sizes, with dinghies, covered cabins, auxiliary motors, and all the gear they'd need. To those, we'd added salvage from the marina, of new sails and cordage, paint and varnish, RTs, inflatable boats, and anything else the Culbertsons had thought useful.

Now Jay glanced across at us. "Yes, now we have a boat shed built and that pulley to take the yachts right up to the glen mouth, we shouldn't have problems with storms. The yachts won't last forever, though."

Teresa nodded. "We've sufficient supplies to keep them repaired for a generation, maybe two. After that, they'll deteriorate until they're unsafe."

Donal pursed his lips. "I know. So make a list of what's needed to keep them going as long as we can. It may be that in fifty years, we can build replacements." He changed the subject. "Edinburgh, do we circle through Glasgow as well, or not?"

It was decided that we'd visit Glasgow too – while we had the petrol, the roads were open – if barely, some hadn't deteriorated as fast as we'd thought they would - and we had a summer that bid fair to be a long and warm one this year. I pounced once the council left us and Donal grinned at me.

"Didn't think you missed that. Yes, I've a mind to spend the whole of it salvaging." He became serious. "Look at it this way, love. It'll be a long warm summer from what we can see, and when it's like that, then often the winter following is a bad one, storms, floods, really cold, and what will that do to the roads?" I saw, and he knew I did. "Aye, this could be the final time we can do this, and there's another thing, we're a bit like the roads." I sat up indignantly, and he smiled at me. "Not an insult, but we have to be realistic. You know how old we are, and we've been fortunate."

"We have," I agreed. "And one can never count on fortune."

"That's so. I'd think we have a few years yet, but not to do more than lead here. Ricky was twenty-four last birthday, and I think he'll be coming to us to talk of a wedding any day now." Come to that, so did I. "So, one more major expedition, maybe even two or three, but all over this summer. Then we cut back to going no further than is possible, and in a few more years, that'll mean just the coast and locally."

I made lists, reminding me of time's passing, so I looked about me. Cassius and Bruce had died three years ago, and Tai was fifteen. Laddie, I thought, could go next winter. Esme Pemberton had lasted much longer than she'd ever expected, but she'd left us this past winter. I'd encourage Ricky and Alex to marry once summer's expeditions were over. They could move into the main house in Johnny's Glen, and Ricky could start taking more of an active leadership role. It would help if he were wed, and more so if there was a child on the way. Minister Giles was fading. Better to have a wedding while he lived and then quietly establish a civil ceremony. I reached for my pad and began writing again.

****

Summer came early, and thanks to my lists and talks with those who'd like some item in particular, we were ready the moment the weather improved. This time, we all but stripped the glens of the able-bodied to staff our convoy. We'd leave just enough to defend it at need, but they'd have the guardhouses. We'd reached fifteen hundred in population at the end of our twelfth year. Small numbers had continued to trickle in. Most in some vehicles, although I knew that would end once the main roads failed. Afterwards, we'd get fewer as time went on and reaching us – or even knowing the area where we were – became impossible.

I mentioned that to Donal as we checked off lists, and he chuckled. "Aye, it's as you said years back, things that were part of our lives become stories then myths. In a hundred years, our glens could have become a sort of fairyland to the south, a place where people live without fear, with ample food, in fancy houses, and with great sailing ships that come now and again to those who have the fortune to see them." He glanced to where, like many, we had an arrangement of weapons over the mantle. "In time, guns won't work, and after that will come a time where no one believes they ever did."

"Or because they were fairy-given," I said smiling. "Twelve years and already people are forgetting some of the songs I changed to fit the glens weren't always that way."

"Aye, and that's something else to put on your list, love. Music in any way, shape, or form. Instruments, sheet music, books on making or repairing instruments, disks of any music, while we have electricity and players. Particularly any Scottish items or music."

I nodded. We'd always looked for that to some extent. By now, we had enough bagpipes, both the great-pipes and the small, along with sufficient items for repair or replacement, that anyone who wished to learn could have their own. I'd like more of the great drums, however, and during this trip, I planned to talk to those who taught about certifying more people as music teachers. I bit back a sigh, so many things to do, so little time before what we had was *all* we had; and all there was to last us down the generations to come.

Still, we had sugar beets growing and hives thriving. In Sea Glen, we'd a set of salt pans, and while we got little salt from them as yet, in time, we'd have more. Sufficient, if all went well, to provide enough once salvage ran out. We'd gone hunting the previous year for a sheltered glen where the land caught the all-day sun and found a place. There we'd planted the whole glen with coffee and tea bushes, and they were doing well. Not as well as I thought they did in their native habitats, but sufficient for us to have both. I had lists of things we could produce in time and which would be not just wanted but needed. And I hoped some of those might be provided in this last great expedition. Oh, yes, add safety pins, hair clips, needles, and other items for sewing to the list. Note to self: *some museums or displays might yet have hand or foot-operated sewing machines.*

Time flew past, and on a bright morning, we began to gather. It took three hours before we were lined up, then the great gates opened, and we drove through. Each of us knew this could be the final time we ever saw our lowlands. I drove our Landcruiser, Cheryl beside me with Meli in the back seat, while ahead of us Ricky and Alex were on motorcycles, and Donal in the Landcruiser we had never returned from its rental. There were no plans to halt short of the cities, and we did not, driving far into the night. We stopped at last above Glasgow and parked.

Donal pointed. "Down in the dip here. That way, no one in the city will see lights."

The camp was abustle as we settled in. We had six hours to sleep before those chosen for the job went quietly from place to place, waking us, with food cooking once more. We ate, and the column unwound as the drivers and vehicles fell into line. We drove slowly into the city, and I stared, making a sound in my throat at what I saw.

"Aye," Donal said quietly. "A sad sight. I remember coming through in my twenties. Something to see, it was, but not now." Groups of half-a-dozen vehicles were breaking off the column, people who'd joined us from here going in search of those they'd known.

"Will they find anything – or anyone?" I wondered, watching them go.

"Maybe, maybe not. All we can do is look." And look we did for a week, finding people here and there, not many and fewer still interested in joining us. On the second to last day, I talked to one man with two daughters and their four children. A sour old man in his late fifties, living in a vast mansion with antiques and fancy furnishings, but the children all looked peaked and nervous. The daughters would have been in their twenties when the virus hit, and their children not much more than babies.

The grandfather eyed me as if I had come to steal his silverware. "We've no need of you, and anyhow, I was born here, I'll die here. This is my house, and I'll not leave it to be plundered or burnt down. We do not need charity. We're managing."

I met the daughter's look and asked. "Your husbands?"

"Overseas, never got back," one said. "Daddy took us in here. It's as he says, we manage." Her eyes on me said that this was a lie, that they were not doing well, and when my gaze turned to the children, I saw her wince and make a decision.

"I'm glad to hear it. So many others are starving or sick," I said, my tone bland. "We live in half-a-dozen interlinked glens far to the north. We have fertile land, one of the glens opens to the sea, we have livestock, and," I laughed. "We have a school, a library, a health clinic, and cottage hospital, we have a dentist and assistant, and we even have monthly concerts. We have music teachers too who take private pupils – we have spare instruments for that." I saw both women's gazes flicker. "However, we want only those who want to join us."

"What do you give those that do?" one asked, and I recited the items.

"A house on half an acre if they have a trade we can use. If not, then a smallholding with a house, barns, and animals. Either way, we give them vegetable seeds, fruit or nut tree saplings, and we encourage them to have a pet."

Their father snorted. "Filthy things, mange, fleas, scratching furniture and having to be fed, digging up the place, making a noise and a mess."

And under his breath, one of the children said, so quietly, I think that only I and the women heard. "I'd like a puppy, and so would Joey. Sissy wants a kitten. It isn't fair. Just 'cos it's his house."

The women said nothing, but I saw a hint of red show on one's cheeks while the other looked down, but not before I saw the flaring anger in her eyes.

I spoke politely to the older man. "I understand. We'll be in the city another day, the morning after that we go on to Edinburgh and then home. We won't be back, the roads are falling apart, and it's been decided that after this year, we'll stay closer to home."

The old man glared. "So why do you come here, woman?"

I smiled pleasantly. "We're looking for people if any want to join us, and for salvage. We take nothing from anyone that has it, but where shops or houses or businesses are empty, we may take some of what is there."

His face twisted into a snarl. "You'll take nothing of mine. Get out. Go on, get away from here before I get my gun."

I looked at him. "I want nothing you own," I said carefully and from the corner of my eye saw one woman register the words I'd used. "Since this is your place, I'll do as you bid me. However, all tomorrow we'll be at the hotel on the corner of …" I gave the address. "We leave the next day at eight a.m. After that, we'll not trouble you ever again."

"Good, if I see you no more, it'll be too soon for me. Now get before I help you along."

I nodded to each adult, in turn, left, strolled across the road to my Landcruiser, climbed into the driver's seat, and drove off. Donal straightened up from where he'd listened, hidden along the back seat, gun in hand. "What do you think?"

"I think the daughters had enough of their father's demands. They heard what I said, what we offered to those that joined us, and they looked at their children. I'd guess food's been getting short from how thin they all are, and the old man hates pets, won't let the children have a puppy or a kitten."

Donal looked at me. "And where would they get one in this place?"

286

"They'd find one. Children do. Anyway, they're not allowed a pet, and their mothers seem to have accepted the father's rules up to now. I made it clear this is the last time we'll be through, though, and I saw them registering that."

"Eddie was right," Donal said, referring to one of the women we'd taken from here in our first run. "Said she knew them and the old man. He's a snob, counts whatever he owns as his, and he'd kill for it. Wouldn't ever leave the house because it's his, and he can't take it with him."

"She was right," I agreed. "Although I wouldn't be certain that his family feels the same way. We'll see."

We spent a day loading the possessions of those who wanted to join us, and most of us went to bed after an early dinner – with a substantial guard out just in case. By seven the next morning, after an early breakfast, Donal started us lining up. By half-past eight, I was ready to lead off with Ricky and Alex scouting ahead. I was about to put my vehicle in gear when a large van towing a tall covered trailer shot into the square. One of the women I'd seen earlier looked out of its window at me and asked a question.

"Should we wish to join you, would we be welcome?"

"How many of you?"

"My sister and I, and our four children."

"Join us and be welcome," I said formally. "I'll tell you we expect those who join us to accept a pet. One at least, although two is better." I heard cheers and squeals from the van and grinned. "Fall into the line and see me once we stop again, which won't be until Edinburgh. I hope you have enough petrol?" She nodded, and I moved off, while in the rear-view mirror, I saw her join our convoy a dozen vehicles back.

I kept my word, and we drove all of that day. The roads we used were major ones, so we hummed along with forerunners and few delays, and it was dusk when we came to the city's outer suburbs and halted at what had been a campground, I thought. There was no one there, and I noted that some chalet buildings could be taken back. I sent Alex to the sisters with a dinner invitation, and they arrived quickly. I had them sit down, food was brought, and I asked questions.

"I'm Moira. This is my younger sister Shania. We want to come with you." She introduced the children, who gazed at me hopefully.

"You said we could have pets?" I nodded. "How, when?"

"Unless we find something here, then when we get home. You put a notice on the community board, and people will tell you what they have. You can choose from those or wait for new litters. No charge, but it's considered polite to leave food to help out."

Moira stared. "On the community board?" She laughed then sobbed, and Shaina caught her up. "I'm sorry, it's just I think how we've been living, and all the time we could have come to you. We wanted to leave the city, Daddy wouldn't hear of it, but it was getting impossible to find food. Eddie had told us people came through looking for those who'd join them. She said she was going. I tried to get Daddy to go, but he wouldn't."

"And this time?"

She looked as guilty as a cat in the cream. "Sometimes Shania and I don't sleep well. We found sleeping pills in a pharmacy, so last night, we gave them to Daddy in his cocoa. He slept like a log while we loaded up everything we wanted to take. He was still asleep when we left."

"The van and trailer?"

"They belonged to a neighbour. Shanna said they'd be better than one of Daddy's fancy cars, and we could take anything from there too when we got the keys."

The back of the van was solid salvage, and the trailer was packed high with a tarpaulin lashed over it. "Sensible," I commented and watched the women relax. "Now, what did you do before the virus?"

And that turned out to be good. Shanna had taught music at a primary school and privately, favouring the pipes herself and teaching three other instruments. Her father had thought it a ladylike occupation. Moira had been a librarian – also a lady-like career – and both were anxious. "Will there be jobs for us?"

I reassured them. "Jobs, homes, pets, and the children will go to school. I'll see they have a medical and dental check once we're home too."

They left with goodwill on both sides, and I looked after them. Something in the way Moira had talked of the sleeping pills, something in the way she'd said her father was "asleep" when they left, made me think of another interpretation. And I'd seen the look shared between her and her sister. I'd ask no questions, they'd done what they had to do, and they weren't the only ones who'd killed to survive if that's what they *had* done. It was none of my business, and I never did ask, then or ever. That was our new world.

CHAPTER TWENTY-THREE

Carpe diem – seize the day. ~Latin motto

However, one beware that now and then, the day seizes back.
~Sheila McArn

We took another route home. As I'd reminded Donal, there were two reasons for doing so. One was Kipling's story, and the other was that if we swung nor-nor-east, we'd be in a territory where we'd not been as yet. He'd agreed, and it was a good decision as we discovered. We stopped at a small village when Cheryl called over the Radio Transmitter.

"Sheila, I can see alpacas." The convoy halted while I went with her to look over the paddock. Cheryl pointed, and I saw a grazing flock that looked back calmly.

"They're too tame to have lost everyone that had them," I commented, and she nodded.

"Let's go and see?"

We strolled towards the farmhouse that most likely was the one where the animals belonged and were almost at the gates when a voice demanded, "Stop right there."

We stopped. "We saw the alpacas," I said. "And we wanted to talk to their owner. If they're yours, we could buy some or swap if you'd rather. This lady here," I indicated Cheryl, "has fifty in her flock, and they're the same type as yours."

"*Suris*?" said the voice incredulously. Cheryl nodded. "And you've got *fifty*?" She nodded again. "Where are they? Do you live near here?"

He'd edged into view by then, and Cheryl commenting on the quality of his flock had him disarmed in minutes. He accepted an invitation to eat with us and got into a deep discussion on alpaca breeding, wool quality, and the difficulties of seeing they didn't become inbred now that other flocks were almost impossible to find. We found that his circumstances were those not uncommon nowadays.

"I went to a fair I wasn't supposed to," His grin was hard. "I raided my piggybank and sneaked out. Came home with a sore throat, didn't I. Then everyone started dying. Mum and dad believed in being stocked up. I stayed here, and I and a couple of their friends buried them in the back garden. People around mostly left, said it'd be better in the city, I stayed. I wasn't gonna leave the alpacas to starve, and," he stammered. "Mum, and Dad, I didn't feel right leaving them either."

So he'd stayed, he could shear, and he'd fed and looked after the animals. Meli asked their names and grinned at those. One of the two lines – the later one – all had names beginning with Al. (Alphonse, Alys, Alonzo.) The boy had been named Alun after an uncle, and his parents had named the new line with an Al both in his honour and as an in-joke on alpaca. I listened and thought he'd done well. From the looks of him, he'd be around twenty-one or two, so he could only have been a child when that happened. How had he managed? I asked.

"Like I said, some of mum and Dad's friends were okay. They stuck around for a few years before they packed up. They didn't leave until about five years ago. They did want me to come, but I wouldn't."

And for five years, he'd stayed alone, looking after two graves and twenty-six alpacas. I left it to Cheryl and Meli to convince him that he – and the alpacas – would do better with us.

When we left the next morning, our convoy was increased by one human, twenty-six alpacas, two alpaca floats, and a large covered trailer containing all their gear. He knew where there was another breeder on the way back as well. We stopped, rounded their alpacas up, took all that were of an age to be domesticated again and of good quality, and when at last we arrived back at Glen Mhairi, Cheryl said in an aside to me.

"Two kids who already like each other, and a total with this lot of ninety-three alpacas. I think I've got a head start on two dynasties." I grinned. I thought she had too.

We cleared our salvage off the vehicles, made a trip to a larger town where we hadn't been before, and collected all the linkable storage barns there. We took even those on farms where the barns were in good condition and set those in lines across the glens, including the one with tea and coffee bushes. Then we made another run to Edinburgh. And a third before the winter set in, after that as Donal said quietly to me one evening.

"Another winter will do for the roads there. We can try next year, but that may be it. Best we get what we can while they're passable." We did, and when the winter came, it was unusually stormy, and I knew he'd been right.

Ricky and Alex went out with scouts in the spring and came back to say the roads were finished without many people working for weeks. We discussed it with the advisers' council that night, and the consensus was that it would be unproductive.

"We have all the people who want to come here," Ricky said. "The ones still in the cities are those who'd come reluctantly, and do we want them? Most are staying because it's easier living still or because they can't take what they don't want to leave. Better we check the smaller towns, we know there are people there, look at Alun. And there's still more salvage in the towns and villages than we could take before it's ruined."

So it was decided. And in the spring telling, Ricky stood to say before our people and the graves, what we would do, and to be married to Alex. Meli came forward then and declared that she and Alun would marry in autumn with Cheryl's blessing. I was pleased to hear that. And when Cheryl came silently to our home late one evening in the sixteenth year after the virus, I listened to her decision.

"They're good kids. They love the alpacas, and if you add a chalet or two to the house, they can have those as private rooms. I want to leave this with you too."

She handed over a sheet of paper, and I read it. It left everything she owned to Meli and Alun with provisos. If they divorced, it would be split, a third to him, two-thirds to Meli. Since this was a form of entail, neither could arbitrarily sell the property or the animals once they'd had children. If they divorced after they had children, Alum could remove the chalets as his; everything else would go to the children in trust, but to Meli for her lifetime, after which, the property must remain intact as to the original property.

I initialled the back of each page to say I had read and agreed to it as Glen Leader. It had become the custom that wills and other such things are given to the clan leaders for acceptance and recording, and we kept copies of them all. I added to this one that in view of the provisions, the glen would provide two chalets free to the alpaca farm, known as Cheryl's Place, but that any work done with them was to be at the farm's own expense, and that as the animals were an acknowledged advantage to the glens, that we would also provide free a further five barns for storage or shelter.

Cheryl grinned at that. "I was saying to the kids just last week we could do with more barns for storage and winter shelter. I'd make that three and two – storage and shelter."

She departed smiling, and I reflected how well things had gone of late – which sent a shudder down my spine. Note to self. Do *not* say that sort of thing. The next thing that happened made me forget the shudder. Claire called me from the gatehouse where she was keeping watch with Ann and Kin Yarrow.

"There's people here asking to join us. A *lot* of people, Sheila."

I grabbed my tricycle and hurtled at its best speed for the gatehouse where I saw that Claire was right. There were indeed a *lot* of people. I counted over forty vehicles, all of them utes or the three ton-lorries. The utes had full trailers attached, from the sounds the lorries had livestock, and I saw children's faces at the windows.

I stepped up to the gatehouse window – made from bulletproof glass, with a microphone outside – and spoke. "You'd like to join us?"

A man walked up and nodded. "We would. May we come in and talk about it?"

"You and four others," I said politely but firmly. I wasn't taking chances, and I wasn't sure that what I could see was all the people there were. Five people would tell me how tolerant he was. He hesitated, then accepted that I wasn't going to change the offer. He came in, bringing with him a range of voices so that I warmed a little. He was, I thought, in his late forties, with him was an older woman, two younger people, a man and a woman in their twenties, and a girl in her mid-teens with shaggy hair and a rugged look. The spread of ages and both sexes indicated he was reasonable.

"I'm Dylan, and yes, after Dylan Thomas, my mother was a fan." I suppressed a smile. No doubt he'd heard all the jokes on that. He said the names of those with him and wasted no time explaining the circumstances. "We all lived around the town of Quayside. We've been doing well, but there was no place we could fortify effectively. A bunch of lowlifes in the area got together and started raiding us. Stuff that could be scavenged was less, so they stole more. Others joined them, and lately, they've just about been living on us. The final straw was when they broke into a house and took everything, food, medicines, guns, and ammunition, and they…" He paused, and I spoke quietly.

"Assaulted those whose property they stole?"

Dylan looked relieved. "Yes."

The girl – introduced to us as Isobel, Iz for short – stared at me and made a spitting motion. "Fancy way a' putting it. My best friend Bessie was, as you put it, assaulted. Four 'o them had her, and she killed herself when they left. Her sister told me. I know which they was, too, and if I ever get a chance…" Her eyes were alive with hatred.

Dylan gave her a weary glance. "If they're ever that close, you better hope you can get away, not stand about trying to shoot one of them." He turned to me. "We heard about you a while back. You have land that's safe, someone tried to get in, and you handed them their heads." He looked for confirmation, and I nodded, smiling reminiscently. "We packed up everything we've got. If you won't take us in, we'll go on along the coast and hope to find someplace we can fortify and be safe, and where that lot maybe can't find us. We'll do anything you want us to do that's reasonable."

I laid out terms. We'd talk to each family. If accepted, they'd come in group by group with their possessions. Until a family was cleared to join us, they could stay in the chalet homes outside the gates. If our council deemed them suitable, they could enter. If we didn't, they left – with everything they'd come in with, we weren't thieves. If only part of a family or group was suitable and some weren't, they sorted it between them, and we'd abide by their decision. And we had laws here. If they broke those or persistently behaved badly, the council would again put them out of the glens with their possessions. I clarified a few questions of "bad behaviour" and saw the girl nod approvingly.

After more discussion, they went to take the good news to their people, and Janet, who'd joined us, looked at me. "Three hundred? If most are suitable, that's great. Not the least that others didn't come but may follow."

I knew, and I hoped hard that most of the three hundred would be suitable. Most were, once we'd finished talking, questioning, and accessing them. One family we split, the mother was an old harridan, and the men her daughters married kowtowed to her and, as I saw for myself, ill-treated their wives and children. Janet drifted off quietly after we both saw some of it, talked to the women, unseen by husbands or mother-in-law, and they made application to the glens to be accepted as the three sisters and children, exempting the mother and husbands. We had a quiet word with Dylan, who said it was none of his business and stood aside while we sorted out a fair share of possession and livestock.

The husbands and the harridan went on their way, calling down a wide variety of curses on our heads, and that was that. Two other families demanded to know what religion the glens followed and how we stood on the Sabbath. They didn't like the answers and left voluntarily. Several of our children had been circulating amongst the incomers too and bringing back titbits of information. Using those, we weeded out other would-be settlers, and they too departed – one way or another.

But of the over three hundred come to us, we took in two hundred and seventy-four. And another forty-seven a month later when those who had stayed found that, when what was stolen by the gang that preyed on them, was spread over three hundred and fifty people, it was barely tolerable, but not when that is spread over a fifth of the number. They'd been careful; they promised those who preyed on them had no idea of their route or destination. They settled in, most choosing to live in Sea or Blind Glen, and when winter came, we were one people, the glens of Clan McAlister. With spring, they too came to the telling, and some spoke. So all was well, and we rejoiced - until the following summer arrived; and with it problems.

****

I should have expected trouble. I knew that when it arrived. Any time you sit about thinking you have it made, that's when things go wrong. It was late spring, and we had the scouts out, including young Iz. We didn't accept anyone under sixteen as scouts, but she had just turned that a month back, and Donal had checked her out.

"She's good, no doubt about it. Shoots a bow like she was born to it, says she spent all winter learning, and I believe her. She can stalk, she's good sense, and she rides horses, motorbikes, or an e-bike. I said she could go out with Dan and Jackie."

She did, and I should have remembered what she'd said a year back. I should have told them so they'd know to watch, but I didn't do either of those things, and she paid for that. Jackie and Dan came in one day in late summer to report.

"There's a group moving around the area, not Thurston way; they're southeast. About seventy or eighty of them, mostly men with a few women and kids. Jackie and I don't like the look of them. Iz said she'd watch, and we came back to report."

"What don't you like about them?"

Jackie frowned. "I didn't get much of a look at the people with Iz's original group, but she recognised some. She said two were ones you sent away. They seem to be guiding this lot, and she said we should get to you fast. She thought they were coming here."

I asked a couple of questions and groaned. From the sound of it, the two were the old woman and one of the husbands from the family where we'd taken in wives and children, sent mother and husbands packing. And from further descriptions, I believed Iz was right. They were with the group that had preyed on the women. Just how much had the duo told them of us? Not that it mattered right now. I sent Jackie and Dan to get a meal and a night's sleep and called in more scouts.

In an hour, they were on their way. Morning came, and with it, Marni Gilson, Jackie's friend who did some of the stores'

297

administration. "I don't like to tell you, but someone's stolen things from the weapons barns."

I asked the obvious question. "What?"

"Case of hand grenades and a bundle of bolts for a full-sized crossbow."

"Have you any idea when they disappeared?"

"Could be as far back as ten days ago, just about the time the previous scouts left."

There was an almost audible click in my head. Iz, her best friend, what Iz had said when I first met her, and a group who lived on others. I went to find Donal. I talked briefly but enough to tell him what I believed, and he looked at me.

"I'd say you're right. That's why she practised all winter. That's why the grenades too."

"Do we go and look for her?"

"Aye, we may not be so fast afoot any longer, but we're good drivers, and we can shoot. Load for bear, lass, and we'll see if we can save her."

We found the gang baying around an old tower, one of those types of old tower that was little more than a staircase winding up to a walled platform over fifty feet up, composed of un-reinforced concrete and old. I'd climbed up something similar when younger, and if this one was of that type, it would have heavy doors that blocked off the upper platform from the stairs and a ladder most of the way down the outside from the platform.

I scanned the situation with powerful binoculars and groaned. "She's there."

Donal scanned in turn and nodded. "Aye, she's had blood for her going already. Look to the left, by that blue lorry."

I whistled softly. "I can see eight. Who would they be?"

Donal snorted. "Men who raped a friend of hers and two traitors most likely."

"That would make it six. I see eight."

"Targets of opportunity, keep them trying to get her, so we have time to prepare."

I felt the blood drain from my face. "Jamie Tamman, Donal, she's doing a Jamie."

He spoke heavily. "So I think, and not much we can do about it. There's open space between our cover and them. If we attack head-on, they'll slaughter us as we cross it while they have shelter. Even if we pulled some away, others would stay there to take her. She's done this twofold for her friend and us. We don't make that worthless."

"No." I picked up the small hand mirror, I knew Iz had learned Morse for the scouts, and I flashed it over and over at the tower until a flicker said she'd seen. I got one word.

"No."

I sat back. Donal grunted. "Her choice, her life, and let's see nothing's wasted."

Iz had started shooting again. A howl of rage went up as a man fell, then a second before a large bunch of them charged the tower. I was counting back. "Jackie said there was about seventy or eighty. Iz's killed eleven so far as I can see."

"And there's a lot more trying to get into that tower," Donal confirmed. He called in Ricky, gave orders, and Ricky trotted away. Our people spread out, moved forward to the point where they'd be seen in another two yards and held, waiting. I went back to the hummock where I'd been and sent more Morse.

"Iz, ladder outside." I used my binoculars, saw her circle the platform and locate the ladder. I let out a long slow breath; thanks be. She moved back to the side where most of her enemies were congregating and started shooting. More dived into the tower, and I could imagine them racing up the stairs, hammering on the bolted door.

The stairs must be filling with men trying to force the door by now. Donal's fingers were flicking in silent commands, and our people closed in. None of the enemies noticed. Those behind

their vehicles were focused on the tower, shouting encouragement to those within. Our forward scouts had come in on the
opposite side, so they were screened by the vehicles. Iz continued to shoot, and the shouts from the tower were abruptly tri-
umphant.

Ricky gave the bird call that was a signal, and our people
were racing forward in silence. From the tower as I panted down
the hill, I heard a howl of glee, an explosion, and, on the side of
the tower towards me. I saw Iz's body fall from the walkway, the
building crumbling. The vehicles vomited men who made for Iz's
body; one tore it over. I saw the bright knife blade coming down
… and the body was flame, the men flying backward.

Dylan went past me and vanished into the dust, I had my
handgun out, but there appeared to be no one left to fight. Ricky
had people herded together under guns. I stumbled forward,
feeling every one of my years, and found a dust-shrouded Dylan.
He sat by Iz, an Iz who was grey concrete dust, her body torn
and rent, and I sat by him, my legs unceremoniously dumping
me there.

Dylan looked up and spoke quietly to me. "Iz never knew.
Her mother's husband was sterile, and she was desperate for a
child. It lasted nine weeks and five days until she knew, then she
was nice about it, but we were over. Iz never knew…"

I remembered how Iz had talked to me several times in
the library, and I offered the only thing I could. "She liked you,
she admired you, she told me you were a real leader."

"She did?"

"She did. I think if she'd known who you were, she'd
have loved you."

He touched his face to hers before starting to straighten
the body, laying her out with gentle care. "How did she do it?"

I sighed. "Iz stole a case of hand grenades. I think she
booby-trapped the tower, so she could bring it down if she needed
to. And I think she did the same with herself. She didn't jump or

try to climb down. She fell. I think one of them shot her, and she knew she was done. She fell and pulled the tower pins and two in her hands in her last breath. It fits the time it took for them to reach her and turn the body over."

Once we sorted out the bodies, it fitted with my hypothesis. There were few left alive on that side. Three women, two older children, a baby, and a badly wounded man. I picked up the baby and handed him to Lachlan McHain, who'd come towards me.

"Teach him to be a better person than this lot were." One of the women snarled wordlessly at me. I had a guard put on them, and a morning report came that the wounded man had died. I let the women and the children go when we were ready to leave, giving them the vehicle they chose. Nor did I ever tell anyone – even my Donal – that I'd checked it alone first, found food, and added some of Mac's pills to it. I'd not risk them coming back or their children growing up to return with allies, hell-bent on repayment.

We took Isobel's body home and buried it where Dylan wished. I talked to Donal, and we spoke with Ricky and Alex so that the following spring, we formally surrendered as clan leaders and joined the council. Laddie had died the previous year, and Tai died that winter, held in my arms as we stroked him. We would take no other creature into our house now, we were ninety that year, and I felt as if shadows were closing in on me.

CHAPTER TWENTY-FOUR

Hither and thither moves and mates and slays, and one by one, back in the closet lays. ~The Rubaiyat of Omar Khayyam

But in the end, we make our own choices, nor will I believe otherwise. ~Sheila McArn

The twenty-second year after the virus was a good year. Tommy succeeded in duplicating solar panels and batteries, so we need not fear losing electricity any generation soon. Our numbers had risen to well over two thousand, and the trickle of those coming to the gates continued. We were, so it appeared from their reports, the only group who had and obeyed fair laws, with sufficient land and population, in northern Scotland. Some groups had begun well, but the rise of someone strong often left that group in a civil war. And a people divided cannot stand.

The roads to the far south were long impassable, but we salvaged from those areas we could reach, and the long rows of storage barns stayed full. That would continue so long as there was salvage we could find, and even more importantly, salvage we could not make. Sugar beet and bees flourished, and even when salvage of that sort was gone, we would have something sweet. I was writing in my official diary when Ricky came in.

"Sheila, it's Donal." He choked, and I stood up, knowing the truth.

"Take me to him."

He cupped his arm about my shoulders, and together, we walked to where my love lay. He had walked out with her from the library, Janet said. He had halted, made a sound in his throat, and slowly slid to the ground. He lay there, and I knew, looking at him, that there was little time left for us.

"Carry him to our house and place him in our bed…"

"Not to the hospital?" Janet asked, her tone sharp.

"No." We had talked about this day, and I knew his wishes. "Take him home." So Donal was carried carefully to the bed in which we'd slept together so many years. I removed his clothes, washed him, and redressed him in a long nightshirt. Then I sat in a comfortable chair alone beside him. He opened his eyes some hours later and looked at me.

His voice was weak, barely a whisper. "What happened?"

I gave him the truth unflinchingly. "A heart attack."

His smile showed in the corners of his mouth. "I canna complain. It's been a good life and a long one, and you beside me for all of it save those years you were away. Will I get better or not? Tell me true now."

I bowed my head. "I gave you the medications we had, but we both knew this time would come. Once they stop working and you have the first attack, it's a forerunner. It's likely you'll have a second fatal one within days, a week or two at most."

"Yes, start calling them in, lass. I'll talk to the council first."

One by one, they entered, Donal talked briefly to each of them, making clear he valued the years of friendship, support, and their abilities. And one by one, they left, many weeping. Once that was done, I fed him, lay the night beside him, and in the morning, I called in those others he wished to see. He talked to them, remembering some good thing they had done, some way in which they had contributed to the glens, and for three days, they came while he lay in our big bed and gave them the last of what he could provide.

We were alone again after that, and he turned to me. "Can you say how much longer?"

"Another three or four days, I think. Not much more."

"Do something for me, love, go to where the Rosses are and see how they do?"

I stared. "Why?"

"Claire said Daisy Matson told her that Ruth wants to marry Kinley Yarrow. He's asked, but she put him off. Daisy says it's because Ruth's afraid her family will send more trouble here, and she doesn't want people to blame her and then Kin for it. The roads are still passable that far. Go and see."

I stood up and stretched. I was weary, but a night's sleep would repair that. I had little strength left, but I could rest in a car all the way. Besides now that my love asked, I could do no other than what he wanted, and I admit to a sudden curiosity about them myself.

"I'll leave in the morning."

I was rested by morning, and Ricky, appraised of Donal's wish, had a scout group along with several lorries waiting as soon as we'd finished breakfast. At his heels capered his new puppy, a terrier/Shetland sheepdog cross named Charli. I smiled at the pup's overtures, stooped to pat her, and felt a slight dizziness. It was gone as I straightened, but I knew it for my own warning.

It was around midday when we drove into the town where the Rosses lived. I gave Ricky directions, and while we stopped, looking over the town from the outskirts, I made a suggestion. "We may not come back. Take anything useful your people can find."

He nodded, gave orders, and the lorries fanned out with scout vehicles as outriders. With them gone and with three vehicles remaining, we headed for the address I remembered. The place was silent, the door shut, Ricky honked the horn, and there was no response.

He helped me out of my old Landcruiser. "I'll go first. You hang back a bit."

I obeyed, smiling at how far a small boy had come. Charli, before we could stop her, scampered ahead and halted at the door, barking.

Ricky opened the door, stood motionless, and looked back at me, beckoning. I joined him and nodded. After all their scheming, their foolishness, that was how they'd ended.

The next door, too, was shut. I opened that and looked at what was to be seen, unsurprised.

"All four of them."

Ricky moved closer. "Not naturally. If these are the sons, they've both been shot."

We returned to look over their parents, and Ricky's eyebrows went up. "No indication on either of them. What do you think?"

"I've no idea. Was there a gun in the boy's room?" We looked and found one, two shots fired, lying on the floor between the beds. We checked the kitchen and found no food. Ricky went back to the parent's room and managed to move the bodies a little. There half under Joe's body was a razor blade, I noted something else, and then I knew.

I sat on the old sofa and looked about. "No proof, but I'd say Meg died naturally. Joe found her dead, looked at his future, and gave up. They were both near sixty. What had he left? So he killed himself. Their sons found them. I'd say they gave up as well. There's no food in the cupboards, no electricity, nothing works here any longer."

Ricky shuddered. "You're right on that. Have you looked at the bathroom?"

"I have a nose still," I said dryly. "So, the boys had few choices. They'd have had to leave and scavenge further afield. Then what? Wandering, scraping food where they could find it, with less and less that's edible. They were thirty or thereabouts, and they could look forward to nothing. Save coming to us perhaps, and begging on their knees."

Ricky, who'd known them both, snorted. "They'd not have done that. It would have meant working honestly, keeping glen laws, and everyone at home knew of the family. There were grudges, and laws or not, some people would not have been kind."

I nodded. "Truth. So they decided to die on their terms, and they did." I sighed. "Look round, see if you can find something to take back to Ruth as a memento."

I found a locket, nine carat gold, at the bottom of the jewellery case by Meg's bed. It was initialled and contained a tiny sepia photo of a woman. I pried that out, and in minuscule handwriting, on the back, it declared that it was Grandma Merin. I searched the other case beneath it and found that she had been Meg's mother's grandmother. I replaced the photo, took the papers that proved it and the locket, they would go to Ruth. Ricky found a vase, glass, vibrant and lovely green with gold accents, and we added that.

Then we walked out of the house, and I turned to look back at the gate. "I'll not have Ruth ask about the bodies. Burn the house."

Ricky grinned. "Always fancied a bit of arson. What about the rest of the town?"

I shrugged. "I saw no one as we drove through, no signs of anyone either. There's no wind. The town may survive, but the house burns."

"Once we have everyone assembled again," Ricky said practically, and so it was. The others came in loaded with salvage and reported they, too, had seen no one. However, they found a storage business, forced open everything, and sifted out enough of use to fill most of the lorry space. Ricky drove us back from the assembly point where the others waited, removed a large can of oil he'd brought, climbed the stairs, poured it around the bodies, and left a trail along the landing and down the stairs.

I stood in the tiny entrance and waited until Ricky joined me. The oil trickled down, and once it was near, I lit the taper I had and tossed it. The oil caught, burning as flames crept up the stairs. We left, Ricky shutting the door behind us. I climbed into the Landcruiser, and we waited until I saw through the door's glass a red glow that brightened. I nodded, and Ricky touched the accelerator. By the time we'd reached the others, a column of smoke was rising, and I sat back to be driven home.

Donal was awake when I returned and demanded chapter and verse. I told him.

"So likely Joe and the lads killed themselves, and you have a couple of things for Ruth. A good job well done, love. This vase, though?"

I laughed. "There's little doubt the locket belonged to Meg's Great-grandma Merin. The vase? Probably something Meg took. If so, it was hers by right of salvage, and if I tell Ruth it belonged to the Merins, she'll have something lovely to hand down."

I called in Ruth the following day, and we presented her with the papers, vase, and locket. I said of her family, only that I had found all four dead and given them to the fire. She listened dry-eyed and looked relieved. She clutched the items to her as she left, though. I thought her happy to have them and to hear her family would never return.

Donal looked after her. "She can wed now, something else well concluded."

It was so, and closer to the conclusion that I knew. We talked much of the night since he could not sleep, and it was just before I would have started breakfast that his eyes turned to me. "Stay." I met his gaze and knew, diving to ring the bell. Ricky came running, and we held my love's hands as his gaze turned to us.

"Good lad, I love you," he said to Ricky. "Hold the glens. Hold the laws."

Ricky spoke softly. "Everything as you wished, now and forever."

Donal looked at me then. "I'll wait for you, lass, but there's nae hurry."

His breathing changed to hoarseness, and we waited, holding his hands. His eyes closed slowly, the breathing halted, started again, stopped – and Donal was gone. He had turned ninety-three two months and nine days ago.

I rose from his bedside, gave orders, and all was done as I wished. We buried him by Mac and Johnny. I would lie there when the time came, and in his grave, I placed urns with the ashes of Cassie, Bruce, and Tai. He lay in McArn tartan, a *skean dhu* in his sock, a sword in his right hand, while his left cradled the urns. There was no coffin, but beneath him, a quilt made by his mother and one I had made covered him before earth began to fall.

Joss MacFiernan made sketches and did a painting of him a month after. She called it *Heart of the Glen*, and it showed Donal as he was in his strength looking down at the man who'd died. Beside the younger Donal stood Cassie, Bruce, Tai, and me in my youth also, my head bowed, while I knelt by Donal in the grave. She gave it to me, and I knew I would value it however long I had left to live.

That was something I told no one but Janet, who was practical as always. "You think that was a sign?"

"I do. I know the symptoms, and I've been giddy twice more. I think I have little time left, but I wanted no one to know and for them to think first of Donal. Now he's buried, I can spend my time sorting out what needs to be ready or done, and I ask your help."

Janet took my hands in hers. "Whatever you want, whatever you need."

So for weeks, I was busy. Quietly I gave away things I owned. I prepared a funeral kist, a chest with clothing I wished to wear, items to go with me, and I wrapped parcels for friends. I rode my tricycle through the glens, talking to those I cared for, watching the colours of the land, and loving every inch of it. I spent time with Ricky and Alex, remembering how they had come to us, thinking of Ricky's sister, Kaylie – and found to my pleasure they planned to call the new baby Kaylie if a girl, Kaylen if a boy.

Then it was time. I knew the morning I could not rise from my bed. I called Ricky, said my farewells, and made a request. "I've long since kept a sachet of hot chocolate by me that even if none were left elsewhere, I would have one last mug of it to drink."

His gaze met mine, and I knew he understood. "When?"

"When I've said my goodbyes," I said them as my friends came and went. Alex received the containers of tiny pills, Claire those of my books she loved. Janet received some of the paintings I owned. To Ricky, I gave my love, Joss's painting of Donal's funeral, my own book, and the glen diaries. Then I savoured the hot sweetness he brought me, and I knew I would see again the man I loved, who would be waiting. Donal's word was ever good, and I would see Tai and the dogs once more, and that was very well.

****

From the Leader of the Glens of Clan McAlister:

Five days gone, my grandmother died. Near twenty-three years ago, Sheila and Donal McArn took me in as an orphaned twelve-year-old. They loved me, raised me, and then released me to be all I could be. Into my hands they gave the glens and a trust. On Sheila's death, I found this book and all the diaries she had written of how we survived those first terrible days and months.

Of the diaries I had always known, and they are a valuable record, but the book surprised me. I knew she'd had friends who were writers and that she too had wanted to write. Life, she said, often takes you on another road. So it was for her, but I think she chose to be that thing she'd wanted in this book. It may also have been she knew some would more willingly read a book than ancient diaries, and I will see that happens.

It was a project in her later years when they found machines during the last trip to Edinburgh to reprint books that were perishing or where they had only a single copy. You placed supplies into the machine, added a unit with the manuscript, set systems, then pressed the main control. Soon thereafter, whole books came from the other end. She used one machine at a time, saying it would be long before we could replace them, keeping them clean and in working order. Use one until that failed before using the next, and once all stopped, we might repair one from parts of the others that had failed.

Thus far, we are still using the first, they seem to have been very well and sturdily made, and I hope the five will carry us through to a time when we may be within sight of when they can be newly made again. We also have a line of barns with supplies to feed them. And so I have set this book, written by Sheila McArn, into the machine and produced copies of it. These were stacked up in the library after her funeral and taken by our people within hours. I printed more until any who wanted had a copy. This small addition has also been printed and may be read in the library records.

And to elucidate a minor point: In the years that I knew Sheila, she said things, as did my grandfather, that seemed to go against standard army service. I believe they did not serve in the regular army, but in some aspect of it that was unofficial, although I know they were listed on the army rolls. What they did, where they went, or for what purpose save that it was at the behest of the Government, I do not know, but I know they served long, retired, and received a pension, and in the end, all that is important is that to their last days, they lived and died with honour.

I would have asked Joss to paint another picture of my grandmother, but when I looked at the one made for Donal's funeral, it seemed to me there was no need. Both were there, in two ages, and both together were the true heart of the glens. However, I asked her for a copy. While I have the original, which will always hang in the Leader's home, the copy hangs in the community hall so that all may see their faces and never forget.

As Sheila often said, it being a phrase that always made Donal laugh, and as those of us today that still watch discs on the television, and who will yet know it well; to all the glens, and the people of the clan –

Live long and prosper, Ricky Black McArn.

****

From the Leader of the Glens and the Clan McAlister:

I add this to the records that any may turn to it and read. My grandfather, Ricky McArn, died three days gone, his wife, my grandmother, Alex, having preceded him four years before. He was Clan Leader for forty-nine years and will be sorely missed. It was his choice that I should follow him, and to that, I am sworn. Matters have changed here little since he took up Leadership. We remain, we hold the glens and the laws, and we have spread a little so that we have people now in what is named Sweet Glen, for the sugar beet there, and the bee skeps. The great-grandson of Tommy Branson holds his house and workshop in Thurston yet and does fine work. We have paramedics trained by Alex from the teaching of Sheila McArn, and that is very well.

I have often read the diaries and the book my great-great-grandmother Sheila wrote, and I ask those who follow me to read and make copies of it available to all of the clan. Let no one forget how the clan survived, what we owe to Johnny and his brother Mac, or that we hold the land in trust.

One thing I shall add, that despite alpacas coming from far lands as Sheila recorded, they have taken this to be their home.

They thrive well under the guardianship of the Cheryl family. Tigers, however, unwanted and unwelcome, have lately moved into the area from the south so that we held a great hunt and killed all we found. Their skins adorn the clan hall, recently built, while our dogs and cats found the meat palatable.

Donal Ricky McArn
****

From the Leader of the Glens of Clan McAlister:

It is now three hundred and nine years since the virus. We have grown to be a mighty people, covering all the land of the original glens and far to the north of Thurston, being at the last count fifty-seven thousand, nine hundred, and twenty-three adults – an adult being sixteen years or more. It is custom that once in a lifetime, each Leader writes a piece, which is added to the book of Leaders. This was begun by the first who bore the ancient title, and the custom has continued. Thus, there are two books that Lady Sheila McArn wrote, and this other encapsulates the letters of all a leader might wish to record. Her book has the first two, and whatever the last may have been to date, that one being replaced each time the leader dies and another rules. All speak the truth as attested by the people of Clan McAlister of that time.

Of the items my ancestor mentioned, we have many alpacas, and they are a much-valued animal. The tigers we see now and again, at which time they are always killed. Our voyages south along the coast have increased steadily, and we begin to relearn the lands beyond us. And one final thing I should record. The book of Sheila McArn is a treasure to the clan, it was regularly reprinted, and in this past year, we have found a way to rebuild machines to do the work. It was a joy to me to read her wisdom again, and of those she loved in other places and know that if or when the time should come, that those in the lands beyond are like us and that we may one day meet them as kin and friends.

Alex Cheryl McArn,
Leader of the Glens and Clan McAlister.
Buaidh an àird, no bàs le glòir! Lean a dheòin do Rìgh.

ABOUT THE AUTHOR

Lyn started writing in 1990 and, within a year, had short stories and poems published. In 1993, her first book, a humorous true-life work (*Farming Daze*) about her farm, friends, and animals, appeared, followed by six others in that series. As a joke between them, a longtime friend of Lyn's, Andre Norton, was given a book Lyn had written set in one of Andre's worlds. Andre was impressed with the work and took it to her agents, who sold it to Warner books. This led Lyn to write another six books in Andre's world, published either by Warner or TOR. Lyn has won seven short story Muse Medallions from the (International) Cat Writer's Association and six Sir Julius Vogel Awards for her books. Since the original book, Lyn has seen almost fifty more books appear plus over three hundred short stories and says she has no intention of stopping so long as she can write.

www.ingramcontent.com/pod-product-compliance
Lightning Source LLC
Chambersburg PA
CBHW020223260626
47156CB00002B/513